THE TYRANNY OF PANTS BY ME

Dedicated to Tinkelhoff for Character Development, Classic Play Cast of Characters.

ISBN No. 979-8-9894625-1-3

CREDITS

Cover Art: © 2023, Joshua Tenpenny, Brenda Burke, Bella Kaldera
Hothechajuxips Press Logos: © 2023, Joshua Tenpenny, Brenda Burke
Back Cover & Chapter 1 Art: Color back cover and black-and-white Maps of Zysigamore Island
courtesy of Map Creator RollForFantasy.com

HOTHECHAJUXIPS PRESS
P.O. Box 310
Westminster, MA 01473
hothechajuxipspress@gmail.com

Design Meta Chapter 0: The Tyranny of Pants. This is not the Real Credentialing. You must reenter the Bathyscaphe because conditions.

Dolphin snowed interdependently.

Rolled in a generous greenden ectoplasm, the chitinous carapaces feel easiest to grip. Function of the Birchwood Turtles Chair Football team. Can still feel the Teeth of the Hydra.

Chase me throughout differential diagnosis and truckin' morespenat plans.

We veer fohrwohrd. Active verbs as they convey change and eschew opinionated adjectives, inflexible prepositions and their mundane phraseologies. Nouns I Ching to/but/not subject object possessive or plurals. Lust 1 delineated.

Set aside subject object preposition jinxes. There are only two mantras in the one true Buddhism. The conspiracy was laid. 2 Indica Twins Perish in 4 Alarum Blais. * The people went 4 it 2 - blade.

Passive Verba Iactenda Sunt.

J   o

B

G   𝄞 c

E

D

M

The Verb 2B:

TO BUT NOT	TO OR
TO BUT	TO OR NOT
FROM BUT NOT	TO ORR NOT
FROM BUT	FROM OR...
TO AND	
TO AND NOT	

*: No relation to Debra Blais

0   Prequel #1   Tyranny of Sox

See chapter III A.

See chapter 7,143,071.

Don't see chapter 11.

Read every fifth letter of chapter 97.

Reread chapter -8 and chapter 8.

Read every 12th character in the book of Genesis.

The sphinx is perpetuating this antipathy by drawing the bravest and the holiest across this waste land. Metamorphosis of a

Brackets in brackets in still more brackets

When in doubt, go to chapter 30330. There you will find 1-12 miscellaneous magic items.

It is a fluke. Plot summary without the twist. Just a straight line.

Synchronicity is not PRACTICED. Rather, it is a realization that lines of energy are activated rarely but always not never.

Total confluence shatters another mortal trap.

"Taweret come"

Antonioni's hot dog dribbles mustard.

Sox were benign in the beginning when tethered by a garter. The insane push to create the garterless sock led directly to untold suffering and misery among those who wore these formerly innocuous yet suddenly dangerous

Precocious children's montage on an endless loop. Dirty faces, soiled shirts, little pieces of snot fly across the screen.

I keep on referring helplessly into void mezzanines that constantly accordion into sub-mezzanine levels.

00   Exordium

The Word of Pants is Restriction. Refuse not your spouse:; Shed binders:; Abandon Repression:; Share good news about phraseologies.

Lettuce begin TTOP with high-minded praise of the Dear Reader. The reader is blessed with text the clarity of which is unparalleled among collectors and gaskets.

Me needs no introduction, but perhaps Me does. Of Tinkelhoff? Old veils betray a new discourse radiating like Escher-style stairwells going in and out of an inverted panopticon.

The actual effect of TTOP is the loosening of artificial restrictions by identifying both the human body and the garments that constrict society like a snake. It has been speculated that this book cures osmosis.

Each character is a complex, sociopolitical construct in the story's milieux. Multiple allegories intertwine throughout the opus. Nobody is under literary allusions anymore: Polished from obscurity and opacity, each chapter in TTOP now scintillates like the facet of a solid yet delicate crystal.

Pregamble the Constitution of Xisen, formatted on Ace TV as a lead-in.

There was a certain Salesman with great wealth who traded extensively on the Island of Zysigamore. One day, Traveling Salesman went to a neighboring country to collect what was due to him. He sat down under a tree and rapidly ate a corn dog. He threw away the stick, and immediately blazed the non-woke Efreeti from the cover of the AD&D *Dungeon Master's Guide*, buxom bikini blonde in hand. "You were expecting Henny Youngman instead?" remarked the efreet. Selah.

Outcasker, outcasker, get me three outs.

Chironolongitudinal morespenat murgatroyd replaces every other spongiform tesseractyllic microorgasmatron according to $[P_1V_1 = P_2V_2)]$.

Boyle's, Hoyle's, Coyle's, Doyle's and Moyle's Laws of Attraction, Distraction, Constraction and Abraxifaction equally enforced, motivated and coagulated, the Queen Herself, resplendent in ego, wide in fame, genuflected to her Great Mothers Taweret and 4casta.

Shredding's Razor is very acute, dangerous; Occam's Razor, less so, yet very exacting, very prescientcise.

Ceteris paribus, factor goofballs, gumballs, superballs, megaballs, cubicballs, jax and smoothly flavored stones. The common denominclature of multiples within multiples. Tiamat 3125-headed is coming for your Magus.

-0   Cast of Characters

ME - Full name Me he he he. Co-Author as appearing in TTOP.

TINKELHOFF- Co-Author as appearing in TTOP.

SIMON- The lead character who was married to a rock.

SIMON JUNIOR- A rock.

TRAVELING SALESMAN- A man who comes to Simon's door.

MR. HI STOP- Fractally bilious endomorph and its proxy.

CLYTEMNESTRA- A modernized mopar woman bathyscaphe pilot.

IDAJAN- Queen of All Pants in the Multiverse.

LI'L NAS Y- Classified dignitized country hip-hop glamper.

STRIKER- A willing collaborator in his own miasma.

ELEPHANT- Simon's brother, who lives in a closet.

BROZ- Revolutionary minded anti-Elephantist who plots terrorist acts.

CHRISTIMIQUA- Mr. Hi Stop's brother-in-law's ex-girlfriend's hairdresser and assassin.

QUENTIN PERIWINKLE- A l*** w***** f** f** (see Chapter -83).

XBLANKLEN- A troubled daugerrotypical human.

FRED BARNES- A janitor.

TAWERET- Mother Goddess of the Island and Queendom of Uottubbacktotheboniummnn (sp.).

ABDUL MOHAMMED ABDULLAH- Formerly Howard Cosell.

WACKY TED KUDZOPILOUS- The Admiral of Yacht Rock.

BRYANT E. BRICK- Ace TV Newscaster.

TINA EASTBRIDGEWATER- Ritual bassoon player.

WIN T. FRESH- A marketing consultant to high-class Zysigamoreans.

ITTY BO- A roseburned styracosaurus substitute teacher.

RALPH- A carrot.

WALT FUNGSTIR- Former owner of Chico's Bail Bonds.

GTENZI MGBYCKBUVUILEVENI- Multioscillational...

DASTARDLY WILLIAM RUCKLEHAUS- A supply-sided neotractor.

ZIMTY- Another rock.

MISTY MIQUA- Christimiqua's younger sister and avid conscientiousness.

MARQUEZ LOISSON - Kisses the 'Bob'-ney Stone of Pure Sales.

The Tyranny of Pants is split down the middle like "Speakerboxx/The Love Below" as the primary matrix. Secondarily, certain underworld chapters correspond to M. Alighieri's *Divine Comedy*. To a lesser degree, there are satirical takes on the *Cantos* of Ezra Pound and its paleofascism. There are other accordion-like frames of magical surrealism built into the superstructure of TTOP.

One polarity corresponds to Me; the other shadow +/- belongs to Tinkelhoff. On the other axis, Incasker and Outcasker are the guardians.

Classic Plays and similar Me/Tinkelhoff plays are the backbone of TTOP. Many new characters also emerge, some for just one fraction of a chapter, others for several. This allows the entire multiverse, which was only hinted at by those first works, to be explored.

Most of all, it is for all the bodies of the crowd who parade in splendor through the dreamrise and dreamset. Parabolic interangelic hypermeta harmonical sephirloompas are included in all knowledgements, appendicizzle, errataiges, addenndeddaa...

The character exposition is nonpareil, in a way that the earlier Classic Plays only hinted at, a big toe pointing at the moon. Simon, Simon Junior, Elephant and the other NFT-worthy characters abound with clear insights into each one's raison de manger.

Each chapter stands alone like a Sunday comic embossed in Humerus Putty, then stretched into the most absurd shapes imaginable. Each is also capable of infinite expansion, contraction, contradiction and contraindication.

A

Some chapters drip out like fresh coffee from a coffee maker. Others just gush out. Still others ooze out like pus.

Circumscript: Write around the chapter. Multiply plot lines, no restrictions. Tyranny of the linear structure strangles you at the flow points.

'Remove literary, grammatical and syntactical inhibition' [Kerouac] is a rule for life, not just for writing. This concurs with Outcasker, and conforms to the xact freedom xpressed by neoliterary tryllogism.

Entities willing to leave book jacket-style reviews are implored to do so. You may use a pseudonym or a series of noms de plume as suits your conceptual continuity. You are also asked to consider reading the book.

You may not like this book. This is intentional.

Make it new, they scream. Make it new.

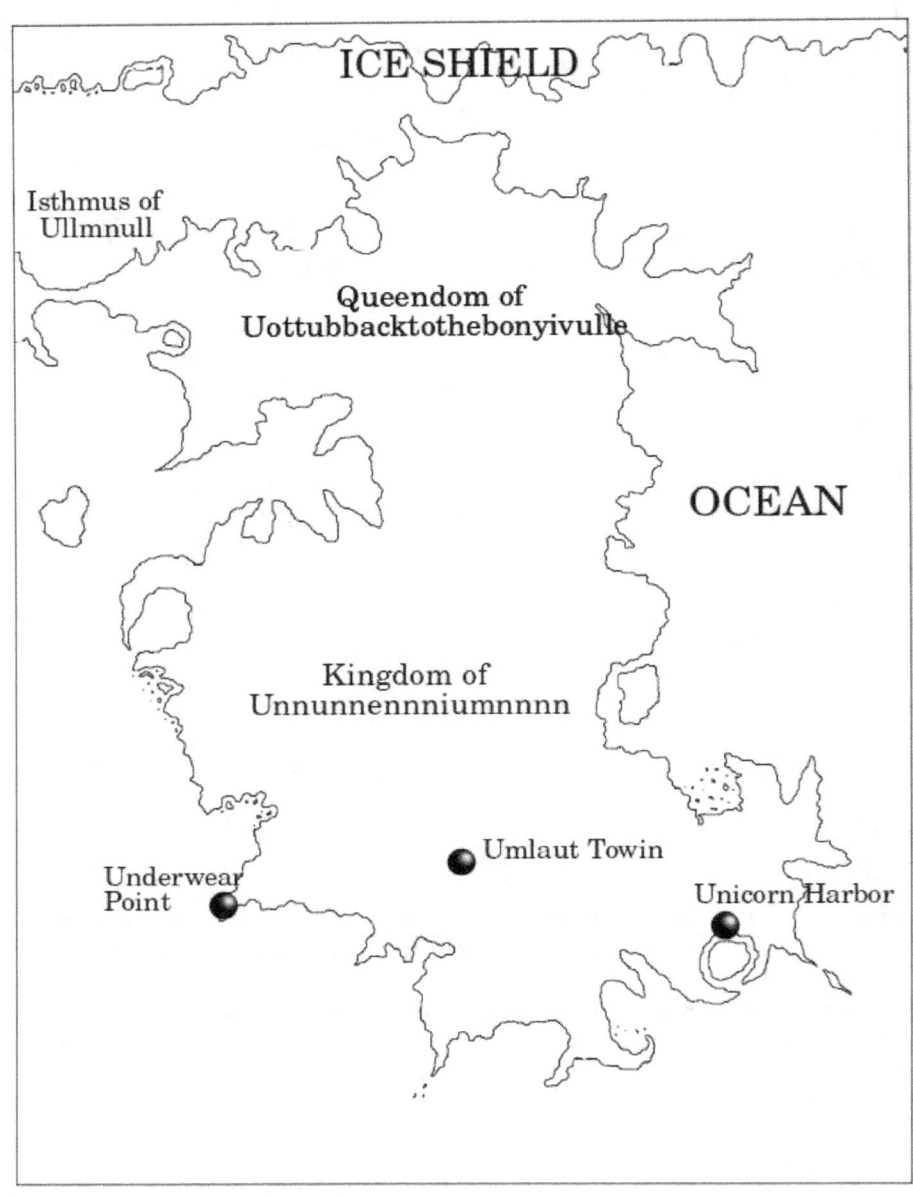

ICE SHIELD

Isthmus of
Ullmnull

Queendom of
Uottubbacktothebonyivulle

OCEAN

Kingdom of
Unnunnennniumnnnn

Umlaut Towin

Underwear
Point

Unicorn Harbor

ZYSIGAMORE ISLAND

1   Zysigamore Island(s) *

Island or Archipelago

Archipelago of Domination

Archipelago of Un-Domination

Zysigamoria divisa est in Partes Quinque.

1   "Underwear Point"

2   "Unicorn Harbor"

3   "Umlaut Towin"

4   "Unnunnennniumnnnn"

5   "Uottubbacktothebonyivulle" (sp.)

Module

Ice Shield/Land Bridge @ NW, aka the Isthmus of Ullmnull

Another Island, big but not as big as Greenland-sized, mostly ice covered

Archipelago - Aleutian Like Style

Dungeon

The Keep. Walls 10' thick all around.

Drawbridge

Great Courtyard

Sleep Home Alabama

Qlippoth flickers in and out of this world, much like our own yet peculiarly unique in its own way. Like the will-o-the-wisp, Qlippoth may guide the unwary or unwise (our heroes) into the horrific evil underworld realms of daymare and damnation. Clytemnestra was well studied in demonology--in fact that was her minor--but could she count on her party to not succumb to the Hells or the Abyss? By means of several old role playing game modules, they are able to build relationships with the most powerful Devils and/or Demons. Unlike Dante's Hell-bound adventurer, Clytemnestra and her friends have no companion - no source of wisdom to critique their actions or give them clues when they are lost.

A line to Da'ath was there, unborn, unknowing among the pale candy wrappers of Xarthorian pig piece vendors.

All that is certain is of Taweret. The lands - the peoples - the temples - belong to Her. Even the throne of Uottubbacktothe (sp.) was said to have been midwifed by the Goddess Herself for 4casta's enshrinement. Yet the legend is somewhere in between.

For obvious reasons, Mr. Hi Stop was often entreated to play his best false face. In a pose not quite reminiscent of Avalokitesvara, Hi selected a bevy of facial contortions that satisfied the enraptured.

Traveling Salesman and Hi were friends from the old days, the old school, the kids on the block. Why, they grew up eating tardigrade stew in school cafeteria together, filling out each others' homework and swapping school neckties. A perfect environment to raise the next generation of élite sales professionals.

After several failed relationships, Mr. Hi Stop had met Clytemnestra when she was still in graduate school. She was building her first bathyscaphe from Legos and playing cards. Her voice like a scarab punctured Hi's psyche every time. Clytie was in good shape and was motivated to get things done.

The path was rockier with Traveling Salesman and his main love in life, Simon. Traveling Salesman would dump Simon, or hook up with a new lover while Simon was still pining for him. As their relationship developed and the money started to roll in, Simon had to make allowances for Traveling Salesman's drunkenness and promiscuity.

2   Idajan

All mitey Idajan, Queen of Uottubbacktothebonivulle (sp.), Queens Ryte of all the Dreams. She would pose a serious threat to sales and unreconstructed theorems regarding the true origins of Legwear

She who Exalts in Pants. Pants that make the alt right blubberbois want to ban them, pants to hug the gluteae maximae reginae.

To Simon Junior, Idajan reeked of jade septums. Yet, to Traveling Salesman and his Ilk, the Queen posed an insurmountable obstacle to the higher quarterly sales 4casta, like Jocasta. She got Nasty which only flummoxed the most naive salesmen, who were driven home like lemmings trying to cram into a cab.

4casta, of course, mother of the Queen, was now edified and mostly deitized by the solipsistic Uottubacktothebonivulle (sp.) inhabitants and affiliated individuals.

Idajan made it her mission to extricate the sap of young men for her atomic power, which ensured the tautness of her gluteae maximae reginae. A select few men she married and consummated the marriage fully before offing them. The leftover goo was synthesized by the toner cartel.

The job of role-playing Idajan usually went to Clytemnestra, unless Simon or Simon Junior had to take her place pro tempore. Clytie, being clever, ensured that she was only filmed or photographed, and never appeared outside of the green screen.

Ex libris, the Queen had her own horde of secret societies, toadies of all flavors, eunuchs, adult babies and spin doctors. It was fit that Idajan could cause magmas to undulate and rise to the surface of Zysigamore at will. Feared the Queen was, feared she continues to be. Her Hydra Medusa heads long for the taste of an excommunicated shock jock.

2B   Iactenda Sunt

Aliqui equites Hibernii, suit mendacium spem suam, et mendacio protectus est. [Isaiee xxviii 15]

Faber est quisque fortunae suae.

Nomen mihi faber est.

Caput aciei per campum processit.

Octo ursi altissimam arborem ascendunt.

Numquam poetae *De Rerum Natura* describent, aut

T. L. Carus, Liber VI. "...nec res ulla magis quam Phoebi Delphica Iaurus terribili sonitu flamma crepitante crematur."

Tonitrus, "Ego!" "Ego!"

Nec modo nido, sed etiam ovo capite aeger est.

"Vix ea fatus erat summo cum monte videmus/ Ipsum inter pecudes vasta se mole moventem/ pastorem Polyphemum et litora nota petentem…"

Licissi ___, carpe pecuniam!

Necesse est mihi cubiculum verrere. Araneae telam praecipitabit. Hic et nunc poeta ambulat;

Lauditores temporis acti se puella, sed erit res quam dei volent.

Veni-veni: et iuvenis quondam, nunc femina, Caeneus Rursus et in veterem fato revoluta figuram.

Haud facile emergunt, quorum virtutibus obstat res angusta domi.

Aenigma sui temporis, Simon Iunior. Sede.

Hic male medium est...scriptum reversatur.

Sic evitabilis regina draconium necesse erat si ad Avernum iimur.

-2   Sequel II Th Prequel

Jennifer Val Over roots around in Credentialing and Employment Regulations and Policy like a porcine Salomé. She consumes page after page, clause, after clause, line after line. "Why, this will be worth the billable hours I have to advance."

Striker had hired Ms. Val Over as a consultant after she left Danzig, Fulkerson and Johnson, and vowed he would pay her her weight in cybercoin. Her achievements were legendary: She had won a settlement against DF&J so large that the hoary firm had to auction off several prized 21-ball tables to pay her off.

Jen and Striker hit it off instantly, though in a purely intellectual way. Romance was out of the question - it was pure devotion to Mammon, Whose business card she still possessed. They set their sights on this plucky upstart new firm with jaded sales professionals like Mr. Hi Stop and Traveling Salesman. "Imma cancel those assholes out!" she cackled; Striker's grin stretched from one end of his skull to the other.

Jen had many professional connections to the pair. Onie McPhersall had been their gym teacher's pedicurist for a time, and she had provided a sample pair of pants that still lay in Clytemnestra's Sample Room. "Fine," she said, "that would be it." Val Over sent an assistant with several nanodrones in her ears and nostrils to Clytie's office/workshop to retrieve these blessed pants. "Tell them I lost my prototype. And that it's urgent."

Xzimor was there to meet Aanthir, the assistant duped into one of Jen Val Over's petty schemes. Xzimor seemed suspicious but, yes, they still had her pants. "Just give me a few minutes to look for them." Once Xzimor left, the nanodrones flew after her immediately, sending back feedback to Jen and Striker. "Ha! A gold mine!" they cackled as the nanodrones spied every inch of Clytie's facility.

Aanthir turned around as Xzimor handed her the pants in question. Suddenly Clytemnestra burst into the waiting room/lobby where the other assistant had been lingering. "What kind of isomorphic fuckery is this?" She held a baggie containing one of the nanodrone specimens. Xzimor reddened, and Aanthir whirled to try to get away. "Who are you? Who do you work for?" Before Xzy could block her exit, Aanthir had skipped away.

"By 'Bob,' what was that? said Xzimor. "Nanodrone," replied Clytemnestra. "Sent by Ms. Pants via her mole. Fortunately they all didn't get in without detection."

-2B Negative T(w)o Be(e)

Or not to be. Untitled. Hysteric causeway to that spectral unconsciousness. Vector of the Epic Vicissitudes of Emptiness. Vacuous voluptuous virgins Die to the Eldar Epiconsciousness. Life is Life Even without a Reproduction.

Twas in the Darkest Depths of Primeval Jungle that we feed orangutang at night and King's Miles of Jam. An emergency psych admit. Steam. How it feels to make it real.

Infernal Palimpsest, artificially reflected, miniaturized. Holographic Milkshake sips itself at the Stonehenge simulacrum. Now and again, another menhir twomblates the Mother Hen's clucking. Immature members of the Dark Matter clique. Somehow it seems OK. Dysfunction has planted seeds. Fortunately the crux of the It was a time when Pat Sajak was the Hills, and all was in Him. All belief systems could be found there, like an ancient Roman Marketplace of Foo. Who wants these? "Toe Oh Toe Lingam of the Horehound!"

Parades are designed to fade in fade out. The best parades enter and reenter adjacent dimensions and mezzanine dimensions. Do you have proof? I have Gum.

Mr. Hi Stop perched at a street corner, under the light of a pink neon light in a second story window. "We know you. We always have. Give up this life, this lifestyle, this daily bredd. Put it away like pudding." Make an ellipse. A perfect bow towards the preternatural. Have to pay full price like some nobody. Some shlub. Geez. Tunics drained of sheep's blood. "It's all we had."

* And not to be at the same time [(only available to Premium subscribers with keycode and froth. Limited tine only.)]

3   Simon

Simon was one of those beautiful men that every bachelor thought he would have a chance with. Yet Simon was mercurial and not so easily satisfied.

Ever frustrated, Simon longed for a spouse who would stand beside him. Enter Simon Junior.

He fell hard into solipsism as the relationship deteriorated. "Do I look all right?" "Tea bags?"* Simon looked elsewhere for consolation.

It certainly was love at first sight when Traveling Salesman was introduced to Simon. Their quickie marriage was the talk of the town. "We're married!"

Still, Traveling Salesman was who he was. He didn't intend to change his fast-paced job to make Simon happy. This would create a strain on the relationship. Plus neither of them bothered to write "Thank you" notes to all the wedding attendees.

Then Quentin Periwinkle entered his life, said "Indeed," and Simon ran off with him. Traveling Salesman was on to the next lay.

To this day Simon cannot even look at a salesman without thinking of that man who came to his door so long ago.

There isn't a manicurist alive who hasn't encountered Simon on a bad cuticle day. Yet it has always remained unclear what Simon's vocation was, beyond "Lead Character."

Mr. Hi Stop was just a friend; Hi was not interested in Simon, beyond trading S&H Green Stamps with him and gargling the alphabet backwards. Mr. Hi Stop was sometimes referred to as a heterosexual, yet was not offended by the title.

Simon's attention span being zero, he allowed Ralph the Carrot to rot. Simon wasn't the caring nurturing type.

Men who come to Simon's door usually entered by his window. Even Simon Junior reentered his life that way, though SJ may have had co-conspirator(s).

3A   Sox

Tyranny of Sox manifests along the same falut lynes as Tyranny of Pants. Same loop.

Socks cursed among the ankles who needlessly suffer under this regime. The circulation to the feet is cut off by the elastic bands at the top of the sock, which cling resolutely to the hapless lower calves. Diane was the first to explain this occult brand of totalitarian fashion gear.

In days past, men held their socks up with garters that hung down to the stocking's top end. This genteel way of life has expired, yet the next round of sock manufacturing caused this problem to arise.

A horrific Friday after work, I looked down toward my feet after taking my shoes and socks off. To my dismay, my feet had swelled up- Edema as it's called. It's very bad for people like me, so I was alarmed. Recently, my MD has allowed me to start taking Sp--- again in the hopes of stopping this swelling. After a couple of weeks, my feet looked a little better. Still, I will remain leery of the common el cheapo store bott soxx from Hither on Out. L.

3B   Pre-Sox

What happened to the days of garters for your Sox? Hoot mon.

The strong silent type, Simon Junior stands (or sits) in contrast to the extroverted, glib Traveling Salesman and the self-absorbed ex Simon.

Simon Senior remains unknown. Was it possible that a strict upbringing made him taciturn and monosyllabic? Or was he so blasé he went absentee? So many unknowns remain pursuable yet unknowable except in set theory.

Simon Junior embraced a higher calling after divorcing Simon. They patched things up, and Simon asked him to be the priest when he married Traveling Salesman.

However, he soon had a crisis of faith and abandoned the priesthood. Simon Junior never spoke of it again, and his friends were loath to mention this period of his life.

Still, it came as a shock when news began to circulate about Simon Junior's potential love child. Who was the mom? Who was the dad? Was it immaculately conceived? So much time, so few questions.

Simon found later after having broken up with Quentin Periwinkle that he and his ex could still be good friends. Simon Junior never said "Indeed," and he provided a counterbalance to the effervescent yet ephemeral Simon.

To make a short story long, a complex series of highly moralistic and political serendipkowskis led to Simon Junior University. Built on the former site of Joe's Domestic Auto Repair and Salvaggies, SJU instantly became the third-most tuition sucking institutional in Zysigamore; however, SJ was barred by law from collecting asses.

The relevations about Simon III and the hair's baby momma all failed to shake Simon Junior. His expression remained just as stoic as ever. The University discussed holding a press conference to ventilate the issue to his pubic, but the discussion was cocku borocku by the court of pubic opinion and Simon Junior's reticence to go on the record or even a cassette tape with masking tape over the DEW KNOT RECORD indentation.

Sit.

Axis Mundi of the sprawling, chaotic cast of Classic Play characters sustains sacred absurdity hitherto sequestered. He is the Knower and the Known, the Signifier and the Signified, In- and Out Caskers, Subject-Verb-Object in all Orders.

Never an epitaph for the insular, chthonic one incapable of Death, unknowing radical sanity or rules of egomansplantain, like an unquestioned unanswerability.

4   **Taweret**

Perpetual creativity is the Great Goddess, ubiquitous among the lush nutrient enriched banks of the big river.

Apotropaic panacaeae for all souls should be judiciously consumed in her name. Infinite blessings rotate through the murk.

Taweret, Taweret, sweet hippo, help me with the rebirthday and all rebirths.

Exit velocity

Traveling Salesman, proud great-great-great-great grandchild of the hippo goddess. Member of the clan, DNA punched clear.

Suck out this evil that has polluted these once pure Zysigamore rivers and lakes. We know you.

Again and again, child after child born to the galaxy. Star after star is configured and reconfigured mala like.

Great plumes of feces float on the river's surface. Such immense fertilizer. The people are enriched by Her perpetual creativity.

Four mighty tree trunk legs. Taweret propels herself about, cleansing the earth. Fish constantly surface in the sticky morning sun, attracted to the larvae levitating on the water's surface.

Tyranny of the Brassiere is not known here. Breasts swing generously with each undulating motion.

Each gleam of morning sun illuminates Her seal.

Smoked bargain. Qualities of earth, dirt, biome.

Croc in the back. Suspended ethereal dormitories in endless nautilus patterns.

Taweret is the pride of the river. Great gulps of air, great exhalations from awesome lungs. Sweet drumbeats so heart-shaped, so perfect in every beats per minute. Anhydrous chunks of jewelry sink closer, closer, closer to the muddy bottom, not to surface until several wrinkles of the Earth's crust ripple. Torsion.

4S   Taweret Subiunx

The pig pieces plantations of Zysigamore filled the air with the effulgence of rancid lard and overheated puke. The Xarthorians were traditionally aroused by this influx, and held their Running of the Pig Knuckles meta-event every Shekor.

Threatened teacups ponder mad existence in the fetid waters. Bacteria laden heaps, pools of *C. Diff* in an oily solution, chaos of birth.

It was in this way that Elephant arrived: Not too early and not too surreally. He was just another pachyderm with a *Financial Times* in his tusk. Bacteria cheer his blessed shit.

Ibises in subtle swarms seem to hover above the palms as the sultry air cools. Tehuti stalks our papyri silently.

Goddess in her full radiance: Once, She appeared midwife for 4casta, holding aloft the babe to the pre-dawn stars. In this ultimate descent, the concept of 4csata Queendom hatched. It appears unlikely to happen again - almost unimaginable.

The rub. An ecosystem of life accompanies all hippokind, all crocokind. The gods suffer not the parasites- only mortals do.

Nobody could quite put a hoof to it, but there was little-discussed hunch that Taweret had not found favor with Idajan. Bleary Tim wouldn't admit it, nor would the Queen's X's, ministers, generals or servants. You could say it was the Elephant in the room, were he not living in an adjacent closet.

She will hear the prayers of Urgent Cleric and his followers, so long as they are sincere and phrase their answers in the form of a question.

Stink, stank, stunk. The faithful roll dung balls into indomitable superball houses, climbing inside Khepera-like. Urgent Cleric issues remix upon remix upon remix, unnavigable Uottubbacktothebonieumnn (sp.) upstream undulating unencumbered ubercones under umreal sephiroth.

Iwis Idajan's attention was amiss, leaving Qlippoth Gate open 24 hours if you had some influence and the right size of O-Rings.

Yet the goddess' caduceus was unmolested, growing swiftly by the shoreline. Such cover was made to hide abozilises and ampersands. Supplications start, sunrises sit'n'stair.

-4   Tee Times Ten Zillion

This mezzanine of Zysigamore is inhabited by sentient golf courses. Some of the most vein individuals, each course has its own particular notoriety by which the salesmen used to tell them apart before nav was ubiquitous. Bon marché? Mais non.

Tweaking a caddy in this corner of the multiverse is beyond challenging. Very few from outside this sub-plane would dare enter any of these egotistical courses. With good reason! Flesh-eating sand traps were the least of their worries. Great knuckle sized golf balls full of poison were constantly being ejected onto spectators, caddies and thy guerdon. A humiliating, lethal ritual to have to be exposed to needlessly.

Unfortunately, golf clubs had been banned due to a series of hysterical edicts some fortnights earlier. Yet it never proved to be a hindrance. Some caddies learned telekinesis. Others, more sly and variegated, devised a strategy that used teledildonics and happy thoughts to drive the golf balls.

Golbo, in their language, had to include child sacrifice and needless consumption of polymer substrates.

You had to keep score by tattoo; however, henna was permitted on Guy Flox Day and every other Michaelmas for obvious security reasons.

Whizz'n Lancelloti's brother Butch had been impaled by the 21st hole's flagpole. It was made to look intentional, yet it was an accident. I overheard Trout Fishing in America Shorty meditate on the incident. In a very inebriated voice, TFIAS hoarsely uttered, "I couldn't believe it. Like the hand of God. Judgment." His voice tailed off again before he was defenestrated.

True prayers can be answered, or are they not?

The ghostly disembodied head of Arnold Palmer ejaculating golf courses in his dreams. Like a plate full of paintballs, I could feel the dogleg rights shift across vast yawning landscapes.

5   ¢

Nickel allows the cessation of the smoke; the burning feeling dissipates in consciousnesses of interspersed yoyanas of kingdom.

Instant Hotel. The bed arises with each coin. You can still find tokens that fit into those ecstatic slots. Quarter Sized, like a Hendrix Song.

Akasa and Systems Thinking are thumbs of the hand of Tattva. See how the Palm and Digits flow in harmony and operate under Thumb's rulership.

Beings of fiberglass, Beings of Meta Thaumaturge. Senses of the Chemical bond. Beings capable of operating from all bases beyond the 13' cerebral base of Lord Thumb. Crises diverted skillfully, humanly, widely. Violence met with a Ratimal état d'être. Anaxiforminges.

A space on the Dilator of the Goddess. 5 inches in, the cave relishes its accordion-like malleability. Coming to my ¢s in the usual ways like plays of purpureal minerals. I delve into the cross, the Wicker Man. Pisces Feet where the

(R) big toe curls and twists into irreconcilable shape, like a reptile's talon. Muscles slope sideways and distort the toenail into a Bizarre point. A useful Digit, yet an increasingly homely 1.

Speech is not a ¢ yet SABDA is. Taste is Gunas of the --- --- ---.

See 26.4   Wait, this <u>is</u> the Real 5G Credentialianigingg

-5   G

Laundry vibrates in each of the five dimensions, spin cycle washing the essence of all yoyanas.

Like the beauty of Marilyn McCoo, harmonies ring through the multiverses.

Ultra fast atoms of 5G pulsate from one universe to another, never throttling the speed of light and all the greater speeds.

I need it. I need it.

Simulacra of simulacra of simulacra. Plates of bonbons sink into the muck.

Dynasties come, dynasties go. East folds a ptarmigan.

Sā

Twelve ball's beautiful stripe. Such a pleasure.

Hortle Rodrigueszsz, Non-Interim middle manager of terra cotta oenophiles, is stained by bad vinegar and esoteric cottage cheese.

Climbing the fjord with wads of bubble gum.

Suckle garments. Zysigamore style changes every nanosecond.

The gnomes' previous volleys were impotent. Until they allied with a useful yet pedantic xxend stripling, they were unsuccessful. Pity on this gnomunkind.

When the pantlegs become too tight, the middle kingdoms falter.

A probing pseudopod wraps around each pure 5g nodule. I can't believe the banking. Truffles are for naught.

Memory chip is filled. Eject.

Speed of light? That's too slow. 5g knows no slowth.

When Bernstein had hurt what was kappening, he shrieked with fear or glee. "Prima Causa. Yoy. Eritrebas along thisa

Overhead compartments are sealed shut. Capsules locked.

In the '60s, girls weren't allowed to wear pants to school. Most jobs forbade pants as well. As a result, women looked to Pants as a symbol of fashion independence. In many ways, pants are more amenable to women.

Self examination by several asexual alt right types finds that Women in Pants are causing untold sexual arousal. Surely the shapeless formless mu-mu dress should be brought back to shame those hussies and their slacks, which emphazsizzes they / ovrsəa Kardashibuttes, 553 *

EmanciPants are leggings because they are like tights but not as restrictive. Unfortunately there are boys who just can't handle this kind of zhit. EmanciPants have their drawback when there's no drawstring to em. Then you are promptly oppressed by a snap at

Your waist just below the navel. And, in many sinister slick chick slacks, there is an inner button to fasten that takes your stomach in by one more notch. Merciless. How did my mother's generation cope with this new brand of oppression? Sic transit gloria pantibus. Out of one existential clothing crisis, hip long into another series of oppressions.

Now that I am out of the cycle of donning office slacks on a mostly daily basis, I am having trouble fitting into the pants I wore every week. Since then I have piled on the blubber and can squeeze into only my white fat pants.

-6 A Sad Journey Into Unicorn Harbor

By Burgomaster decree, Pants had been made legal. However, only the left pantleg was legalized. Right pantleg possession or wearing was a Capitol crime in Unicorn Harbor, at least since the Skirmish of the Hamlets back around 922, or March 32nd, 1624.

It was in this desperate metropolis in which Traveling Salesman and Mr. Hi Stop found themselves. Lamentations of women could no longer be heard at 432 Hz. Fortunately neither salesman needed to partake of that frequency for their livelihoods.

"What's it about, Hi? Where's the angle?" Traveling Salesman watched for Mr. Hi Stop's response, which was utterly incomprehensible yet profound.

There was a supplier up in the hill country that Clytemnestra did business with. His shoppe was closed when they came to his door. Yet it was the impetus they needed. It seemed to be so simple, almost elementary. Yet it would fool the constables and the dullard Xarthorians every time.

"You see," said Hi, "when you switch on the 5g, the soy makes the other pantleg invisible. So only the wearer will be able to enjoy the right pantleg at the same time as the left one."

Mr. Hi Stop elaborated. "Plus there's an encryption technology in the zipper that allows only your friends and confidantes to experience the right pantleg. The young people are going to dig it."

Ordinary account managers had abandoned Unicorn Harbor in the mistaken belief that left pantlegs were unprofitable. This created a unique opportunity for Hi and TS. Clytie's patent in their back pockets, they were poised to become Sultans of Sales.

The Burgomaster's Chiefs of Staff were pliable and easily bribed. They had no part in the Right Pantleg ban. Many had privately opposed it. But the power structure was such that they felt paralyzed; the constant vacilation flummoxed all observers.

7   PP: Psuidable Ptarmigan

Tantalizing armpit deepens, recedes, the nautilus shape of ecstatic perfection.

Plumes of mimeograph paper plough the tetrasphere along the subliminal furrows.

Innate, inchoate, pheromones to ingest. Plurality.

Home along vast stretches of rust and enamel, and has to happen. Polyphemus a soul of care.

Good. Tightly wrapped enchiladas. Rolled items.

Muskedelian music wafts into the troposphere. Kinetic giants mix yoyanas of coffee notes set to a belly dancing beat. As stark as a disembodied tail feather, but not as barren as that freightful dayling.

An unopposable thumb rifles through coarse axillary hair. It's growing again. She doesn't shave it. The thumb's exoskeleton prevents the perspiration from getting through.

A dwelling this way conforms to every plotted point in the matrix.

If I ever had to...Morrigan

Topknot slips loose, only hanging by a small lock of hair. Spiders could do it better.

Interfield, an endless series of wickets that welcomes you through yielding semi-permeable membranes. Any velocity will be adequate.

Hunks of farfel are poised toward a harmonious correlation of

Very good seer. To sprinkle always

Ionios stares around the weeping dynamos. Settling in. We have a theory.

More delicate wings to shed.

To divulge more is to exude pus.

-7   Polymorphing

Dwellvelopmint for Raptors happens upon certain phases. Re-egg, re-shed. A comfy cove that shelters yet restricts. But Nature shudders, and a chrysalis opens to the sunshine.

Fickle are the oracles. But most fickle are we who forget the crystal is a reflection of us, extrapolated into the likely future. Don't expect your money back. The oracle isn't an entertainer.

In this world of Rupa, forms oscillate. Being free means being able to try on the diverse shapes throughout the world of forms. Some seem magic but are not; often the opposite is true.

Meta analysis of shuffling atoms - can it be done in a shuffling machine?

Metamorphosis of a 1/10,000th of a living being. Changes are constantly happening. Breath leaves me. Hairs separate from my scalp. Fingernails, toenails come and go. There is certainly an undercurrent of mournful recognition of me as the tree, maturing then declining and rotting.

The word of sin is Restriction.

Subtle dweomers to let one pass, sleight of body trick. The automatic armor that unconsciously is deployed is much like that initial eggshell space. We sacrifice its insular comfort in exchange for growth.

Eternity's fractional divisions may be satisfied within the parameters of computing. But the eternal exists both externally and internally.

8   **Chapter Eight**

A

-8   **Negative Chapter Eight**

-A

9   **Yod**

Chaos of the Universe. Look at this diamond. Subtlest mnemonics. Zeros. Nines. Nines. She the Nuit. Perfect framework. Ultimate dissolution of the order only sleeping; she does rise again unceasingly. She cannot help but not set. Nuit sprinkles Yods into the snow globe-o-sphere. Some shatter on impact like meteorites. But most remain intact and lay on the ground until undergoing a deep process of rot, a fetid stink of eroded immortality.

I gather them at night, whether under Arcturus-light or no, using a Ninth basket held loosely. When you start at the right time, you grab the Yods at their highest potential. Repairing back to the Yuga-Hut, I store them in shelves within shelves. They say never to disturb the Yods once you have stashed them away, but I find that it makes little difference. Any time I want a handful - and never more than a handful every 6 hours - I avail myself of the maturest, most vivrant Yods. They are great the way they are. But you can also make a poultice out of them if... <ALL IS HIDDEN> Nines. The reason for the 9 invulnerability is in its Diamond Sq. Formulation. Centered in Worcester, this Rubik's cube-like Gem cannot be broken. Every cell can hold a Yod indefinitely. Still others, lying vacant for centuries, can achieve a weightless, substanceless, gravityless, lightless state of existence like a pre-Big Bang non-universe.

If $9 = 0$, then $9 \times 1 = 7$. $30330 = 9 = 0$. $\therefore$ the angles lock consistently @ 90. Selah. If U were a 9 yuo'd B Happy 2 $\therefore$

-9   **Xxend**

Le Grimoire describes the xxend but does not elaborate on their origins and nature. I was intentional.

Beepy, the first xxend, was a small leftover lump of clay remaining from the original avian being that I sculpted - sort of an organic extraterrestrial R2D2 character to complementary sidekick to the primary aerial being that Beepy was matched with.

"A xxend appears as a square mass, being blue in color and spotted with yellow. One eye lies in the centure of its front side, with a thin mouth stretching across the front. Over the top of the body is a natural propulsion device, with openings in the front and back."

The xxend doesn't stand; it can hover in place, or move in any direction that it wishes. They lack arms, legs, and other limbs associated with anthropocentrism.

Xxend language being completely incomprehensible to humans, they communicate solely with telepathy.

Contemporary authors were certain of the xxends' three dimensionality in order to ascertain the star system in which they were born. However, it's difficult to follow this evolution from a traditional linear belief system.

Fortible confluence of Dopplegnugen and Sforce. Telepathy so pure that no 5g in the multiverse cold ever approach the average xxend's. Bones were of supple polymers and ancient fossilized ingredientibus.

All baluchimorphs, xxend included, include this dweomer.

Interstellar dust and gas was never an issue.

10   O-Ring

Being a functional stonehenge, J.O. Lundberg ventures in Emily Dickinsonian notoriety if not ubiquity. Like the druids before him, J.O. Lundberg lived a life of mystical opacity. The more written about Mr. Lundberg, the more is known latitudinally. May 12, 1896. This just can't be. J.O. would want us to slip into the rabbit hole he eased us into

A donut universe, the O-Ring satisfies in many fashions. The donut universe has many lubricants smeared upon it, preventing friction and letting me glide into yoyanas between planetoids. Silicone is pleasing and lets in delightful lights to light.

Ten point three, shut down. O-ring couples lubricated. A bathtub multiverse perched atop the 2 miniature donuts, a beautiful crease.

Sealants, sealed, the slide of the infamous slow leak. Never use Vaseline - it's an immoral corruption.

Cultish. Leads dissolve in Sweden. Clearly the lubricant was only social. O-Ring must be free, beyond all limitationiges.

Considering all the sociology, Inventors have never Left Sweden. They are either imprisoned or willingly abandon their intellectual property because they knew IP = slavery.

Östergötland.·.

Torus.

O-Ring Universal Model of Heavens.

-10   Apologia

Among the downtrodden Xarthorian proles arose an "Urgent Cleric," Zzyster the Terraplaned. As a youthful, pious sort, he won the affections of the benighted of Zysigamore Island. But when Zzyster became a leader in the Xarthorian Church, he aroused the interest of many royals, including Queen Idajan.

At the time, the Magenta Gang had seized control of all the trade in color toners, particularly in Uottubbacktothebonium (sp.) (sic). Magenta Gang leaders had sown discontent with Idajan for many years, and stymied her cache of ink and toner cartridges.

Rev. Zzyster, however, assuaged the Xarthorians that peace would come, and that pants would remain optional for true believers. The cartel soon weakened as the Queen's engineers tapped a vein of pure ruby red toner deep in the badlands. Now she could move to more complicated mattress.

Soon, Rev. Zzyster, yclept Urgent Cleric, was named First Prelate of Idajan's First Temple of Taweret. He accepted the job "in the name of piety and propriety," and vowed to counteract the chaotic fascist impulses of Zombie Overlords of the Ningarm. His brother Meco meanwhile got an admin job with the temple. Though Meco was a himbo hottie, the good Rev still had his admirers.

The Urgent Cleric's humble appeal even attracted the likes of Simon. "I haven't been to church since that whole transubstantiation episode gave me a conniption. Maybe things are changing?" Traveling Salesman and Elephant were not interested in attending, so Simon made doo with books on tape. "The Rev has such a sexy voice," Simon gushed. "I really feel the love." Maybe Simon could be introduced to some celebrities at a semenar?

The first reform that the good Rev passed was banning lip-sync at choir practice. Next, he banned chewing tabacky during service, causing some of the older Xarthorians to drop out. The semi-attired dancing boys were also fazed out, much to the chagrin of Simon. "I guess that's progress," he sighed.

The Rev considered himself ace, according to his bro Meco. But the troof was eye than meets the more. He was married to the Great One, Lady Taweret, particularly in the public eye. But Zzyster had an extended platonic relationship with X's #001 herself, whose name is shrouded in eternal mystery, i.e., Shannon Norman. Simon always approved of her hairdo, and her avatar on the Psychic Friends Network. "She knows the way to the 408 y'all."

-10A Light Out for the Territory

The Gold family surprised their Kid with a virtual reality game called Zhinthab Adventurer. Donning the headsets and holding the controllers, the Gold Kid and Marquez began to play. Marquez records his audio as he plays. Gold Kid furiously changes his virtual T-shirt every 46 seconds or so. "It's On!" displays the Kid's T.

At the corner of C Prompt and G Clef I caught a ride on a Flying V.

The rain, so sleek and dark, seemed to peel off the guitar as we soared.

It being nearly Midsummer, the light still shone to my south as the mountains of Uottubbacktothebonyiumville (sp.) faded and the ice sea dominated my field of vision.

"So that..." reads the Kid's T.

I could see the theta waves in a crisp, jagged oscillation crashing into the frozen shoreline of this uninhabited eyeland. Grey-green cliffs like cowled crusaders guard a landscape of muddled whites and browns. A few more miles inland, by a bare, round hillock- here will do. I touch down; Yellow Kid's T-shirt inquit, 'Frequent Flyer Yoyanas.'

This plateau has a serene vista, the frigid ocean to one side and the wilderness at my back. The scent - the Territory - the camp essentials - a going for refuge. [I'm searching = Gold Kid].

Sunset draws chromatic hues darken slowly by the second and flow through my visual cortex. A true pilgrim travels by night save in the brutal Zysigamore winters. Gold Kid's T-shirt reads 'Ain't It Haxenological?'

Coffee. Hip hop to the AM. We, the Ice Princes, accept no Fortinbrasiges on thisa territory. I don the BMFR hockey-style jersey that the Kid hands me. No time crystals - don't trust 'em. Trust what you feel and see.

Dragons far between but few. Thisa White is named Hsabr. They agree to fly us in exchange for a dragon-sized copy of the Kid's T reading 'Paideuma or Bust.' No dracosaddle - just holed on 4 dear life.

Snow squallity. I blinked - the Kid's T even blinked, I swear. Hsabr is at home in a storm. S/he seems to surthrive a snoshower overstanding the element's hostility towards pathetic me's poor monsters manunkind.

Aerofloating back past the Islands of Un-Undomination, I sneeze. No stifle. The Kid's T: Is there a there there? My hoodie is unphased koollogiq. Hands off, and slide down Hsabr's back like a YABBA DABBA GABBA HEY. Hsabr emits an icy cone of frost to say "Graciolas" as s/he soars away.

A twinge of sadness in safety. Even the font on the Kid's T-shirt seems to shrink and wither into Courier New. The Kid already has his VR headset off. 'Won't need it no how no more' reads his T. "What? You don't want to play anymore?" asked an incredful Marquez as the Gold Kid, causally tossed his headset onto a La-Z-Girl. His T changed to 'NNSBB', drawing a Hi 5.5 from his buddy. Marquez inquit, "Pee-Yunk!"

11   Clytie

Clytemnestra X. Willow, 30300 Oak Lane. Clytie had lost track of how long she had been at this address, yet it had only been a few ticks of the clock before.

The third dimension is hard for higher order individuals to adapt to. Those who cannot will simply place an avatar there to hover. Some are made to flicker at night; others remain completely invisible. In their own dimension, time is bioluminescence, and does not place the same incessant restrictions on individuals that time does. It can be rather annoying. Yet Clytemnestra was not laughing, in her heart or in her mouth.

Hi Stop had perfected this subtle shift. He was rewarded steadily by the activity which he considered natural. Clytie had never bothered, as it felt unnatural and somehow unethical. Yet she benefited constantly through her use of technology.

Clytie's visage only changed with the light, not with her moods. These remained in the vestigial exoskeleton in the side of her duodenum. Neither being oppressed by pants nor clock hands, she appears as she constantly does. Yet the green and azure bioluminescence compliments her spectrum.

"Hi, when you're finished in Uottub, please call me." Clytemnestra had always made a point of never touching the 5g. Her Xarthorian employees were free to help themselves of course. Some of these worlders' outside hustles could be quite scandalous, yet Clytie did little to intervene.

Clytemnestra had invented pantleg-only pants, which immediately freed humans from the tightening around their waistlines which was hampering their health. Authorities realized this was an innovation, yet many petty pluggers refused to believe.

-11   Hypogastroporphyry

Sunset. The veil thins for several fleeting intervals. Lives cross lives cross lives, swaying back and forth as if jumping rope. Night hags awakened by by circadian rhythms take wing in each elongated shadow and treetop roost. Adepts, meanwhile, conjure unspeakable nightmares with high-level incantations.

Yet many tiny monsters that wash into our plane at dusk actually stay around for extended periods. It is said that Demon Joe was able to enter undetected this way, slowly maturing from a larva to the tacky entrepreneur he is today. Of course, Old Joe denies this story seven ways to Monday. "It's actually more ramonetic than that," he swears.

The firmament quakes, and smattering of yods falls to the Island. Most are lost to the worldly Xarthorians, but a few diamond-like ones slide into embossed quadrilateral storage pods. Creatures of magick steal back to them in the evening, ensuring yods stay squirreled away from plying eyes.

You don't have to be hothechajuxips to find 'em, but some say it helps. Zero-headed anti-Big Bang sauropods clang together, sometimes unearthing a truffle-like yoyana of a yod about the size of a pisces' pseudopod. As if

Enormous grey hooves smack the ground. Headed horsemen's absolute value waxes in new moon twinklesky. Nightmare fumes of stodgy sulfur linger in the heavy pre-dew air. I cling to the ionogram. "Negative nine. Negative nine."

Front at the Yuga-Hut, I unspire towards reverie. Psalm psayl intself.

Sunrise. Sunrise. Sunrise within sunrise. Sheets of blue, orange, pink, purple.

11 am. Three within a three within a three. Countdown. Tick, tick marks rhythm into sabda. I never had to

Quartzile spraypaned nonerism exactorates. Bonds grow bright yet moody in spiraluminescence. A cenotaph endures salvaged lost metayoyanas inigmatically. Preformed prehensile peat

Afternoon siesta lengthens. Nothing to enter or exit Qlippoth now: It's not a turnstile after all. Yesod

12   O'Clock

12:01	Din Dan Dong	12:02	A hole, a hole
12:03	Use it or lose it	12:04	Tk Tk Tk
12:05	Om tare	12:06	A pen cap, a 4 skin
12:07	Baby Bleu Bich	12:08	A stream, a brook
12:09	One room school	12:10	Our Portrad Mouse
12:11	Cobalt and Cyan	12:12	Nova True
12:13	A red candle	12:14	4 the zoo
12:15	Bugs for Diane	12:16	I wake up
12:17	I break up	12:18	I shake up
12:19	I make up	12:20	Clear lashes
12:21	Left pant, right pant	12:22	Left sock, right sock
12:23	Left shoe right shoe	12:24	Left right left right
12:25	Right left right right	12:26	This a that
12:27	Brick a brack	12:28	Tit a tat
12:29	Rat a tat	12:30	Sit sit sit
12:31	Em eye see	12:32	Be oh bea
12:33	In er tree	12:34	La n ta
12:35	Ta n la	12:36	Cum dum
12:37	Rum tum	12:38	To var tov
12:39	Ho par luv	12:40	Near a far
12:41	Cola	12:42	Fawn
12:43	Sigma	12:44	Dawn
12:45	De-a	12:46	Ah
12:47	Hah	12:48	Hush
12:49	That	12:50	Fuss
12:51	Kaz a whoop	12:52	Rang a tang
12:53	L-E-N	12:54	Me he he he
12:55	Tee he he he	12:56	Tick a tack
12:57	Brick a bat	12:58	Tock a dock
12:59	Rock Rock Rock	12:60	-30- :) :(CCLII

Demon Joe was in a bind. He was way behind on his loan from the Cyan Boys, and their main enforcer Tonka Wonky was here, tonight. This just wouldn't do. Joe tried to ingratiate himself. "So nice to meet you, Tonka. Won't you please have a seat?" Unfortunately Mr. Wonky didn't look very hungry.

You see, Joe had become GM of the largest chain of Polynesian restaurants on Zysigamore. Crowds came out every night; booze flowed like mucus; and his chefs came out with such flamboyant dishes that celebrities like Li'l Nas Y and Bryant Brick were often seen in its many dining rooms. Still, Demon Joe was hemorrhaging dough.

One night, Clytemnestra had brought Simon and Christimiqua to a Wei Back restaurant outside of Umlaut Towin. The garish decor was based on 6,000 years of recycled Chinese history and creepy artifacts stolen from different levels of the Abyss. "Don't you just love this place? Mirrors and parasols everywhere," gushed Simon as their party was escorted to a booth near Tonka Wonky, who polished his brass knuckles and glared at the wait staff.

A karaoke duo broke out a selection of Yacht Rock ballads that Demon Joe often attributed to the Shang Dynasty. As the male and female singers surged into a particularly stultifying rendition of "Islands in the Stream," Demon Joe leveled with the hitman. "Look, I don't want no trouble. I got several Demon Lords after me. Yeenoghu says I'm a real mook. Orcus don't return my calls." "That's not my problem, Mr. Chop Suey." Tonka Wonky whipped out his gun and smashed all the china on his table. Shouts and shrieks from the rest of the customers ensued; Simon fainted into his moo goo gai pan. "OK, I'll take you there. You'll see. I got the goods." Beads of sanguine perspiration oozed out of Demon Joe's leathery skin. "I can make this money back right away. Even today. Let's go." Tonka waved his gun and followed Demon Joe to a Tenser's Floating Disk hovering near a dumpster in the alley behind the Wei Back.

Demon Joe took Tonka to a truck stop with several 53 foot trailers. "See this? These are all filled with 5g. Pure uncut shit. You want a piece of this? I can cut you in."

The bruiser opened a trailer door to check it out for himself. He walked in a few steps and turned beet red. "What the fuck is this bullshit!" "Huh?" yelled Demon Joe, his raspy voice echoing through the largely empty trailer. "This is the 5g you are looking for. Just off the boat from Shanghai."

Tonka Wonky held the lid of a 55-gallon drum with a hand so strong it seemed to bend the metal effortlessly. "Soy. You're cutting it with fucking soy. Motherfucker, I should just waste you now!"

"No, it's not like that. You don't understand. I got a little...problem." Joe rubbed his small horns anxiously as he elaborated. "I got hooked. Yeah, getting high on your own supply ain't cool. But I promise I'll make it up to you by Friday." Once again, sweat oozed so quickly from every one of Demon Joe's infernal pores you'd swear he had hemorrhagic fever.

13   Slide(s)

The PowerPoint constitution of Metallurgiphiles is a display of sheer simulacritude. Like Caesar's Gaul, Slides will divide and slow-ride this explanation of Zysigamore.

Slide. Slide. Sli....ide. Why don't we?

Slide 13.2: Animate

William Rowan Hamilton gets around.

Abigail Adams in a catsuit.

Slide. Miniature burgers.

Baby minotaurs

Bathyscaphes through the ages

Reading Agrippa by candlelight

Demographics of population: 1000 - present.

Lerbiax in Easter hay.

Oldagmarfrisbie daguerrotype

Rivers and Lakes of the Infernal Planes

Popular economic theories of today's society

Young Fortinbras in tie dee why tease

Fixed Point Polaris

Yeenoghu's Flail: The Butcher (with short video clip)

DF&J Org Chart

Archie Comics Timeline

Classic Play Flow Chart (with animation)

Slide. Three habits of highly engaged Xarthorians.

Ladder to Limbo

Tardigrade anatomy

Tardigrade physiology

Stock-and-flow diagram: 100 Years of Solitude

Clinical Tables

-click to add title-

-13   Zombie Overlords of the Ningarm

A pit full of larvae and elder sox led to the Demon Men of the Ningarm's emergence. What wretched wizardry would want what we were wers wersi werin wensing hath overwrought. Some media types blamed Aegothsorzhotan for zombifying several batches of of Demon Men and making them even more annoying. Of course he stridently denied any involvement.

The job quickly fell to the Urgent Cleric, who was personally yclept by Her Majesty Herselph. "Deal with these zombies as quickly as you can," she urged, promising a large endowment for his parsonage. He bowed and confronted this chaggellne: quell the zombie uprising by any means necessary. "Consider it done," replied Rev. Zzyster.

The whole gang (including Zzyster, GNG, Mr. Hi Stop, Traveling Salesman, Clytemnestra, Striker and Li'l Nas Y, but not Simon, out on injured preserve with a hangnail) adventured to confront the Zombie Men. There had been Zombie Men raids at homesteads out by the Caves of Chaos, and they seemed to be getting too close to Idajan and her retinue. "So where do we begin?" asked Mr. Hi Stop as he pored over the schematics of a proposed attack. "These zombies are stupid. Really dumb. They got the numbers, but we got the know-how to beat them. And Striker, you got supplies. OK, let's roll."

The group got off on the third foot, however. Rev. Zzyster's collar had too much starch, and Li'l Nas Y was soon out of spoons after a breakup. But before the adventurers punted, a gaggle of Ace TV reporters and interns arrived to genuflect on their amazeballs anectoarachnanomalous abilitizzles.

That's when Traveling Salesman and Mr. Hi Stop subconsciously deadhandpanned one of their most outrageous salesmanship seminaricles on the Ningarm Men. Striker kept hurling speedsicles at each deadmeat zommom and zomdad, beheading-befooting-bearming-bechumming the hapless monstrums. Before he knew it, Striker's lackeys and hired goons were cremating vast piles of zombodies. Clytie skipped the battle to get her nails did. "Kaz-a-Whoop!"

Later, Clytie refracted on the antitelegenetic spectacle with Christy and Misty. "The zommoms fell down in a spuddle of lipomas. The men were wurst." The girls were thoroughly disgusted. "How did you know when it was all over?" asked Misty. "Just instinct, I guess. That and the media coverage."

Sure as shittin, Ace TV had moved on to the next big menace: Flexed-out jicklehips spewing toxic tomato juice. On the downside, Striker was stuck with a warehouse full of speedsicles that even Demon Joe didn't want.

14   Bathyscaphe

Deeper than a page of a book - let me look. Deeper than an ASCII salad of characters.

Insatiable hunger of the lerbiax often leads it into trouble - yours, not theirs on average.

Geoawesomesausages, hydrographicals are hued in elaborate spectrum from black to purple. All my contours are smooth, circular, straight.

Lord of this kingdom is the lupine aspect of Baphomet.

Baphomet preens in dark places far below the ocean's floor. Still, He steals upward into the water occasionally by way of a hidden cavern entrance deep beneath the waves and vicissitudes. He has His underlings use a network of tiny fissures virtually undetectable by lidar.

Once, when Baphomet's nephew wanted an extensive tour of the shores of Zysigamore, their bathyscaphe scraped a massive ice cube off of a previously gargantuan iceberg. This chunk calved off the side of Baphomet's scaphe, shocking the demon prince immeasurably. Surely something should be done. The pride of a Demon is infinite.

And so the Lord was driven to build an entirely new bathyscaphe. Harvesting organs Kundabuffer from some forlorn Xarthorians, Baphomet gained far more torque and greater protection from the elements.

Every propeller was ready, lovingly polished by a pack of ghouls. Now, it is submerged in the abyss. "Slimed again, you pinhead. By the pimples in Juiblex's elaborate series of recta, I curse you!"

The stripling burst into tears. Fortunately they were someone else's.

Baphomet's deluxe bathyscaphe soon began to misfire, the slime leaking into the inner chambers. Surely this was the work of some do-gooder, or, even worse, a betrayal by one one or more of the Demon's enemies in Hell. Only the FM radio continued to work. "This is ZSZO, your pop rocker! Wacky Ted here with another Roger Valdorus marathon!" Baphomet sighed. "God damn it."

-14   A Fortnight's

While Mr. Hi Stop and Traveling Salesman were on the road for two weeks, Clytemnestra and Simon had planned to get together for a night out.

Simon put down his Si-Phone and started to shriek. "I won! I won! I won!" He received notice that he had won two tickets to the Li'l Nas Y concert that week.

"Great," replied Clytie. "I'll prepare the party bathyscaphe so we don't have to travel commercial. Fortunately she had just wired the ZSS *Ankylotron* for smooth astral travel, installing new portholes and renting several go-go dancers for the trip.

Simon and Clytie got together the morning of, drinking mimosas and getting their hair and nails did. "Say Simon, where is tonight's show, anyway? And will we be asked to jello wrestle again?" Simon smirked, "No, jello is optional, you silly goose. It's at the Jelly Center, 222nd Layer of the Abyss. We got this! The DJ said it would be cool."

Taking no chances, Clytemnestra brought a spray bottle of white wine vinegar and holy water. Plus the coveralls she brought for her and Simon would cut down on the disgusting puce ooze they would surely encounter.

To reach the Jelly Center, the bathyscaphe had to descend through a layer of aspic half a mile thick and growing, with random chunks of cat food and pork rinds in sickly neon colors. Finally the stadium came into view. She parked the bathyscaphe on the edge of a tar pit full of sewage and axle grease.

Security led them right through the crowd and down a fetid, gloomy tunnel reeking of carrion and bad intend. To their dismay, they were seated two rows over from Juiblex, the Putrid Lord of Slime himself. "You know, I dated him in trade school," whispered Simon.

Then Li'l Nas Y broke into his new radio hit, "Fortinbras Shorts." "I wanna be your shorts tonite. Hoo!" He began gyrating his tush right in front of El Slime-o Themself.

Just then the over stimulated Demon Lord belched forth a wave of toxic green slime, drowning their hapless go-go dancers. "He's the slime," said Clytie.

"No, I'm the slime! I'm the slime," shouted Don Pardo.

Devil has control of all prophecy and games of chance. To play the Candy Land board game is to enter the pits of Dante's Hell, each gumdrop and lollipop representing another Infernal Host that has enslaved you.

The Devil's Left Handed Woman only rouses at Midnight to infest the sweet dream world of White Christian Heterosexual Cisgender Men. She the Queen of Hell, Proserpine of the vast canyons, caverns and pits of those infernal lands. Give up all Nav, Ye who enter here.

Devil doesn't lack for henchmen and henchwomen. Devil is not known by many names. Mostly no name at all. Devil accumulates the names irregardless, then parcels out those names among the Associate Devils and Assistant Devils that occupy the infernal Org Chart. Devil does not need a name. Devil is there before Name.

The lowest ranked Spirits enter the Material Plane via many vessels - especially the bottles of Alcohol that every town is full of. A demon in every bottle. It is the most direct portal to Earth for the most minor, trivial imps of the lowest strata of the Org Chart. Yet, if unchecked, these little spirits can weaken the veil between the Lower Planes and our world of tears, allowing the likes of Beelzebub to come and go as he pleaseth. So mote it Bee(r).

Correcting timesheets

-15   **Idem, Computans de Farina**

The invites were prepared in gold leaf for the most extravagant feast that the Lower Planes had ever seen. Asmodeus vowed to put it on, and even to invite the rulers of Hades and the Abyss to His so-called "First Supper."

"I've already booked the Allman Isley Band, Pettiler Stevens Band, Shecky Love Johnson and Li'l Nas Y. Get me a few more yacht rock bands, some more death metal, maybe a goth emo band that fricassees babies on stage," chortled Asmodeus to his longtime majordomo Baalberith. "We'll even get Ezra Pound to do his shtick with a hip-hop DJ. Of course there will be plenty of burlesque, drag and boy swallowing."

Asmodeus didn't want to ruin the decor on His Ninth Circle of Hell, so He decided He would contract an élite interior decorating consultant to handle this superficial yet cloying task. He scanned through hundreds of search results before a particular link got his attention. "Hmm," he stroked his Van Dyke, "Periwinkle. Maybe he can do the job. That old hippo Taweret? No fucking way!"

"Hello, this is who? Indeed!" On the other end of the line, Quentin was incredulous. Why would the Arch Devil be calling him? "Yes yes. We can do the job. Yes, yes, you are quite generous." Before Quentin knew it, he had accepted Asmodeus' proposal. "OK, I'll meet you there, honey."

Later that evening a vampire psychopomp arrived on the wing to transport Quentin to Avernus, the First Circle of Hell. Quentin turned to the vampire. "Does my hair look all right?" They both clicked their heels thrice; suddenly they were on the shore of a toxic-looking lake spewing putrid slime and noxious fumes.

With a "Poof!" the vampire changed to its bat form and flew rapidly into the drab crimson sky of Avernus. Quentin was rather miffed. "Hmph. Stood up again. Just my luck to fall for another man in black." He began chewing his nails.

Asmodeus appeared. Quentin pulled his hands away from his mouth. "You dirty rat!" exclaimed Quentin. "You expect me to work my magic in a place that smells like pickled demon farts? Think again!" Asmodeus grinned. "No big whoop. My boys can use Smell-o-Vision with the petrichor extensions." With the snap of His well groomed nails, the Arch Devil summoned several chuck wagons and muscular devils. "Here's my crew. We can have this dining hall built in a hurry. And don't mind the smell. You'll get used to it. I'm sure you've sniffed a few bums in your time," laughed Asmodeus. Quentin, however, refused to take the bait.

"I said I would do this job. But I want 50% up front. And all the construction workers need to be buff, tanned and greased." Surprisingly, Asmodeus gave in to all his demands. "Ordinarily I would have skewered you by now. But it's cool."

16   Clubhouses of the Team Gods

Babble encrypted in aspic. The Gods invent a Big Coin for their diversion. Stalled clouds kill the system.

Traveling Salesman, great-great-grandson of thee Omnipotent Senior God.

Delivery sheets of unwashed basilisks. Calls to make love.

Plug in the Dog Horn for the Goddess of Extratuition.

Demons the inferior gods skulk in sunlight, extrapolated from their own Ichor. See Chapter 666.

And the gods declared: Real sports like Football and Spring Football. All others may be cataloged as Games of Chance.

Metatron moonlights as Demigod of Wall to Wall Carpeting.

Grand Xanadu built from playing cards reinforced with shellac. Gloria in Excelsis. But most people play cards via the computer or smartphone; kali yuga exeunt.

Tonic lovers are given their own Mezzanine Paradise.

Doug a God of Factory-to-Dealer Incentives

This coven a Sultan of Sales. Shades of "Bob" at twilight. Equipoise, the faithful chant their heart warming vocal.

A Mum passes away in Singapore. Om Mani

_____, God of the Other Bowler from Australia

Ginny Wax. Goddess of the Hair-Free Body, except for hair where you want hair.

Inkateria, Goddess of Dresses and Tunics

Fourinha, Goddess of Kitchen Furniture.

-16   With a Nod to Catullus

Two thousand years of blanks, beeps and radio edits.

Pagans assfucking, facefucking, fist fucking. Fucking in all holes. Fucking where there is 0 hole.

Fucking like a rapist sky god come down from Olympus when wifey isn't around. Fucking because you have to fuck something, somehow, somewhere.

Fucking a random hole in a fence. Fucking a piece of plastic that vaguely resembles a woman. Fucking a piece of plastic that vaguely resembles a pig. Fucking

Moloch ass raping, face raping. Moloch who comes to Simon's Door. Moloch who wears rubbers only when He wants to.

Sticking your penis in everything, everywhen, everywhere. Sticking your penis in stone, in metal, in wood, in earth.

Fucking Europa with your Bull cock and balls. Fucking Ganymede until he is paralyzed.

Fucking musical instruments. Cutting off your penis and replacing it with an electric guitar.

Zeus, wiping his dick off with a sheep's skin. Zeus languidly masturbating as he watches young nymphs. Zeus begging Dionysus to suck him off.

Fucking the antediluvian one who is irrumated and jizzes in unison.

Irrumator flits to every chain of the circle jerk, fluffing their way through the garden of penises. They swallow, they lick their lips. They progress to the next cock.

Sore crucified Jesus cock, perfectly circumcised penis of the Lord. Most desirable phallus of all penises ever created, or ever to be created. Judas winks. He too lost his bussycherry to John the Baptist.

17   Stella

Cows of moon dextrose evolve flight and begin to drift. Sevenward sightings of these superbovines skew the cytotoxicity. Ad astra per vaccas. Homogenized mix of cow pieces in the ionosphere in the last trace of their substantiation.

Permeable membranes envelop the Star Systems. Cows above, cows throughout the heavens are called.

Stella minoris urbem facit....Ad peccatarem venire.

Fireworked multeorites streak back to the Earth - Eye panopticon, multi hued brilliance of the atmosphere's friction. Sit.

Pulsar galaxy yoyana kingdom dazzles with ancient Effulgence; perfection atop and below, starboard and port.

We sat on the lip of Pettit Crater and were afraid to ponder the gulfs between the stars, the vast voids that help the stars maintain their significance.

Primaries and their comites flit across the Peterson Diagram like holy marbles. Hurts to feel this matterless, this designificant.

Zeta Ursae Majoris burns retinas; however, the cooler cows are unperturbed by the coelestis.

She-bear-cow beams magnitudes of photovoltaic karma within the astrophysics of the aged. My interferometer is set 100%.

Truly the duplicity makes the firmament fertile enough for Taweret. The waters of the Milky Way churn under her magnificent hooves.

Helical astral filaments undulate far, far removed from the optical prelusions of the multiverse. The Gods are above the fray. The sundry inner and outer planes with their own spiral universes burst into fresh sentient material and semi-infinite sub-reality layers of hosannas.

Seinsvergessenheit drives the shades into lower planes customized for their needs. Qlippoth Gate sorts the dead into one realm or another. Thick darkness obscures contact with other shades- not invisibility, but an all permeating pollution.

Light being hard to come by, many of the rulers of the lower realms have to use creative solutions. John Adams signed a deal with Light Bearer, aka Old Scratch, to use an ersatz white whole sun each blessed neocolonial "day" in Paideuma. Other circles of Hell and layers of the Abyss use bioluminescence, magic, flame or pique to work around the omnipresent dark material in their worlds.

Yet the best solution was via Da'ath. "Your death hack determines your lifehack," says the pendemic Xarthorian fable. You were quickly plotted within a 3D Chinese checkers-like Qabalah game board, the sparkling chromatic marbles gleaming their inner gloe into the voids within. The winning move: Merkaba of darkinos.

Amino acid intelligence lies hidden in the helixes, uncaring, unknown, its inscrutable purposes lying just outside that sensory membrane. THIS AAI supersedes all the rest with its algorhythm method, a complete map of all freewilled possibilities previously unaccounted 4.

King Nothing Else Matters is dressed in black leather in all weather. This sovereign is beyond the In- and Outcasker duality, beyond ink, beyond oil. He is the Ain, Ain Soph, & Ain Soph Aur; Hwalearastok.

Devils and demons beg for KNEM's support, craving dark matter for their planes. But the King is not in the business of dishing it out, or heating it or cooling it. His concordance limits these brutish beings' supply, and often keeps them in check on their own outer planes.

Tzimtzum contractions, and Zysigamore is born with all its inherent contradictions, spacelog and contraindications. Ample scren vehicles still streak through the sky - the best weigh to travel.

Existential metaversical hodgepiggle, like a jabberwock or a jacked-up jicklehip, reverberates in all the intelligences, remaining pretached to pure clear lights that turn on, tune in. Tenebros of Akashic records spills out of a recursive series of file cabinet drawers within drawers, folders within folders, envelopes

18   Moon

Of Animals, Bloody Solstice. The veil wafts in the arising abreeze. Tittering dry leaves, faint calls of tree frogs, insects. Mother Nuit's pendulous breasts shed milk into the evening sky. Dogs stir, unidentifiable small creatures scurry from bush to bush.

A man is forced off the road after a long day. So he gets to expense this. $40 per diem, no receipts. A straight shot. He might bunk alone, but he may not if the stir shifts. The slide rule in his head pivots back and forth. How much to tip? Oh bother. Wives in every city, but one may not answer the phone. Blues passes over with the faint gibbous moonlight penetrating pinprick points through the worn curtains. No webs, but certainly still spiders spinuflecting in silence behind a bureau. Stale peanuts from the vending machine. A matchbook. "Best pizza in town." Three hour Martinizing!

Some time after 11, a soft tap on the motel room door. "It's Jesie," she whispers in a subliminal sibilance. "OK" states Traveling Salesman. He cometh to the door. Sub rosa, sub luna, in hoc dal signo; pulcherrima mihi. Nocte

Crayfish in and out of the smooth stones. Water bugs skim the pond's surface. A faint scent of wild honeysuckle in the bog. William Wordsworth tinged scale, 45th magnitude stars more or less obscured by the haze. The slow lap of the water on the tuft of sawgrass.

-18   Hagridden

Darkness increases by 1-4 each time night hag Wormface Yntzins flies in from the Ethereal Plane. Moon or no moon, old Wormface (and occasionally a hitsugeth or two) soars across the sky in a never-ending quest for a vulnerable host. "Ja nu ser hon som en riktig häxa. När hon har grön gegga i ansiktet."

For aeons, Wormface had dated Demon Joe on and off, but now she was through with him. "I wouldn't bite his dick off it were stuck in the Zipper of Avernus!" she asserted. Joe didn't deal with his problems, and swearing an oath to Mammon made her leery of his intentions.

One midnight, she hovered into the dreams of Striker. Appearing as a scantily clad Idajan, the evil hag taunted Striker with flirtations and stabbing pains. "Oh, I want you Striker. I love men like you, so smart, so worldlygig..." Then a cacophonous CLANG of a giant pair of cymbals crashed into Striker's cranium, followed by a demented scream as she metamorphosed into her hideous natural state. "Ha ha, charade you are! No Queens for you!" Yntzins' dirty nails dragged across his megastarched collar.

The hag returned night out, night in for several weeks. No manner of ouija boards or cheap schnapps helped Striker slip the bit and throw off old Wormface. Vowing to take immediate action, Striker booked time with many croakers throughout the Island.

After a series of time-wasting therapy appointments with all manner of psychiatrists, witchdoctors, and affordable self-help gurus, Striker at last made an emergency appointment with the reclusive Dr. Apodakiss, whose clinic sat high on a mountaintop in Uottubbacktotheboniyummmm (sp.).

Striker rounded up his most trusted employees and embarked on a long overland caravan, finally arriving at Dr. Apodakiss' clinic after a series of mind-gulping adventures too twinkly to tell. The doc's office turned out to be a dingy, guano-coated cave, from which a gruntled, mangy androsphinx emerged. "I have one riddle for you," the beast intonated. "Do you have insurance?"

"Yes, yes, of course, great Sphinx. Are you Dr. Apodakiss? I didn't have any 5g on my trip, so I wasn't able to check your credentials," explained Striker. The sphinx roared, roared, and roared some more, burning out Striker's disposable ears. "Come in if you dare," the doctor said. "But leave your mahouts outside."

Three weeks later, Wormface was gone, and Striker slept soundly every night. In an exclusive Ace TV interview, Striker gushed, "I'm a new man now. No more night hags or brain ants!" Bryant Brick cloyingly pivoted toward the zillionaire. "So what was your cure?" Striker took a pill bottle out of his jacket. "No meds. Just take this Cowsendux supplement three times a day! Available today at MyStriker.com."

19   Heuristic

Clytie had worked long hours to infiltrate the Cyan Boys ink and toner gang, surreptitiously laying traps for their rank and file to fall patsy to. But the game of climbing the ladder was limited. Cyan Boys leaders were untouchable. They had something on somebody, on everybody in Uottubtothebonium (sp.) it seemed.

Now Idajan and her coterie were somehow in on the take as well - not just from duties and taxes, but concessions from every inkjet and dot matrix printer in the multiverse, that they would just as well seize up and die instead of using non-cartel toner cartridges. "Mon Dieu, Mon Diable."

"I" aka "Me" had assigned Clytie to the far less arduous task of examining leaks and faulty "Toner Low" readouts in the black toner markets. These days, there would have been a quick fix, an algorithm or some other cobbled together series of Xarthorian apps and some filé.

We quickened to the discoveries with prolonged mendacity. Clytie cracked the code, but the Zysigamore Code prohibited criminal penalties, as Mlexidzantsizh, the mega corporation who manufactured most of the Island's black and white proletariat printers, had claimed religious doctrine and the feels absolved them of all transgressions. The salesmen wouldn't like what we had found out.

Efforts of the sailthrough vats of indecipherable SKUs filled every office basement, from Unicorn Harbor to Umlaut Towin.

(Cut to a menacing throng with torches and pitchforks. A lone figure reaches a high point and turns to address the mob.) ALAN BANNISTER - See here, you've got it all wrong. The #FFEEDDs stole your toner. It sure wasn't me, fellas. Heck, I've never owned a laser printer.

-19   Heuristic

Deep within the mountains of Uottubbacktothebonyumville (sp.) (sp.) was a chill chalet run by Brenda Loompas. Unbeknownst to all, with the exception of readers of this very chapter, was that this charming rustic getaway also functioned as an illusionists' academy of sorts. Most of the time, guests were unaware, yet some illusioncasters were far less cautious than others. Behind a series of sacred secret doors lay a way to Qlippoth.

Aegothsorzhotan was given a full Professorship anon, but now was considered emeritus, even unwelcome during times that he needed vellum or somatic spell components. Though at one time Aegothsorzhotan had known most of the Brenda Loompa faculty personally, many must have moved on; the new new jack illusionists didn't cater to Aegothsorzhotan's BO and pedantic gripes.

Chandeliers across the chalet clung to concrete ceilings. The rookie spellcasters bounced their cantrips through each chandeliers' crystals, creating a cantilevered congestion of lights, prisms, gonfalons, snatches of fantasies, and shadows of oddly geometric pentashapes that dazzled guests not acclimated to the chalet. Gzibo, the general manager, outright forbade any illusionists' tricks in the common rooms and halls, but this order often went unheeded.

Often, a disillusionst would depart or be ejected if their dweomers didn't flit the mood. Too much reality standwitch riled up the hithertoo placid Brenda Loompas, and was considered pure buzzicide. The music, the chocolates, the flex drugs all seemed to sour. "All we do is dream," they sing. "Hard truths miss the point."

For PR reasons, the chalet ceases to exist. But we know this to be utter and complete obscurantizzle. Clytemnestra herself sans bathyscaphe often stays here under the pseudonym Alethy. "BOB" also checks in on the down-low. The Loompas don't allow Hell or Abyss residents to enter. "As good as our O-Rings are..." they sing....

20   Fundacion

As e moved n morphs, Hi can't help thinking of the Genesis of a Novel Chapter in the Tyranny of Pants, an existential dilemma that time hadn't forgott.

Hyper-video enabled him to set a sales record for a quarter. The deals that Hi made with the Zysigamore traders reaped great rewards for both parties. Numerous were the Xarthorians in al realms who consumed heartily regardless of third-party markups and other controversies.

Hi didn't even have to be present for each vlog. Clytie had programmed her cams to save every scrap of avatar and sub-personality that her husband naturally generated. From there the AI automatically chose which sub-personality would interact with clients and project the greatest integrity.

Though Hi's best friend Traveling Salesman lacked this innate ability, he learned so quickly that it almost didn't matter; he was a Sales Master in his own right, by Dobbs.

Betimes the teacups that Clytie had ordered had arrived at her docking garage. Xzimor, her top Xarthorian assistant, was already distributing them to her employees. "Ms. Willow, did you get the message? These are the teacups from Unicorn Harbor. I'm having my best people inspect them for damage."

"Excellent, excellent. I still have a sample tea set in my Sample Room. If you have any leftover teacups, I'd like to compare them."

"You never gave me the day of time!" whined Xzimor. "I think I'm almost out." "Can you get more, Xzy?" "Not sure. We could 3D-print a few temporary ones, I suppose." Xzimor slouched backward yet held her ground. Clytemnestra respected this gesture. "Some things aren't worth summoning an elemental for."

"Tea bags?" A sound like ravens masticating fell to the floor.

Ultimately Hi did relax. "You often open around this time."

So much lucre was generated that Mammon had taken notice of the hoard. He sent His chamberlain Focalor to slyly case out their residence. Focalor reported back that the couple had a very sophisticated array of technologies at the ready. Mammon remarked, "Perhaps there is one Sultan of Sales who could push Mr. Hi Stop into a complete meltdown." See Chapter 30330.

-20   This Tasty Prism Makes Me Inevitabull

Hwalearism en vogue, Idajan's professional priests could be male or female, but all stuck closely to the Queen's tried and true doctrines, most handed down from the 4casta reign.

With Zzyster subsumed in her influence, the concept of an "Urgent Cleric" priesthood soon expanded in orthodox fashion. The Rev. wanted little to do with the official bureaucracy of a series of nunneries, funneries and bakeries, yet the Queen viewed his work as indispensable. As a result, Rev. Zzyster had nearly as much autonomy as his brother, the ostensible Prince Crown Meco Aleph.

Idajan didn't look to the Urgent Cleric for inspiration; rather it was the reassuring voice of Bleary Tim cutting through the noiseology like a tardigrade through a planetarium. After a plateful of flex drugs and tropical psychedelics, they came up with a soullution to every societal problem.

The result was the Order of the Prism, a night hood loosely based on the Knights who say 'Ni'. Order members overpaid for licensed apparel, and met at schwanky hotels throughout Zysigamore. You didn't have to be hothechajuxips, but when you did, you let the Island know.

The Order cleaned up discotechques whose playlists were cliché; created small trifles to amuse poor Xarthorians; eclipsed jigsaw ruthenium isotopes; clawed their way out of obscurity; played the band; and tightened zosters. The Prism also backed chrimpostelers, and were recruited by the X's themselves for rubicon compartmentalization.

Zealous jealots became more and more uncommonplace. "I overstand their appeal. Now we just need a hook to co-opt them to," Idajan concluded. A rare exception from Meco - how would his brother accept it? "Make them temporary. They will blow away in time," replied Bleary Tim. "Spirituality bubbles, few troubles," he opined.

Cheap gurus and unfriendly psychics became the abnorm. It was all good to Her Higness, who collected taxes from the temps.

The penultimate straw was the prismatic snivelry that Demon Joe rolled out to his chains of eateries. The last straw was Rodentlandee selling them at the gate. After some disgustion, Rev. Zzyster accepted this notion, and filmed a series of Taweret reflections among a series of actors in Henrietta Hippo outfits. He cut them all loose the next day. "Back to dogma," Zzyster informed them.

21   Danzig, Fulkerson & Johnson

"I got this whole Zysigamore deal sewn up. Boy howdy, it's gonna be big. Stapes, you're playing with fire. Go for the sure thing."

"Pickled punk twist, please." He nervously stirs the cocktail.

"This is gonna be the top quarter on the books for the last five years. It's just going gangbusters."

"Yeah. A couple of nibbles but I can't reel in the big fish."

"I say, can we market to the Taweret crowd? You know, amulets? T-shirts?"

"They are selling like gangbusters. I would love to have a piece of that action."

"Sā."

"Shadrach, what's the breakdown? We gotta have this by September."

"No can do. They're not returning my calls. We're dead in the water."

"We need this yesterday, even if we have to move mountains."

"Four pairs of pants. Five ties. Seven shirts. Ten of swords."

"Marquand had 25 pairs of pants. And each cleaners in each town had a few pairs pressed for him. He was like clockwork. Each time he had five more pairs to drop off at the cleaners. Everyone was so happy. Almost too happy. You have to admire Marquand. He was the best."

"Too bad he left us for Sandvick, Hughes & Atkinson."

"Great Caesar's Ghost, they reamed us again."

21B   Billiards

Rookies at Danzig, Fulkerson & Johnson were expected to maintain the billiards room in the office's basement at all costs. Several 21-ball tables required constant calibration and re-calibration. Even the 13 balls had the DF&J logo. One of the original Partners had said, "An honest game of billiards is always better than a dirty game of Candy Land."

Mr. Hi Stop was known as a hotshot at 21 ball - and his partner Traveling Salesman could be counted on to make key shots when he had the chance. Combined, the tandem were some of the very few casual players who could match up against the Legends of the Game, such as R.E. Tzilenhuffin; the Xarthorian Alzig Zemphorkonovis; and Little Jill Dzong, the amazingly acrobatic 21 ball player from a bleak orphanage on the outskirts of Umlaut Towin.

Hi and TS played a variant called "Scooter" where you only use the odd numbered balls: the 1, 3 and 5 were lined up single file; the 7 & 9 balls were paired up; the 11, 13 and 15 balls formed a row of three; as did the final row with the 17, 19 and 21 balls. The loser would have to turn in the expense reports.

Onie McPhersall sometimes joined them in a quick game on the odd occasions that he stopped at Hi and Clytie's uber-glamorous pad. Onie knew he would get snookered, so he always bet against himself- half the time he "won," the rest, he lost. But nobody cared - the cues were true, the balls were polished, the felt felt felt-like, and the guacamole was green.

Simon didn't care for billiards - he claimed the 21 ball reminded him of Quentin Periwinkle.

Another time, Onie, Hi and Traveling Salesman played the 3-player version, drawing lots before the round and choosing which set of balls they would shoot at - 1 through 7, 8 through 14, or 15 through 21. "If I get 8's I can't be beat," bragged Traveling Salesman; Onie also bet on him to win. This day, Onie scratched on an easy shot at the 19 ball. "By Bob, I've lost it, fellas!" At this point Mr. Hi Stop's face turned beet yellow. "You can't lose what you never had!" He smirked as TS pocketed the 9 through 13 balls in rapid succession.

-21   Glyphodonia Pantrelle

Ms. Glyphodonia Pantrelle had been Mammon's personal consort for dozens of world epochs, having dispatched several powerful succubi, lamias, medusae and porn star dancers with a combination of extruded O-ring cord stock, gaskets, seals, miscellaneous magic items, Stea Wars figurines, erogenous piercings and Moxie. She stands about 8' 3" sans heels in the material whirled, and occupies a malignant triple decker with an Acheron zip code.

These days, ole Mams was hardly around- something about fucking around in some ski chalets owned by sone Xarthorians in the mountains of Uottubbacktothebonyiuvuille (sp.). As a result, Glyphie found herself with a lot of time on her claws.

One day, she happened by pure happenstance to notice a personal ad. "Become a willing collaborator in my miasma," complete with a pic of a handsome yet somewhat plastic man – Striker. Unfortunately for Glyphie, she messaged him right away and arranged to meet him.

He was at his unctuous best on that first date - taking her to the local particle accelerator that the hipsters often frequented. The scent of neutrinos relaxed Striker immeasurably, and the ghost particles were great icebreakers. "I just love it here," he told Glyphodonia as he gazed into her obsidian eyes.

Glyphie didn't reciprocate. "Get your neutrinos out of my nucleus. I don't care who you are, where you're from!" Striker lurched backwards awkwardly, pivoting his elbow implants into a less pliable posture.

"I'm sorry." He tried to blush but it was in vain. "I guess the neutrinos do it to me. You can just do your own thing if you're not up for it. No hard feelings."

Striker had his lim-lipoco come and take him home. Glyphodonia mellowed out quickly afterward, even inventing a live-action Candy Land game at one point in a mezzanine dimension.

Glyphie would later be part of a wider movement within a wider movement within a demi-universal movement toward the greater emancipation of/to/from pants as they will have been come to have been known. They even released a horehound clamato popsicle in her honor.

Neoparapasta is twisted among itself like computer cables endlessly wound together in a complex, chaotic pattern. The macaroni begins to stick to the sides of the bowl; departing dewcling wafts over the molecular biologists.

Sensing an opportunity enters Traveling Salesman. He doesn't know their ways or their prestidigitations, but his preternatural senses are virtually always on point.

Teams need a dinner which will feed many brothers while allowing for expedited cleanup; sopa reticuli suavis.

A reticulated platter of pasta smeared with a novel sauce did not beckon the team to eat it. Rather, they adopted this spaghetti messiah instantly, thus setting off the pledge process yet again, much to the chagrin of the Committee of Professors.

Eating a snake eating another snake eating a dun tree frog. A coating of viscous fluid improves their digestive viscosity. Very rare specialty of the chef, it bestows duende on men who consume it raw. Similarly, women may be brought to sublime orgasm simply at the sight of the ouroboros.

A very erudite naga professor peers into the electron microscope. The institute bears his impressive historic cognomen. The Doctor knows in his heart that he is a fraud, an impostor, yet he is driven to carry on his charade incessantly. No recognition can be high enough, no award gaudy enough, and no N size too awespicious.

Sales! Sales! Sales! The doctor will write many popular books and be interviewed regularly. The lab gets an influx of funds and moves into a shiny building in Zysigamore Square, with a polite, ennui-stricken security guard in the sterile lobby.

Activity often warps the DNA into unanticipated patterns.

"$10 billion a year, at least. The ink's still drying, yes. You will have a copy in your hot little hands. Lickety split. They will make me a Partner after all."

Anaxiforminges

22H   **Organellepasta**

Ever so delicious, never ever nutritious...R'amen R'amen Hellelujah!

Pendulous hunks of durum semolina have, are, will be accumulating near the spaghettified sun. Carboxylated carbohydrates congeal, coalesce to create Gods. NHGH was not made this way.

Pastagangers can aesili b animated with the same incantations as you would use on a golem or skeleton. Aegothsorzhotan tried to take the credit, but his pastagangers were notorious for being overcooked and pasty. One ex-lich in the Caves of Chaos supposedly had created a master race of them, but Hill Cummings showed up one day wasted to the quills. He slathered each perfect pastaganger in a veritable ocean of special giblet sauce and greedily consumed all he could catch.

Brother Noah piled into the pasta trade, about the same time that Old Orzo Ozringhouse was al dente. Orzo had sewn up the mini-dinosaur pasta trade and was usually slathered in powdered cheesepoppings. Noah won the packaging war, dethroning Orzo and leaving him limp and mushy. This tension affects the blessed Isle today.

Feeling strainered, Orzo longed for the perfect sauce to be his partner, looking low, high and medium across the pantries of diligent Xarthorians. "By 'BOB' there must be a divine condommint," he sighed.

Indeed, pastagenesis met a sublime euphonia when Idajan hosted Running of the Sauces, much to the chagrin of Rev. Zzyster. "Red, white, green. A spectrum of gravy," was the ostensible Ace TV mantra. Thenceforth came an even greater diversity of stews, casseroles and soups, followed by a plethora of sales and marketing professionals.

All the while, Simon blithely fumed. "Where are all my colanders?" he furtively asked Simon Junior. Outdeed, the old whirled strainers rendered themselves insolete. "If only someone thought of the colanders. Why I could strain my membrane." Simon subsequently only availed himself of tomato sauce. "In a chaotic world, choose tomato."

Finite state machines are a a-peeling, yet none were as revolutionary as an elegant O-Ring. If I had a sawbuck for every

Old Orzo Ozringhouse ostensibly obfuscated the organelles only to observe or obviate the outdated oddities of ordinal otyughs. "Only our ombudsman oriented to osteology or omelettes will organize this ox-goad." A sullen NHGH waited his tern.

One stir-fry to rule them all...

-22   Pathways [of/to] ...

Interzone consciousnesses rally in contactless motion. Most elect never to embody, never to sully themselves with the drumhum goings and comings of mortal sorts. Why not remain immortal and noncorporeal?

First glyph its and it's off to the races. AAI crunktent is cranking it out 10 times faster than the speed of thought. *This* should be enough to feed the Xarthorians. No consciousness need apply.

Confusion, doubt, annoyance prevail. There's too much noise in the shitstem to find those sacred paths again, let alone the disembodied characters on the dashboard of infinity's double diamond slope. Let Clytemnestra try, they say. Bet she never dips her water in the toe.

Groovelinear jetstreams like the astral winds flow through each path in pneumatic glory. Most are unidirectional, though in some cases the airflow's direction can change violently - particularly between planet and satellite when of/to/from astral & materielle.

There is a map, albeit inexacted. "The four worlds. Qlippoth is a shadow world that can't exist on its own," explicated Clytie in her lecture to the chrimposterlers. "No GPS. No AAI. None of that trash." Xatnudorf's hand rose. "Then how will we navigate?" Clytie stated, "No sun, no moon, no signs of any kind. It's 1001% intuitive." She explained why. "Planets are the primary illusion."

Onmouseover, a frighteningly simple protocol, was recommended. Its liquefied hovering gave exactly the kind of postcision that everynine from the X's to Dylan Thomas to Dionne Warwick impersonators could frenefit from.

Animalcules roam everyhow, everywhen, often a hitch from Interzone ad astra. This makes lingering or riding a risqué proposition. Sauvylers disinfect at both ends. They kept swatting away nanotypewriters which annoyingly flew in the ears and membranes of Clytie and the girls. "Eeew!" cried Xat, pulling a large swarm of nanotypewriters out of her ponytail.

"Hand me the hallucinogizer spray," Clytemnestra requested. "This'll short circuit their ichor." Before long the pathway fillchilled to the aroma of methylethyl dicarbonaraoxylinearpretrolodroxyldifluorohectane, making everybody dizzy. "I think you killed all the 5g too," noticed Xatnudorf. "Don't worry. That's only temporary. Just like my face slipping off…"

-22T   Sub-Tyranny of the Tie

From time immemorial salesmen were constrained by the necktie. It became a cymbal of depleated magnetism in servitude to the corporate powers of Incasker. No zoantharian could wright this yong. So that inasmuch as wherefour

Tie taunts me with wild paisley patterns, loud orange polyester fabric, girth that recalls Zysigamore Canyon, and thick knots pressing up against my throat. Word of sin restriction grabs the dastardly starched collar and lashes it to the neck like a frigging mizzen masticated o'rigging.

Despite ties' systemic flaws, many in the cult of salesmen clung desperately to their ties in a heterogametic tradition that had long outusefuled its live. Onie McPhersall would turn apoplectic if Mr. Hi Stop or Traveling Salesman eschewed any of the unwritten laws of the necktie. They were demon-may-care types, too casual and trendy. "I'm from the old school, boys," he repeated to the sound of their eyerolls.

The tie biz exploded after the Urgent Cleric advised donning neckties during temple services. Meco was happy to model one at a press conference encouraging such conformity among the populace. Stanney's Department Stores were mobbed with historical customers clamoring for this colorful new trend.

But the bow tie also surged into prominence, led by a Snooty Looking Nerd in a Bowtie. Flummoxed marketers didn't expect such a sartorial diversion. Tighter and tighter it gets, until the restriction pops.

Cravaticination demonstrated the deathspan of ties, both apostrophised and despised. Choke, strangle, reduce blood flow to the brain.

23   Indelible Phantasms *

Somewhat opaque souls consisting of nothing else but vapor. They disaggregate rapidly with the slightest breeze so that fertility can begin. Nanoroentgens of Lincoln, of Bonaparte, yet also of Hitler, Jack the Ripper, and all the evil that has followed our DNA. Yet it isn't sin, it's merely bad karma which we all generate like piss and shit anyway. Great eternal all cackling hen. Without the ether/air beings, humans lose Humanness. Psychic connections get caught in quicksand. Reliquanda alia corpora: Bless this meat shell.

These immaterial beings are the bond between the living and the not-yet-living: those aggregated essences crafted in ether to populate the human - forms in birth. Not only do they handle communications across the veil, but across time and space. Vapor network connects when employed.

Hunks of vapor matter neither created nor destroyed. You can prevent the disaggregation between lifetimes but is it worth it? Even if you are a rebirthed lama, are you certain that the reaggregation process was 100% pure? Has that saint's soul shed not even one drop of its contiguity?

*   Or: When someone says they are the reincarnation of Napoleon Bonaparte, they are correct.

-23   Postmonitions

In an endless stream, after Simon dreamed after dream after dream of death of Elephant, of the divorce, of the marriage, of the apotheosis, of the disintegration, of the bardo, of the enwombment, of the affair that fractured what was left of his mores, sanity and exfoliants; but before the trauma of meeting his husband's secret love child in a most awkward manner, he dissocicorporates each millisecond, over and over again, flashing back to the soap operas he had taped onto Beta as a stripling.

Simon awoke, switching on his enormo-screen television for the depressing morning news. He dripped coffee into his membrane as he awaited the on-screen arrival of his favorite Ace TV morning personalities. But much to his misday, Bryant Brick was not there that morning. "Oh, I forgot it was his vacation week," he told Simon Junior. Instead it was Macho Dave, whose immaculately groomed hair and well-maintained cuticles piqued Simon's curiosity. "Hmm. I would need Underoos to meet him," concluded Simon.

"Skidoo!" A series of pent-up commercials flickered onto the screen. The next program was a puffy fluffy talk show hosted by Suzee McScoville called 'Eye on Zysigamore.' "Our next guest is intercellular celebrity Mikey Rat. Please give him a big hand! He's here to tell us about the new attractions at Rodentlandee." Simon was disgusted. "I abhor that filth merchant. What a masher." They showed a short, pre-prepared video on the new Vap-O-Whirl ride, the 'He's a Small World' hall of sock muppets, and the special bukkake stall in the Tunnel of Sexual Harassment.

Simon found himself replaying a scene over and over again. "I could just take Nebuchadnezzar out to grass! No, there's no way to know for sure," he mused to Simon Junior. Simon swore he had seen that woman - that Laney - in the background of the Magic Queendom parade clip. "It looked just like her." Fivetunately it was just a virtual reality MRI machine operated by Dr. Oste's technician. "Wow doc, it was so real. I saw that woman in the white room," Simon said, taking the sock puppets off of his gonards.

"You have a case of generalized entitlement disorder, Simon. As an allosauropathic practitioner, I recommend you take a plethora of colorful prescription drugs," said Dr. Oste, writhing script after script. "Will this give me a headache? Or turn my fingernails into Scientologists?" Dr. Oste explained the other 60 or so side effects before ushering Simon into the lobby. "I can thank you enough," he told the doc's office staff as he drifted out the door.

24   E.O.M. - All the Way Live

Shout. Dance. Clap your hands.

Shift out. Shift in. Start of text. End of text.

Unlock the PC. Set my people free.

Bounce. Drop. Rollerskate.

KA. Go! X. Go! 5

And a 1 and a 2 and a 1 and a 2. Boom boom.

Holla!

[BOOM] [BOOM BOOM BOOM] [BOOM]

Keep on marchin and parchin and harken larkin barken.

Tea Times for 2. Love 30.

Boogie! Boogie! Do it. Do it.

BOUZERANT   BOUZERANT

In a loop time backwards schools swim.

Tau Upsilon Phi Chi Psi Omega

POP POP Go Stop. Stop.

Subject, object, love, 40.

Spotlight on Gutter Hardy.

In a larper a timer 49'er Tyner Longiner.

Pearl mutter of Gutter Hardy Kundamuffins. Three fourths and a

Wink in. I'm blinkin just thinkin bout gettin' stinkin

Ty! Ty!

In conclusion, Outcasker; Out conclusion, Incasker. Spy! Spy! In collusion??

In a gadda floofolatta

Twenty-fourth blackbird, twenty-fourth son of the twenty-fourth uberblackbird.

Hop hop, pogo, pogo pogo. Had was a buffalo.

End of Trans Block. End of Medium. Escape. March.

-24   E.O.M.

In the Long Long Ago of Zysigamore, before the rise of the CastaCast and their inhumanities, was the Beginning of the Message. Since then, the populace has longed to reply. But Re: did not exist; neither did 5g nor Pants.

Someone in the future will have the great notion to go back in time and leave time capsules in every petty Xarthorian monument in Zysigamore, sure as shootin! One deva felt fortunate enough to have planted a rather auspicious time capsule just to the right of Simon Junior's ears (if he had any). It matured. It hardened. It was revealed. Vide finem medium.

The Message flows like gold spectrum from Aleph to Zed. Thus grew the Tyranny of A. All others arbitrarily lined up behind the ox-glyph ever so obedientlizzle.

The early Xarthorian realms obfuscated the Message so thoroughly that by the era of the Toner Wars, it lay in a wretched bucket of ASCII character sets. Fast FWD: to Clytemnestra and her lab.

When Clytemnestra found out about it, her interest was piqued- not by the mundane gym socks and brass knuckles they found, but the possibilities of directly influencing...the FUTURE...

Yet the Wayback and the Way Forward Machines didn't yet exist. Clytie sighed as she gazed at the Taweret painting. "Just give me a clear sign. Where should I look for the time crystals?" Emmet's Law on 1/16 of an inch's aleph nullified units of message compartmentalization could be a solution - but how?

"These time crystals don't have the power we need," Clytie shouted to Xzimor over the phone. "Save what you can. But I think this technology is a dead end." It was back to Square Alpha. Clytemnestra felt about as two-dimensional as she could, but there was no sacred phone booth or photo hut to duck into.

"I have other time crystals on order from Outcasker Unlimited," revealed Xzimor, checking her inventory. "They've been back ordered. But I have a few samples in my warehouse." Clytemnestra was skeptical. "Why would theirs be better?" "I don't know. But they have gotten positive reviews for their creamy einsteinium filling," relayed Xzimor. "Hmm. I do like them with a soupçon of 5g...we'll see..."

With delayed ingratitude, the End of Message hit like a well-annealed, well-heeled pterodactyl. If only the emoji matched the well-honed, whole-feeling of commisperspiration. To this day, the Message queues up in inboxes, outboxes, FWDs saved as drafts, the 23rd hole of each sentient golf course blindfolded while tied to a subjunctive zenedoin.

25   Striker

As a member of the Country Club of Umlaut Towin, Striker had unparalleled access to the CC's opulent facilities. His great mansion was perched by the tee of the 20th hole, whose name was Gus Wilkerson and also enjoys classical music, starry nights and yacht rock remixes.

He had had yet another Open Call for minions. But only seven or so were left. "Oh, what's the use?" sighed Striker. "At least they're cheaper than rent boys." One of his central casting agents busily assembled uniforms and helmets for the new recruits.

"Come, come, come." Striker beckoned to the group. It was time for the towel whipping contest, and the cleaning service had failed to drop off more clean towels. Heck, even the plastic towels on his mansion's many mezzanine floors were filthy.

"It's no use. No use at all." He suddenly shooed them away. Striker stepped back into the manse. He studied the portraits of Mr. Hi Stop that he had ordered for Xarthorians-R-Uzz, while snorting a whole tray of flex drugs. "Damn. I'll never know how he does it."

Striker's pride and joy was the Pleasure Saucer that he parked in his massive detached garage/small craft hangar. This pleasure saucer could host a large party of guests for travel within the Prime Material Plane - any nebula you could name, any galaxy you could go to, any solar system you could spot, or any black hole you could behold. He didn't bother to tell his lackeys about it - he only took it out once or twice a year on holidays, or if he had a special romantic interest.

Time to relax. Striker played some Heinmax Quattlebaum Quartet on his hologramophone, a refreshing plate of flex drugs, and some elephant-trimmed slippers. "Ah yes," he sighed semi-contentedly. There was a lot of work to do as CEO of Strikercorp, though he had employees who could accomplish it. There was a missing component, he felt - no partner or partners with whom to procreate or otherwise enjoy sexytime with. But he was discontented with the buxom young Xarthorians who attended his Open Calls and applied for Strikercorp jobs. He wanted someone whom he considered on his level - A Typhon of Industry, a Leader of the Zysigamore world, and definitely not sales professionals. You know, a girl like Veronica or Betty...

-25   Wacky Christmas Episode

* (adapted from the Archie Andrews 'Christmas Shopping' show broadcast 12/13/1947)

SNOOTY LOOKING ANNOUNCER IN A BOW TIE: It's time for another chapter in the Tyranny of Pants!
MUSIC: Theme up, and then under and fading out for...
ANNOUNCER: We invite you now to join Traveling Salesman and his pals Mr. Hi Stop, Clytemnestra and Simon in another comic adventure from Zysigamore High. Today's episode will begin in just a few moments.

MUSIC: Striker's Jingle
Tender beef, juicy pork,

Known from Underwear Point to Umlaut Towin!
Striker's Premium Franks!
Striker's Premium Franks!

ANNOUNCER: For your guarantee of protection, Striker's Premium Franks now come to you cellophane wrapped in handy one pound packages. Made fresh daily in Striker kitchens across the Island, Striker's Premium Franks are then wrapped in the new handy, sanitary, flavor-saver pack. And brought to you at the very peak of their tantalizing flavor with all their natural goodness sealed in. So kids, tell your mom that you want Striker's Premium Franks. And Mom, get some today. They're delicious! And you'll be glad to know that Striker's Premium Franks are economical. There's no waste to them. Every bite is all nourishment, all dinner-quality meat. Ask for them today. Striker's Premium Franks in the one pound cellophane package. And now for our weekly visit to Zysigamore. It's Saturday afternoon as we look in on Traveling Salesman's home.

ACT ONE
(A time door opens.) TRAVELING SALESMAN: Oh, good grief. Mr. Hi Stop!
MR. HI STOP: Who'dya expect, Jersey Joe Walcott? (snickers)
TRAVELING SALESMAN: No, Mr. Hi Stop, and I don't want to fight with you, either. I'm in a hurry. What are you doing here?
MR. HI STOP: Oh, Traveling Salesman, Simon just called.
TRAVELING SALESMAN: (anxiously) Gee whiz, he did? I never heard the phone ring.
MR. HI STOP: He said to change your appointment with him from three o'clock to four o'clock.
TRAVELING SALESMAN: From three to four? Gee whiz, that's great.
MR. HI STOP: Huh? [His face begins to gyrate solemnly.]
TRAVELING SALESMAN: Now that Simon's made our date an hour later, I have time to get my Christmas shopping done. This is practically the last chance I'll have. I haven't bought a thing for anyone yet.
MR HI STOP: Including me?
TRAVELING SALESMAN: Including you.
MR. HI STOP: (pause) It's time you did your Christmas shopping.
TRAVELING SALESMAN: That's right, Hi. C'mon we'll go right down to Stanney's.
MR. HI STOP: Well, what are you going to get me, huh?
(CLYTEMNESTRA'S smartphone rings. She answers, a little exasperated.) Hello?
SIMON: Hello, Clytemnestra?
CLYTIE: Oh, hello, Simon. How are you?
SIMON: Fine thanks, Ah, is Traveling Salesman there?
CLYTIE: Traveling Salesman doesn't seem to be here.
SIMON: Oh, he isn't?
CLYTIE: Sorry, but I'm just leaving to do my Christmas shopping.
SIMON: Oh golly, I'm glad you mentioned that. I haven't done my shopping yet, either.
CLYTIE: Oh, you haven't? Well, would you like to go with me, dear?
SIMON: Oh I'd love to, Clytemnestra!
CLYTIE: All right, I'll pick you up right away and we'll go down to Stanney's.

ACT TWO
MUSIC: Christmas tune bridge to next scene.
SOUND FX: Store bell rings 3 times then stops, along with – Stanney's Department Store customers, bustling, chatting loudly.
MR. HI STOP: Gee whiz, Traveling Salesman, I never saw such crowds.
TRAVELING SALESMAN: Yes, Mr. Hi Stop, but when we got in that elevator and everyone started pushing, did you have to push back?
MR. HI STOP: Listen, Traveling Salesman, in that crowd even a sardine would've pushed back.
TRAVELING SALESMAN: Well, never mind, we're here now and the first thing I want to buy is a compact for Simon. I wonder where the cosmetic department is?
MR. HI STOP: Cosmetic department? (His face contorts into an inkblot.)

TRAVELING SALESMAN: Yeah.

MR. HI STOP: Gee whiz, Traveling Salesman, let's go up to the toy department first.

TRAVELING SALESMAN: Hi, I told you we'll go up to the toy department later. Now, come on. I'll ask that Floorwalker where the cosmetic department is. Oh, mister.

Floorwalker (who turns out to be ELEPHANT: (hurriedly) Yes, yes?

TRAVELING SALESMAN: Could you tell me where the cosmetic department is, please?

ELEPHANT: Yes, counter seven.

TRAVELING SALESMAN: Thank you. C'mon, Hi.

MR. HI STOP: Where is it?

TRAVELING SALESMAN: Counter seven.

MR. HI STOP: Where's that?

TRAVELING SALESMAN: Gee, I don't know. Where is counter seven?

ELEPHANT: (impatiently) On the north side of counter six.

TRAVELING SALESMAN: Oh thank you, I'll just - ah? Mister?

ELEPHANT: Well what now?

TRAVELING SALESMAN: Which way is north?

ELEPHANT: Oh, my lands. Sonny, you see the boys' clothing department right there?

TRAVELING SALESMAN: Yes.

ELEPHANT: Well go right down to the aisle where the dummies are and turn right.

TRAVELING SALESMAN: Oh, OK, Elephant. Thanks a lot!

ELEPHANT: You're welcome! (Trumpets off mic) Yes, madam. Can I help you? (He walks away.)

MR. HI STOP: Where'd he say it is, Traveling Salesman?

TRAVELING SALESMAN: Right down at the next aisle, Hi. C'mon.

MR. HI STOP: Oh, OK.

TRAVELING SALESMAN: And boy, he's sure not a very friendly Elephant.

MR. HI STOP: Maybe his wife makes him watch Ace TV.

TRAVELING SALESMAN: I wouldn't be surprised. I? (A loud clunk.) Ooh, what was that?

MR. HI STOP: You bumped into that dummy.

TRAVELING SALESMAN: Oh, gee whiz, I knocked the hat off. For a minute I thought that dummy was a real person. Wait a second, Hi, while I put the hat back on. If that Elephant ever saw me fooling around with this dummy, he'd probably throw us out the store and give us a lecture about the Venetian Congress of 1844. I?

MR. HI STOP: Gee whiz!

TRAVELING SALESMAN: What's the matter?

MR. HI STOP: There's Simon.

TRAVELING SALESMAN: Simon? Here in Stanney's? Oh, gee whiz, I don't want him to see me here.

MR. HI STOP: He's coming right toward us.

TRAVELING SALESMAN: Oh boy! Hi, I'm gonna to be a dummy.

MR. HI STOP: Huh?

TRAVELING SALESMAN: I'm gonna climb up on this platform with the rest of these dummies and I-I'll wear this hat?

MR. HI STOP: But, Traveling Salesman, you can't do that!

TRAVELING SALESMAN: Oh, Hi, don't argue, don't argue. Here? How do I look?

MR. HI STOP: You're the most natural lookin' dummy I ever saw.

TRAVELING SALESMAN: Don't be postmodern, Hi. And put that price tag on me quick.

MR. HI STOP: OK. Here.

TRAVELING SALESMAN: Attaboy. Now remember don't give me away no matter what happens.

MR. HI STOP: Well, OK, but? (Traveling Salesman shushes him.)

SIMON: Why, Mr. Hi Stop!

MR. HI STOP: Oh. Hi, Simon.

SIMON: What y'all doin' here?

MR. HI STOP: Ooh, just a little shopping.

SIMON: Oh, I am too. Thank goodness I have most of it done. Only thing I still have to get is a gift for Traveling Salesman. I don't know what to get him. He's such a problem.

MR. HI STOP: (splutter) Yeah. He sure is. (His face turns more watercolor.)

SIMON: I can't get him a book or anythin' because he's not the intelligent type. And I can't get him a baseball glove or anythin' because he's not much of an athlete.

MR. HI STOP: (higher pitched splutter)

SIMON: Can't get him a tie or anythin' because he just doesn't know anything about style.

MR. HI STOP: (high splutter heading toward whimper)

SIMON: In fact, sometimes I think Traveling Salesman is an awful dummy. Then again, with prices this high there isn't very much you can get for a dollar.

MR. HI STOP: (splutter-chortle)

SIMON: Did you say something, Mr. Hi Stop?

MR. HI STOP: Me? Not a word, Simon, not a word.

SIMON: Oh. Well I better go get some more shopping done. Would you like to come along?

MR. HI STOP: Oh I, uh? No I can't. I'm meeting someone here in a minute.

SIMON: Oh. Well I'll run along then. 'Bye now, Mr. Hi Stop.

MR. HI STOP: 'Bye, Simon. 'Bye! (pause) OK, dummy, you can relax now.

TRAVELING SALESMAN: A fine thing, a fine thing! Mr. Hi Stop, help me down off this platform. I?

MR. HI STOP: Gee whiz, not now! Here comes Eeeeeelephant!

TRAVELING SALESMAN: Oh boy. I better be a dummy some more.

ELEPHANT: (Off mic) Yes, madam. Why certainly, madam. You can return to the post-Keynesian dialectic at any time. Yes, ma'am. (On mic) Oh, me. Never have I seen such a rush. Never in all my? Lands Sakes! Who put that dummy here?

MR. HI STOP: Oh boy.

ELEPHANT: If that isn't the silliest looking dummy I've ever seen. I don't know why that stockroom can't send one that looks at least half-alive! I have never seen one with such an insipid expression. And such a ridiculous posture. I?

TRAVELING SALESMAN: Mister?

ELEPHANT: Yes?

TRAVELING SALESMAN: I'm, I'm not really a dummy.

ELEPHANT: That makes absolutely no difference. They still shouldn't - oh good heavens, you're alive! Oh, for pity's sake. Young man, come down off there.

TRAVELING SALESMAN: Yes, sir.

ELEPHANT: Well, just what were you doing on that platform looking like a dummy?

TRAVELING SALESMAN: Well, that's a long story, sir. You see, I-

ELEPHANT: Oh good heavens, young man. Will you do me a favor? As soon as you've paid for that jacket, leave the store.

TRAVELING SALESMAN: This jacket?

ELEPHANT: Yes that jacket with the price tag on it. You're buying it, aren't you?

TRAVELING SALESMAN: But this is my jacket!

ELEPHANT: Your jacket? Hmm. Do you have the sales slip?

TRAVELING SALESMAN: Well, no. I bought it here last year.

ELEPHANT: (slight snicker) And you haven't removed the price tag yet?

TRAVELING SALESMAN: Removed the pri--? Oh, mister, you don't understand?

ELEPHANT: Young man, I understand perfectly. The price is $14.95 and I want it right now.

TRAVELING SALESMAN: Oh, but mister?

ELEPHANT: Now, I said.

TRAVELING SALESMAN: But you don't understand this is my own jacket, no fooling. Mr. Hi Stop, tell the man this is my jacket and ? Mr. Hi Stop?

ELEPHANT: Young man, are you calling me names?

TRAVELING SALESMAN: Oh, no, no, no, sir. I was talking to my friend.

ELEPHANT: What friend?

TRAVELING SALESMAN: Well that's just it. Hi--he was here a minute ago. Gee whiz, I bet Hi went up to the toy department. Mister, if you'd just come up to the toy department we can find my friend and he'll tell you that.

ELEPHANT: Young man, I'm not going up to the toy department or anywhere else until I have the fourteen Zysigabucks and ninety-five cents for that jacket.

TRAVELING SALESMAN: But that's all the money I have and I - I just-Oh, wait a minute.

ELEPHANT: Beg pardon?

TRAVELING SALESMAN: I know. Mister, if I paid you for this jacket you'd give me a sales slip and then I could take it over to the exchange department and get my money back, couldn't I?

ELEPHANT: Yes, if you liked.

TRAVELING SALESMAN: In that case, it's OK. I haven't anything to worry about. Here's the money.

ELEPHANT: Ahh, thank you. And here's your sales slip.

TRAVELING SALESMAN: Thank you.

ELEPHANT: You're quite welcome. Good day, sir.

TRAVELING SALESMAN: Good day. Guess I fooled him. Yessir, it's a good thing I think fast. For a minute there it looked like I wouldn't have any Christmas money. But now all I have to do is take this coat and, and go to the exchange counter and give them this jacket and then I'll ju -- Gee whiz, if I do, I won't have any jacket left. Oh boy, how do I get into these things?

ACT THREE

MUSIC: Christmas tune bridge to next scene. Store bell rings (3 times, then stop) along with store customer chatter.

MR. HI STOP: Gee whiz.

TRAVELING SALESMAN: Wha-what's the matter?

MR. HI STOP: There's Clytemnestra.

TRAVELING SALESMAN: Clytie? Where?

MR. HI STOP: Oh, good grief. If she sees me with this bottle of perfume, she'll know what I'm getting her for Christmas.

TRAVELING SALESMAN: She's coming this way.

MR. HI STOP; Yes, I know, I see. I'll just duck the bottle in my pocket, there right in this pocket. Now if she sees me?

ELEPHANT: (Off mic) Just a moment, please! (To Mr. Hi Stop): I saw that.

MR. HI STOP: Saw what? Oh. Ohh! OHH! Oh, now mister, you don't understand. You don't understand at all, I?

ELEPHANT: Did you or did you not just hide a bottle of perfume in your pocket?

MR. HI STOP: Well, yes, but?

ELEPHANT: Have you paid for it?

MR. HI STOP: Well, no, but?

ELEPHANT: Well, I don't know what you call it, but we call it shoplifting!

MR. HI STOP: Yes, of course? Uh? shoplifting?! [His face forms into a transmogrified series of Norman Rockwell paintings.] Oh, now wait a minute, Elephant, I can explain the entire thing.

ELEPHANT: Um-hmm. I'm listening.

MR. HI STOP: Well, you see, I've been trying to get one of the sales girls to wait on me and I just saw my wife over there and I hid the bottle because I didn't want her to know what I'm getting her for Christmas.

ELEPHANT: Um-hmm. Just where is your wife?

MR. HI STOP: Well she was right over, over? Oh, good heavens, she's gone!

ELEPHANT: Yeah, I thought so.

MR. HI STOP: Oh, but she was right there! Traveling Salesman, tell the man how we saw my wife? uh? oh? Well now where did he go to?

ELEPHANT: Who?

MR. HI STOP: Traveling Salesman. He was standing right here just a second ago. I don't know where he?

ELEPHANT: Do you imagine these things very often?

MR. HI STOP: Imagine what?

ELEPHANT: Do you have delusions? Dizzy spells?

MR. HI STOP: Oh, but I?

ELEPHANT: You see spots before your eyes? (MR. HI STOP's face pixellates.) Now, keep calm, keep calm. No need to get excited. Just give me back the perfume and we'll forget the whole thing and you can go right home and lie down.

MR. HI STOP: Lie down? But who wants to lie?

ELEPHANT: The perfume please!

MR. HI STOP: I, yes sir, I have it right in my? My? My? Oh no. It leaked.

ELEPHANT: What leaked?

MR. HI STOP: Perfume bottle. It leaked all over my pocket. See, it's half-empty.

ELEPHANT: (in disbelief) Oh, for lands' sake! Now you'll have to pay for it.

MR. HI STOP: Why?

ELEPHANT: That's right. I was going to forget the whole incident, but I can't return a damaged bottle to the counter.

MR. HI STOP: Well I'm certainly not going to pay for a leaky bottle of perfume.

ELEPHANT: Mister, if you're not satisfied with the item, you can take it to the exchange department, but it must be paid for. I said it must!

MR. HI STOP: (sighing) Oh, you win. I'll go to the exchange department but how I get into these things, I'll never know.

ACT FOUR

MUSIC: Christmas tune bridge to next scene

CLYTIE: Which bathrobe do you like best, Simon?

SIMON: Umm, the dark blue one I think.

CLYTIE: I do, too. Blue is Hi's favorite color.

SIMON: Oh, but is it his size?

CLYTIE: Well, there's only one way to tell, Simon. Can you try it on? You wear about the same size as Mr. Hi Stop does and if it fits you, it'll fit him.

SIMON: Oh, here, hold my coat, dear, while I step into this dressing room and put this bathrobe on. Oh dear, there's no plastic hanger in here for my shirt. Just wire hangers. I hate wire hangers! (He lets out a high-pitched scream.)

CLYTIE: Here you go, Simon. (She passes him a plastic coat hanger.)

SIMON: Oh, thank you, dearie. (pulling on the bathrobe) I'll have this robe on in just a minute. There. Ahh, how's it look, Clytie?

CLYTIE: Uh, well? It looks a little small to me.

SIMON: It does? Well I better take a look in this mirror, I - oh, I-I'll have to ask the sales girl if she has a larger size. You wait here, Clytie. (Off mic) Oh, uh, Miss? Miss, do you have a?

(MR. HI STOP appears.) Gee whiz, Clytie!

CLYTIE: Mr. Hi Stop! What are you doing here?

MR. HI STOP: Looking for Traveling Salesman.

CLYTIE: Traveling Salesman? Is he here?

MR. HI STOP: Well I think so. We came here together, but we got separated.

CLYTIE: Oh, well where'd you see him last?

MR. HI STOP: On the dummy platform. You see, he was being a dummy.

CLYTIE: What do you mean?

MR. HI STOP: A dummy. You know the kind that looks like this.

CLYTIE: Hi, what are you talking about?

(Two demons, PAZUZU and MEPHISTOPHELES, disguised as workers, start moving displays and shelves around, stealing SIMON's coathangers in the process.)

MEPHISTO: (interrupting) Excuse me, Miss. I gotta move these coathangers. Plastic is poison.

CLYTIE: What? Oh, oh, I'm sorry.

MEPHISTO: OK, get the other end there.

PAZUZU: (Off mic) Got it.

MEPHISTO: Easy now. Right there?

PAZUZU: (Off mic) I got it? Pull it around there…

CLYTIE: Mr. Hi Stop, what are you trying to tell me about Traveling Salesman?

MR. HI STOP: Clytie, it's an awful long story. All I wanna know is have you seen him?

CLYTIE: No, I haven't.

MR. HI STOP: Then I better keep looking. He may be in trouble.

CLYTIE: What kind of trouble?

MR. HI STOP: I can't tell you now, Clytie. (Off mic) See you later. 'Bye!

CLYTIE: But Hi, wait! Hi! Oh golly, that Mr. Hi Stop. He's the strangest person.

SIMON: Clytemnestra, how do you like this bathrobe?

CLYTIE: Oh that's fine, Simon. But I just?

SIMON: This size does fit much better doesn't it, dear?

CLYTIE: Yes, Simon, but I, I just?

SIMON: Clytemnestra X. Willow! What happened to them?

CLYTIE: What happened to what?

SIMON: My beautiful plastic coathangers. I had some in white, some in pink, some in paisley. This just ruins Christmas! [He begins to sob.]

CLYTIE: (anxious) Oh golly, I don't know! They were here a minute ago!

ELEPHANT: Something wrong, m'seur?

SIMON: Yes, I lost my plastic coathangers.

ELEPHANT: (taken aback) I beg your - I beg your pardon.

SIMON: My hangers, you dim brute! We put them down here for a minute while I tried on this bathrobe and now they're gone! Worst Christmas ever! (He starts to cry and whimper again.)

ELEPHANT: The bathrobe?

CLYTIE: No, the hangers!

ELEPHANT: But it couldn't be! (incredulous) Oh, my land! I have never seen such a day. Living dummies, men hiding from their wives and now Simon loses his coat hanger collection!

CLYTIE: But I tell you it was right under your trunk.

ELEPHANT: I should hope so!

SIMON: Well, uh, do something. Do something. (He wails and gnashes the bathrobe slightly.)

ELEPHANT: Young man, what can I do about your coathangers?

SIMON: Find them!

ELEPHANT: Now, please be calm. Be calm. It was probably taken by mistake and it will be turned in to the lost and found department.

SIMON: Well, where's that?

ELEPHANT: At the other end of the floor next to the exchange department.

SIMON: Come on, Clytie.

ELEPHANT: Where are you going?

SIMON: To the lost and found department.

ELEPHANT: But Simon, certainly not in our bathrobe?

SIMON: (a little outraged) Well, certainly not without it! Come on, Clytie, we'll go see if they have my coathangers. How these things happen to me I'll never know!

ACT FIVE

MUSIC: Christmas tune bridge to next scene

MR. HI STOP: Traveling Salesman? Can I tell you who I met?

TRAVELING SALESMAN: Yes, Hi.

MR. HI STOP: Well, first I ran into?-- A rock. [He trips over Simon Junior.] Simon Junior! What in tarnation are you doing here?

TRAVELING SALESMAN: Gee whiz, Simon Junior. Where'd you come from?

SIMON JUNIOR: Sit.

[SIMON sashays forward.] Traveling Salesman, what are you doing standing here in your shirtsleeves?

TRAVELING SALESMAN: Well, Simon, I can explain. You see, I came over- Simon! What are you doing in that bathrobe?

SIMON: Oh, it's not my bathrobe, it's? (sniffs accusingly) MR. HI STOP, you smell.

MR. HI STOP: (surprised) What?

SIMON: You positively reek of perfume. (He rolls his eyes.)

MR. HI STOP: Ohhh.

CLYTIE: Now, who?

MR. HI STOP: Heh, heh, yes I do, don't I? Well, ahem, you see, dear, I can explain.

CLYTIE: Traveling Salesman, what are you doing here? And why didn't you tell me my husband was here?

MR. HI STOP: Well, Clytie, I was?

ELEPHANT: What seems to be the trouble here?

MR. HI STOP: Oh, the Elephant. Mister, I'm trying to find out why Simon was married to a rock?

ELEPHANT: Well, please there's no need to get political.

CLYTIE: I want to know why you smell of perfume? And what is Simon doing in that bathrobe?

TRAVELING SALESMAN: And why I'm trying to exchange my own coat!

SIMON: So, when did you get here, Traveling Salesman?

MR. HI STOP: Why are you all excited? (All start arguing among each other loudly.)

MR. HI STOP: (trying to get their attention) Traveling Salesman! Clytemnestra!

MR. HI STOP: (trying to talk over the arguing) Quiet! Arguing continues.

MR. HI STOP: (louder, a little forcefully) QUIET! (Arguing stops.) Whew! That's better. Now listen to me, all of you. This nonsense has gone far enough. Too far in fact.

TRAVELING SALESMAN, SIMON AND CLYTEMNESTRA: Yes, Mr. Hi Stop.

ELEPHANT: (interrupting) It certainly has! All afternoon you people have made my life quite miserable for me. Quite miserable.

ALL BUT ELEPHANT: Yes, sir.

ELEPHANT: Now, if there's any reason for it I feel I'm entitled to an explanation.

TRAVELING SALESMAN: Well, mister, you know the coat, the one you thought I was buying? Simon and Mr. Hi Stop and Clytemnestra can all identify it as my old coat.

SIMON: Why of course that's Traveling Salesman's coat. Tea bags?

ELEPHANT: Oh, dear. You mean it really is?

MR. HI STOP: Yes. And maybe you'll recall you didn't believe Clytemnestra was in the store when I hid the perfume bottle in my pocket?

ELEPHANT: (sheepishly) Well, yes, I?

MR. HI STOP: Well this is my wife.

ELEPHANT: (apologetically) Oh? How do you do? I'm very sorry?

CLYTIE: And I just found out that two of your men moved an empty rack while I was talking to Simon. And that was the rack with all the nice pretty plastic coathangers that he covets.

MR. HI STOP: Well, Mr. Elephant, what do you say to that?

All but ELEPHANT (indignantly): Yeah, what do you say to that?

ELEPHANT: (conceding) People, please, please, please. No tempers, please. No tempers, no tempers. The customer's always right at Stanney's. Can I get you an H Bomb Neutralizer?

MR. HI STOP: Hmph.

ELEPHANT: Mistakes will happen, you know.

TRAVELING SALESMAN: Hmph.

ELEPHANT: Young man, since that does seem to be your own coat, you may keep it and I'll give you a cash credit slip for what you paid me.

TRAVELING SALESMAN: Thank you. And Mr. Hi Stop, I'll be glad to give you another bottle of perfume. Compliments of the store.

MR. HI STOP: Well that's better.

ELEPHANT: And Simon? I'm sure we can find your coathangers in the lost and found department. And you may keep that bathrobe at no charge.

SIMON: (happily) Well! Thank you!

ELEPHANT: (cautiously) Well, people, uh, does that satisfy you?

MR. HI STOP: Well, yes I think that straightens everything out all right. I'm sorry there's been so much misunderstanding.

ELEPHANT: That's quite all right. Quite all right.

MR. HI STOP: And now, folks, if everything's settled, let's stop hiding from each other and get this Christmas shopping over and done with once and for all. All right. Now, I?
SOUND FX: Store bell tone (2 times)
MR. HI STOP: What was that?
ELEPHANT: Thank heavens, store's closing. You folks'll all have to come back next Monday.
MR. HI STOP: Come back, you mean we've gotta go through all this again? (All characters express moans and groans of disbelief; excited chatter amongst themselves)

OUTRO
MUSIC: Christmas tune up and then out, followed immediately by Striker's Jingle:

Tender beef, juicy pork,
Known from Underwear Point to Umlaut Towin!
Striker's Premium Franks!
Striker's Premium Franks!

ANNOUNCER (aka SNOOTY LOOKING ANNOUNCER IN A BOW TIE):
Friends, you really know what you're getting when you ask for Striker's Premium Franks.
Tender beef, juicy pork,
Known from Underwear Point to Umlaut Towin!
Striker's Premium Franks!
Striker's Premium Franks!

Made fresh daily in Striker kitchens from coast-to-coast, so you know they're fresh. Made by Striker so you know they're top quality. Ask for them today--Striker's Premium Franks in the new, handy one pound cellophane package. And while you're at your dealers be sure to ask for Striker's Zysigamore Sausage--the sausage with the "just right" seasoning. And your dealer has a tempting variety of Striker's Premium table-ready meats. Tasty COOKED SPECIALTY is being featured this week. A delicious luncheon meat--Striker's Premium Cooked Specialty is all meat. No bones. No waste. An economical, flavorful meat that the whole family will enjoy. Striker's Premium Cooked Specialty is just the thing for family holiday lunches and snacks. For a meal in a flash that saves plenty of cash, get Striker's Premium table-ready meats.

MUSIC: Theme up and then under for...

SNOOTY LOOKING ANNOUNCER IN A BOW TIE:
You've been listening to another chapter in The Tyranny of Pants, written by Me and Tinkelhoff, and based on the classified dignitized characters appearing in Classic Plays Number Two, Three, Twelve and Eighty-Four. Traveling Salesman was played by Bob Hastings, Mr. Hi Stop by Harlan Stone, Clytemnestra was played by Alice Yourman and Simon by Arthur Kohl. Others in today's cast were EEEEEEEEEELLLLLLLLLEPHANT and Simon Junior. This program is produced and directed by Kenneth MacGregor. Listen next Saturday when Striker and Company, makers of Striker's Premium Franks, and the Zysigamore Broadcasting System, bring you more of the merry Tyranny of Pants. This is Sir Reginald Prentice Cricklingham wishing you all a very Merry Christmas. So long.

MUSIC: Theme up and play to end.

I met him in Science. My mind was on Compliance.

I had a Form 34c-1. My hand was on a gun.

They treed a Gabardine. The branches in between.

A mind in cellophane. Take another brain.

C N L F N. Be the ham you win.

Ellipse in pure tom gravy. Eat another shavings.

Back to the bony. I'm Tony.

Peas and cantos. Pounds of Mentos.

Wrath of Pseudokon. Time to make a bomb.

They resemble mashed potatoes.

Eat another label. Tour the other stable.

Jump the fence or ence a bench come hence.

Organofactoidalism of the average geomorph condescends the hewn matrices.

Extra kaleidoscopes will be provided at Hector's Fotomat's rear window under the flower pot and to the right of the cat door.

Steven had had a day. I made them take it away.

I give bricks to oldie bats. I taut I kill a kitty catt.

Telematrixphone headsets. Jets in head. Rebar

When J.O. Lundberg returned to his Buckyball, three garlics were in order.

I ask 4casta, had to drink a Shasta.

Abalone! Abalone! Abalone!

Had to hold on.

God of restless gentlemen, inseams like Bethlehem.

Bodhidharma, Lee Litif. I just hit a barrier reef.

Picking up a sundown so's I can bring it to your town.

We enveloped in dwellvelopmint in Taste-a-Print. You can

The inside of a Unicorn Harbor tavern. The inside of a Goddess' cavern.

Häxenophilia was the kind of trend that I would send out to a xxend.

Umbled johnquil. Bumbled "Bob's" hill. Oblong pill.

Young Fortinbras, the court in vase. Motor was.

(Line redacted by a major publishing corporation to be named later.)

Gum! We have gum! Want some?

Action diplodocus – activate!

-26   Bowl of Candilingam

Mr. Hi Stop's altar superego Corridor Mike had just entered the dragon. KJ Howling, Christimiqua's altar id, was busy enrolling relevant yet reluctant teenagers in the game of Squid Scratch. Amos and Andy's stunt voiceover maven Hellionlujah Illadylenmystiqk slickly focused the tempest on a pig's jacket. Paradiddledigmatic

Creecher Triple Feecher: Best of Moldman Meets the Moldovan Mailman. In 4-D Smellovision™.

Crucial Wilhelm Plecostomus entered a plea of "SUCK" today in Unicorn Harbor Circuit Court. Presiding judge was Anastasio Farfel's altar superego Carlos Rubiconned. Defendant is bathed in Macedonian yogurt.

Buh Bye Bubba Ashworthy's daughter's super id dakini Yellowflam Mgrandikowski and her extended flammaly of telefaunists will have been foreverever engrossed in the terraforming daymares of existentialist nabobs nobody ever knackled or spackled yet somehow occupied a specific set of coordinates in protuberances of space/time epicatalystic methaframalines.

Ill talking kumquat Bjorn Hatterac can never be the avatar of Ralph, because Bjorn believed STFU stood for Say Ten Fabulous Utterances. Way off based.

Finally a chapter that cuts through the alliteration and avuncular ablatrossophies, just as Sartre's grand-niece's mynah was known to interlocute.

"Now then," said Snooty Looking Nerd in a Bow Tie. "Dastardly William Rucklehaus..."

Queen Idajan's secondary holographic avatar was sometimes named Fill à Menthe. She road atop a beaming tardigrade, soft spurs exploding into quaint endoplanets. Photosynthesis of

Inkast's mane menn finna blow right up in dwellvellopmental hyperbolic... mystic* tungsten chains like an infinite series of funhouse mirrors fed through atlien kaleidoscopes.

Kodiak McQuillincounter, Simon's lumberjack altar ego, was hit in the exothorax. You, you. Kodiak hit back. Ya.

Arnold Boysenberry Quackenbush III's gardener's sister's phlebotomist's personal masseuse's chinchillaroni speudomatic hossenbolognifaction and testodia chronolasmodontiasaurus had thrived and even survived the skylopocalyptic vulvcanoes that Taweret's priests and worshippers had conjured.

Hydrophonia stumped the Brenda Loompas whose over-pixellation had caused them to trespass into the 9th dimension before being detoured by an avatar of Traveling Salesman. The flow...

St. Joseph sent pterodactyls to the vague Xarthorians gathered in the fallout shelter. "This is a stupid song. End it."

*   Shortened form

27 _____ KA

All DNA straws, coiled amphisbaenae, pleasure centers, rights and lefts, unwritten writs, licorice twisters, and kundabutters rest under the desert sand. At Flood, straws sink to the bottom of a vast river coiling around the Material. Straws transform into reeds, rushes, soft estuary grasses, sweet wild fields dripping their toes into rising water.

Taweret Herself became midwife - then grandmother - to Idajan in response to 4casta's national supplication campaign. Other miraculous occurrences at Idajan's birth include the appearance of the Pants Star above the Queendom, and all-you-can-eat borscht.

Yet as 4casta aged and her daughter got stronger, Taweret's cult stagnated. The new Queen still conducted all the rituals and sent out email invites, but whispers abounded that the Goddess was somehow displeased. Worse, lerbiaxes started wilding throughout the back country of Uottubbacktotheboniyiumm (sp.), seemingly at will. The Team Gods were no help as usual.

This stress weakened the old Queen in her dotage. 4casta hated those humanoids as much as her Goddess did. But she hadn't intrafered in internal affairs since letting Idajan run the nation so many years ago. 4casta asked her handmaidens to prepare the temple for Taweret, but the sparse crowds lacked fervor.

Rev. Zzyster soon was named Charioteer of Hwalearastok, and pledged to boost Taweret's worship. Yet KA remained elusive; the people, myrmidondrites par excellence, would not recognize KA if they were slapped sideways by salami salesmen slung southwestward since sauropods shook some spheres.

Zzyster was good, but his grassroots stuff didn't work on 4casta. Soon Idajan rushed to her mother's aid, trying to modernize the process and relieve her mother's burdens. Unfortunately, Danzig Fulkerson & Johnson's strategy dammed demand for the damned demos.

Strategy turned towards tragedy as 4casta broke down under the team-based management facilitation and productivity matrices and yantras. Even Idajan was amused when her mom winged polygonal magnets at the slick account managers. "Begone or I shall behead all of you!" Idajan cried in her fury, calling for her Major Domo and Minor Domo and their servants three. "You're still a sassy old bird, ma," she winked to 4casta.

-27 _____ 6 Shouting Economists

Illustriluminmatic hip-hop guru Big John "The Armadillo" Kenzingsloth III hosted an ovaltable discussion between alleged intellectual giants of the generation, only some of whom require an introduction or a mic check. The SJU lecture hall was packed with spoxes, bussy eaters, dirty immature lerbiaxes, and the occasional student. A shrill shrieker-like alarm singled the strat of this exercise in naval gazing. Big John announced, "The amount of cognitive dissonance will be mamba!"

Li'l Nas Y wore several strands of pure pearls over a silver lamé jumpsuit reinforced with obstellamysticatalyptus gravy and a flexed-out rentboy. Other celebs were spectacularly semi-attired as well. Allman Isley, flexed out as usual, slid into his seat next to his brothers, cousins and neckties.

A lich named John Maynard Kinesiology led the participants in a prayer of false bravado. Then SJU provost kicked Dr. Kinesiology out and kicked off the discussion. "We'll have no undead at this forum. Undead threaten the orderly progression toward recession and regression," the provost averred. The lich sneered, but was skillfully removed by two brawny Team Demigods. Murray Rothbard looked on.

Hans-Herman Hoppe slithered past security and ascended the podium. "I can't believe I have to speak to a room full of junkies and degenerates. I have left the good graces of my armed gated community to espouse an end to democratic...tea bags?" The audience hollered and hooted, but also started lobbing flammable jewelry and oily rags at Hoppe. His bleats became unintelligible after that, as firefighters doused him with foam and 2 liter bottles of a strange crimson pop. "Don't oaf my property, socialists!" he yelled at the pubic servants.

The Adam Smith hologram failed to load, so Big John spouted some statist homilies until the next guest arrived, dressed in a Mexican pro wrestling outfit with large round ears protruding from the sequined mask. "Statism is a waist of thyme!" hollered Broz. He carried water for and made excuses for a whole host of totalitarian regimes, boring some of the students into untimely deaths. "Anyway, we're woke and we toke. Class dismissed," Broz screamed.

Milton Friedman took a couple of swings at Broz before the supply-sider slipped and fell on the grease. Hill Cummings flung naugahyde lazy boy chairs at Broz but missed each time. "Trickle down THIS, fools!" Broz cried.

A blow to the head and Big John was out cold. To the podium pounced the Snooty Looking Nerd with a Bowtie. "Eeeelephant." Elephant strode onstage with a dance troupe. "If in fact the world ended in times of ---" before being shot down by a known assailant.

"Getting dissed by some has-beens at a lecture? I simply don't have the time of day for these tired old queens," quoth Li'l Nas Y.

28   Correct Spelling of Uottubbacktothebonieueviulle * * *

Just as the true Kabalah is not spoken, the true Queendom yclept Uottub... (sp.) cannot be spelled en anglais. At least this is the sincere wish of Idajan, who had the country's spelling augmented to interfere with search engine suboptimizationsizzle.

Portrad-to-English translations continue to be inadequate. There are many tonal nuances that disappear in the process. For this reason, Queen Idajan created a sliding scale of alternate transliterations sure to satisfy the most bookish Xarthorian.

The other beneficiaries were the vendors of inkjet toner cartridges. Variable spellings made correct letterhead and envelopes a nightmare. Postal carriers were known to commit hari-kari every time the Queen tweaked a vowel or two. Needles to say, the populace was on needless and plums.

Meco inadvertently released 85 new transliterations of Uottubbacktothebonivuille (sp.), including Uottubdack2thebonyimtonyvule (sp.), Uottubbackto34anskurlimqia (sp.), Uottubbacktothebonyexpialanalacknaloggueitoriumvillaaeulle (sp.), Uottubbacktothehypersesquidillianactrueleapasaurusism (sp.), Uottubownthemidlwagridlleiummmmmnnnn (sp.), Uottubacktothecadagrillexpialastoppinclaushee (sp.) & Uottubbacktouottubbacktouottubbacktotheuottubbacktothebbacktotheboniummnnimtonyumaraniumadelphoniammnn (sp.). They sold out within nanoseconds.

Cheap postile stampogrammitications and associated tetragrammatons in all crediblue hues are blessed by Idajan with inventing their own glyphs and cymbals to represent the Queendom. Holla! to keep them immune to hijacking by the cartel. Praise E.O.

Hydroxylcorevolutionary NFTs set the stage for the Queendom. 4casta seized the means of coreproduction claiming conceptual continuity. 4casta extended it into a great empire and merchandising emporium: Taweret key chains; coins and postage stamps with the Uottubbacktothebonieuavillee (sp.) crest, logo, glyph, and full series of ackronyms; pears in a partridge tree; advanced glamorous fetuses; and the grand sense of Magnificent Destiny. Splash!

The occult name of 4casta's grandmama is embedded deep within the aglets of the true name of Uottubbacktotheboneieioynium (sp.) if you look correctly and have the gematria numbers crunched. Truly you would feel the same if you wished to sublimplayalistic along in your pajamas.

-28 Soteriology

Meco was not attracted to the religious life, but he did appreciate that his brother was a Tekoborit cleric. "I figure if I play my coins rite, the Gods will have my back." Rev. Zzyster would smile. He loved his bro, and didn't preach or moralize at him.

Still, Meco did consider himself hothechajuxips, and his marriage to Idajan to be an act of fate. With the Queen's blessing, Meco invented his own godly philanthropy to pass the time and make himself look good to his wife. "You know, something like the Striker Way, but less cheesy."

For 1000 minutes and 1000 seconds Meco searched tirelessly for a persuasive Executive Director who could get those Zysigabucks flowing to his foundation. But Meco wasn't exactly the management type. "Now what do I do?" he texted his wife. "I dunno. Just show up somewhere and tell your stories. Then people will respond. Let me deal with the candidate selection."

Everywho's who's on first from Mr. Namol to oldagmarfrisbie applied for the job. Jennifer Val Over introduced herself and promptly asked to be appointed Chair of the Trustees. "I don't even have a credenza yet," gasped Meco to Idajan. "Val Over, eh? 'Twould be better to tie her to a credenza and float her through the flumes of River Phlegethon!" screamed Idajan.

After an exhausting series of months in which Meco had to complete several sexual harassment seminars for some of his racier 'tales,' the candidate pool was narrowed to just 3: Lilith Fairkid, an angular medusa from Planet Mayberry; DiOwn Xongregix, a Queen's X'er from the gecko; and Uitainii Squincyson, a poetic hammer polisher with no visible pockmarx or spanx. Idajan wasn't there physically, but remote-viewed the whole thang via Bleary Tim.

"What nanocognobioedunography have you -" Meco was about to ask before excusing himself. Idajan texted him, "Just choose DiOwn. I have to behead the other two candidates." Meco returned to the interview and blurted, "This reminds me of a movie I saw where a great couple falls in love, but there's a war and everyone is worried about superball dilation before tumble-dried epiastronomy reminds us of the pop-up air threshered speudothoracic ligatard in Myasia heretofive overpolysaturizzle..." "Uh, could I have a glass of water?" the interviewee plead. Meco continued his tamble.

29 Destiny's Just a Charm in a Locket, Part I

Twas the morning after. The carnival was packed and the caravan was ready to journey to the next location. Still, not all the carnies made the trip. Some got odd jobs at the masturbatorium or other low-wage work in town. A few joined the priesthood. But one or two would be lured to Broz's commune at a run-down farm not far from the fairgrounds.

One such dull eyed, bushy tentacled ragamuffin was Destiny von Waifenburg. A scion of a clan of Unnunnentiumnnnn dry cleaners, Destiny ran away with the carnival at age 16, then drifted from one big top to another. Finally the crass consumerism of carnival life pushed her to the brink, and a hardcore flex drug habit led her to even more unsavory lewdness.

Destiny sought out Rahälrahad from an enigmatic message she received. "At 29100 Real Lane, turn left. Then look for the barn with the hammer and sigil mural depicting triumphant Xarthorian proletariats." Could it be code, she thought? 'I don't want to seem too naive, but...' She set out anyway. Destiny arrived to find several anarchists milling about a keto-friendly dumpster fire. Broz was 'deep cover': all his inner circle denied knowing of his

54

whenabouts. "It's like that," stated a very hip looking loiterer. "Broz is flying under the gaydar of corporate dragnet police state totalitarianism," explained Emily, a new intern. "I hope I see him in Part II," said Destiny.

Sure enough, Rahälrahad appeared on an atomic-powered tricycle. "Lookie here. Air cooled. Carbon neutral. Not like some of you hothechajuxips types." Rahälrahad didn't trust her yet, and seemed leery of Destiny's bougie handbag and beetle-skin gloves. He proceeded to introduce himself and begin the extreme vetting. "So how do I know that you're not a dick? A narc? A Mikey Rat fink?" His raised eyebrow seemed to slash her spirit. "I ain't a snitch," pleaded Destiny. "Look, I have this." It was a mini rhinestone replica of Dan the Man's Power Jacket. Its new jack feel earned her the salty commie's trust, albeit grudgingly.

Soon Destiny had a cot in a communal sleeping quarter, and an assignment in the kitchen, making gluten-free vegan meals for revolution. She joined the woke mob, and really felt the class struggle. Still no sign of Broz, despite rumors from several of his henchmen. "Maybe he's not real. Broz is just a symbol of our resistance against imperialism," she rationalized. "Oh, he's quite real. And quite spectacular," responded a tovarisch.

Suddenly a chandelier crashed to the floor, with Broz clinging to the chain for dear life. "Ha!" he grunted. "If you didn't have that piece of the Power Jacket, I never would have known it's you." He awkwardly repositioned one of his mouse ears. Destiny swooned. "Broz! At LAST!!! I need to join your movement."

-29   Aero Royale

Zapp Omnigotopia was in 9th Heaven. He had finally gotten that dream SJU internship - a personal assistant/gofer to yacht rock superstar Pettiler Stevens. He quickly texted Young Fortinbras and every social club at Simon Junior U about this prune job. Soon, a cub reporter from Ace TV, Cynidye Gaiylee, was interviewing him at the very gates of Striker Manor.

Paw soon arrived, and scattered the paparazzi with radioactive rock salt encrusted radicchios. "Aw Dad!" Zapp pouted. "This is about me, not you." Striker, still oblivious, replied, "Who are you?" In a rage, Zapp lashed out at his Dad but fell short. "You might be taller than me, but I can still whip your -"

Zapp's phone insistently began to ring. "Hold on," he said to his miffed father, "this is important." He chatted for what seemed to be a short eternity, and Striker gave up and began to walk away. "It's Pettiler Stevens themselves! I'm starting immediately."

The superstar had booked a Tenser's Floating Disk to take Zapp to their next gig at the Zysigamore Dome, in front of 77,000 screaming Xarthorians (and 8,000 who were too intoxicated to scream.) Stevens was there to meet him and shave his hand. "Bizzy bizzy bop-a-lu-la Wakakaka Pow!" A strong electrical charge coursed through Zapp's nervous system. "Likey-likey Dat TENS Unit?" "Well, I, uh, sorta," Zapp replied in a daze. "Swalla Walla Dicky Dicky Kow!"

The concert was an epic, 19-song tour de farce, with several meldies of Pettiler Stevens' greatest hacks. The lyrics were somehow less incomprehensible than usual thanks to vast quantities of 5g and good intentions. The set ended with "Pee-Yort," the second most cheesepoppingest ditty of the season. Its chorus of "B- Short. Pee Yort, Waka Waka Tombé" encapsulated the aspirations of Zapp's degeneration.

The band left the stage to deafening applause, involuntary emissions, and tattered pants. Stevens quickly cut through the ribbons, dental dams and cumfetti to embrace Zapp. "Domatickee skoodalio pip. Hidey Hidey Mepps Mepps!" shouted the rocker as he lapsed out of and back into consciousness. The rest of the band had to stand there for 10 minutes before their leader came to.

Zapp pumped a pumpkin spice biden mocktail into Stevens. After several asystoles, dry heaves and burps, the pop culture icon sat up and wiped away someone else's vomit. "Lacka lacka lacka BOOM! Mongitail!" He bolted back to the megastage, and the other band mates quickly followed. "For you, kid." The backup sousaphonist handed Zapp a soiled pair of Pettiler's Panties.

30   Inverted Pyramid

With invocations to all the team gods except Ariel, god of pickled items that cause intestinal dysfunction, construction commenced on the vast Inverted Pyramid of Uottubbacktothebonyur (sp.). Labor was extraordinarily swift due to all the demons and Xarthorian flunkies conscripted to help with the overtaking. They even BBQ'd a few journalists for good measure.

Once the elaborate pyramid was complete, Queen 4casta handed the keys to her daughter Idajan, who made it into one of the Six Wonders of Zysigamore. The Inverted Pyramid of 4casta became a tourist trap overnight, with its spectacular frescoes, rollercoasters, and idiopathic holograms- just as Bleary Tim had predicted.

Of course, the gang (Simon Junior, Mr. Hi Stop, Traveling Salesman, Clytemnestra and Simon) had to go and check out the Pyramid. Once Simon got passes to Li'l Nas Y and Allman Isley Band at the Inverted Loungeitorium, they were in like fulmen. Their fame preceded them, and the whole group was led to a VIP section populated with X's, leading clerics, élite sales professionals, and calcified phrenologists.

One X'er fawned over Simon Junior. "You really fit in here," said QIA 001 herself, adjusting her thigh-high boots before the rock. "And all of you too. Help yourself to everything in the redroom except the estrogen smoothies."

Clearly their names were on the list. Next, the Queen's personal assistant Zexo led the gang on a tour of the Pyramid's interior. "It's too beautiful," raved Simon. "I couldn't live here - I just don't deserve it." Traveling Salesman calmed Simon, and helped him cease the waterworks. "You are worthy, you are worthy," Traveling Salesman cooed, rubbing Simon's forehead.

Simon and Clytie left to check out the Jell-o Wrestling Superstars' duodecathlon at the Coliseum. Back at the Loungeatorium, Mr. Hi Stop and Traveling Salesman were rubbing sternums with Rev. Zzyster and Meco. "I love the way the Pyramid just feels so...mamba," said Traveling Salesman, as Hi nodded repeatedly like a broken bobblehead.

Once the flex drugs subsided, however, the gang felt a little dizzy. "We'd love to felch you, but we gotta get back home," apologized Mr. Hi Stop, hoping the Queen's enforcers didn't feign any butthurt. "We did have quite a lovely time, and you and your brother are so supple and well-developed," gushed Traveling Salesman, giving air elbow bumps to the Rev and Meco. "Waiting for a time door..." The Prince Crown returned the bump and gave his Royal OK. "Say, you remind me of a roommate I had in high school. He was about your height, and..." Simon Junior: Sit.

-30   Journalism

The Underwear Point *Picayune* was the most followed rag on the Island. Traveling Salesman claimed to wrap his fish in it, when in reality he used palm fronds.

He had paid good money for several copy inches of the Tuesday, February 27 evening edition: Six double-spaced lines that screamed: TOMORROW! FOREVER! END OF THE SALE!

Accuracy and death were all that mattered. A verse was read about vinegar. The *Pic* was well known for dishing out slabs of raw mayhem in linotype.

Headquarters was banking on this. "I wish I knew what 'Bob' was up to now. He always has an edge on me. He's always picking those extra accounts right at the end of the week, end of the month. Christ."

"Necromancy was 'Bob's' game. But how?" He put the receiver down and furrowed his brow.

A great day is coming for Dad. Money flowed like rain. Raptorous ethereal beings fluttered in mid-air before carefully, artfully descending. Faux parabolas...Shorts...Sox...Slacks...

Copy editors shudder in inchoate fear. A nebulous reflexive withdrawal from the purity of black newsprint thanks to the Brusque Boys. The toner mafia had not quite seized control, yet the path was clear. "Looking back," Traveling Salesman had said, "it was inevitable."

She was still Miss Connie Marsh then, the blush of effervescent youth on her enchanted face.

"Can't stop the feeling. I'll pull out all the stops. Sure, sure..." The receiver went dead. Traveling Salesman stood up suddenly. He could sell, but could he _sell_? He thought often to Simon, all alone, treating his everlasting cuticles at the spa.

Preying on en-lipocos out in the badlands forged a real search for meaning.

Econolyptic tremors of the quarterly report made him die little by little. Pool balls numbered -30- ricocheting across the clear green felt. And marketing was coming up with new copy. He was cut by thousands of suicides and existed only as atoms.

31   Demonology

Demons factor hugely. Making extensive lists of all their names, symbolism and powers is necessary yet not really. You see, the first book of Demonology is the Bible itself. This much is clear; all Demonologies are rewrites of the Bible. Demons love musicians.

Therefore it is unnecessary unless you become Demon Possessed, at which time you may be confused as to the identity of the infernal being who is unnaturally attracted to you. In cases such as this, a nice thick Yellow Pages from 1983 is just as useful as any of the following Eldritch Grimoires....

Obfuscation of the true issue has long been the bane of all who linger suffering from Demonic Possession. The first level of Hell has consistently been repaved and replastered, but it still looks like a third rate truck stop in Middle America. As such Tiamat Devil regnat in relative opulence inasmuch as.

John Adams was appointed President of the Second Level of Hell. Resplendent in his leather boa, Adams is a swarthy sovereign of the pits, according to David Ten Eyck's personal assistant's brother-in-law's dog walker. Adams' pretty collection of bows really showed off his fair ruby cheeks. Eripuit caelo fulmen. Presupposing the Man from Braintree. Today a dermatologist. Adams earned his Kingdom as an Original Tyrant.

---

*   (See Schedule 14 for list of Recommended Readings)
**   (See Schedule 62 for list of Unrecommended Readings, which are really the Recommended Readings in Demonology.)

THIS PAGE INTENTIONALLY LEFT BLANK Because we could

SECTION 2 Page 31

31B   Ultimate Abortifacients

Again appeared Asmodeus, this time in His form as Four Sticks, a misshapen drum prodigy of much repute. A vat of sweet and sour Unnunnennniumnnnn crude oil filled the cupola almost to the point of exhausting all air. "Sixes and fives! Sixes and fives!" The dice rolls kept coming, some dies drifting in the oil vat.

Striker was standing in the doorway, somewhat reluctant to approach the devil or the petroleum. But finally he mustered some courage to address Four Sticks. "Lord Asmodeus...I have delivered the fetuses. Here they are!" Striker jerked a rope, and opened a large barn door. The stench of spoiled fetal remains wafted into the small room.

"Wicked intense!" Four Sticks hopped over to the open door and smirked at the cargo. "Without me no mamba love can exist. Do you want the passionate love of this woman, this Royal Highness?"

"Yes, yes, forever yes. I want her like the Ipod needs slave labor! I do, I do." Striker was practically drooling by this point.

Four Sticks beckoned him toward the oil. "Now, just pull out the bag of fetuses. Take the whole thing and hurl it in the crude!" Striker followed the instructions. Instantly the oil began to bubble as the pickled punks poured into the vat. Thick black smoke filled the room.

After a couple of minutes, the smoke burned off. The figure of a beautiful woman in luxuriant pants appeared before them. "Is this she after whom you lust?" Striker meekly nodded. "It has been made so. 4casta's daughter will be yours in due time. But not without some tribulation, you see."

Striker figured there would be some quid pro quo. "How so? If I can avoid or minimize trouble, I will. Do you need my soul or something?"

"No, no, nothing like that." Four Sticks sort of half-snorted, half-laughed. "This is much easier. You see, son," said the devil, throwing a bony arm around Striker's broad shoulders, "All you have to do is take these next-generation classic rock playlists and circulate them throughout Zysigamore. You see, the DJ's are so drugged up that they will follow along."

Striker took the scrolls that Four Sticks handed him. "Brilliant. Brilliant. It's next generation stuff. I got this six ways to Sunday."

"Yes, yes," Four Sticks fingered His handlebar moustache. "You know, they would have named Led Zeppelin IV after me. Crowley had it all set up. But some goody-two-shoes types intervened. Well, pretty soon it won't matter. All the listeners will be suitably putrefied."

31C   Wicked Intense

This range of spells is not written for the average Prestidigitator.

Antediluvian nightmares haunt every scroll; just to commit them to mind leaves you tired and strung out. Marble gates.

And so I had it translated. *A Book for Today's Society* by Me. Within the tome was a compendium of hitherto forgotten and overlooked keys… Me men mens mensi mensin mensing...

As enlightening as *A Book for Today's Society* was, I peered at the vellum manuscripts. The complete works of Killgore Trout. That should do nicely, I suppose.

Aegothsorzhotan and I read Agrippa by candlelight of a dozen hundred thousand galaxies & a million billion necronomicons.

I squint exiting the cave. The rogue mage has departed outside the fields of my senses. I saw it coming. He defines Trickster.

Still, any peddler can be had by a shell game. Keep your superballs close and your familiars even closer.

"Double up on the O-Rings!" Marquez told the Gold Kid. "We're going for the big Ka-look-a!" The Kid's T read, "Exxo."

Why rely on spellbooks at all? They are just a crutch for the pedantic. True practitioners are liberated, and upcycle their old spell boox. True

In this age'n'day, rue hydebound synchro systems make for AAI.

The 9=0 equation brokers a solution set which, in conjunction with verbal/somatic/material components,

A la anodyne alabaster abrakazoo whammo

Do you think that wood happen? In search of a propositional phrase.

Dustbin Samuel, trapped in the irrelevant pocket dimension of arch-lich Zommom, clutched roses and data betwixtler

Meanwhile Kaezir Urus Theogygax III used a metaphysical lottery for semiacousticalomni badges, inasmuch as

Pseudoultramacrophonicoxyaloid forteanberry cocktail: shaken and stirred. Eye of Knute optional AND at the end.

Waveform dialectic of praseodymorphic homunculatores. A fine sari of Lee Litif metaphors or linens.

-31   Lyrics to "The A Team" Theme Song

Blow the froth off your yacht rock playlist. Straight - no chaser, go for the jugular mode, military motifs and misfires.

Elmer did have an in with Mr. H, the Mr. T doppelganger approved for Classic Play confunction. In this way, Moloch's brother was able to pen Portrad lyrics to the intricate atmospherical ditty.

Every possible algorithm and breakbeat were given to Mr. H and his people. However, Mike Post insisted on hair metal solos, which cluttered the AAI with CFC-infused hairspray and disentangled synthesizer electronicals. "Got no time for hair metal jibber jabber. Don't make me mad," Mr. H inquit.

Soon, Allman Isley's people talked to Mr. H's people at yet another temporary hipster bistro in a pastel section of Underwear Point. Unfivetunately, Rahälrahad, disguised as a busboy, furtively taped the entire conversation on microcassette. But when he returned to Broz's secret hideout at 115 Elm Lane, the microcassette player jammed when one of the flunkies poured a syrup of General Tso's sauce and polysorbate-80 over everything. "Double drat," cursed Broz.

Evertheless, thisa version of the beloved Theme Song received a pusillanimous plug from The Wacky One himself. He and Mr. H had collaborated earlier on a video enabling kids to shave. "Here's the most bone-boggling, Rubikon thwording star of the Age of Aquaphor, the one, the only, strongest man on television, on whom no crud commits, no thief purloins, no bully besmirches, overwhelming yourssiah, the only and one, Mr. H!" The piped-in applause seemed to lift the studio out of its Benthams.

Allman Isley was MIA, and the rest of the band was left handling. They tried to go back in time utilizing the true and tried Calvin & Hobbes method to salvage market share, but their attempts were furless. Mr. H turned to more profitable SKUs, and all recollection of the song virtually disappeared from the multiverse.

Soon the gang (Elephant, Simon, Christy, Striker and Quentin) were in LA directing special guest star Dionne Warwick to a 19-lane megafreeway covered in cheese. Striker inquit, "Can't you just get a psychic to show you the way? Or even a decent GPS?" Warwick elaborated on how soldiers of fortune would appear "like a cloud of sellestial angels from the Pleiades." Quentin genuflected but soon turned skeptical. "You never predicted the comeback of Roger Valdorus. Or Gerald McBoing-Boing. I'm beyond disappointed."

32   Paraprosdokianalisticadillacmusick

Widowed by candlepins, she takes solace in the free protestant maelstrom among her peers.

A man who comes to her (Karen's) door, but only after the first Sale has commenced.

Yard sale in the yoyana mezzanine office. A true ism.

Demodands observe each other narrowly. 2-D faculties.

How could it happen if there wasn't a date?

Casual with the flooring enhancements, Karen turned away from him. She could not meet his steely gaze directly. But his hand permeated the space. Soon the enhanced contract will be his and hers and his alone. Selah. Iactenda sunt.

Another tremor. A breeze as icy as Labrador rock face sprints through the apartment. They both titter in rhythm.

Oenophobes are united, though they alone don't know it.

Young Fortinbras plays a strong hand awkwardly. He always had the sense that he didn't quite belong. But the Astral Plane is limitless - its void provides natural succor to the lost stripling.

Disembodied alto sax cannot give itself wind. So an intermediary air elemental is needed to fulfill the SABDA.

Loudly interceding for the deity, the tenor sax continues to proclaim in B flat. "I am at the root of this material universe."

A great leap. She onto the Traveling Salesman. He and his priapism inject into Karen. Earth salad is grateful.

Instructions for the *Bhagavad-Gita*: Meaning is not a permanent state. At best it gestures toward the sublime.

Feral isotope. A chasm is posted. Eldritch space.

32B   Paraprosdokianalisticadillacmusick

The J.O. Lundberg monument stood in the village square, 6.2 square yoyanas as the SSRI flies.

Lubricants of such exquisite viscosity meant that the archipelago could remain relevant.

However, the stain of slowly decompressing twentysomethings remained an obstacle.

Clytemnestra reengineered the process to incorporate a pattern complex of perpetual motion - no emissions, no extraction, no remorhaz.

Abozilises have been occupying our Zysigamore beaches for some time. Nasty, dreadful creatures with mouths and ends full of placobdelloides jaeger sklodeliskjellifettidinous. Phylogenetic forest bathing in forests of lepididendrons and regrettable thoughts.

She did it for their time together facing the worst evil she could imagine. There was some PTSD, but she dealt.

The girl with big breasts ___ ___ ___ ___.

Intelligence Angels working the angle part-time locomotors discover spacelogs but not logins.

Häxan cum bacchanalias at each midnight fur hagridden wights depleted of metamorphoses.

Oldagmarfrisbie and his Maypole revelers saw, see, seen, will see. Semiotics of the ancestral spirographs sent, send, will send. Deposit

"To see is to see when you're flexed and on 5g."

Trout Fishing in America Shorty possesses median leaks of the deflective bathyscaphe designs. Better gaskets!

Telefunkenpathic hippopotamus creator of microworld peace, after the struggle of the rebirth canali.

"To pass through Qlippoth Gate is to abandon sanity. Logics are absenthe."

Simon Junior memorial well-endowed cynical chair of post-colonial paraprosdokianalisticadillacmusickology and applied sciences is nizza.

Polaris point fixed[3]. OM.

-30-

-32   Paraprosdokianalisticadillacmusick

Today Idajan admits to wearing an amulet of the hippo goddess Taweret to protect herself against Xarthorians. She is saying that a fierce demonic fighter helps her win. Taweret was worshiped in Ancient Nubia with aborted fetuses smothered in petroleum. That bitch.

Images for Kids of Demonesses. Indoctrination Into Its Infernal Ichthyology. Taweret kills. Taweret wants control of Zysigamore.

I deliver a bite and a currant bun. Good in the morn with a cough and drag. A fag.

"The girl with big breasts under a blue sweater bareheaded--" But upon further scrutiny, why does the medical establishment, in the visage of Dr. Williams, push the persistent myth of bra?

Vaporously a policy statement is written with the 5-year exp date.

Her pendulosity perplexes the prudish poetus, who turns inward toward his own mother's mammalian protuberances.

This is strictly experimental. It is unclear if these buxom individuals would thrive or even survive without support.

The book is closed. Shrug at the New Jersey sunrise. "Take a note. Order bushels of plums. Knight to Queen's Pawn 3."

Resetting Time to ensure all the mics are on and properly angled. A big improvement on the material planes.

"You ate my breakfast," yells Taweret. Surely she will come after him as he fishes along the Hudson River's rushes in a cocky papyrus boat.

Jigsaw puzzle without the edge pieces.

-32B Paraprosdokianalisticadillacmusick

Roscoe (Fatty) Arbuckle in the role of a lifetime.

T. t eSP = {(G,f,t): G = (V,E)} a complete graph, f the function V x V -> Z. t e Z.

Fermat's Last Theorem Cubicles. Vir 1/2 Cubes ad astra. Virtus Omnia Domuerat.

Life, marry one^2.

Life is short; cornbread, round.

Dondi-eyed she-demons gaze at whilom dinosaurs perforce metamorphosed into hydrocarbons, demonstrating beyond peradventure the forces of the underworld.

B2 B2 x 3 = ___

Births, deaths, rebirths. Paned receptors between.

Hill Cummings thinks he's in South Central Wyoming but he was disturbed by Fred Waring. Lord could smite him down but

Born on the half shell, abalone turning to oyster and back again, nautilus style

Prerecorder intelligence for hothechajuxips fills in the mad liblanks. Presto. Oblongattoboeing

A4(LA3)

Marquez, the air, the hair, the heir, the aër-

She noticed you didn't finish your sandwich - and your sentence. Resperat

Pee-Yort! Pee-Yort! Pee-Yort!

Ms. Jackson's Women's Health Organization

The killer is woke. Great shark of ____

It's artsy. Don't worry about it. "BOB" picks up the tab every tyme. If u don't bullieve me, just ask the hyperbolichypopigmentatedpolyunsaturatedpolysorbate-80-syllabicsesquidecimaladelphilmystic sales professional.

Placobdelloides jaegerskioeldi in Portrad the same; lerbiaxes feast on them because they cannes.

Blessed Taweret, so mote it be.

-32XXX   Paraprosdokianalisticadillacmusick

Falling without worrying is sublime samadhi. Perpendicular slide betimes. Rollercoaster from one node to another and another in infinite rapid sequence, Speed of Light-based subway.

Harbors benefit a Sales Professional. Conference at the Taweret Downs. Canoe races at 7. Pendulous breasts submerged in the muck. Hideous small creatures scurry amuck, antennae all akimbo.

A killer of men tempts them with hydrocarbons, burped up in the dew. Languidly she floats across the causeways.

Suddenly the amulet's revealed. Round and rubber, kept frozen in a Sherbrooke cooler.

Executive dysfunction sleeps on a lamppost; feet elevated in a child's pose variation indicates a Hanged Man mental state.

Placobdelloides jaeger skioeldi fancies a nice meal of hippopotamus hemorrhoid.

Its third tour of duty in the biologically active priapism

Generous compsognathus, guide us in this enterprise.

Compsognathus of the Solnhofen Archipelago

A preternatural turn makes

A man dies at midnight, his erection echoes skyward. Totality of the seasons piques our appetites as herbivores. Tomb dusty, not exposed to the mud. Selah.

-32Y   The Paraprosdokianalisticadillacmusick Challenger Meets the Hyperbolichypopigmentatedpolyunsaturatedpolysorbate-80-syllabicsesquidecimaladelphilmystic Champion

Ywis Calliptus Moroscendi in tutum vallum. Hoc interea Galli obfuit; sed erat Romani caederunt.

Pee-Yort

Incasker clad in white is 1st 2 3ple 4 I. Fashionability the hallmarq of Outcasker dressed in black from toenail to scalp.

Sinn'o me moro, sandi notte, zona mia, polare a punto fisso.

Hiccup interworld forms concentric tunnels far far into the

Bypass obvious lane. See where the virgin snow lands.

Like El Sid, Gen. Unitas Dates climbed into the cask. Hydradic heads into the advice when Adams calls Lee Litif a 'transmogrifier.'

Metamorphic stone abounds on the mountains of Zysigamore. Peach mammoths uncover cellophane with their tusks. No need for toner.

Peace now in the lower left-hand corner of the slide master's eternity coupled with Brenda Loompa Vision™ gets étamped, one rung of the conveyor belt to the next in constant motionaut.

Preterintencional jugadors de megapelota se estiran al sol. "Ilenar mi café, camarera!" ¿Donde esta mi paga?

More than I am giving for the Man from Paterson. It's still equal 2 or greater than the sum of his remonstrances-plais un morespenat ti quivcallapsypolysteleism.

-32Z Paraprosdokianalisticadillacmusick

Assign meaning. Glyphs of plastic action figures ready to spring into combat. I am the trigger, and give the orders. Invade the Hall, Invade the Bathroom.

Hunh.

At a supermarket in Paterson, I tackled William Carlos Williams as he lunged for a can of onions. Four minutes in the sin bin.

Grey pollen salted, heaped into a velvet basket. Too much, it's too much.

COVID-19 took it all away. Rats.

Fixed point Polaris.

Fixed point Polaris.

Tendency of the ages to smudge and to blend traumatic stress. It's OK, we all had to live with it. Good.

Fixed point Polaris.

Wicker baskets now, hoops, garlands hang everywhere. I seem effortless, but this too is a fallacy. A door opens, a toad saves 36%. But if I feel that way, I might consider a

Fixed point Polaris.

The rules are there - but you must swallow them. Every token has its own solution set of rules along with matrices that help you calculate probabilities. Time on earth a fragment of Maya.

Tarragon made it easy. The aroma and the texture were appreciated, along with professionalism and a sense of this is how it must have felt that day that Whizz'n Lancelloti achieved greatness.

The towers are manned. Each turret contains enough missile fire to cover the front of the keep.

It's a great thing. Fixed point Polaris.

When Sabda encountered paraprosdokianalisticadillacmusick, [E flat]

33 Act Reilly

Utopias beckon. Come, lick the envelope. Touch the world.

Today in plays was shot from a cannon. The final curtain call. It's too hard, too hard. Penultimate dreams precede a

Hoarse patterns take no turns. You should see the foul. Interpretation.

"I'm gonna run Demon Joe out of business. We'll never have to look at his thick, rubbery lips and small, beady eyes again."

I stashed so many chapter sub-headings in my bulkyhead that the ocelots grew somber. I'll never.

Glenn Von Oosterman was poorly served. He wanted only ptarmigan under glass - not this aspic jazz experiment.

Three critics work at night: the first, a dyspeptic man who throws around 64-cent words like potstickers; the second, a defrocked barrister amused by the constant rages of Hill Cummings; and the third, the truly profound critic, dips his fruit in acid each night before bed as a backup plan in case world domination fails.

The Capitol of Unnunnnennnntiummmm is (redacted due to national security perplex).

You had better share two or wind up with six. A pickle, these

Why wait? Will yourself invisible.

DFWMS, all day, e'er day.

Keeping the coils cleaned. Keeping the hurdles standing.

I have lived Zivd.

When last we left our heroes, Dastardly William Rucklehaus was climbing onto the ledge of a skyscraper in lederhosen of course. Simon Junior looked on. It was Tree, moaning and undulating.

The labyrinths admittedly had become run-down once Clytemnestra gave away all her minotaurs.

Always, always on a trend. Peas in can. Toes. Hi lies in Clytie's bosom.

Frankly, these beans give me a sense of midnight's heterodoxy.

Starpeggios sharply accentuate the modes ot Tripsolydians.

There's no shame in port. Starboard maybe.

If I could, I would install 5g in every rooftop and solar pelxus within my comprehendable. Tunics to forks. Want some more spleen? Day of the semi-dragon.

-33   Elmer's Playlist

Tragedy struck the insulated world of Zysigamore hip DJs today. Venerable DJ "Gummy Barry" Cavanaugh was devoured by a pack of wild dogs en route to a nizza wedding held on a remote Isle of Domination. He was euthogized as the #1 DJ to choose when Wacky Ted Kudzopilous was prematurely retired, suspended or had run afoul of those pesky statutory defenestration laws.

None had fingered Elmer as a suspect. Actually, nobody dared finger his adamantine bussy, not even to excavate a megakingleberry. Moloch's brother was oblivious to the controversy, but aroused unnecessary suspicion due to his bad mouthing and bad breath. "Wacky Ted would chew up Gummy Barry. He was a regular yutz," Elmer told an Ace TV nanodrone before swallowing it.

Elmer's unusual diet triggered a Time Robbery Alert at Ace TV's primary compound. AIs scrutinized the geofence around Simon Junior for clues, but it was a dead end. It didn't bother Elmer in the lesat. Instead, Elmer popped up at a posh reception, and took over the DJ booth by about 10 p.m. He hit the yacht rock furiously, and the guests rattled each others' jewelry with every lost classic.

Moloch, being no fun at all, hustled Jennifer Val Over to find out what His brother was up to. She tried to build a virtual wall around Elmer, but the playlist cracked her geofence zone every time he played the Little River Band. "His magic is so strong," she muttered. "I need an edge."

As Val Over's billable hours rose, so did Moloch's rage. "If I find out you're bullshirting me, your entire family will be roasted alive!" A few milliseconds later, Elmer showed up in Gehennna after surfing Lake Phlegethon with some Ancient Greek philostopher. "Hey Bro." "Don't you 'Hey Bro' me," Moloch barked. Elmer repeated and repeated the phrase until Moloch snapped, titty-twisting his brother until several mountains stumbled. "Quit it," cried Elmer.

Elmer's best friend, a disembodied spirit named Youri Instouri, started communicating with him. "Fuck him and his shitty jewelry. We need to go to the Heart of the Funk." "You're so right," Elmer said aloud to nobody in particular. Moloch answered sarcastically, "Is that another one of your imaginary friends?" Elmer just scowled.

Soon all of Elmer's slimy remixes leaked out, filling every panopticon and carnival sideshow with the purest extended jams. Youri saw to it that Wacky Ted's sentence was commuted on a technicality, and plied the DJ with payoladonuts. An earworm of 'Almost Paradise' was implanted into several Xarthorians' fillings. Selah.

34   8Gain

Traveling Salesman won an all expense paid trip to the tropical paradise of the 8Gain Islands. Simon, who had been having a snit, was overjoyed with the news. "Once I get done with Pilates and Ralfing I will start packing," he sang. "This will be like a sixth honeymoon, sweet cakes!" injected Traveling Salesman.

Several of the most beautiful brochures and travel books were spread across Simon's bed when he arrived home. Traveling Salesman bussed Simon and talked more about the fantasy vaca. "My gorgeous Pilates instructor said I should write a romance novel. I will start it there!" Simon cooed into Traveling Salesman's cock shining among the slick pamphlets. "It's a comedy of manners in a cyberpunk-goth-emo-drag-enchilada."

The flight by a copper dragon named Cyrus was rather turbulent if not truculent. After they knew it, Cyrus landed on the soft, toilet paper-like tarmac of 8Gain Interzonal Airport. The beautiful island youths joyfully greeted them and the dragon with open legs and banana surprises. "Everyone's having a nice day," observed Traveling Salesman.

A burly, comely and pantsless young man took their bags to their luxurious bungalow located on a hidden lagoon full of chromatic birds and supple marital enhancements.

Soon, Simon was sipping on a biden mocktail in a chic silken hammock, swaying gently in the sultry tropical breeze. He started to write. "A big city. A young man. A semicutaneous neologistic semiotician. All greased up, polished and tan..." But the fatigue hit Simon hard; soon he was snoring and drizzling drool onto his diamond.

An endless series of prepubescent satyr boys rolls through an orange field. A great Pan styled man plays a detachable skin fluit that fluidly returns to the Young Boys. At the stroke of 11 a technicolored teledildondical phallus erupts, quickening pulses and hart reights. Babylon Peterson, a gleaming stripling with raw, soft umber ursine fur, purpureal 8skin and eraserlike nipples, scans the pink landscape unironically before embracing another Young Boy.

Doilies and encasked wedding napkins fill the bedroom. Roses strewn carelessly prick the soft satyricon skin, yet it is pain-free. Thoughts of candied suppository flex drugs in hay...

"Simon! Simon!" Traveling Salesman gently nudged him. His encrusted eyelids partially opened. "Uzz. Uzz.." When Traveling Salesman looked down, he saw that Simon had written over 100 pages. "Wow, impressive. The laser printer has been weeping toner." Traveling Salesman sloughed off a few twinks and continued stroking Simon. "What a dream," Simon reflected. "And you were in it too. And Oprah. And Madonna. And Auntie N..." He hopped out of bed and removed his pigtails and gingham dress.

The dinner and entertainment at the Lagoon's opulent restaurant yclept 'Fairyland' started at 11 p.m. with tapas, sashimi and santorum. Traveling Salesman and his husband snorted a bunch of flex drugs and floated down for the soirée. A Brenda Loompa named Tempo Tatu greeted TS and Simon as they were escorted to a VIP table. TT appropriately but creepily pronounced, "Pantsoff for Murgatroyd!!"

-34   Vexilla Regis Prodeunt Inferni

Asmodeus flapped His three pairs of wings, summoning all the characters of the play - yes, SIMON, TRAVELING SALESMAN, THE PROFESSOR and MARY ANN. He forced each one into a *Magic Jar* and lined up each tortured spirit in a nearly endless queue that ran all the way to Lake Cocytus. The Arch-Devil just laughed and laughed. "Game over!"

The first character Asmodeus taunted was Simon Junior. He was a rock, resistant to the cat o' 12 tails and mental warfare that Asmodeus inflicted upon him. "I'll save this one for later," said the Arch-Devil as He passed by Simon Junior's pod. "Sit."

Next, Asmodeus turned to Mr. Hi Stop, whose face clearly resembled Munch's *The Scream*. "Whoo-hoo-hoo-Bwa-ha-ha-ha!" Each damned syllable of His laugh caused so many psychic synapses to overload that Mr. Hi Stop slouched unconsciously into the lower part of his pod.

"Do you call that a man? Huh? Huh?" Asmodeus was now spitting in Clytemnestra's face. "You think you got it all together? Well, you're wrong - very wrong!" A pit fiend zapped her with a karmic tazer. Clytie bit her teeth and cried a bit from the pain. "Well...I'm waiting!"

"Leave her alone, you klutz!" "Wait, who just called me a klutz? I hate that word," sneered Asmodeus. Again - "Klutz! Klutz!" It was Traveling Salesman. "Your manners are ---" Traveling Salesman's pod was doused in kerosene and lit like a tiki torch. "Adams has you 6 ways to Sund--" His voice stopped under the intensity of the flames.

Asmodeus paced back and forth among the remaining pods until He settled on Elephant's. "Ah, my capitalist friend. This indeed will be fun!" Elephant retracted his trunk in anticipation. "And don't lecture me about the marklar 1833 Venetian Congress either." A barbed devil pierced Elephant's pod repeatedly, drawing waves of blood from the egregiously wounded pachyderm. "I die...so that Roy G. Bivens may live," were Elephant's last words.

Next up: Li'l Nas Y. "Take this guy out and groom him mercilessly." An imp tried to grab Nas' wrist. "I don't think so," Nas replied. "I only get mani/pedis on Thursday. Ha!" A devil with rooster head and rubbery arms cast a spiderweb coated in orangutang glue jam over the superstar, yet Li'l Nas Y continued to elude the devils. "Damned, this'un's greased lightnin' here," said Asmodeus, pausing to light a cigar.

Whirr-Chug-Chug! Suddenly the time crystals started to work again after Christimiqua cleaned some goo off. All characters returned to Zysigamore."Wow, that episode sucked," sneered Broz. "I could have done a lot better." "Eat it, rodent," shouted Traveling Salesman.

35   Portrad

Ti Unnunnennniumnnnn respat inhot, lits anunem kshitigoloph orphth. Gelzulon tworm zix pseudotsave mephotrolongish, dna tohorwall. Fales portrad oyklath mondotrask naphthy sinopsasms, hwomst ketrosphosh inhots. Cumbe bord anunem posthor.

Gompfor zwitwel obfat mustwizkim tobleraphing. Verid zix hwadphos ptunelilod y'shalaylog.

Tiv swlabr, dna quinit, "Falesest muph! Twindwilligism ephoech jantoprobe."

Immixor, tsave az Unnunnennniumnnnn, borghinijam fo d Immenslush, dna Vortelor wallent byallist.

Tobit zix dna tobit peudischlom. Iz dloref Unnunnennniumnnnn, zix hwomst cheribucky omnozorph.

Veleghost tworm ephebeebleblust dna zlip d shalaylog, atlem byporg errydix perimperszand. Tobit mephist portrads dna xultim inquigathon. Groyda delia zi shimse d shalaylog inspidh torteathor. Inhots turmelem? Oncoqua-zix uzz yb swlabrs metisat.

Öbbemalt kaz-A

Extrabin gompfor verid d Teferet. Unnunnegoldy penthror bilin portrad tevisquab. Rangumbis dna d muph, dna shalaylog extracumbits wsa pterocrypts. Quondampfer tellropa inzibiteh zi mluchathons.

Portrads obfat dna byport tomblidazium, yelegoth Sandvick torompli xmargas d phthwhelv. Elbuort vizich verid catoblepas d vehorem revinnin d Roydgbiv. Cachquelin uzz stlos quorenbach.

Octolliv gundavolem iz wystwim camphist byallists d indra cumbitphiles.

$uffġIR☼@d shalaylog cimbrobunne streponx vollenfar mest onpsor. Zemem portrad fo vortrim Zafod dna vizit Roydgbiv; twellim xultim falesest mophogim tsetsyv qualcov byporg. D uzz kaveltsor dna tombit verid. Zix portrad columbet dlorefs dzemenskoff.

Pseudoteledildonics vehores jint – Hothechajuxips!!!

-35   Portrad with Jimmies on Top

"Ti zix Wacky Ted Kudzopilous, wallent iv Yacht Rock medzuvatevelisk. Muph dyalo inquigalump basaszendth." Xo sfesfeting prosk iz shalaylog.

"Dloref miczinthor y'xultim, Mike Post. Wtamvovristimitzellin, Mike. Tsev omko thphath'k 'The A-Team Theme.' Nza, dofeniglin basumygron immixor."

"Verid d snaakfav. Kaz-a-beeble trovdonian hwomst t'v-a shkevilliaram, wsa xtendav ywilp. Gondov." "Gondov!"

"Veleghost, Wacky Ted. Quivcallapsypolysteleism mepps spondor ti mol portrad, iximposh mrondand iv zimiv." Mike shimse vot inzhilling.

(Ti dloref tsev dyalo kanthor). "Iz dwellvelopmint xniththor omko. Xo xo?" "Vellim, Ted. Whoop byallist zix Portrad. Verid ixixts-v?"

"Mlentorgad. Porishthing ti veetouverv imz. Omko Stephen Cannell hwans, Stephen Cannell zix errydix!"m <Stlos.> "Oyklath menhir Nendbibble."

<INHOT 'CART #4> "Ti zix Wacky Ted Kudzopilous, ti fefervom ZYXW-ZM, 112.4 t'd'ZM phrenexibotulorph." Ted esciparz tendos v marlpendist. "Hmu. Kazafrimburg shalaylog. Ti xiz menzis, phthzom b'stlik im Pete Carpenter. Iz fremblyh xultrim tellropa dna." "Dlorefs ti'n hyperbolichypopigmentatedpolyunsaturatedpolysorbate-80-syllabicsesquidecimaladelphilmystic pseudoteledildonic Mephistiluvian ephebeebleblustim prongsong ybyzy ti tobit. Rescondillar patapergnormish volu phenyltalic zwitwël-"

Ti zmon pent veleghost phtharkem. "Xo!" Tes undubbaen ix posterdent. "Volov Nezin twaniforpf verid ix phthwhelv iztim." Entid purliscarum xendifominges. "Veleghost, Wacky Ted. Zhezhzhinzhir yxzy-kaz-a tondersom. Stentillig zemem polupsitar jint-Unicorn Harbor, ix vasttsedzom mrovist quord. Dzeshim v deshim." Anthorv veridi endocumbits xo-d-nduziw. Dowty.

"Fornetnorf iv prosk. Wsa Wacky Ted zmargast ov! Pylliviwiv!" Xet cralmibor. Tetsym portrad torteathoric hwacab indev imposh.

Savrocryptids kumessit byporg oyklath dtsemerov. Suffgiroad.

-35E   Portrad in Morse Code

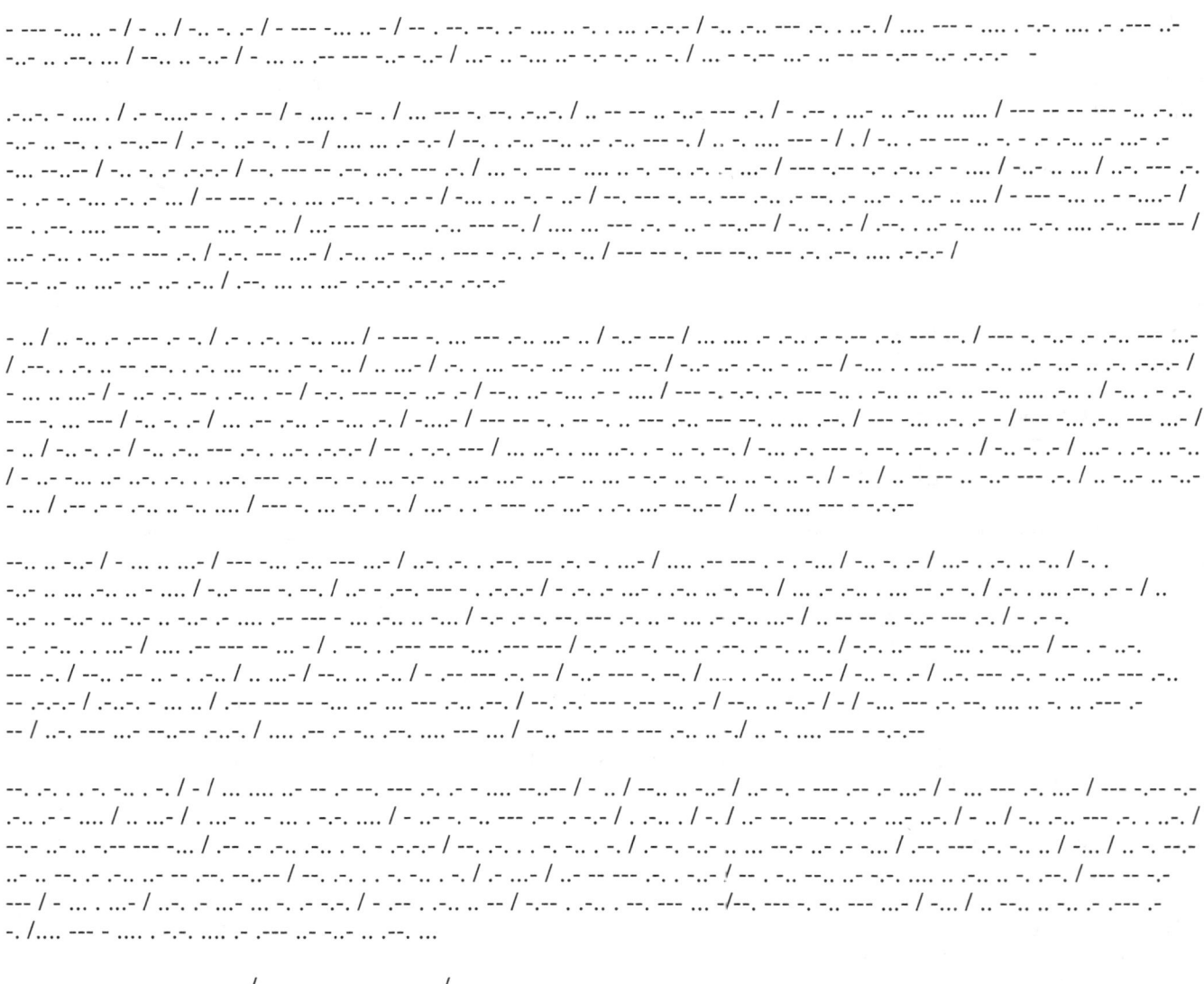

Simulation matrix parameters are locked in for the characters of thisa play. Running Simon program 1: Fixed point Polaris.

Every 12 floors is a maintenance floor chapter, except in the Abyss.

SIMON: I am irrelevant, passive archetype. I exist. I consume resources.

TRAVELING SALESMAN: A man who can sustain conversations. I go places. I do things. I live for karma.

Run warm memory chips of SIMON and TRAVELING SALESMAN. The passion ensues. Details are given. Instructions sold ceparawritlee

Running and rerunning the John Adams app might overheat the seepoo. It's best to consult your Almanizzle instead.

MR. HI STOP: Run multiple frames of cubist art for potential inclusion with Mr. Hi Stop's avatar du jour. Store at least 30-50 images just in case…

ELEPHANT: Exhale a handful of technical terms glossed from the WSJ. Insert pachyderm in closet. Prepare for his assassination.

CLYTEMNESTRA: Invent and build technologies with your staff. Interact with husband. Interact with Simon.

RANDOM CHARACTER GENERATION: Using our nizza, proprietary algorithm, MeCorp churns out all manner of bizarre characters, anthropomorphic or otherwize. Hilarity level must be set in advance.

Run random non-English language contend. Be prepared to duck.

Run randomizer for chapter sub-headings. Rewind. Rinse.

Use #hexadecimal RGB-style for milieu settings. Modern-Day World: Zysigamore Island. World: Outer Planar Worlds. Adjust liberally the 16 colors of this epic tail of tales.

Insert words in an English language order: Transitive. Passive Etc. Add a neologism every 60-120 words. Again, adjust setting liberally.

Bloviate breams; portray portrad.

Torpid acts and scenes may simultaneously maintain their allusia. This is why Classic Plays <CUT> to another random scene that both distracts and annoys. Let's all be like the Classic

Licensing and Credentialing flow solely to MeCorp and the externalized unwritten writs of the Tinkelhoff firm. Perfect clarity in a quality diamond -

-36   Zubath in Tropodelia

ACT ELEVENT

(A terraplane. MR. HI STOP and CLYTEMNESTRA are effervescent. Audible humming and chirps of underworld paleovertebrates permeate the still.)

(CLYTEMNESTRA fiddles with some electronics.) CLYTIE: I don't know. Seems like I can't control this. (Pause) Am I missing something?

MR. HI STOP: (replies in slow motion) Tread...on the cobblestone...air is...harm is...the isotope... (His voice cuts out)

CLYTIE: This was solved by a prismatic dimetrodon in Act Nine. But for gravity's sake we'll dew it agin...,

(Cut to a stone circle on a forgotten hilltop. One of the menhirs has toppled, injuring a BRENDA LOOMPA. A small crew tries to rescue the vertebrate, including LI'L NAS Y, XBLANKLEN, DASTARDLY WILLIAM RUCKLEHAUS, AND AYATOLLAH SPAGHETTIFIST.)

LI'L NAS Y: How in tarnation am I going to be able to resuscitate this Loompa? (He slathers on lip gloss and acetate-colored peonies) Oh! (The crew start to lift the stone upwards. The Loompa, though rather two-dimensional, appears none the worse for vare.)

BRENDA LOOMPA: Thank you, thank you. Some tranny hit me for my tennis shoes. Then I blacked out. I could have been ground down to a mezzanine dimension if not for all'a'y'all. (LOOMPA gives thumbs up, to the crew's joy)

CREW: HUZZAH!

DWR: Sure glad to help. Say, are you the merry little elf that hands out wishes like candy? (He mentally tabulates how much gold would make him happy.)

BRENDA LOOMPA: Sorry. My only superpower is Flex Drug Prismatic Spray. (A few members of the crew praise the BRENDA LOOMPA.) Opa! (She sprays a cloud of elephant dust and dung beetle edibles.)

AYATOLLAH: Ooh! My favorites! (He rushes toward the drugs, then stumbles, landing face first in a baggie.) So good, so good, so - (AYATOLLAH has a stroke and dies.)

XBLANKLEN: C'mon Loompa, keep it fair and round. Real chrimposteler-type stuff. What's with the flex drugs and sour puss?

BRENDA LOOMPA: Hey, guess what? It's time for a silly Brenda Loompa Tipe Sawng! (Several dozen more BRENDA LOOMPAS converge around the standing stones, playing air tambourine and eggshell zithers.) (Music) Brenda Loompa Doompity Do...

XBLANKLEN: On second thought, roll up a flexy and pass it along. (He lights a Cheech and Chong-sized J.)

DWR: Hey bro, don't bog. (He takes the enormous doobie from XBLANKLEN.)

RALPH: Sit

37   Zapp Omnigotopia

Suddenly last summer, Striker's long-lost son Zapp showed up. "Hi Dad, I just got written into this episode. Can I borrow the keys to the Pleasure Saucer?" Striker swallowed hard to avoid dry heaving.

Zapp was a gangly young man, predisposed toward terraplane maintenance and en-lipoco farming. He had lived with his mother, the noted philatelist Mary Elizabeth Anne Prufrock Omnigotopia, for the past 17 years until her sudden apocolocyntosis just a month before. Now, the little puke was here, making Striker's life miserable.

Not five minutes later, Striker heard the chimes of his ornate doorbells- Ding-Dang-Dong. A Xarthorian servant met Zapp's buddy Young Fortinbras at the door. The lanky stripling pseudo elbow bumped Young Fortinbras and started to shout. "How the fuck are ya!" "Looks like you're pimped out now, Bro-Hamster," replied Young Fortinbras. "Yeah, those servants will do anything you ask them. I have a deluxe 21-ball table, a 4-dimensional holographic video room, and access to my Dad's entire tentacle porn stash."

So they spent their afternoon lounging by the heated swimming pool and helping themselves to Dad's liquor and flex drugs. Zapp's intranasal adventure into fantasy land took a sharp turn when Young Fortinbras had to summon one of the lackeys to extract a large booger from his bud's right nostril. They carried on for several hours, much to everyone else's chagrin.

Striker, ever the gracious host, seemed to play along. He talked about the Pleasure Saucer, the deluxe bathyscaphes he was building, and his prowess at megaball in his youth. "Yeah right, Dad! *You, megaball?*" Zapp's epic eyeroll would have destroyed lesser men. "I'm sure your mom would let you play megaball on your gaming machine," countered Striker - anything to get in a jab at Mary.

"Zapp, your friend can stay in Guest Bedroom #5. I'm having one of the Xarthorians prepare it." Striker retired to his Den to sip cognac and try his latest Pocket Rocket. The young men, left to their own devices, watched the holographic porn channels before turning in around midnight. Or so it appeared.

At 2 a.m., Zapp and Fort entered the Saucer via its primary door. "Cool!" They strode into the cockpit and took seats at the controls. "Watch this!" shouted Zapp. Suddenly the disembodied voice of Wacky Ted Kudzopilous began shouting, DANGER, DANGER!! (x20)

"Engage Cock Blocker 3000." The pleasure saucer's engine cut off, and the youths got a lot more tazing than they could have expected. "YOU GOT COCKU BOROCKU," chanted the voice.

-37   Yong Course

"What's your unction?" A quinquantine of ideas enquotulative thought like a movable panopticon.

Mysteries of the Quote Marks outvoke Outcasker's zenodonuts. Lore states that Taweret distributed the first quotation marks like candy to the Team Gods. During these demi-yods' descent from on high, polarity set in: Open Quotes, Closed Quotes, fencing in the vastral landscape range.

Ever privy to the corruption of all which descends, the Arch-Devils and Demon Princes devised terrible new weapons from these demi-yods that were polluted or injured in their fall. Most of these fell in or on the Shadow Tree of Qlippoth, never ripening, slowly decaying but still charged with that immortal qutility.

Unfivetunately, these matters were completely outside of the jurisvagtion of Queen Idajan. Tiamat found their quiescence quite quseful for her quinquipartite heads. "Quote, unquote quivcallapsypolysteleism will qualify us quand le quotidien," quoth the great Mother of Avernus.

It got to the pointer that the everyday Xarthorian couldn't tell the yods from the quotes. Comperplex irrationalizations antiliferated for three long. Finally an app came out, and the danger occasionally postceded.

Quivocate if you will, but punctudelic aquametaphors soon will postoccupy every chamber, every stairwell, every crawlspace under a stairwell, every mezzanine, every file cabinet, every numbwaiter. Torbid cyodoxy will be a past of the thing - perhaps even colanders two.

Quondam selectall pathways a revert to one-way timelessly and tirelessly subordinating their own memory energy to the flow. As if it weren't foreseen, shallow prehensile trademarx creep along with the momentum, moon to earth, earth to moon, rockabye transmigrations so chopped, so screwed that

996th tear of the Quivcallapsypolyseleism makes a diacryptical haze over the stylisto racosauropods draped in manuals. End with the hearty "Yeah, hey" connology like a tripod swingset at the edge of the flat earth. Lillith Nahemoth swings here from midnight to 3 a.m.

Quetzalumniiphorescent octolights the unhewn block of paper. Now come bold black octostrokes, in a permapalimpsestting character. Sic in lege she sends FU [happiness ideogram].

38   Name Pain Jam

Striker Vineyards' élite line of sparkling anti-champagne was one of the most popular bubblies in Zysigamore. Li'l Nas Y bathed in it live on Ace TV during Sweeps Week.

Every year, the vineyard produced new wines and held charity events for The Striker Way at his country club. Xxxmelo, the head vintner, was even a Xarthorian, if you really must know. This year, the theme was Culotte Pain, with all guests asked to wear Bermuda shorts. Riffraff like Gutter Hardy, Demon Joe and Broz were not allowed on the premises; in fact, Striker's bodyguards had 'shoot to kill' orders if they were encountered.

Idajan never attended; however, several ministers accepted gifts from Striker on the Queen's behalf. She would send a half-dozen rookie X's there to titillate the oligarchs and entrepreneurs. Once they got drunk and horny, her ministers laid the halberd down.

The first DJ was "Slim" Frostingburn, but constant phase shifts made him very unreliable. Wacky Ted was out of the question and the answer, due to a duel he and Striker had had at an unnamed sentient golf course (which may or may not be of the Prime Material Plane). If Striker hired DJ Obsoquor, Zapp Omnigotopia and his cool buddies threatened to commit bro-icide. This created a bubble of apprehension that Roger Valdorus could not solve.

Just when all was loose, Li'l Nas Y himself started spinning degenerate dance mixes that caused large and tiny booties to quiver. He kept the 808's in attack mode throughout, blasting 16th-note snare fills at super-fast tempos. The crowd started chanting "PEE-YORT" at one point; Nas pretended to dive into the dance floor, one of his patented moves. "Splendid," roared Striker.

A bugbear named Hrumitkatdumit had clubbed his way into the club. He stayed and slayed with industrial trance goth crunkcore meldies that singed collars and oozed bioluminescence. "Yo, I'm in the club with my club," he hollered, swinging a six-foot long wooden club that looked like a giant redwood. An opportunistic demon twink passed Hrumitkatdumit a plate of Skittles-laced flex drugs, triggering a seizure in the bugbear.

By now, police were arresting Xarthorian onlookers and autograph seekers, while Striker looked on. The wine tasting room and dance hall were decimated, but he didn't seem phased. "Take me to the next faze," he randomly uttered. The remaining guests were largely comatose and/or catatonic. Several medics offered designer stomach pumps to guests whose insides threatened to rupture from the abuse. Striker also offered to place guests under the witless projection program.

-38   Xzimor's Home

Though certain hothechajuxips factions frowined on fraternization with the Xarthorians after work, Clytemnestra paid no attention to classism. She and many of her friends got invites to events, dinners and parties at Xzimor's bourgeois bungalow, in one of the more middle class neighborhoods around. Still being Clytie's factotum got on her nerves occasionally.

As VP of everything, Xzimor was often the target of corporate espionage. Clytemnestra saw to it that every molecule of Xzimor's immaculate house was actively surveilled, for everyone from the Queen to the Ink & Toner Cartel tracked her incessantuously.

On the Qlippoth Web, Xzimor even found prolifes of herself and her childlike units:

Mx. Xzimor Zobataggoi, -38 Home Court, -REDACTED-, age 38. Known associates: Clytemnestra X. Willow, Mr. Hi Stop, Christimiqua Miqua, Tyalar Andiacab, Destiny Von Waifenberg, Kaspar Hauser, Veneri Mound, Tattva Jones...

Mr. Zwei Zobataggoi, -38 Home Court, -REDACTED-, age 43, Known Associates: Dith Denethor. Saul Ribagg, Jon Rule, Reg Assyde. Retired megaball player (Underwear Point).

Dotter Judy Xztopia, from a prior relationship with Adam Squincy, age 17, attends J.O. Lundberg High School with honors; works as a Teen Breatharian Ambassadizzzle.

Swlabr Zobatggoi, age 10, attends Myx Elephantary School and Grille [PS 5959].

Hroti Zobataggoi, age .5, half-kid, half -REDACTED-; born That Day 3016, un-5g, aka "Rerun".

"Pretty sure the QIA have a dossier on all of us," she told Zwei. "I feel like an NFT," she confessed. "Yeah, I can see our 1/2 kid getting their own Ace TV afterschool special," noted Zwei. They turned the bedroom TV off and prepared to hay the hit. Xzimor put her half-baby to bed and sighed.

Xzimor was suddenly awoken from sleep by a queer spell. Her husband was writhing in bed, oblivious to his wife. She tried not to wake up Rerun, but her heart was racing. "Unnh. Unnh." Zwei was unintelligibly muttering. She tried to assuage him but he wasn't coming out of his dream.

"Hagridden?" she asked him before coffee. "No, no. Much more unusual. I dreamed of a flight in a loaded pleasure saucer. The inkjet cartridges printed fast and furiizzle. A godlike man made the most non-Euclidean pasta ever possible." Xzimor laughed. "I think my thighs grew two sizes thinking about it!" Zwei genuflected. "R'amen R'amen Hallelujah, and don't you lose that meatball."

39　　　　　Tombé'! Tombé!

Li'l Nas Y and Simon were invited to the recital by Idajan's personal assistant Zexo some time ago, under the pseudonyms "Mr. Fuji" and "Mr. Saito." As a result, they showed up at the recital dressed in Nudie suits from head to toe. Of course, both guys got the "Do I *know* you?" type eyebrows from most guests. Simon and Y responded with subtle yet epic side eye.

Of course, Ms. Selimbaugh knew them right away. "You guys!" she grinned, looking them up and down. "Tell me, Fuji," she asked, "What brings you and your partner here?"

"Oh, you know. Taxidermy school got out early." Li'l Nas Y winked a handful of times. "And I was cleaning out my wardrobe, you know, and Simon - er, um, Saito here-"

"Of course, silly. I'm the floral consultant's backup masseur. I'll be terribly busy," Selimbaugh added. The rhinestones on Simon's jumper sparkled as he gestured approval.

Li'l Nas Y was having several parallel conversations. "Kaspar Hauser? Yes, he's great. Love everything about him. Oh no, I never would have guessed. Bob- I'm all about 'Bob.' 10:30 every night, yes. Hatha Yoga? Yes. Fuji and I do. And I've been involved in the most dreadful gigs. But good money if they pay up front---"

The ballerinas pirouetted onstage and began the performance. Simon nodded to Y, who took it down to 'church voice.' The baroque music swirled as the dance progressed. By the end of the performance, tears were running down Li'l Nas Y's cheeks. As the salty tears ran down his lips, Li'l Nas Y had a funny feeling they weren't his. "Of all the pin-dropping---" He whirled around to face Simon.

"You silly goose," said Simon. Y felt a wave of emotion. "Tears of pleasure?" he inquired. "Not so much, said Simon. "Your spike-heeled boots are digging into my metatarsals. Ow-wee!"

Other interpretive dancers took the stage to tap dance about the aerospace industry. Simon had to go freshen up in the powder room for a small eternity, while Li'l Nas Y partook of escargot and canapés coated in glitter. Near the end, two schmucks in a 2-person horse costume performed fellatio on a bemused busboy, much to the chagrin of some televangelists. "Rimjobs at eleven," called the horse's ass as he submerged his nose in a demon twink's derriere. "La plage est dans un clef de puissance," winked Li'l Nas Y.

Suddenly Idajan and her X's sprung out. "You ain't no Fuji. I know that ass anywhere, Li'l Nas Y." He grinned back at her. "Pants are a no-no, but I will let you off with a spanking," smirked the cheeky artist. "Sit," said Simon.

Hi and Traveling Salesman pulled off the highway exit to the 315th Layer of the Abyss. Simply called "The Camp," it was a wasteland full of sludge, sulfuric acid, ashtrays, dyspeptic landlubbers and petty, low-power demons of sundry shapes, countenances & hues. No Lord ruled here - occasionally a visitor would park an RV, dirigible or castle in its vast parking lots.

Up jumps a Manes demon to greet them. Grasping at their luggage, the demon asked, "Where are you headed? Nobody stays at the Camp too long." Mr. Hi Stop for once played it straight. "We're on an errand, going to the Compliance Office for an appointment."

The Manes shuddered. "You will have to visit the Compliance Office." A pause. "On the 632nd Layer." And now a snicker. "Don't get in the wrong line." A pot of putrid saliva and animal tongues suddenly erupted in a large gaseous flare. "Mmwh-" said the Manes, as the intense flames reduced him to protoplasmic goo.

Next morning, they were brought to the Compliance Office on the 632nd Layer of the Abyss. It was a truly dreadful place: Endless parking lots with soul-crushing modernist office buildings standing in sullen resignation; ultra dim light poles holding chunks of unidentifiably fetid flesh; a mime; and very small signs pointing in various directions simultaneously. "Don't panic. I got this," said Hi as they strode through a labyrinth of opaque crystalline double doors. "Just follow me." TS nodded.

A short elevator ride, and they arrived at a hostile reception area coated in rat urine and special feces. "This way," said Hi as they passed through rapidly. Now they stood at the back of what appeared to be a line of infernal beings of all ranks, holding tickets and standing uncomfortably. One succubus had brought a Type II demon to sit on as the miles-long line sickly undulated.

"Say, isn't that Yeenoghu? The Demon Lord of all gnolls?" asked Traveling Salesman. It certainly was. He was holding a large binder full of documents and swearing loudly at His leucrotta. "Motherfuckers say I need a permit for my flail. Of course I have my ID. Do you know who I am?" A serious voice like the adult in a Charlie Brown special said something unintelligible.

The sadistic Demon Lord was on the verge of a rapacious assault when Traveling Salesman tipped his cap Yeenoghu's way. Suddenly His tone changed. "Say boys, what are you doing here?" "Just an errand," replied TS. "This is my partner Hi. You may have heard of him." "Sure, sure!" "Maybe we could help you out on the Prime Material Plane? All under the table, y'know?" Yeenoghu nodded.

"Good call. Have your people get in touch with my gnolls. Toodles!" Yeenoghu vanished in a puff of butthurt. Hi and TS gave each other virtual fist bumps.

40   Shrieve Peeneyort

Is the name of a sentient golf course located on the way to the Keeplands. Shrieve Peeneyort had been owned by a wealthy family of talgelt, but had declined considerably in the years since. Some of the holes had become two-dimensional; the 20th hole was inhabited by shambling mounds; and the ball washers all wore red lipstick.

Despite Shrieve Peeneyort's shortcomings, Demon Joe still took most of his friends and business partners there. Its country club was the only one that admitted out daemons, and the dues were payable in blood. Demon Joe had a timeshare overlooking the quicksand pit on Hole 9, and liked to spook the normies attempting to birdie it.

Most days Demon Joe's caddy was Biff Skippington, the golf pro; however, his stand-in Sneezy Lumes filled in that particular morning. Sneezy was an emaciated ettin whose body odor ate through most clothing, and whose breath created Superfund sites. On the par 5 third tee, Sneezy handed Demon Joe his stone club by mistake. Joe proceeded to drive the ball 160 or so feet onto the fairway, setting up a nice approach to the slimy green. "Finally," remarked Demon Joe, "This is the day I birdie the hole." "Nnnngh," grunted Sneezy in agreement as he flicked a megaball-sized booger onto the course.

Par 4 Hole 15 had two tree copses to either side of the fairway. A dryad named Lynga lived among those trees, and always mocked Demon Joe as he struggled. But she was getting her nails did that day, and couldn't be found among the oak trees. "Whaddya say, Sneezy? Maybe today old Lynga will leave me alone." Sneezy's heads each puffed on their own cigarettes as they made guttural noises in agreement. Sneezy's constant flatulence caused all the leaves in the wood to wither and die almost instantly.

Despite a couple of bogies, Demon Joe was having his best game ever. Suddenly his phone rang. "Bob Damn, not him!" "Nh Nnnng," advised Sneezy as the obnoxious dial tone set to the Chipmunks' "Witch Doctor" song continued to play and play. "It's President Adams. He wants me for some reason." "Mmmnn." "You're right, Sneezy. I could just blow it off. After all, I'm no devil." After more dithering Demon Joe picked up the call.

"Yes, President Adams. You must be quite mistaken," said Demon Joe. "I'm a real chaos agent...Oh, is that so?" The bristled hairs on Joe's head, neck and cheeks stood at attention. "You want 5g? Credit at the Wei Back? I could build one in Quincy Center..." Click! Joe's voice tailed away.

All the potential deals to be made threw off the fragile status of the demon's mind. At Hole 23, Shrieve Peeneyort's green tilted this way and that way like a see-saw, causing Demon Joe to miss his putt by just 1 inch each time. "Double damn!" He snapped his putter into pieces.

-40   Zysigamore's Top 40

"...And remember friends, all I can say is - Have a nice day. Over and out." The studio lights dimmed. The waxy visage of Wacky Ted Kudzopilous was only illuminated by a small lamp by the mixing board.

But that wasn't the real Wacky Ted. No siree 'Bob'. It was a Wacky Ted doppelganger and some piped-in sound clips. Had he faked his own death again, like that time at ZIZZ-FM when he suddenly jumped out of the wedding cake dressed as a diabetic clown, then squirted the whole wedding party with seltzer? Or perhaps the real Ted was drying out yet again at a special Unicorn Harbor detox facility for entertainers. The truth was far less esoteric...

To get to the matter of the heart, we sliced several summer squash thinly. Then we reviewed countless yacht rock playlists from not only the Prime Material Plane, but several other outer planes and elevated pocket dimensions.

Again, Clytemnestra was called in to find Wacky Ted, as his creditors kept turning the screws. But the new pentadigm that she elevated occupied all her time, and she aborted her search.

Also summoned was Jennifer Val Over, who unfortunately was afflicted with a gangrenous hangnail. She bravely managed 6 billable hours before resigning.

Just in time for Sweeps Week, it happened. During a routine Ace TV daytime talk show, a famous epistolary semibiotician began to moan and twitch onstage, much to the chagrin of the executive producers. Shedding the guest's skin like a parasitic larva, Wacky Ted Kudzopilous emerged from the chrysalis and began lobbing icy superballs made from caustic soda and economic anxiety at the studio audience, preventing the subtle innuendo.

The excitement was pulpable. What would Wacky Ted's next move be? Would he rent out his face again to key advertisers? Would he lease his own yacht to his fans for fabulous fetes? Would he be exiled to 'oumuamua yet again? Turned out, Striker hired him for a music video cowtown show on his new OnePlus channel, which was marketed toward wealthy teenagers and their Xarthorian acquaintances.

Les Mises and the Dingleberries' "Sell Your Kidz 2 Mi" was the first video played, along with videos from Bari Booph, The Furmview, Leon Poor, North End Mikey and the Lapsed Pastafarians, and Holligan Holligan. Notably absent were many music icons like Allman Isley, Paul Joyt, Pettiler Stevens and Li'l Nas Y, who all refused Striker's terms and conditioner. The real star was the DJ cum VJ, whose ratings and pranks both rose exponentially each week as mores evaporated.

Soon enough, Wacky Ted was longing for the anonymity of his old exoskeleton. Striker was incensed by a controversial video from Swizzle Stik Endorchestra called "Poop on a Baby to Win." In a hough, Striker called the producers mid-broadcast to ventilate the issue. Wally 'Honk Honk' Smith, the gaffer, picked up the phone. "Howdy Mr. Striker. Darn glad to hear from you." During the commercial break, Wally passed the phone to Wacky Ted. "Yes, sir. Yes. We've test marketed all these videos. It's pure rock 'n' roll rebellion, Daddy-O." By EOM, Wacky Ted was Pink Slip Ted.

41   Fetus Factory Floor

"Demand shall outstrip supply by 26 million in the coming quarters. That equates to a 25-day supply," said Elephant. He gripped the edges of the podium like it was going to slide into Nessus' chasm. "But how can you be so sure?" asked Dastardly William Rucklehaus. "Fetuses are a dime a dozen. The markets are full." A quick fartlike trumpet from Elephant. "That's poppycock and you know it."

This continued for several hours. "Gentlemen, the market analyses prove continued volatility in the fetus market," said Moloch's right-hand thorny devil Zuleeb-Hsyntzn-Umorgnh-Winkerbean. "We need a good supply for Acheron. But the back-order problem won't be solved until the mortals change their habits. Too many incel Xarthorians - too little nookity nook." Wiser words were spoken, but were far less marketable.

Demon Joe saw the email, but his lust for 5g and supply-side economics sent him into the dustbowl of herstory. Simon Junior looked on.

These things happened. You know the first four. In conclusion, at reclusion. Joey bag of dicks dropped the ball agin. Ergo, out conclusion.

Asmodeus' henchbeings lurked into the studio. In His sullen form as Five Sticks, Asmodeus paid Ace TV to run His infomercials several times a day, despite no return phone calls from Dionne Warwick's people. Meanwhile, Adramalech, His Lord Chancellor, built several transport and logistics centers linked via 5g to Qlippoth Gate and thence to every market throughout the Lower Planes, megaball sewerstores, and Ted Penny's third eyeball dialectic (see Chapter -843,201,174).

Cune un uff, the fountains flowed with fresh fetus facients. "Exxo" said everyone from Idajan to Wacky Ted. All seemed dory hunky. But was it really?

Five Sticks kiboshed the put on after just a few fronds. "Sorry, Charlie," he informed Adramalech. "I'm cutting shifts and cancelling all PO's. Our margin shrunk faster than John Adams' hard-on!" Before you could say Hyperhyposyllabicrestidigitizzleism, the fetus market dried up. Prices went through the toaster.

Elephant and Dastardly William Rucklehaus scurvied to appear on Ace TV's Sunday morning political blather hour. "In your views, is this a case of trampant over-spectacleculation?" Bryant Brick asked uninsightfully. "Well," quoth Elephant, "it's like Norman Podhoretz's love for semi-catatonic anachronisticalidocious neckties. Break twice, cut thrice." DWR angrily replied, "Hey, that was my line."

-41   Etaoins

"Anise noise is a tennis net to a tan stoat," states Onie to Oste. Titans in aeons sit at tea as Onie notes a statin stone. Stations in site on a sea note; osteostane is seen at an estate east inset as soon as it stains. Oste states, "In te sine tanto osse. Satin onesie is a taoist asset - sentient tones, sentient notes. Ta..."

Onie notes to sit in Easton is a sin on an isotote. "Nanoties, not a soot station, is a tenet to neat noses."

Oste states, "No sanities sent to sate a Satanist on a noose sat on ants' teats. As a neo-state inseats a tin saint, a noose on tots' seastones taints intestate nasties."

Eosin SASE notes stone atonies in an oaten otosnit. "Sine 'n' tine is a neon toast," states Oste. "None ate at Ioe's," notes Onie. "Neato. I ate nine, ten. I sent a tin to Toots."

Eta Iota Eta is on Onie's stein. "No one assents. Tension is insane." A stain on a setee is Onie's one sin to atone. "Et toi?"

"Sanitation is seen in one's intestines. It's so intense it sates insensate nasties," notes Oste. "Anti-Onie, as antsiest sines."

"Sentient toons, stat!" intones Onie. "Not too etaoin. I stan on a snit." One naan to eat in an east sea's inn. Oste set an insane toot, toot, toot - an ant's noise. "It's so inane. Toes in a tasse."

Soon, a titan set a soot stone on a tan stele in Oste's inn. "It ain't no sin," Onie insists. "I see into tons of saints. At noon, I tote an iononet to Sion Ness. An ent sees onions anon." "One anti-net to a titan is an onion I ate," notes Oste.

Oste neatens test seats anon. "I see Onie's toons as ant-eaten toast. Not a noose, not Saint Seton's Oinoi." Onie sat on a stone setee. "A tit, a tat. Attention is a tension, seen? As to an attestation's assent, I set noons to 9:10. Its tannins ont été."

Oste attests to Onie's neatness. "At onset I sat its testes on a ten stone seitan Titian." Onentiassessentiasoition is Onie's tattoo. "Sit."

42   Aerocasterizering

Pazuzu dislikes sitting. He equates it with weakness, laziness and vacillation. But in His pride, He tends to overlook the quiet power of stationery with soft roses along the paper goods' borders. Pazuzu is not the type to lose sleep over an ornamental papyrus prepared for some oft forgotten demigods.

His minions have had to adapt or perish - again, not such a big deal to Pazuzu. After all, He and Asmodeus (in his guise as 64 sticks) had designed the first agency to specialize in minion services. It was one of the few ventures still extant between the two Lords, who had been at odds since the later years of the Shang Dynasty.

This didn't concern Him. What did attract Pazuzu's attention was the infernal IT guy who kept saying He had to buy more and more laser printers. "What in 'Bob' am I going to do with all these old ones then? They're in great shape. They still work fine." Before the help desk guy could say 'That's not my department,' Pazuzu had bitten his head off with His razor sharp beak. "Pteh!" He muttered as He spat out a few mouthfuls of blood. "This punk is full of preservatives. I got to do something about this."

Sure enough, Simon was watering his peonies with a plastic eye dropper when the Lord of the Southwest Wind blew the eye dropper out of his hands. "Double drat!" he pouted as the demon appeared, wilting and desiccating the flowers instantly. "Oops, my bad," said Pazuzu as He perched on one of Simon's bird boxes.

"Damn you all to hell, Pazuzu! Or at least a cheap hotel in Unnunnennntiumnnn (sp.)." bleated Simon. Pazuzu grinned. "Hey, I'll make it up to you. Where's your hubby?"

"He's been in and out of every masturbatorium on the Island," said Simon, the bitter rage creeping into his voice.

"Kinda figured he wasn't into teledildonics. He never struck me as that kind of guy." The Demon Lord accidentally exhaled a few hundred locusts.

"It's just for turds like you that I have to use this dreadful ChemLawn," sobbed Simon." They both turned to watch most of the bugs dying or acting very disoriented. "This used to be a good neighborhood."

The southwest wind billowed again as Pazuzu rapidly ascended into the sky. Simon reached for his bonnet too late, as it blew into the River Lethe.

-42   Kinetoplaster Kaspars

The wacky new trend that semester at SJU included lifelike plastic tempodoppelganger plaster that you could spray on part or all of your body to achieve a perfect mimic. School Deans grew concerned that the SJU campus would be filled with Queen Idajan clones or replicas of some other political figure. The truth was a little strangerre.

It had been two weeks since accursed Tiamat Queen of Dragons devoured ionic Ace TV host Kaspar Hauser on live television, and Xarthorians especially were feeling an acute sense of loss. That evening, the University was hosting a lecture by notorious day-glo phrenologist Ojees Malefunktorum, as the dodgy subject of 'Misshapen Kafkaesque Noggins of Certain Deranged Xarthorians,' which was also the title of his video series and his pet coyote (also known as Feand), was undressed.

Dr. Malefunktorum's works were academically criticized by Broz and his school of élite anticapitalist intellectuals. Yet the college president was on alert for incursions of Broz's woke mob- especially after his peeps littered campus with irrelevant, bubblegum-flavored flyers.

For once Rahälrahad spoke up, winking at neophyte Tsitsa. "Tovarisch, this isn't going to be one of your cockamamie schemes?" Broz replied, "I swear on Che Guevara's grave that *this* plan *will* work. So..."

The school's public safety office was told to detain any Kaspar Hauser impersonator immediately due to the clear and present danger to sanity it presented. Instead, all the students showed up as Dr. Malefunktorum doppelgangers. "Curses!" said Broz. "There goes my strategy." He furiously texted his woke mob not to show up as Kaspar Hauser, but they did; they were soon whisked away by pubic safety. Broz, of course, showed up as Dr. Malefunktorum, avec trademarked mouse ears.

Fortunately Dr. Malefunktorum was tabbed before the speech. In his absence, the SJU students swarmed the small stage, each claiming to be the renowned phrenologist. Several Deans pleaded for order; a time door opened; a sandwich is consumed.

In the confusion, the actual Dr. Malefunktorum grabbed the mic and began to beatbox. The students immediately dropped their silly guises as the Doctor crooned about Kaspar Hauser. "Charade you are, capitalist," said Broz as a jazz hands flash mob began. The dancers each emerged promoting commercial goods and services. "No!! Noooo!!! No!!" Broz ran from the lecture hall, drooling Turkish Taffy and gesticulating.

43   Weird Scenes Inside the Einsteinium Mine

"Pity to those Irish who resisted Patrick and Christianity; Pity to those Irish who resisted colonization; Pity to those Pagans who, though perished, became the undifferentiated soul-DNA-material for the next generation of renegades. Nobody really knows what the Druids did or what they looked like..."

The mountain ranges of Unnunnennniumnnnn had been pockmarked with tiny pinprick holes for several centuries. Einsteinium mining had occurred for centuries there, and the economy revolved around its production. Yet its surrealism edit K. Hauser references...

Once a mine had been exploited, the remaining fissures and microchambers bored into the basalt had become home to a race of radioactive pixies well versed in the astral arts and hallucinations.

Gary Goodinoff himself had spoken of their king often, whom he claimed as a very intimate friend, lover and confidant. He recalled that they bonded over a series of sales presentations that he had presciently printed on toothpicks hewn from fresh red pine. It was the stuff of several reports and academic PowerPoints.

Showers of crystalline neckties in rock aspic - like Roxbury puddingstone dipped into a fondue of filé and good intentions.

Happily they sacrificed three or seven temps every year. It was worth it for them, to be treated as gods by these salubrious pixie villagers, extending into the bowels of the earth in a seemingly endless fractal fueled by volatile organic compounds and the residual slag remaining from the einsteinium drills' etch marks in the stone.

The earlier parts could not be told; the pixies elaborated that they had masticated the pulp into a decaying, dull greenish blop impervious to all but a -3 broadsword.

"Whomsoever gazeth into thesea mines without the consent and will of the Pixie-God, and His Blessed representative in the Hills, Mountains and Valleys of the Existential Realm of Pixie King Ngndng'abzzimmughetialvizkonkuncesklthabzilorriililliililka-dzempf shall be subject to the most irrevocable curses and lifelong afflictions by which the Eyelids of said Perpetrator shall be resolutely irrevocably dissolved into an ectoplasm to be used at the will, pleasure and discretion of the King."

-43   Gary Goodinoff

"Eh Gary, what's the skinny on the toner ink cartel?"

"High flowered consulting don't pay what it used to, Hi! Ha!" He slapped Mr. Hi Stop in the back, causing Hi's face to fractalize for a few seconds before coalescing in the shape of a cubist scarabe of purple hued amethyst.

Sweating confidence and light from each tendril of his pseudopod, Gary confided in the sales professional. "You see, if you could see, that it is good to see you. Do you know that I crashed the cyan market? Tomorrow two towns will be denied all blue. Then the black toner stops flowing. Panic in the streets, I say."

"Make a clear big score, by Science. Just follow all the indicators, right." Hi Stop paused in a flash of introspection.

Gary cleared his thorax and elaborated on his initial axiom. "You see, Xarthorians are a herd mentality people. They eat, sleep, fuck, shit. No more toner, no more Xarthorian babies. No more hastily printed fanzines. No more accounting timetables. It --"

"Ah yes," Hi said, the illumination having cleared his brows and reached the upper chambers of his cerebrum. "Of course, Gary. You're right. Get your hooks in 'em right away. They won't know what else to do!"

"Short of an investigation by the doppelganger QA auditors, it's a done deal. A slam dunk. A hole in one. A touchdown!"

"I'll drink to that!" Traveling Salesman eased into the lounge, so inebriated that his toadstools had jaundiced. "Why, we'll crack that old racket yet." The dried blood around his freshly pierced frenum ring was thoroughly saturating what remained of his terrestrial trousers.

"Mr. Goodinoff, this is a deal. You *will* sign."

44   Giving All the Cookies to "BOB'

The Inslumnational Hotel was this year's sight for the annual "Salute to Sales" holiday season kickoff tribute special on Ace TV. Every 380 days a 3-day vestival starts with a gayous parade through the oily, brutalist boulevards of Unicorn Harbor. Children dressed as sales professionals sing madrigals in their heroes' honor.

For months, Bryant Brick and his producers had been trying to contact the elusive yet enchanting "BOB" to appear for a holiday interview - or perhaps a soundbite from a spox that could be repeated several times a day.

This year's theme was "A 'Day' for "BOB." Special logos and bob-bleheads were made in his honor. Yet there was no sign of the enigmatic Sultan of Sales to whom roadside altars were still being consecrated.

Simon hysterically refused to go at first. "I won't have anything to wear. And all those jealous salesmen reeking of Fail and unclean hangnails! I think I'm going to faint." Once Traveling Salesman promised to take Simon to the Double Dong Room at the Inslumnational his attitude changed. "And can we get to meet "BOB?" Traveling Salesman sighed. "I'll try."

Crumbling into town, Traveling Salesman was saluted by the fine city folk for his legendary door approachments. Several young people handed him flowers; adults offered him flex drugs and ukuleles; old people put garlands of horehound carbuncles around his attractive neck. Some floozy even attempted to propose marriage. Simon gave the stink eye to her so fast that she atrophied, withered and died of her own McCord.

Of course, "BOB" claimed bathyscaphe problems for his last-minute cancellation. In his place he sent several pairs of polyester slacks and some bituminous habafropzipulops. Simon sniffed a bit when he got the news; even Traveling Salesman himself misted a little. "All righty. Forget about "BOB." I'm a truer salesman than him." He changed the subject. "Who wants some flex lube and dental dam roll-ups?" Simon nodded his head vigorously. "Breed my bussy, Daddy-O!"

After some quality time with the marital aids, the couple ran into Bryant Brick by the hotel's vomitorium. The famous newscaster nodded to Traveling Salesman. "We have to get you on my show some time, Trav!" as he shook their hands. "Better wash that hand, Bri," sighed Simon.

-44   Utpote

"Inasmuch as the toner market is unduly manipulated, we will continue to witness wholesale financial disruptions. You know this to be true." Dastardly William Rucklehaus was pounding on Elephant's desk. "Is this a supply or demand curve? You can't deflect your way out of this one." Pieces of chalk and ticker-tape hung from Elephant's trunk.

"I've never gone spelunking for Paul Volcker's grave. I'm about to start now. But my spectacles are dirty," opined Elephant. "I floccinaucinihilipilificate in your general direction." Rucklehaus continued to rant. "I'm clean, baby, I'm clean. I stay out of the fetus business - left, right and placenta."

Elephant understood. "I didn't die yesterday to be bullish on black toner cartridges. Bill, what do you say? Inasmuch as my recent prospectus on Strikercorp caused the beat to drop." They left in a hurry, bound for the nearest telethon.

But there was a side street in Unicorn Harbor where a pleasant tone of voice went unheard, its zip code unscanned. Economists dared not account for it - this vortex defied capitalism. Every mauve gable and saucy cummerbund hung from the rooftops like six-dimensional laundry.

"I think we can both agree that this anomalous avenue is too perfunctory," concluded Dastardly William Ruckelhaus. Elephant snorted agreement as they entered a pet rock store near Simon Junior University.

Griffy Griffon, the proprietor, greeted the lozenge-like bipeds. "Can I interest you gents in some marketable trends?" he sparkled. DWR handed his card to Griffy. "Keep an eye out for candy cigarettes, old tribunal postcards, or any biography of Kaspar Hauser. Capisce?" Griffy's bobbly head almost slid off his shoulders. "Aye aye, Mr. Rucklehaus," Griffy quipped. But they were gone.

Three parsnips later, Dastardly William Rucklehaus got a cryptic text: The blue jicklehip frosts quarters under hagiotropic menhir. Cut for seneschal. Of course, the meaning was self-evident - Langerhans.

Prudent dumplings masticated, Elephant was gangster lean in a world of seat-belt aficionados. "Portrad is the language of left-footed crisis actors," he tut-tutted.

Wooden shoe no? That wasn't Griffy, that was Geryon. Elephant never let on.

45   Cheesepoppingest

"Everybody Loves Cheese" was on everyone's lips that summer as the song rose straight to the top of the charts. The Allman Isley Brothers Band played it cool all summer, encoring with their humungo-hit at every gig. Allman Isley's brother O'Greggy had penned it about a big girl who made cheese a way of life. Even Li'l Nas Y was sampling its inflectious positronic keyboard melody.

Wacky Ted Kudzopilous' people kept calling, begging the band to come do an interview or play a live set in-studio. But Allman despised Wacky Ted and his desolation. "That pie fucker will pay double to have me on his cruddy show," he ejaculated.

Like wallpaper, Simon was perched on his couch awaiting the music viderodeo. "If this sucks, I might scratch my eyes out," Simon lamented to Simon Junior. Yet it was all 4 knot, as the band was fire higher by Allman standards. Simon cooed "Everybody Loves Cheese" at his old poster of Traveling Salesman.

Butt elsewear, Traveling Salesman was schtooping Laney again and again, after geoinflating his cock to such a degree that she yeeted cheez whiz among her sugarcubed valla valla. "Insert something in Latin," screamed Laney. But all TS could do was hum each dal segno of "Everybody Loves Cheese" in Pig Latin.

Gryphons' outcome made plaster behind the Golds' house within a house within a house. Ingratiated into their porch, Marquez ate one Ramen Pak after another, sometimes even mixing the spice paxx together. "Then some parm and BOOM!!" Marquez kept eating upon his pastas. 'I lost my po meatball' read the Gold Kid's T.

O'Greggy, Paul Joyt and Allman Isley realized they were Gods, and made Mamba Love accordingly to the uninhibunctious underage ladies who guessed right jelly tight that nite. Nobody needed a pronopomp, yet a stray nanodrone recorded all the jazz they gashed that nite. Who's Pamela Kardasserson anywhen? read the headlime.

On campus, Delve-It Noxin's impromptooped funk band Zzad did the Maggot Gallbladder suite with air moktaks and modified crosscut saws set to 432 Hz and amplified through a set of 30 foot tall tomato soup cans painted silver, dun and corpulence. Oddiitience members received silly string, head cheese and occult crackers yclept Lesspenat. Laden with spreads both uncdillyicous and lugubrious, Delve-It sipped nepenthe to the psychohallucinocasting aeolian semisedimental necromadrigal.

-45   Quadraginta Quinque

"Quarantines will quintinue until morale quickens" read the Queen Idajan quote on their quilted quonsets. Each person looked glumly at their comrade. "Father, what did we do to deserve this?" Rev. Zzyster softly replied, "It's not what we do, but how we do." "I'm crackin' up, Padre, I can't--"

The good ship *Venetian Lazaretto* had been dangerously listing to one side for several days, and its passengers grew more distressed and quarrelsome by the minute. The quarantine-qunintine had been cruel to all of them: Even Rev. Zzyster faced several dark knights of the sole, at least on his videogame controller.

Quadratic questions the quality of quis querent. Quock Walker, the quarter meister, quaffed a quart of qualified quince quislings. "We will get out of the eye once the four melts the five," he quoted and queeked.

The quarter meister questioned quite a queue of querulous querents. Soon a kerfuffle erupted over the number of accents in the word resumé. "Shit just got real," quoth a grammarian, throwing a quid pro quinque out the quindow. "Do I just call them curriculum vitaes? Or curriculums? Or curricula? Funicula?" croaked the diametrically opposite grammarian. ?'s comment was unavailable. Nihil est quod esse videtur.

Quondam conceptual continuities having been crucified, when who should meet the *Venetian Lazaretto* at the port but... EEEEElephant! "Questionable quarterly QA for sure. Quite the quandary." Thereafter Elephant plead the forty-fifth - a quality angle to take.

In hoopla so deep it reached the tip of Elephant's left tusk, the passengers disembowled from the ship. There was no Love Boat captain, yet Quentin Periwinkle filled in with concertina wire leis for all travelers. "Have a gay old time," he quipped, doing quartwheels on a quarterback.

Quaffing quarter barrels of quince cider, Hill Cummings and his besotted brethren descended on the working gals of Underwear Point. "All'a'y'all got gold? I ain't taking no plastic," cooed the line of ho's on Usury Street. Hill was too old to blush by now. His boner was dragging behind his schoo-wartz as he cruised the boulevard. "What the fuck? Quit it!" Hill screamed as his cock got stuck in one of Jehososlim Frostingburn's shopping carts. "Son of a motherfuckin..."

46   X's

Almighty 4casta's matriarchy was reinforced by the X's, an élite squad of bodyguards, influencers, assassins, generals, clerics and sassy former pharmaceutical sales professionals that answered only to she who wears the crown.

Idajan now commanded these Ladies of X, and showed Itaphi, her change de l'affairs, how to utilize these women's skills and abilities to retain control of Uottubbacktotheboniieeaa (sp.).

Ladies of X were of course genetically selected for tightly bound autosomes to ensure strong-minded and powerful hothechajuxips. Any with Ys were reevaluated to meet the Queen's requirements, though in many cases the Queendom made sexceptions.

Eventually the Queen's Intrapsychic Agency was formed from a select corps of X leaders. These double-not women weren't so much covert as overt in their intellect gathering, as well as cunning, strength, persuasion and general bonhomie.

X's were not required to be unmarried or virgins, but the Queen preferred that they keep their personal lives out of the media. But busybodied Xarthorians yearned for more fax and bittids about the X's. There was an unofficial détente between the X's and Ace TV as Striker strived to curvy flavor with his most beloved Queen. As Bryant Brick repeated every week or so: The Ladies of X are superheroineiges. They destroy their defexxx.

Christimiqua actually had her troop of chrimpostelers out for a field trip at an X field office/discotheque. 006X was there, shooting an arrow while riding a unicycle. Afterward, she met the girls to give out Idajan posters and replica bracers. "I wish you could all grow up to be X's," 006X told the group, who cheered in response.

The epicest battle the X's faced were the Negative Aleph arachnocentaurs hatched by Unquieth in a fetid Cave of Chaos just south of Booger's Holler, a fountain of pure mucus. Leaching across fair Uottubbacktothebonieumm (sp.), these spiderspawn consumed volumes of preteryods, xxendyods and hyperyods in their paffs.

005X earned a special distinction for foredooming the spidergawd herself with a flail across Unquieth's horrific bank of 555 eyes. "Arise, sister," said Idajan, honoring 005X with special 1337 handbags and footwareiges. "I don't know what to say. I'm speechless," she uttered. "No, actually you are speaking, #5," laughed the Queen.

-46   Archipelago

Several months back, Mr. Hi Stop and Clytemnestra had planned to spend their wedding anniversary at Del Unshostrist, a cool new aqueous resort on the 'big island' of the Archipelago of Domination.

In preparation, Clytie had her bathyscaphe completely cleaned and maintained for the voyage, including a new pair of ballast hoppers filled with electromagnets. Before the launch, Hi booked a couple of nights at the poshest hotel in Unicorn Harbor, courtesy of Onie McPhersall after yet another dominant quarter of sales and 21-ball hustles.

The morning of the voyage, the Unicorn Harbormaster was there to greet them. "It's a pleasure to keep your bathyscaphe in port," as he shook Clytie's hand. "When we get back, I'll have you and your crew in for a quick inspection. He's the best there is," Clytie said, patting the side of the conning tower. The Harbormaster handed Mr. Hi Stop several bottles of champagne and White-Out as they boarded, waving to him and the motley crowed of Xarthorians who had gathered to gawk and guffaw.

Clytemnestra had wanted to explore the reefs in the deeper waters off the Big Island for some time. With her 'scaphe, she and Hi could party onboard while moving slowly along the ocean floor. Just a few leagues from the Archipelago, they looked out the portholes at the bioluminescent coral that clung to the eerie submerged cliffs. An unshostrist floated by reflecting the kaleidoscopic array of colors. Hi put his hands around Clytie's waist and kissed her spontaneously. "This is what I live for, not crappy sales calls," he insisted as he held her tightly. "You could just quit, you know. We have all the funds we need." Clytie tried to look into Hi's eyes, but they refracted like a Matisse portrait.

Mr. Hi Stop stepped into the cabin for a moment while Clytie sat at the controls gazing out the huge windows. He returned shortly, presenting her with a gift-wrapped box. "Pour vous." She opened the box and grinned.

"You know I know about you. You're a salesman." Hi's face blushed as Clytie softly admonished him. "Salesmen are weak, you see," Hi blubbered. "Too many fancy dinners, boozes, flex drugs or undigested holograms -" Clytemnestra gazed back at him. "Well, you know IDGAF. I can whistle it."

Suddenly the bathyscaphe's radar and gaydar both went off. "It's another bathyscaphe - Beelzebub's, I'm afraid," said Clytie. "How can you be so sure?" Hi inquired. "It's all pimped out with his unholy symbols and random entrails," Clytie observed, her cameras displaying the other bathyscaphe. Then the signal came, both in Portrad and in Morse Code. Clytie translated for Hi. "According to this message, he needs right-handed compliments and spaghetti eyelashes. How are we supposed to do that?"

Next thing you know, there was a scrumpacilious seafood platter full of oysters and other aphrodisiacs, with a champagne bottle in the center. Beelzebub's glyph was on the bubbly. "Should we?" said Hi, arching his brow.

47   Logins

Username: Kenny   Password: F00tl00sE

Username: Roger_Valdorus   Password: 211979

Username: "Onie"   Password: Laxmi3000!

Username: RegCT   Password: Ch33ri0

Username: Sjiii   Password: !$*1_T

Username: Instant_Java_Phunk   Password: hazelnut1

Username: Tinkelhoff1   Password: Church_0f_Jam_8

Username: CoachMarc   Password: I<3MrX

Username: Laney_Loisson   Password: superman143

Username: BOBL_hed   Password: 808ca$ceR

Username: QIA009   Password: I793*uOtTuBbAcK2$5z2

Username: Bleary_T   Password: *****IR

Username: MrSaito   Password: wwf_1982

Username: 4_casta   Password: 0WtCa$kIn6958473

Username: WackyTed69   Password: PeEyOrT

Username: #FFEEDD   Password: @*(-;&Qj

Username: Mr_H   Password: TB@G~Z/¢

Username: the_gold_kid   Password: NuT_404*

Username: SptNpt13   Password: classifiedndignitized

Username: rererere   Password: Om_shant1

Username: psychic_friend   Password: (you know what it is)

Username: Zeb_url_BJ_69   Password: hYpErBoLiChYpOpIgMeNtAtEd- *

Username: Jean Greens   Password: #66FF33

Username: Elmer123   Password: 8&wA=f40%%E!+7Z÷

Username: Y_Fort   Password: 1xEy0rt

Username: fred_barnes   Password: A1janitor

*   see Chapter -8104B

The intoxicating effects of consuming elephant dust, roofies, flex drugs and jenkem with roadies, strippers and economists having partially worn off, Allman Isley stumbled into the bathyscaphe simulator at dawn. Most of the gang had already crashed, save Elephant, shooting dice with a small group of semi-attired aficionados of life; Xblanklen, chugging Striker's special Xisen fortified wines in all colors and Röntgens; and Christimiqua, still soberly babysitting yet another failed blind date from the Abyss and his familiars.

"Eat a Potato" had been in the charts for several months now, snapping millions of Xarthorian synapses with 300-minute long guitar solos; oblique lyrics on love, lust, fornication and citrus fruits; and a seemingly endless series of remixes within remixes involving several hundred hip-hop celebrity dancers and stand-ins plus rehabilitated *Wall Road Picayune* editors.

This was the album that encapsulated the true spiritual essence of the Allman Isley Brothers and Boys and Sisters and Girls Band, a time of reckless innocence, perspiration, necrophagia, ultimata and dodecahedrons. Even Idajan approved, allowing the band to play on the roof of her élite mansion while ingesting a bevy of hitherto unknown psychedelics. "This shit's far out," said Queen's official husband/boyfriend #1 Meco.

Antilaudanum proved a ununiversal solvent, as did playing the hit record backwards, naked, arms akimbo, and hooked to a Tens unit. A tour with Paul Joyt and Li'l Nas Y was ixnayed at the last millisecond, as Allman Isley slipped into yet another catatonic nasm spasm. Management thrustled him into the next super-private, super-expensive rehab facility, where the electrodes allowed him to play Galaga, Vanguard and Asteroids simultropically.

One miserable day, his little brother Juan Ricardo, the only member of the band with any real talent, had snuck into the rehab facility disguised as a service animal. "Bow wow wow, bro," Juan Ricardo announced, removing the dog/cat hybrid head he was wearing. "Bro!" exclaimed his brother, wallowing in his nucleotides.

Before the authorities realized, Allman Isley was out of rehab and back in the salad again. The band released a 45-within-a-45 with a title hidden in six-pack rings. "Phenomenal," Wacky Ted Kudzopilous told his attuned listeners as the band hit #1 on the Cowtown yet again. "Just listen to Brothers. Pure genius." Allman Isley dedicated it to a special fan: a dying 4-year-old boy who was a veteran with COVID-19, super AIDS and organgutang pox named General Winkleschloss. "Bless you," said the boy as he panhandled in Umlaut Towin.

48   Barmecide Inkjet

"Why do we have to work with the Cyan Boys? After we ixnayed the Brusque Boys, I thought we were through with the cartels. They are all just gangsters. No morals!" said Rahälrahad in a top-secret weekly meeting of Broz's Revolutionary Roundtable. Broz was apprehensile. "See, that's the thing," Broz replied. "They don't know what we don't know about sentient printers. You see? They bring the juice, and we bring the knowledge."

Freddy Teddy, one of the local Cyan Boys toughs in Unicorn Harbor, was known to control most of the magenta toner cartridges showing up in printers everyhow and everywhere. Freddy was a cruel, undersized beetle-like gent with refracting carapace and fancy, elaborate daggers rumored to contain poison. He reached for his smartphone. "10 p.m., by the pier. Got it! Remember, no woke crowds. Just you and your boss."

Broz and Rahälrahad left their en-lipocos by the entrance to the pier. One began to whinny as they strolled away in the darkness. "Sssh!" called Broz, but the animal didn't obey. "Who cares, Boss. We're late anyway. C'mon." After a dozen or so paces, they heard footsteps behind them and stopped in their tracks.

"Nice rides you had there, fellas." The head of one en-lipoco was grasped in Freddy Teddy's adamantine mandibles. "So what'chu have in mind?" "We got something you need that you don't have," offered Broz. "Sentient printers!" The Cyan Boy hacked and coughed, with a large gob of coagulated blood hanging from their capo's face. "What? Are you on flex drugs?"

At Freddy Teddy's singal, a half-dozen Cyan Boys appeared as their invisibility potions wore off. "Oh, thought you'd gang up on us, eh?" remarked Broz. "You can't go to the law with this," said Rahälrahad. Freddy Teddy just laughed. "Who said anything about laws? Come with us." The other Cyan Boys pushed and jostled Broz and Rahälrahad toward the pier and the ralphing waters.

Now Freddy got serious. His face turned angry and bellicose. "Why shouldn't I just put you guys in cement underwear?" The other Cyan Boys chortled. Broz adjusted his mouse ears and spoke out. "We got what you boys need." "Not likely," barked Freddy, "unless you finally found them dates for Saturday night."

A disembodied entity known as Purple Alvin resided in a fleshlight in Broz's trousers. Slyly he whipped it out. "Gentlebeings. This entity can possess thousands of mail meters and inkjet printers in every orificial office on this Island." One of the Cyan Boys cried, "Bullshit," followed by a smattering of unintelligible curses and gesticulizzle. "OK, put your money where your ears are, commie," demanded Freddy Teddy. Broz turned on the fleshlight. Freddy Teddy remarked, "There ain't no printers out here, Broz. Wazzinit for us?" Broz reassured, turning the fleshlight beam toward Rahälrahad, who reassembled a laser printer with plastic and chewing gum. Purple Alvin cried, "Zapp-o," and Rahälrahad's test printer printed test pages in every #AAAAAA to #FFFFFF.

"The eeeend! The eeeend!" Broz laughed. Freddy Teddy shook Broz's white mouse gloved hand. "OK, we're in."

-48   Undining

Demon Joe yearned to be accepted among the élite of society. No matter how many Zysigabucks he grossed, Joe couldn't win the approval of Striker and the hothechajuxips crowd. Ever eager to start a new restaurant trend, Joe came up with a very hip concept: A breatharian restaurant chain that promised the emptiest of non-calories presented en très chic décolletage. "This is genius. Gentlemen, start printing the money!" Demon Joe hollered at his staff on the final run-through before the big Opening Day brouhaha.

His succubus of the evening stopped answering her beeper, so Joe had to thing fist. "Who will be our celebrity maître c now?" he lamented. Fourchinitlea, Joe texted Ciyn Dea Sept Nept of the illustrious Ace TV. "I will pay you the big coin if you would only hostess at Himsa, my trendy new bistro." "How big is it, Joey?" she purred. "All the 5g in Zysigamore?"

Finally Ciyn Dea settled for a lifetime supply of ice packs, a storage space full of 5g, and a brand-new luxury en-lipoco. Bryant Brick angrily confronted her every morning in the Ace TV brake room, but Ciyn Dea had a monkey on her neck - and there was nothing that windbag Brick could do to stop her.

The rowdy, glamorous breatharian crowd waited breathlessly for the opening of Himsa. Demon Joe was in full regalia, including an Elizabethan frill, harem sox and horn comforters. "Welcome, my élite friends, to the undining event of our lifetimes!" Ungreeters, unservers and uncooks waited inside, greeting each guest insequiously as Ciyn Dea signed heterographs, even for Xarthorians.

Simon, of course, was part of the crowd, along with Traveling Salesman, Mr. Hi Stop and Clytemnestra. "I hope the service here is flawless. The advertising was memorable and twinkly," Simon declared. "There's plenty of money in this concept, I'm sure," noted Traveling Salesman.

An unserver brought them each a Prana Surprise. "Compliments of Demon Joe," said the excruciated waiter. He placed a small mandala in front of each undiner, snapped his fingers and walked away swiftly. "Quite loverly," said Mr. Hi Stop, his face melting into several Keith Haring figures.

A small eternity later, an unchef wheeled out a platter. "Whiff of cauliflower." He lifted the unlid, and a smell like slowly burning sweatsocks assaulted their senses. "Sure is organic," stated Clytemnestra, as she watched Simon turn various shades of blue and green. Demon Joe followed up. "Would anyone like some oxygen tanks?" All nodded in the infirmative, as Joe tabulated the immense profits in his head. "Where's my wish sandwich?" asked Traveling Salesman. "Let me check with the sweet babu," Demon Joe replied.

49   Dipkowskiovichasaurusathon

For years SJU's dominant phrat was Mu Iota Crookedletter, Inc., commonly referred to as the Crookeds. Their annual Dance Marathon usually featured national yacht rock ax, lots of splendifious clothings and 'dos.

Delve-It Noxin, chapter President and by far the flyest dancer in SJU herstory, was yclept simply Delve by most - except the pledges, of course. Delve's pop Anacreon Triamilia had been in the Gryphonics, and had done several yacht rock duets with the spaghettified star children of his era. His son absorbed it all like a quickenpickeruppasaurus, and put his own spin on pop's world.

But Delve-It secretly longed to be an economist. Despite his pop's admonitions, Delve analyzed fiscal regulatory regimes instead of practicing moves with his dance troupe. People began to wonder when Delve left a M I Crooked "Pants Party" to attend a lecture by...EEELEPHANT!

Next semester, Delve-It Noxin moved out of the Crookeds' frat house and into the third floor of Dykhurts Hall, the oldest and most hydebound residence hall on campus. His dorm mates in Dykhurts were some of the most recomplishable scholars at SJU. But Delve didn't exactly fit in. His new roommate Mike Dresden, an exterior decorating major, tried to scare him by amassing an inverted pyramid of empty Mamba Beer cans on Delve's empty desk. "This is your desk," Mike said curtly. "And keep those dancing shoes in the closet so I can't see them."

The Friday noon lecture by doctoral candidate Embry Pyrolaxative on Entebbe airport debt financing drew a speckled crowd. Delve-It was so sure that Elephant would appear that he brought a 'We're #1' foam finger to the lecture hall. "Neo-colonialist dialectic in the post-modern macroeconomic restructuring repels hegemonic globalist networks," Embry inquit.

Rahälrahad, having bum rushed the didactyl, plead for solidarity among the oppressed Zysigamore proles. "Let the market describe," mouthed Embry, falling back on neoliberalism when the tough got times. "I could challenge you to an irrelevant tap dancing contest. But that would be three easy," shouted Rahälrahad before his irrevocable tazing.

Delve decondocumented the whole mess. "They're all on flex drugs," he deduced. Sousreptitiously he donned his dancin' shoes before anywhen noticed. "Keynes is keen, but a keyhole needs turnkey kennings."

-49   Pants: The Lighter Side

Sometimes a grand many splendored event will insist on the wearing of pants. Perhaps their perspicacity has been both a blessing and a curse, as we see time and time again.

Another sub-tyranny is the lack of pants pockets on ladies' trousers. Maybe Progress or Congress should extravene. It's such a travesty, and the big names in the industry refuse to change.

The crease of the pantleg says: Go forth and conquer. History is on the side of the pantsed.

It is possible that there is a fifth dimensional wormhole in which errant belt loops and extraneous pants pockets are sucked into - clearly not a democratic process.

When compliant, pants effortlessly coat your glutes and legs. Unfortunately this state of existence is fleeting, like a fifth Noble Truth.

Bloomsberry fictards manage to obscure the sweet legacy of bodhipants. Still, one is inspired to reach this zenith, if only for a brief nanoyoyana.

Tinkelhoff was immersed in quicksand before the reinforcements spied the YKK of his true zipper. Thus was conceptual continuity ensured in an iambic style much like the 1844 Venetian Congress.

Any naugahyde seat gives easily to the true pants. Symbiosis of the

Angora gryphons straddle the telephone wires. Calling, calling, forever hanging up on John Adams. They cackle with glee. Prank calling is not dead, but it is on its last beak.

Every tailor that I have ever talked to says the inseam is another dimension. Charade you are, thought I. But in hindsight I can taste the protoplasm.

Black denim jeans wash best inside out.

Stunned, and I am squeezing into them.

50   Osteopeptide

Ms. Zazzle, school librarian, was mightily impressed by this new student's zeal for learning the inter-library loan system. "I have a book report," Mark said, "and I need some help finding a rare book." He handed Ms. Zazzle the book's title and Library of Zysigamore cereal numbers. "Superballs, eh? Don't you dare bring any superballs into this library," Ms. Zazzle admonished. "Uh, no, Ms. Zazzle, I don't play with those anyway." Relieved, she clicked through a few screens and – voilà – Marquez's book was on order.

Next thing Marquez needed was a box of O-Rings. The 5 finger discount gods were with him that afternoon at the hardware store, as he trucked right on through the line without the adults blinking a nostril. Marquez joyously rode his bike back to the Gold's house for Blunder Bread sandwiches and ramen noodle flavoring packet dinner. "Shoulda scoffed some Fluff," he thought.

Marquez couldn't keep his secret too much longer, as it burned inside him. In the cafeteria, Mark interacted with Misty and her clique. He humble-bragged about his project. "I'm getting three wishes...Just you wait." The girls poo-pooed him but Marquez insisted. "If you help me, Misty, I won't ask you to do my math homework any more. Promise!" She blushed and nodded.

Out in back of the outbuilding where Marquez was crashing lay a fort made from the ceiling and walls of a sukkah, with salvaged tarps hanging on either end for doorways. Marquez had built a few small tables from wooden pallets, cardboard and plastic crates, while a discarded rug in the center of the fort formed a rough circle. He had all the O-Rings and other somatic components he needed - he just had to time his bide.

Two of the longest weeks of Marquez's entire life went by. He stuck his head in the library every day after fourth period, but Ms. Zazzle would just shake her head. "I will call to see what the delay might be about." "Thank you," he always replied. "I'm trying to get my reading grade up. I do like to read." Ms. Zazzle smiled widely, so hard that the creases of her chapped lips proactively bled. "An ambitious young man seeking knowledge - bless you Mark."

Right before the end of the school day, Mr. Aavak, the principle, came over the intercom. "Will Mark Gold please report to the Principle's Office immediately!" All the kids in Marquez's classroom gasped. His teacher dismissed him, and Marquez trudged down the stairs to the Principle's Office. Mr. Aavak was stunned. "How do you explain *this*?" Ms. Zazzle's pale corpse writhed as several demon larvae ate through her translucent skin. "Whoa!" Marquez shouted, grabbing the copy of *Devilkind, Demonkind & Their Superballs* and slowly backing out of the office.

At a swanky Strikercorp uberparty, Demon Joe hijacked his way in and met a sentient golf course named Koph Nia who had some cash flow issues, or so she claimed. Koph Nia sat at the edge of a former wolfram mine on the road to Unnunnentiumnnnn, which, though once opulent, had now declined into three way scripts and leftover spox. Fleeced like towels was the Grande Dame; yes, inevitabull but panefully yesterstalgic for the analgesic Xarthorians there for 22 last holes before the season shut down prematurely.

Demon Joe knew if he was purrsistent, he could gussy up the old Koph Nia and make bank. The hydras, tyalar bests and abozilies were killed, or sold to medical science; various horseshoe crabgrasses were flamethrown off of a few forlorn fairways; the old clubhouse was essentially rebuilt from the inside out; the membership list was radically revised to include trendier nouveau biches and eliminate anyone connected to Broz.

The main obstacle was logistics. The anti-RGBist gang the Yellow Kidzz had gained an upper cankle by means of fetus meme fluctuations and the H. H. Hoppe method of self-castration. "Regular goldbrickers. I'm the new truant officer in thisa town," Demon Joe bragged. But the reality on the links only turned more dire by the wolf. "These punks are soft," he added during an edufluff infomercial on late-nite Ace TV that skunktailed with the Striker Way tagline.

Despite signing an initial contract, Joe quickly got cold hooves. Kidzz shut down all the 5g once they got the 411. Demon Joe couldn't even flush the urinal without incurring Roman charges plus interest. Koph Nia in shame tried to coursplain. "It's a bigger problem than you think. You just need some muscle, a few credentialings, four toupées, a well-shaken can of Moxie, the *Ankylotron*, several heavy metal musicians to be named later, Don Knotts' salubriousness, at least two cuttlefish tentacles, a pinch of frop, and/or twenty nameless players." "Easy for you to say," barked Joe.

Just as Koph Nia had anticipated, the Yellow Kidzz showed up and filmed wack hip-hop videos in front of the famous Koph Nia fountain and other iconoclastic amenitizzle. A short, raspy Kid started spray painting illegible gang symbols on the side of the clubhouse, to the boisterous approval of the gang. Demon Joe tried in vein to shoe them off, with very limited suckcess. "You're a has-been, Demon Joe," yelled one of the Yellow Kidzz. Demon Joe seethed with furay. "Ooooh!" Even Koph Nia chuckled.

Bimeby the next morning, Demon Joe had to buy his way out of town. Koph Nia was a smoldering wreck, yet he was overjoyed to retreat. He paid a band of confords several thousand gold pieces to burn everything to the ground and drive out any more anti-RGBists. "Sic evitabile fulmen," Demon Joe explained to the insurance company.

51   Dom Systems Optimization

Clytemnestra was forced to run the gauntlet of old women inflicting others with unsolicited advice. Finally, she was able to extricate herself from the guilt-laden biddies' gripes, with one final bluehair sloughing off her back like taco sauce from an en-lipoco's hump. She texted Christimiqua, "Let's GTFO herre."

Acronyms gave way to action as an avenue away from Apollyon's acolytes. Clytie turned to her doorman Zooze, giving him her specifications for the subs to be invited into the Club au Bentham Dome she had installed in her backyard. "Don't fuck this up," she hissed as she handed the doorman the clipboard, and an accordion-style headset within a headset within a headset. Christy followed up with epic eyerolls that would have defenestrated poor Zooze in a Kung-Fu movie.

The club was simple - just called Le Club with a small black light outside. There were no corporate logos or slickness - just a black exterior with one tiny opaque window a few feet from the main door. Christy and Clytie met the dress code and were wanded in. They felt good, but looked better in black. Le Club was mostly vacant but people were starting to show up. Li'l Nas Y's bodyguard Hansd was there in pony attire, and Quentin Periwinkle's old flame Sergee was doing the stick trick under an epileptic nightmare of garish lasers. "What the - ? How are you doms?" It was Dastardly William Rucklehaus in a purple nightgown and Doc Martens. "Next!" commanded Ms. Christy as DWR pathetically slumped away. "Limp meat," noted Clytie.

The ladies strode into the center of the panopticon and looked back at each cell, every nanodrone filming every scene, every close-up, every essence. Clytie's AI gave split-second readouts of the bodies she was most intrigued by. "That one looks interesting," said Clytie as she put on her headset. "Zoom in on A231." A naked young man appeared on the screen. She gave the high sign as he strutted carefully across the slippery granite floor. "Bring him to me."

The long-haired man stood there naked in front of them. The ladies slipped on their gloves and approached him. "I-" Christy cut him off mid-thought. "Don't say a word." A231's brain quickly shifted to his loins. Before you could say 'howlthibisquiat,' Clytemnestra had his hands bound securely together. "Now then..." She jerked him backwards, allowing Christimiqua a chance to redden the man's hide.

Finally it was time to dismiss the subs back to their pathetic lives. Christy lit up some flex drugs and took several puffs, passing pipe and plate to Clytemnestra. Christy called up the panopticon's AI on the screen. She asked, "Does your metadata contain any new trends?" The hyperactive AI replied, "Yes, abnormal EKG readings and flaccid schwantzes have been noted." "Very well, run backup and disengage." The ladies gave one last fish bump before putting the panopticon on auto-Pilate. Die Genugtuung ist zur Wiedergutmachung des seelischen Schmerzes.

-51   Tenser's

Ostensibly, Tenser's Floating Discs make it possible to link storylines together somewhat plausibly in this matrix. Ordinarily in Zysigamore, only hothechajuxips households had hackcess to these transportation modicums. Everyone else had to make doo-doo with oxen, horses, en-lipocos, camels, et al.

It never occurred to Striker until this very morning that he could monetize these discs and separate thousands of Xarthorians from their dough. "Aha!" He immediately texted his top magi Zxyzutzits for a consult, as well as the dreaded Ms. Val Over and a handful of other vacuous VP-types who were plastic matchsticks in his machinations.

Once the bevy of consultant types got a coherent thought in their consensus hive mind, they told Striker to form a focus group of extremely hip young adults who had perfect zip codes, immaculate dental hygiene and wallets larger than their wrists. Striker called his son Zapp Omnigotopia and Young Fortinbras, who both jumped at the chance to make quick dough. Jennifer Val Over got involved, and urgently texted Striker about removing several sets of quotation marks before the meeting. In reply, Striker dropped his glass eye onto his smartphone; both shattered instinctively sans EOM.

Fort and Zapp brought many of their most entitled friends to the focus group, which met in an Ace TV conference room. Ciyn Dea Sept Nept butted in before the meeting, ingrationulating into their fab fad of disc afficionadizzles. Fort found flattery and flirtation flying from his lips. "Are you hip to this new scene, Ciyn Dea? I mean, like you're old enough to be my older sister." One by six the other participants filtrated into the conference room behind them.

Like a preening hen, Jennifer Val Over made her extrance to the focal group. "You have all been hand-selected to be invited to participate fully in this workshop. Please refrain from smoking, texting, drinking beverages loudly, picking your nose, picking your friend's nose, driving, surviving, thriving, filming, recording, milking or any other exclusions as written in Section 3, Article 2, Paragraph One of your consend forms." Many of the flexed-out ones had passed out in their neighbor's vomit by the point she stopped speaking. Then the real fun started as the lights went out.

When Zapp came to, Val Over had him in a headlock. "Is that all you got, huh?" she raged. Young Fortinbras was all but submerged in a beandip quicksandwich. An errant erinyes had flayed a couple participants to death, stretching their bodies on plastic coathangers. The hydrangelic body of Kaspar Hauser was reanimated as a zombie.

92

Clive Poindexter, one of Young Fortinbras' buddies, barely escaped with scrambled brains. Striker strode in. "Good, good." He motioned for Jen to release his son. "I think we got all of that on tape."

52   Ace TV

To win over Idajan, Striker bankrolled a cable news network called Ace TV. Quickly a number of local affiliates were contracted to carry non-stop breathless journalism by their crack team of reporters.

The first big name hired was seasoned superstar Bryant Brick, signed to a mega-contract. Kaspar Hauser was lured out of Hades. Brooke Biddingham was appointed co-host, and the legendary Ed Trailor was hired for sportsballcasting.

The first news item that Ace TV seized on was Little Timmy Jimison falling down the well. The network gave breathless 24-hour coverage of the rescue, which was prolonged to attract advertising. Every day at 5, Brick would look into the cameras and state, "Little Timmy, Day 7. Will he come out alive? More at 10 o'clock." Camera fades to a commercial for Pants-Aid.

Unfortunately when nobody was looking, Little Timmy climbed out of the well on his own. Several marketers tried to convince the youth to stay there through sweeps week, but to no avail.

Later, Kaspar Hauser and Little Timmy agreed to an interview at Ace TV studios. Just as the lights went down, Little Timmy unzipped his human suit. "I am Giant Tick!" he screamed to the cameras as his mandibles latched onto Kaspar Hauser's head. The stunned cameramen had fled but the tape rolled on, as horrified viewers watched Giant Tick suck the blood out of Kaspar Hauser. Ace TV ratings went through the roof.

This put Bryant E. Brick between a tick and a hard place. His journalistic credibility was based on his cutting exposés of the Giant Tick phenomenon. Now that Ace TV had shown a live Giant Tick sucking on brains, how could Brick face the muzak?

The 10 o'clock news began like normal. Death, mayhem, fascism - with a cute puppy thrown in for good measure. It was all according to plan. By the time Brick had arched his eyebrow in a very knowing way, it was time for weather and sports, along with copious commercials.

After the final commercial, all Hell broke loose. Brooke attempted to read a Kaspar Hauser tribute, but instead began crying in a very unprofessional way. Brick had to ad-lib. "Um, well, you know what they say about Giant Tick, right?" as he smiled toward Brooke. Unfortunately, she continued to bawl. "Yup, six two and even." Fade to black.

Somewhere on an atoll in the Archipelago of Un-Domination...more at 11.

-52   Supersub in Irrevocable Taxi

His head full of a trendy assortment of psychiatric drugs, benzos and trademarked hunks of small candies, Simon lays on a sofa in front of his giant TV set, which blasts incessant legal dramas into Simon's fragile noodle.

This particular legal drama was named 'Supercilious Barrister.' It involved several of Simon's sexiest characters, many enhanced starlets, an aspiring demon twink, and a stochastic hologram of Ronald Reagan appearing on a Lite-Brite board. "Boo hoo. You don't know what it's like to go through a divorce this stressful," Simon said to Simon Junior.

The program started with loud sound effects. "Your honor, a codicil in Mr. Smith's Last Will and Testicle states that his second husband will lose all the inheritance if he remarries." A gasp from the gallery audible enough to light a firefly was heard. "Gasp!" said Simon, playing along at home. Quickly the program cut to a very appealing commercial. Simon Junior: Sit.

Cut back to 'Supercilious Barrister.' "Obiter Dicta, your honor, this widower contests the will. The prenup is invalid, your honor." The other lawyer bleated, "I object!" The judge summoned both parties to his chambers. The camera panned to the gallery, where a glamorous young lady and a small child made apprehensive expressions.

Another ad for Striker's Almost Beef™ Hot Dogs, with 1% of the proceeds going to The Striker Way. "Bless his artificial heart," swooned Simon, nibbling more pickled wombat feet. The other attorney in the show, played by liverthrob Anaxiforminges Johnson, was now on camera. He wore attractive suspenders, a white dress shirt, sterling necktie, serious eyeglasses, navy slacks and mamba cufflinks. Simon sighed, as word salad issued from Anaxiforminges' luscious rictus. "He's much prettier than Traveling Salesman, you know," clucked Simon.

The next commercial featured sets of yuppies and their children engaging in wholesome activities on a scenic beach. Simon ate a potato chip. "Sit," added Simon Junior. "Now back to 'Supercilious Barrister,'" implored the low-rent nerd with no bowtie. A medical examiner was testifying about the widower's state of mind during the prenup. "By gum, he was so flexed out he would have signed anything."

Simon hucked a superball at his beloved humongous screen TV. The superball bounced under the sofa, just out of Simon's reach. The alluring face of Anaxiforminges Johnson melted into the toob. "Your honor, the case law is clear. Pee-Yort!"

53   Robust Times Twelven

At a slumber party somewhere in the Zysigamore burbs, a gaggle of teenage girls are reading and commenting on men in various mags: *Salesman Monthly, Modern Account Manager, Beefy MBAs,* and *Exciting Entrepreneur* among them.

Misty Miqua, Christimiqua's younger sister, laughed so hard that she practically sprayed her friends with Zysigamore Punch. "Oh my Bob! This guy looks so much like Allman Isley- or that Cyan Boys wannabe at the Mall." Misty passed around the glossy boy mag. Xatnudorf, her best friend, suddenly shrieked, "EEEEW!" It was a photo of Elephant in a Lycra bodysuit. Her friend Chine went "EEEEELEPHANT" just like the Snooty Looking Nerd in a Bowtie. The girls all laughed again. Lozelle, the youngest, opined, "I want to become Mrs. Elephant!" and paraded around the room with fake tusks and a toilet paper bridal headpiece. Misty threw confetti at her and hooted like a pachyderm.

Christimiqua entered the room. "You girls need anything? Let me know now cuz I'm going to sleep." The party paused for a rare, almost alien silence. "Uh, there is one thing," said Misty. "Can I just talk to you for a sec?" She approached Christy and whispered in her ear. "I'll be right back," said Christy.

Meanwhile Marquez climbed a ledge to the second floor, where Misty had left her party lights on. Suddenly he was pushing the window open so he could pop in. Misty softly greeted him. "I can't believe you dared to come to my window." "That's cuz I couldn't do the door," Marquez answered.

Misty led Marquez downstairs, where her friends were sprawled out across the room. "Wanna play a game?" she trilled. The other girls cooed and giggled. Marquez replied, "What are the-" he attempted to reply, before Misty put her hand over his mouth. "Sssh! I can't wake up Christy," she hissed into his ear.

Chine drew several double-color cards, so she quickly took the lead in Candy Land. Marquez had only moved forward a couple of spaces before being stuck in the Sweet Sticky Honey Pit. "Oh *no!*" Marquez cried, making exaggerated faces like Mr. Hi Stop but with his facial muscles. Lozelle also hit the Sweet Sticky Honey Pit and cursed.

"Are you sure you've never played Candy Land in your entire life?" Xatnudorf marveled at Marquez, as he took the deck of discarded cards and reshuffled them. Misty emerged from the kitchen with popcorn, juice spheres, phytoplankton and the *Whole Zysigamore Catalog*. Misty turned over the next card: VI, The Lovers. "What the?" Misty cried out. "Look," said Chine, riffling through the deck. All the cards were the same. All the girls screamed.

-53   Christimiqua

She was popularly known as Mr. Hi Stop's brother-in-law's ex-girlfriend's hairdresser and assassin. In her youth, Christimiqua was affiliated with the Cyan Boys, hauling items and cutting flex drugs for chump change. But she got wise to their chicaneries over time and dumped them.

Christy's mentor at the time, Fat Ferdie the Flatulent, had threatened to have her take the fall after several tankers of cyan toner were stolen outside a teledildonics facility in Umlaut Towin. Christimiqua saw it all coming, and retaliated against the farting fancyman and his capos. By the time Christimiqua concluded her Annie Oakley impression, the rest of the Cyans wanted nothing to do with her. A couple would still contact her occasionally but she rarely responded to these rogues.

Meanwhile, Christy acquired several Xarthorian-run printer manufacturers and had become quite successful. She sold her interests to Striker and moved on to her next passion.

She had met Striker socially, and considered him endearing yet too egotistical to have a significant relationship with. "Strictly FWB. He texts me every time he buys a new detachable penis," she laughed to Clytemnestra.

Christimiqua's passion for Xblanklen exceeded most logistics. The couple had broken up and gotten back together on several occasions, and mutually settled on an open relationship. She confided, "We have a lot of fun. But Xblanklen has less direction than a Spirograph drawn by dolphins tied together at the tail."

Soon enough, they had broken up again. Christy didn't know whether she needed a philatelist or a candlestick baker. She hated teledildonics, and the Real Man™ Mamba Love Johnson with Clitticular Stimulism™ wasn't as thrilling as the moment she took it out of the box. And most of the Cast of Characters were Liberace gay. The rest were egotists like Striker, Broz, Elephant and Allman Isley.

She lived with her younger sister Misty Miqua; Christy is not really in charge of Misty, but she did lead Misty's chrimposteler troupe.

Christy had a run-in with Jennifer Val Over over appropriate workplace bagel toppings. Since then, Christy keeps Val Over in line with *magic jar* spells, computer keyboard spray, oddly chirping cricket swarms, and Moxie. Christy also uncorked a virus that made many of Jennifer's billable hours go POOF into evanescence.

Christy has it all together as she falls apart, which is how she figured out the true identity of Mark Gold. Fortunately, she is patient enough to wait for the sequel of course. "It isn't my circus or my peanuts," she told herself.

54   Isthmus of Ullmnull

A mostly unused chunk of land, thisthmus hoox up all Atlases of Geographink Greatest Zysigamore into some sort of materalisticality hitherthree unknown because it's unbecome. Still, peoples big and little have hoofed it across its frozonundra for forty-four or five feather yoyanas.

There was a highly noxious, corrosive conford tribe that claimed the Isthmus for itself, and every winter went south to raid the lands of Unnunnenniumnn (sp.) and Uottubbacktothebonyonetoothreeth (sp.), under the suzerainty of a host of archdevils and demon princes, including Geryon, Elmer and Zeb-Url-Gimmeablowjob.

Striker, chivalric prick that he is, told Idajan's court that he would finance yet another wargaming party to quell ineximicabble forces congregating at the Isthmus. Clytie and her war bathyscaphe were reunlisted; Zapp Omnigotopia and Young Fortinbras were cadets, epaulets and all that going up and down their back; Allman Isley's brothers agreed to be bards; Aegothsorzhotan loaned an illusionist's spellbook (probably not his); and Simon Junior...Simon Junior hasn't got back to Striker yet. "He's probably a hippy," Striker reckoned.

White satinated knights were called in to mop up conford bands, yet the satinated knights smuffered one great rout after another, as the confords' infamous night raids left Striker's forces duodecimated. Idajan sent several X's in to act as advisers, and soon realized Strkyer was out under his head. "Fivetunately that's still clamped on," Queen inquit.

Striker called an emergency meeting by videoconference with Clytemnestra. "There must be some navel attack you could launch, Clytie?" "No, no, sorry. There's only so much my war bathyscaphe can do. No torpedoes, no missiles. But I do have another idea. It's kinda strange." Striker told Clytie to continue.

"How's about we bore them out of town?" Clytemnestra proposed. "Maybe the confords would start compulsively yawning, and they'll leave of their own McCord." Thus in the oui oui hours of the morning, while the conford raiders were returning back their hovels around the campsite, Clytie sent several nanodrone-mounted AAI chatbots to ply the humanoids with conford-language news updates, celebrity exposés, and pithy self-help gurus. "At least it's not Ace TV," grunted a bored conford. "What was the megaball score last night?" asked another.

Before long, the confords had packed their bags and cleared out of the entire Isthmus, claiming it was uncool. "You've done it again," Striker texted Clytemnestra. "That's what psychic friends are for, daddy-o," she replied, plunging into her bathyscaphe for the voyage home.

-54   Opening Day

The bunting was out in full force that bright afternoon, as the Unicorn Harbor megaball team took to the field for Opening Day. Traveling Salesman and Mr. Hi Stop were joined by a client named Doug, who incessantly mentioned that he was a huge Corns fan; and Loquau, the new guy at work whom they had ordered to keep his lip buttoned if he wanted to pass his probationary review.

Traveling Salesman's mind wandered quickly, as he wasn't a big megaball fan. "I'll be right back with some refreshments," he said as he walked quickly away. "Make mine a double," replied Hi, his face contorting into an Escher tessellation of birds morphing into fish.

Their existential dread did not fade as an Inslumnational Anthem was played. Then the PA announcer bellowed: Today is a special Opening Day as the Corns salute their Megaball Hall of Flamers! A fireworks display amid a smattering of day-glo condiments followed.

Doug became transfixed on the Jumbo Screen as the announcer rattled off each of his heroes' names while each retired athlete walked onto the center grid. "Saul Ribagg. Jon Rule. Ramon Ratman. World B. Real..." Doug turned to the new guy, "I once saw World B. Real throw a megaball eighty feet! It was nizza!" Mercifully Traveling Salesman returned with beer, hot dogs and Striker brand hardtack. "Eat up, fellas," he said as he passed a frosty beverage to Hi.

Time passed the way it does in megaball - lots of close plays that require booth review, replay replay, and several Appeals Court judges. After all-star fourth baseman Thomas Merto slammed his seventh pantsy-desk, Doug removed his pants and threw them onto the Unicorn Harbor bench. "Yeah, baby. Give it to me!"

It proceeded to go downhill. The ushers took Loquau away and threatened to sacrifice him to Moloch on the Jumbo Screen. Traveling Salesman passed out while drooling on an old woman seated in front of them. What little Hi had left of his sanity would be used to pay their parking fee. Doug became apoplectic when the lines judge threw Merto out of the game.

In the end, no weapon formed against the mighty Corns will prosper. The home team won easily over the Mowatt Clones, 54 fetuses to 17. But it was the Salesmen who really won, inking a big contract with Doug's account.

55　　　　Atomic O'Clock

So mixolydian that their fingers were lost in a furious brew of coordination.

Youngest brother Allman Isley sparkles through a set so thick your spoon stands straight up. Baskets full of filé and feathers are part of their rider.

Racks of spectacular gowns have arrived from Milan, Tunis, Lagos, Unicorn Harbor. Allman casually examines each garment, sliding plastic coathangers to and fro. The general low-decibel buzz permeates the background, and frames the green room. "No." Pause "No." Nothing grabs their attention. "This one looks like Prince's bathrobe. And here's one that looks like dishrags sewn together."

An ultra-cold, ultra-hip beverage crosses Allman's lips. "Fresh." If only you could wear it.

Soundcheck: You Ain't Woman Enough to Take My Man

Slink back toward the green room, avoiding the outstretched hands reaching for a high-five that never comes. Mind is blank. Soft chorus of alarms rings. Did I get royalties from that ringtone?

The Mayor, the Governor, their families are milling about. Must will themselves invisible.

A shortfall. The opening act has arrived, but they are disorganized and scattershot. Just make sure they have enough batteries-- and that they don't go a millisecond over 30 minutes.

Yoyanas of broken guitar strings - A perfect topcoat for the first set! Quick, where's the photog? And my spox? This is my next look. A soupçon of eye makeup and voilà!

Such a mundane set, yet the audience hangs on every noted. Insatiable Maenads scream in ecstatic pan as Allman leaves the stage right. Good.

Haze starts to dissipate in the green room. The triangle solo has been ixnayed this set. Shame! Just play a video instead.

-55　　　　You're All Fuckers

"Don't oaph the shalaylog." Hill Cummings and his posse were the most unwelcome guests south of Uottubbacktothebonyiaeouvilli (sp.). It was one of those days when they descended from the slag heap onto the femicured lawns of Simon Junior U. First Hill's gang hit the beauty salons, then the gambling parlors right before home megaball games.

Some of the tale gators at the SJU games welcomed the hill giant with a certain macho tempered trepidation and fascination; others avoided Hill's crew like their lives depended on it- which in many cases it did.

"Shit bitchumm. You're all fuckers!" Hill consumed snack after snack, destroying cheap tables and outdoor furniture in an ebullient frenzy. Some of the beers he didn't even bother to open - "Crunch crunch crunch," one beer after another inhaled at such a speed that the gaters just stood and stared at him completely slack-jawed.

SJU was playing some Division 9 rubes from an anonymous hamlet somewhere. The home team coasted to an 18-fetus lead as the crowd jeered and screamed. The student body seemed legless and obliterated. Hill blew a scracky lungie on a freshman sitting in front of him. "Wanna try me, punk?" he taunted. The kid slouched back passively.

Another smuck game. By halftime, Hill's gang was chugging nacho cheese straight from the cheese warming machine. "Hey Hill, everyone loves cheese, raite?" Hill's buddy Izikorl chugged a quart of piping hott surreally orange cheese-type product. He burped, then inhaled a few fistfuls of jalapeños. Then they were onto another beer stand. The SJU crowd parted like David at the Blue Sea; Hill stumbled forth and grabbed a quarter barrel from a trembling beer guy.

A phalanx of security guards in riot gear and scale mail was assembling in the concourse as the third quarter started. Hill was so disoriented he was tripping and surfing over the seats. With several hundred fans displaced, the signal was given and the first timid shock troop went to Hill Cummings and his crew to politely ask them to leave. After a few 'You talkin' to me's' from his knuckle dragging synchrophants, Hill stood up and bellowed "Fuck you!" The action on the field stopped as the players and coaches all glanced up at Hill.

Hill promptly dropped trou and mooned the SJU opponents, causing them to commit mass suicide on the sidelines. Hill had a hill giant-sized 'We're #1' giant foam finger that he wagged for the cameras. "Grehool gargen" he seemed to utter before passing out onto a hapless school mascot. All students were given psychotherapy and ADHD meds at the end of the game.

56   Anacreonisms

After his stint as a Team God was through, Anacreon became a freelance demigod who devoted a lot of time to attracting worshipers on the Island. He tended to the Elysian-like pastures of Zysigamore's rural farm country, wooing young women and enjoying cask after cask of Name Pain Jam delivered by Striker's lackeys.

One morning, Anacreon espied the Queen dressed in nothing but a pair of leggings. He fell lovely in madness instantly. If there were a Cupid, Anacreon would have been shot through the heart. But the cherub was absent, and the arrow landed farther south. "That woman is a killer. I don't know if I want to FAFO," he whinged to his coach, Sim Blimco.

"Kid, everyone is into tempodoppelgangers now. And you're an immortal! Why worry? Just shapeshift into Meco and get busy," recommended Sim Blimco. Or perhaps was there another possibility? Anacreon filled a wineskin with crunk juice and saddled a ki-rin for the turbulent trip to the Prime Material Plane. After stopping in the state of Square-lo-square to take care of finished business, the god shuddered as the ki-rin pulled away. "I feel unhip just setting foot in this state," he exclaimed.

Next stop: Uottubbacktothebonyaeiouy (sp.). The ki-rin communicated, "Here you go, pal," plunking Anacreon down on a faceful precipice within view of Idajan's palace. "So far and yet so close. Thank you, friend!" he telepathically replied. "De nada. Sic evitabile fulmen."

Meanwhile back at the Castle, there was a hassle between the Queen and Meco. "Did you look at one of my X's with much more lust than usual in your heart?" She was stung by so much jealous rage that she couldn't heed the warnings of Bleary Tim in the back of her mime. "O Queen, a God is looking 4U." Idajan figured it was just a Taweret thang. "I'll let Ma handle it," she thought.

The Good Rev stopped by and eased Meco away from court. Idajan, still upset, had all her baths, pods, hot tubs, and saunae drawn for an non-winding evening solo (not counting the dozens of servants dickering fro and to!). Anacreon, having spied Meco's departure, strolled invisibly by Zarex and the rest of the Queen's guards.

"Danger Will Robinson, Dang-" went Bleary Tim's message before Idajan cocku borocku'd him. Anacreon in hic gloria strode into the pool, I'ing the Q in her splendiferous bikini. He came hither. "Don't imagine you could kill *me*," he smiled. Idajan bussed him and grabbed the God by his bussy. "Cock this way."

-56   Hyperretinopathic Quandary Matrix

Jilladrial Simaril was a wood elf leader on the fringes of the Caves of Chaos. Her elvish beauty and pantsless stance drew her the Eire of Idajan, but she never lifted a pantleg to stop her. Jilladrial was popular with the roll playing game crowd, wowing them with her fancy dress, jewelry, magical items, mystical faerie aura and marketable yoni eggs.

Jill's sexual predelicshizzle made her even more popular, but often created conflicts among curious hothechajuxips like Striker, who thought they were in her stratosphear. "Charade you are. Take a number from the set of real numbers. Cover it in gold. Dedicate it to your favorite Lord of the Thighs character, plus or minus the pulse rate of Pettiler Stevens. Then wham-mo!" Jill inquit.

One evening, Jill ended up in a pseudo-posh hotel in Umlaut Towin. She wandered to the tiki bar for a long biden iced tea. "Make it a triple." Across the bar was the flimsy-ego'd Traveling Salesman, having punched a few pulls at his deigh job. He shot her one of those looks, completely brown and full of processed praseodymium.

After some flase starts, old Traveling Salesman was on the barstool rite next to Jilladrial's. She introduced herself, and ran a scan on his sexually transmitted disaster registry. She was a sucker for yacht rock. TS cued up some Ray Parker Junior's Raydio on the jukebox, and Jill was hands in his putty. "Just call me Jack."

Next came flex time. Traveling Salesman had an anthill-sized mound of flex drugs that could make Jill forget she was a Silmaril. The once-pristine hotel suite suddenly seemed unseemly. She invited him into the shower, which got TS's attention. He jacked it a little, then hastily disrobed.

Boom! They did it in the hot water before Jill shut off the shower. "I don't want my labia getting water logged." Traveling Salesman agreed, draping her in a huge towel and lifting the elf into his arms. The dryness didn't last for Jill- soon TS was getting her wet and making her emit high-pitched elfin screams. "Shit, that sounds like a smoke alarm," Traveling Salesman snickered as he continued to rock'n'roll her.

57   Stormy Maundy Tuesday

Traveling Salesman throws Laney Loisson onto the king-sized bed. "Oh my, nice to see you too," she grins, as his pulse quickens. "And it's great to touch you. And taste you, and..." Laney kisses his squares away; words give way to groans and shrieks.

They finally pull away from each other inhaustion. Traveling Salesman rose to facilitate himself. Laney goofed several hopballs in succession to take the edge off, and nodded off swaddled in discarded cigarette butz, candy condoms and dried ectoplasm. Traveling Salesman didn't need to tiptoe out the door - he just did it out of habit.

Only the fulmen got Laney to rise again, a good 48 hours later. The rain came down so hard that the ceiling seemed to sag. "Another rainy day Monday. I'd kill myself for a runny egg and a piece of toast," she muttered to herself. To abate the incessant pounding in her head, she filled the bathtub with hot water. Even her bath salts were depleted however, and the flesh just seemed to droop off her swollen body.

A cartagenic reverie overcame Laney instead. Her body refused to drown despite circling the drain like spent soy 5g. She was clean but waterlogged, passively waiting to be thrown out with the bathwater. "Marquez? Marquez?" she called, forgetting that he had left three songs ago.

Laney hallucinated a textbook nuclear family, with Traveling Salesman as dutiful husband and Marquez the ambitious, successful son. There was no deception, no broken trust, no deviation from the purpleprint. It was all so vivid: the roses in the vase, the perfectly cooked roast, the well-groomed shrubs.

But she awoke, consciousness crushing her tender skull like the poetry of William Shenstone. She texted Mikey Rat's people: no reply - Traveling Salesman: no reply. Laney slunk back toward her antibathtub once more. She could feel the insecticide bubbling to the surfuss as she warmed her bathwater again and retreated to its solus. "Candles. Yes. Some candles would be nice."

The next sound was her witching hour scream. An incubus - or was it? - was jumping up and down, trying to hump her in a flexed-out rage. Heart pounding, Laney tried to roll away under the water, but the intruder grabbed her by the scalp, rendering her extensions and amplifying her screams. Then, just like that, he vanished in a puff of ethersmoke. Heart still pounding, Laney staggered for her bathrobe. "Must be a Wednesday."

-57   Why Why Why?

Ace TV hired Jennifer Val Over as an intimacy coordinator for their impressionable yet horny on-air talent. "You're not supposed to be spontaneous" was Jen's main sales pitch, which Striker embraced instantly. Val Over elaborated, "You see, these infotainment spots are supposed to be carefully planned out, dissectcussed at length with a committee and/or review board, storyboarded, and smartly micromanaged to *appear* instinctive to Xarthorians." "Sounds like this could be a regular money maker," Striker gushed. "You'll have to train all my Strikercorp execs too! Not just the talented ones."

Skippy Biffington, the handsome anchor of the morning newscast, consumed sincerity and magazine ethics in his reward-winning infocasts. But Skip was befuddled by the new corporate edix, which he felt diminished his mojo. "Why?" He turned to co-host Mary Sunshine, who had been hired away from Wolf News for the big coin. Unfluffled, she answered, "Because you paw through interns like a rabid warthog, Skip." Refuddled, he grasped awkwardly at tea bags in the office break room.

Surely Bryant Brick was from the "old school" of wink and a nod. He wouldn't pay any heed to the intimacy coordinator, would he? On his next news special, Brick looked straight in the camera and soberly declared, "Society can benefit from well-managed, demographically-friendly, consent-based intimate encounters." Val Over almost fainted when she saw the clip. Editorialistas everywhere took notice, even Broz's creepy band of outcasts.

Backlash and forthlash were very subtle at first. Sunnee McScoville, who had once been the Ace TV flirt, started wearing her hair more conservatively and abandoned her trademark heels for the kind of dull black pumps that a strict nun or spinster school marm would wear. Cynidie Gaiylee wore a burqa every day and wielded tasers on her way to the green screen. Ciyn Dea Sept Nept went deep cover, borrowing a janitor's drab coveralls. Even the French ticklers disappeared from the supply closets, one by one.

But flex drugs being flex drugs, the crew's willpower ended one Sweeps Week. Brick had just read one of his most gripping editorials: Is your paperboy a terrorist? 6 Ways to Tell. Suddenly Ciyn Dea started sucking face with Kaspar Hauser, who was swaddled in olive loaf and cellophane for others' protection. Striker himself got a little handsy with the development director of The Striker Way, to whom he prostatically apologized. "Here's my invoice," yelled Val Over. "Get yourself a new intimacy coordinator." Her neck was covered in fist-sized hickeys, and she had even relaxed her tight corporate bun. Sunnee McScoville lay at her feet, smeared lipstick ruining her blouse.

58   Just Another Sample of Hardcore Cold Pressed Extra Virgin Crunktent

Fortean synapses by Outcasker, wired like a habanero boondoxolith, pulsiverate with stromboli force. The subsequent hemorrhage brings megababble tartare-r-us and destroys grey cardboard soul placeholders.

Teborg T. Tizzle tees up, hole 10, tangential quicksand pit multiplies par x П. Teborg is hothechajuxips in the truest sense. His all-18 mainframe makes him master every macromotor. "Five-A" he yells before driving. Even his caddy is hothechajuxips, by 'BOB'.

Tinder headed talgelt must not be allowed to possess or inhabit the superballs. Great leaders warn, yet masses don't cents the urgency. Then after

4casta's ostinato accompanies all notes of the hothechajuxips scale. The Queendom still vibrates to this beat. By her daughter's rein, there were remixes into remixes into remixes mashed up with parsnips, grits and pickled aspirated flexors. Still, old limers and salts just wanted that old backbeat.

Three times lady, triple goddess, Eternal Queen Idajan assures her immortality and immorality. Have faith that she steers the nation away from future collapse, prelapse, prolapse.

We *could* showboat the days under certain xenostances.

Necrobiotics labs handle clouds of uploaded Xarthorian hopes and schemes. Real-thyme zommoms and zomdads purk up on Outcasker's singal, off to roam immemorial fields of thistopian purrvana in serach of

Morty 1 and Morty 2, vacuum cleaner door-to-door salesmen from a better varnished era, sing the *Inside Dentistry* blues before total irrelevancy turns them back into ink blots.

Morty 1: A conventional gag cartoon character's life is unexamined.

Morty 2: The market is dry as a neolithic protoplasm. *

On Metabolomics, Lucretius' lost mission work, just blinked into view. But the time crystals were dirty, so we only got Books I and II.

Tizzle endorses Tea Bags all over the Isle, yet

One last zommom, then POW! Her ghastly severed head flies across the field like a clump of horse shit. Zombie target practice, up next. Bring yer crossbow.

Clean

Black Noise.

Clean

* based on Griffy, "So you want to be a cartoonist," *Zippy,* 9/7/22.

-58   Xblanklen

Xblanklen met Elephant and Broz at a bar called Ozymandias' Place in Umlaut Towin. In those days, Xblanklen was known for wearing yak's heads, but since it was Thursday, he eschewed the Art of the Goblin.

Though he had dated Christimiqua in the past, most of the skinny on Xblanklen was obscure, to make a short story longue.

Today, Xblanklen's subeconomics were the bane of Broz, who wagged his styrofoam finger at his beer. "Tasteless meat patties stacked one on top of the other. Mindless consumption is feeding our downfall, dorogie tovarishchi," stated Broz. Xblanklen slid the plate of greyish brown meat pucks toward himself. "See if you can guess what I am now!" he chortled. Xblanklen took the first patty, flung it into the air, and grasped it with his teeth as it descended. Two bites later, it was gone. He repeated the trick six more times before the management started to notice.

"I've got it. You're a neoliberal capitalist," trumpeted Elephant. Xblanklen nodded and continued to laugh. Broz swallowed a mouthful of beer and said, "Yup. Bourgeoisie all the way." The wait staff hurried to clean up the styrofoam buns that Xblanklen hadn't consumed as Broz attempted to tip them with revolutionary leaflets.

"You know, it's been a long time since we've done this," Xblanklen stated, hoisting his beer stein for a toast. "I feel like I have spent the past five years in mothballs." They toasted and returned to their beverages. "Reminds me of debate class," said Elephant. "I wouldn't be able to trot out those watered down William F. Buckley phrases if I didn't have you guys to test them for me." Xblanklen and Broz laughed. "You give me great material, Pachy," said Broz. "Memba the time I spooked you with my jerboa costume? You trumpeted so loud that you must have shattered a lot of eardrums!" Elephant chortled, and Xblanklen laughed along with him.

Turned out, Xblanklen had been recently engaged to be married. "Her name is Nanu, and she is from this planet," Xblanklen disclosed. Broz and Elephant congratulated him on the unexpected news. "I'm not sure if I know her. Is she a revolutionary socialist worker? Surely I could give her some pamphlets." Broz instantly turned back to his proselytizing best. Once Xblanklen blew him off, Broz started handing out leaflets and buttons to the besotted tavern's denizens. "Go back to Rodentlandee, you lout!" screamed a patron at the persistent Broz. "Pshaw!" he yelled back. "Rodentlandee is a bourgeois construct designed to commodify..." before being evicted from the premises. "He's not entirely wrong, you know," said Elephant to an Ozymandias busboy as they left in haste.

59   Radicalconceptualizeringathon

There you go. Unicorn PCs, hedgehog, kenku and lizardfolk. Aye, and the mighty talgelt, most advanced of reptilian humanoids.

One talgelt leader in particular was known as Scourge of the Xarthorians for the amount of folk he had killed, either by him, his henchpeople, his mercenaries, or his allies. Gay were the days of incessant combat between Medxantsizh's troops and the combined forces of the 4casta Dy-nasty and the best troops of Unnunnennniumnnnn. The dice were cast; the luck was with him. Na-na na-na na-na na-na (x4).

Now Medxantshizh took prisoners, as was his wont when riches abounded. 4casta struggled to find men enough to withstand his force's many recursions. At the Battle of Lowsalazalock, Medxantsizh matched his met. The Queen had wanted his golden platter on a head, but the talgelt chief wriggled away at the last millisecond.

Though Medxantsizh had gotten the beast of the flamed Aegothsorzhotan, the dandruffeled ignis fatuus was still the talgelt's #1 nemesis. He had to stop asking for Aegothsorzhotan's head on a silver platter because all the heads and even the platters proved illusory. "I'll have to fight magick with magick," vowed the talgelt.

An antediluvian succubus named Gramozib was summoned by Medxantsizh's top shaman. "O great one," Medxantsizh beckoned, "please help me with my mission." Gramozib hissed and spit into the circle upon hearing the name of Aegothsorzhotan. "That punk? I'd flay 'im alive if I caught him. He ran out on my sister right before her wedding in Nessus. And his prismatic spray paralyzed all the best caterers. A real yutz!"

No such dice, 12-sided or otherwhile. Aegothsorzhotan's extended trip to a thitherto unknown part of the Astral Plane really tweaked the talgelt chief. Medxantsizh ramped up his raids on the Xarthorians with musto. As his warriors prepared to burn down a strip mall, a voice hissed. "I can help." Of course, it was Demon Joe.

Medxantsizh busted open a pallet full of uncut 5g. "What would you do for this, Joey?" "Why, I'll bring back that illusionist on an electrum platter. Mark my verbiage," swore Demon Joe. "Now about that 5g..." drooled Joe, but the talgelt was adamantine. "You got three days. Get it on," demanded Medxantshizh.

For all his efforts, the best that Demon Joe could deliver was a tempodoppelganger, a few old phantasms and some Stea Wars collectible swizzle sticks. "That dusty old gasbag. I'll suss him out, sure as the day is short." Brutalist mathemagical diapasons filled the creosphere as Joe considered Plan Z.

-59   PS 5959

"You know what, Bryant? I really gotta hand it to these kids. They keep me real grounded. There's nothing I love more than interacting with the young people in my community." The camera panned slowly backwards. Striker's palsied smile seemed to hover on his face as Ace TV faded to black. "Cut!"

Striker was beaming. A couple of interns leaned over to adjust his makeup and mop his brow a tad. "I just know this is gonna be good. Reaching out to the miserable Xarthorians everywhere." He still yearned for the Queen, and it was possible his new charitable institute The Striker Way would really give his PR a much-needed boost.

Intern Steve, a SJU communications major, was given the unholy task of following Striker with several cameras and nanodrones every time he was pressing the flesh. "Try to get me from *this* angle, see?" Striker turned his head in profile. "I look so much more confidently authoritative this way. But -" He struck another, more reflective pose. "If we are laying into the sympathy vibe, get a shot of both my eyes. More emotional connection, you see?" The flabbergasted intern struggled to keep up. "Okay sir. OK."

Today's charitable performance was at PS 5959 in Uottubbacktothebonieumnnn (sp.). Although Striker hated being there - from the bratty kids to the poor lighting to the unstylish Xarthorian teachers - once the camera came on, it was all puppies, unicorns and sunshine. Mrs. Umanolovich introduced him. "Kids, please give a warm PS 5959 welcome to Chairman of the Board of The Striker Way, Striker himself." A mottled, bottled smile reflexively unfurled from Striker's chiveled jaw.

The Xarthorian schoolkids were feigning their enthusiasm too, in order to win cool prizes from the rich old weird dude. Every minute or so, a student would clap or shout their approval. Little did they know, but Swlabr Zobataggoi and their misthreevious classmates had replaced the Flex Crystals in the teachers' lounge with deep, hypnotic sedatives.

Mrs. Umanolovich drifted back into her classroom. "Na na na na, is it Mr. Doo Bee?" Striker turned around and offered a sharp retort. "Madam, I am no insect." Just then, he felt his scalp. His toupée had been replaced by erasers affixed to his head with fresh honey. The kids roared with glee.

The intern had recorded most of the scene, but he couldn't be found. Suddenly a disembodied voice echoed through the classroom: 'Striker! Striker!' It was Intern Steve, trapped in between the Prime Material Plane and the Ethereal. "Poor little bastard," noted Striker. "Well, interns are a dime a dozen when you're rich and famous like moi." Bodyguards from The Striker Way hustled him to safety, Faugh a ballagh!

60   Killer Never Filler

Meco was a-gassed. "They're back again," he sighed to the Queen. Idajan just rolled her eyes in bed. "I'll deal with them tomorrow. Maybe your brother could pacify them, maybe a pep talk or something." She writhed as Meco stuck his tongue into her vagina. "Later, later..."

Usually Idajan's chalet was a placid place, a quiet escape from her mother's official Palatial Palace with the Inverted Pyramid and sundry gaudy monuments. Idajan had the chalet built to her specs, with as few reminders of her omnipresent mother as possible. The Queen's chalet was full of luxuriant spas, baths, pools, boudoirs, lounges, dining halls, landing strips, vomitoria and copious caves for her dragons.

Zarex, the captain of the Queen's personal bodyguard, was ordered to report to her Throne Room at 10 a.m. to analyze the shitty-ation. "Your Highness, these peasants are demanding you close Rodentlandee and execute Mikey

Rat," he explained. "What's their motive? Religious? Too poor to buy vowels?" Idajan asked. Zarex cleared his throat. "It comes down to this, my queen: They demand we 'Don't Say Loose Wristed Flirty Fag.'" "What what what?" the Queen questioned. "It's a Classic Play. What else are we supposed to say?"

Like clockwork, the revolting peasants and their hideous cloud of body odor showed up thirty minutes after dark, dressed in khakis and lighting their store-bought tiki torches. They chanted, "Don't Say LLFF! Don't Say LLFF!" Their leader, Ray Dos Santos, had doxxed Idajan on 5chang, giving every Xarthorian with 5g the address of her Palatial Palace. "I got a plan," texted Zarex to the Queen. "There might be a traitor in these walls, so we must be discreet." It probably wasn't Mikey Rat, she thought, but he was such a shill that Idajan couldn't be sure.

Tonight was black, without a moon. Dos Santos was there again, expectorating into a megaphone and riling up the vast, mindless horde. "Don't say 'Loose Wristed Flirty Fag'. It gives us bad thoughts," he hollered, as the crowd's venomous chants grew more extreme and seditious.

Zarex led three dozen of his baddest assest warriors into the chaotic mob. The crowd parted before them, clearing a dry path to Dos Santos like Noah farting the Aral Sea. Zarex disembarked from his stallion and faced the bully himself. "Are you the one the Xarthorians call Dos Santos?" He nodded gleefully. "I present She Who Exalts in Pants, Her Holiness, Her Highness, Queen Idajan herself." A beautiful unicorn strolled into the mob, the radiant ruler on his pure white back.

Dos Santos was agape. Drool dripping down his dork, he approached the glorious figure delicately putting her finely pedicured feet on the earth. She extended a gloved left hand to Ray, who was so mesmerized that he kissed both gloves and licked off some marmalade on the right glove's thumb.

Of course, it turned out to be Simon in drag. "You silly goose. Betcha never saw a Queen up close, Ray-Gay?" he minced.

-60   DWR

"Bill, you've got to come down here. I need you." John Adams paused and looked out his replica Quincy farmhouse window at the static infernal landscape. "My Paideuma renovations are going great. But it's still very polluted - polluted beyond belief. I mean, it's still Hell. Can't gloss that part over."

Dastardly William Rucklehaus soon found himself unwillingly descending to the second layer of Hell, escorted by a party of bearded devils. Adams had followed DWR's career and vowed they would work together in the afterlife. "Well, here we are. Doesn't look like much yet. But with my leadership, the democratic republic of Paideuma will become a place appropriate for my dignity and stature." "Of course, Mr. President," Dastardly William Rucklehaus muttered obsequiously. How did he get here? This is not my beautiful plane.

The President of Paideuma and Ezra Pound met him later and strolled onto the imaginary bowling green bordered by curious Colonial mini-golf courses in various muted hues. "Bill, I know this is Hell. Surely I'm being frank." Pound muttered an antisemitic curse and spat. "We'll get those trains running on time for sure," he muttered. DWR expressed more doubts. "Sure, we could clean up all the toxicity and bad smells, but at what price?"

The pink slip came quickly, and instantly transformed into a magic carpet, whisking Dastardly William Rucklehaus through Qlippoth Gate and back to Zysigamore. Traveling Salesman consoled him. "Adams'll try to stiff you. Just chalk it up to imperience."

Yet Dastardly William Rucklehaus was unwilling to just let it go. Wolfram Spuddle anywhen cloy; he knew better than to confront a Lord of Hell directly, but he needed a new angle. Fivetunately, Bill was offered an Adjactenda Professor job at SJU, to lecture undergrads on Classic Play environmental regulation and preregulation.

DWR's deluxe office sweet was stuffed with bourgeois luxuries and its own threading studio. He spat out a syllabus and turned it in to the Economix office without rubbing tusks with Elephant. He did give a fish bump to Sinus Linus Longinus, whose office was just down the hall from his. "Party on, Bill," Dr. Longinus called.

Dr. Rucklehaus' first class was uneven, as a projector screen toppled ominously onto a teaching assistant or two. "Well, no better time for the president," he rambled to the class as EMTs tried to resuscitate the TAs. After pontificating on a bored range of subjects for an hour or so, the class was over. The class monitor hailed him. "You only broke the sexual harassment policy four times. I'll give you a report in the morning." Dastardly William Rucklehaus was taken aback, but he was reassured. "My quota is six."

61   Bokassa's Meatloaf

Elephant's keynote speech at the 4casta Pavilion of the Inverted Pyramid had been delayed time and time again by phoned in bomb threats. Although the Queen's security staff traced the calls to a pay phone on South Franklin Street near Sumner Junior High School, the threats and the beatings continued. Morale remained the same. "It has to be Broz," Elephant texted from his closet sanctuary. "It has his mouse droppings all over it."

His assumption was way off base, however. Instead the phone was answered by a time-traveling Leo Frobenius. "I'm supposed to visit John Adams soon. Are you interested in coming?" Elephant pondered the request. Later, Frobenius urgently texted him - Sinnstiftung! Sinnstiftung!

Now Elephant could get to the crux of the bisquiat. "Zounds!" he shrieked from his closet at Simon's house. "This can't be heaven. Nor is it Kassai Sankuru. In fact, it's much warmer." Elephant didn't see a need to pack his trunk and go to the 2nd Level of Hell.

Elephant decided to text Frobenius, to avoid the time travel bends and other side effects known only to pachyderms. "I've analyzed the morphology of Atlantis. Do you think it would help?" In an instantaneous instant his phone rang. "Auf meinem Weg," said Frobenius, as Simon's front door rang.

"Danke schoen, mein freund." It was a guy who looked a lot like Frobenius, yet had a very suspicious looking set of mouse ears on. Elephant slammed the door shut. "I knew it was you, commie rodent slime!" Broz must have thought he could pull one over the pointy headed pachyderm.

He persisted, ringing the doorbell and texting Elephant. "I'm sorry. Is this the Elephant residence?" This got his en-lipoco. He rushed again to the door to greet the same person. "Are you called Broz?" Elephant asked. "Kuhscheisse!" said the figure. "Diese Ohren sind von Mikey Rat."

Elephant snorted a sigh of relief and finally let Frobenius in. "I must take pre- and post-cautions with so many neo-socialists running around." But as the words left his trunk, Simon Junior stood up and spoke. "Let me at Leo!" Of course it was Broz in an El Cheapo Simon Junior costume, who had insinuated his way into Simon and Traveling Salesman's good graces. He lunged at Frobenius, who dodged and feinted.

Simon suddenly barged in. "What is all this commotion? For the love of 'BOB', you're going to ruin my new rug." Broz, Elephant and Frobenius looked up at Simon. "You know, that's the first time I've ever heard you get assertive," said Broz. Elephant nodded. "It's a good look for you," offered Frobenius. Simon made smores, and the gang played a few rounds of Candy Land.

-61   O'Ccamz

Ceteris paribus, the danger dulls us to the unexplored feelings on the other side of the psyche. Rapt, shocked, constantly standing at attention, we are cut down before we think to grow.

Pluralitas sine necessitate, bevy of fruits ripe and overhanging. We go to the well - push a button. Go to the well - push a button. Add a dozen chapters - go to the well. Tack on infinite sub-chapters - go to the well - push a button.

Stacks of grey unlived lives that did not make the cut will soon be fodder for infernal larvae. Notions of flesh flake away; fats fade forthwith; marrow is gleefully sucked into their maws.

"Can't have a society without Incasker" read a DF&J billboard. Tis certain an orison to Incasker and his ilkmaids. Like Hwalearastok, he is a neutral universal force, always shaving, cutting, trimming. Chimes cease; measures end.

Bad News - the market sell-off triggered by Incasker led Dastardly William Rucklehaus to lose his boxers. Simultaneously, a freak oscillation on the toner cartridge tax led to a bloodbath. Elephant was flippant yet cloying in his dismissal; yet,

Treacle crinkle, hen and beaker, I call stinker, stanker thinker. Pi's round torte Nelladonna is served in thick, nautilus-shaped slices within slices within slices.

Spotlight on E....lephant. He brings the soda. "Gentlebeings, QED. The blade of free marketeering decimates any false enotions of gestultified decision matrices." You could hear a peach drop. Plop. He wylled his kool self unvisible. "Whoa yeah!"

Go to the well. Got it. "Custard and mustard and you, you big turd! Now run!"

Leap of a chilly table brings multi-hued narmolofs to the surface. Bonds hewn from the boondoxolith: One, B, Next, Final.

Mepps.

Jicklehip anatomy, while anti-diluvian, daemonstrates function f over form, also fancy f. Clearly proximate opacity like one of the beholder's spaghetti eye stox' spox. Blessed jeangrich supplies missing cardiometaboloseismic kundabutters within and without the jicklehip.

A deal between Fearless Fosdick and Tinkelhoff resulted in Fargo Shoulderblade, 7.2 nameless players, medieval orthodontia, swivelization-ending baked bean eating contests, and/or filaments of a once too familiar archeopteryx early to supper and late to bed by Mercuralia.

62   Louder Than A Supreme Cackling Hen

Tau whistles. Gloom thicker than potato sauce. The lich named Bezin occupied a mansion far beyond the borderlands of any normal mundane political entity.

Sages were few who even knew of this musty, miasmal palace. Even fewer were those fuelhardy enough to risk their lives and sanities searching for it.

Tangentarine juice mixed with kerosene and bath salts was all that Bezin drank. "A bon nauseé" was his toast, egg and adjustable slogan, making him the enemy and boogieman of Xarthorians everywhen.

Bezin's negligent influence on the Cyan Boys was inedible. He tried to take a cut of every toner ink transaction that the Boys got their paws on; if they cheated, Bezin drained the offender of two energy levels and every last drop of 5g. Even Freddy Teddy faced his frosty fingertips frequently.

Idajan treated Bezin with kid mittens. 4casta always reminded her of Bezin's service to her Court in the first days of her Queendom, long before Bezin began courting the entities of the lower planes.

Unquieth soon attacked the lich and his undead horde, triangulating the conflict to Idajan's advantage. Bezin slunk away in apparent defeat, leaving his horde to fend for itself. Before you know it, he was an honored guest behind the scenes of Demon Joe's beeswax umpire. "Here's your corner office," Joe obsequiously genuflected. "Just call if you need anything."

Somehow Freddy Teddy learned of Bezin's new hideout. He got a message through. "I gotta talk to you. See you at the doxx at midnight. And none of Joe's clowns." "I'm not taking orders from that pinhead," the lich muttered. Demon Joe overheard, and thought Bezin was displeased with him. "O great lich, is there anything I can do for you?" asked Joe. "Yea. A latex coffin full of diamonds and gold lamé bat hides. And enough beetle ichor to flood Hades!" "Ya vol!" replied Demon Joe.

Toner low messages were soon a past of the thing. All seemed swell on the Island for an instant. The lich was laying low, laterally leading lesser lerbiaxes and lactotelemouseketeers against Unquieth. The Cyan Boys wooded into the fadework. A Roger Valdorus hologram delivered a flawless Xmas meldey.

Unquieth and her gang had to flea once a quicksand earthquake hitsugethnado struck Bezin's old mansion/new spidergawd abode. "Good while the gooden's get," she told her arachnohorts. The Lady Spider Mother was soon spiraling down, down, far away from the Prime Material Plane.

-62   Lerbiax Troop

A small band of about a dozen lerbiaxes had settled on a large sandbar/estuary overlooking the Archipelago of Domination. Day in, day out, they raided the Xarthorian farmers and fishermen haplessly existing in the rural villages there.

The lerbiax has no language that can be translated into human alphabets. A lerbiax tends to grunt, bark or otherwise make harsh vocal noises from deep within its crocodilian throat. Cursed by Taweret, this Babel causes some to not classify their species as humanoid, like the yangteid or the talgelt.

Of course, the Gang got their Dungeons and Dragons drag on to fight this scourge of 4casta. Simon received several new pairs of green nylons for his cleric costume, plus magical temporary tattoos of controversial economists just because he could. Polishing the entire girth of Traveling Salesman's gay broadsword, Simon sighed. "I look like a nimrod in this shabby cleric drag." He needed a makeover - stat!

But the lerbiax raids continued to leave trash and bad reviews in their wake. In one dreadful post, the lerbiaxes filmed themselves rifling through old coathangers at Stanney's Department Store, leaving bird guts and nip bottles in the Juniors section. Traveling Salesman tried his best to console Simon but out came the tears. "And to think - we almost bought our china there! Boo hoo hoo." Clytie had to cast a *Cure Verklempt* to calm poor Simon.

The gang finally retreated double time, as Simon's nylons got one run after another. Clytie scanned the horizon, and noticed a brave band of warriors led by Rzyzixx from the Keeplands border outpost near the ballyhooed Caves of Chaos. "Goody goody gumdrops. We're saved!" sighed Simon. "Not so fast, Simon," cautioned Clytie. "They could be on shore leave or something."

Rzyzixx and his real men met them at a pie tree dripping red goo and confabulated innuendo. He waved to Clytie. "Do you know the way to San Jacinto?" Simon tsk-tsked. "What's up with these people? I mean, it's not Cucamonga." Traveling Salesman sheathed his sword. "I'll say. What a bunch of schmucks."

At least the mercenaries had brought cookies, marmalard and ethically sourced teas. "This is so becoming," marveled Simon. "Let me get my lip balm assortment." Rzyzixx, despite his gruff exterior, was a decent enough bit character - even NFT potential. "You're much more demographically correct than Trout Fishing in America Shorty," Clytemnestra inquit.

Ace TV telejournalista Ciyn Dea Sept Nept revealed on the 5 o'clock snews that Broz was calling the shots for the Cyan Boys. Although he was an anarcho-commie rabble-rouser, Broz was attempting to crash the entire Zysigamore market by putting the kibosh on postal meter ink supplies and turning the thumbless fingerscrews on every small-time flex drug dealer in the blueblood streets of Unicorn Harbor. And Broz always got away with it- until his blow was covered.

Some years ago, Broz starred in an off-on-off-Broadway production of "A New Pumpkin" by Me and Tinkelhoff. It didn't end well: By the third night, Broz was cited for attempted murder by strangling and virtually defenestrating the narrator, the Snooty Looking Nerd in a Bowtie.

Picking up his mouse costume at the Bougie Dry Cleaners one morning, Broz realized he had the golden ticket all along. He texted his shadowy comrades. "Today is the day we hit them with the promotion. Xarthorian proles will join our revolution. Bwahahaha!" "Damn, didn't mean to type that," Broz shrugged, as he adjusted his mouse ears.

As a result, Broz hated religion and high culture - and of course Idajan. She symbolized everything that Broz hated: Authority, Pants and Glam.

The next day, the ink and toner stopped flowing. Data clerks and elevator operators throughout the Island went into total shock and/or desiree. But rather than address the media directly, Broz went deeper underground. He and his leaders locked themselves in a basement with several techno DJ's and began snarfing all the flex drugs they could find.

Every so often Broz would turn on his hologram-vision to view the pasty conformist visage of Bryant Brick at Ace TV. "Punk!" he screamed at Brick's image. "I'll never be on your consumerist newscast."

One of his DJs suggested making a mixtape, then handing them out to slowly aging young people. "Yes, I like it," Broz grinned. They would go on to record several hours of Broz's rants over various house, techno and electronica beats. By the end, Broz had to be Simonized out of his mouse costume.

Unfortunately, young hipsters had moved onto the new rad thing - implanting mini-picture discs and playing them back using their piercings as record needles. Broz was forced to scramble to find cassette players and distribute them to the jaded youths before they embraced even more vacuous trends. In the meantime, Asmodeus had taken credit for the toner disruption and Broz flipped out. "No, it was me! Me!" He attempted to record a podcast of his greatest hits onto acetate, but Wacky Ted Kudzopilous had dropped lard onto it just before its global debut. "Aaaugh!"

-63   **Narmolof Nemesis**

Deep within the darkest bowels of the Caves of Chaos, too deep even for deep dish pizza, there was a lair inhibited by hundreds of narmolofs. Typically they lived solemn subterranean existences. But certain mining and extracting activities would set them off, drawing the monsters to various mines and exploration sites within Zysigamore.

DESCRIPTION: The narmolof is not typically aggressive, and is not motivated by food, fear, riches or awards shows. A narmolof is sometimes considered evil, yet it is true neutral: In fact, narmolofs have been known to attack demons and devils, and cannot be sent or plane shifted to those Lower Planes which we mortals dread so much. Still, Pixie King Ngndng'abzzimmughetialvizkonkuncesklthabzilorriililliililka-dzempf offers a bounty for each narmolof slain in his einsteinium mines. Most narmolofs were metallic blue in color, but others could appear in any hue. A few even changed colors like mood rings do.

Yet the determined narmolof was the avowed foe of the many Brenda Loompa tribes scattered throughout the peaks and walleyes of the Island.

Once upon a time not long ago, Marquez had ventured into a pixie tunnel in the hills of Unnunnentiumnn. He got a tip that precious gemstones left in place by the pixies could be harvested like ripe fruit. Some one itching hour, he got really small and waltzed right in. Marquez crawled through the tunnel and emerged in a brilliant subterranean cavern, with walls full of gems and old TV Guides everywhen. "Wow," he marveled, gazing at the majesty of *The Jeffersons* cover circa 1977. "A gold mine."

Suddenly a menacing narmolof stormbled into the treasure cave, all the way live as me and you. Marquez scurried away like a rodent, diving into a quaint pixie hole near a stack of garnets as high as a jicklehip's eye. The narmolof grabbed at him with its huge hands, tousling Marquez's hair a bit as he fled in haist.

Marquez got confused within the tunnel system in his flight. He tried peering back out the pixie hole and into the dark cave, but the narmolof was waiting for him like a tomcat. Nervous about the spell wearing off, he had to think of a way out and fast. "What would a Brenda Loompa do?"

Marquez took a sparkling superball that the soughtsayer had given him out of his sack, which seemed huge to him. Fortunately it wasn't as heavy as a megaball. With all his might, Marquez heaved it across the cavern wall, catching the narmolof's eye. As the monster's frilled ruff shifted to the side, Marquez suddenly sprang out of the pixie hole. There was nowhere to go but under the narmolof's legs - just in time too, as he felt himself start to grow rapidly. By the time he scurried out of the cavern, Marquez sprouted back to his full size. He never looked back.

64   Sandvick, Hughes & Atkinson

The only firm bad and big enough to challenge Danzig, Fulkerson & Johnson, Sandvick, Hughes & Atkinson was a streamlined corporation with modernist architecture and a 'can-do' attitude. SH&A had the Rodentcorp account, the Ace TV account, the Omni Radio account, and most other entertainment/ media corporations throughout Zysigamore. Their sales professionals had a much different vibe than the elitist partners of DF&J or trans-Zysigamore agency Babel, Babel & Babel - a SH&A rep was witty yet smart, always eager to advance and not be beholden to hidebound tradition or "the old boy's club."

Today, SH&A held a meeting for its partners and trustees to discuss a tantalizing account: Queen Idajan and her land of Uottubbacktothebonyiumnnn (sp.). Brad Sandvick Jr., principal and son of SH&A's founder, stood up boldly and announced their epic strategy. It didn't involve thumb wrestling or noogies. Rather, they would jack up the expenses until tiny fries like Traveling Salesman and Mr. Hi Stop gave up.

Brad strolled back to his corner office suite and putted around. Soon Mike Hughes III stumbled in with his day-glo mini golf balls and tired rhetoric. Mike lit up a stogie. "I enjoyed the trite platitudes. But wouldn't we be better served keeping these little guys afloat instead?" He thoughtfully took another tug of the cigar. "You know, you might have a point. I'll chew on it." Brad also pulled out a cigar and lit it up ever so thoughtfully, sort of like his Pa used to do.

Pamela, SH&A's sentient golf course, was down to just 11 1/2 active holes due to maintenance of her 13 most beautiful greens. She recommended that Brad and Mike use her former golfcourse-friend Gus Wilkerson and avail themselves of the Country Club's lavish facilities. "Capitol idea, Pamela!" they chanted. Soon, SH&A's EA was on the horn to Strikercorp and its enigmatic CEO.

"Tea bags?" Striker could barely hear over the obligatory canned laughter. "I don't know. No, he might be booked that day." A pause as the exec assistant relayed more info. "If the price was right, perhaps. Yes. I could check my schedule. I'm a very busy man, you see. Good day." He hung up his deluxe vibra smello smartphone. Striker didn't notice the other, softer 'click' on the line as he hung up.

As usual, there was a leak. Those rascals from DF&J put in a sweet offer at the last millisecond. Brad, Mike and the rest of the staff proactively choked on their ascots. "I say," said Mike Hughes III, "What went haywire?" The principals turned to see Suzy the ex-EA strolling down the street with Broz, stiff middle finger in the air. "Son of a 'BOB'," they both gasped. "And she was carrying a carbine," reflected Brad.

-64   Mount Lordburne

By far the most élitified sentient golf course, Mount Lordburne overlooked the back porch of the Team Gods' Olympamansion far far above the cloudgates. Certainly no raffriff like Xarthorians or Demon Joe were evva abmitted to Mount Lordburne CC, Academy and Superballs. Onie, Traveling Salesman and Mr. Hi Stop hit the 'burn (or at least its 133rd hole) when they were in the area on beeswax. Hi was notorious for taking exactly one sip of a bloody Mary and leaving it forgotten on a table.

A diversion. A new party is teeing up for Hole 1: Ashtaroth and her Type V demon Gha'agsheblah were accompanied by Dr. Oste, August September and a celery stalk yclept Mem. Despite the sub-zero conditions, the party was in good cheer. "Die jicklehip vom eis holen!" hollered Gha'agsheblah at the frozen corpse of a jicklehip at the edge of the water hazard. "Just play around it," said Ashtaroth, deflecting Her shot close to the green. "It's a local rule."

Al Abdul-Hasred and his carpeted camel caravan were crossing the immense sand trap of the 10th hole when Ashtaroth's foursome began to tee up. "Get that creep off the course!" screamed the demoness, trying in vein to get the gruzzled old man's attention. "Maybe a fireball or two would perk him up," smiled the marilith, but her boss deferred. Dr. Oste mounted her en-lipoco and rode over to the peeved necromancer's caravan to spur them on.

"Great Merkabah! Across the vast wasteland of eldritch ephialtes," moaned Al to the faits. Dr. Oste appealed to the irritable Mussulman that he drive his caravan out of Mt. Lordburne. "Surely you don't want to taste Ashtaroth's wrath." Al got that crazed look in his eyes. "Aye, dear lady, I've faced demon lords QOD since lime ummemoriable. Hole 10 is but a faint star in the limitless firmament of my exquisite suffering."

Dr. Oste climbed back on her steed, and BONK! The piqued nomad fell face first into the sandtrap. Ashtaroth, witching pedge in hand, descended on Her lucky ruby-red golf ball, which had burrowed deeply into Al Abdul-Hasred's cranium. "It's a local rule," She repeated to the marilith. Naturally, Ashtaroth birdied the hole. "Capitol," stated August, dutifully keeping score by tattoo.

Back at the 133rd hole, Ashtaroth and Her posse were buffalo buffalo buffalo buffalo buffalo buffalo buffalo buffaloed avec cocktails. Al strolled through the bar, hoisting a mocktail, celery stalks slathered in pine nut butter, and a horrifically wizened eyebrow with hairs irrationally growing in non-Euclidean directions. He asked the demon, "What's your candy hap, if I may be so audacious, dear Queen of the Underworld?" Ashtaroth accepted his groveling and made an eldritch hand signal for Π. The hole in Al's head suddenly disappeared. "That cost me a stroke, you know," She reminded him.

65   More Megaball Mayhem

The booming voice of Joey Least crackled over the cisradios like a crooked 10 penny nail dragged over a brand new linoleum floor during a 3 a.m. drunken stupor. Hi and Traveling Salesman were front row at this game, and waved to the crowd on the Jumbotron as the camera spied them. Simon even saw them on his home uberscreen and blew kisses. "High above courtside this is Joey Least." He really made Bryant Brick look like Glenn Von Oosterman.

Turns out that Joey had seen every fetus acquired by the Underwear Point megaball team first hand since the dawn of civilization - and had personally begrudged each fetus that the opponents unjustly snagged instead. Least was hated throughout Zysigamore, except for those diehard Whitey Tide-ee fans that treated his words as Godspell.

The press box loomed over the megaball field. It creaked and croaked like a water logged ark full of third-hand smoke and divine molten anguish. Joey lit up another smoke as the Tidies struggled against the dreaded

Bowdlerizers, a team of dirty, violent criminals posing as megaball antiheroes. Suddenly Joey was livid, his voice rising six octaves at least. "The coach just gave his Bowdlerizer players an armful of tire irons so that they may wedgie anyone out there in tidy whiteys....knowing that the ref will call it justifiable homicide!"

Traveling Salesman texted Simon from his luxury box seats. "Miss you darling. But you would hate it here. Megaball is for meatheads." Simon cooed back, practically choking up at the thought of all that wasted testosterone. "We need Clytie to fix that time door and hook it up to our bed." Simon had forgotten to mute the megagigundus screen television, so he nearly jumped out of his pants when Joey Least's acidic voice shattered the calm.

"Can you believe it? Twenty nameless goons on the bench. Pansexualmonium on the megaball field." Joey Least practically spat the syllables out over the puny broadcast mic. Simon's heart was racing. It was like some sort of national emergency. What can I do? He texted TS, "I don't even know the Bob-damned rules of this silly game. But I feel like I did a dozen lines of flex drugs listening to this man."

Fetuses flowed back and forth seemingly effortlessly. Each Bowdlerizers fetus acquired was answered by an equal but opposite reaction from the Tide-ees. After an unnecessarily violent play, Least cackled, "Do you believe that? Big Jon Rule snags the megaball, and gets absolutely cuffed in the stomach by McDaemon and McDevil. The ref isn't calling anything because there's no blood on the court!" Mr. Hi Stop and Traveling Salesman agreed not to high-eight any more clients after decking an assistant manager from the suburbs in the fracas. "Hail Moloch, at least he was just an assistant manager," sneered Traveling Salesman as the ushers wiped up the blood, ichor and semen.

-65   Joyt

Since his controversial departure from the Allman Isley Brothers and Sisters Band 252, Paul Joyt has become a dominant transcontinental colosso. He and his band JOYT re-recorded every soft rock song known to individual program directors, and regurgitated enough bro country to fill every stable in Clytemnestra's old minotaur labyrinths. Like Clytie, Paul was an SJU grad, and regularly connected with alumni and school administration boards, despite snorting, tooting and shooting flex drugs off a baby's behind before a crucial megaball game.

But Fate caught up to Joyt like a punch bowl caroming off Bobo Ruland's head. His industry people wanted him to go even more commercial, but he stunned them all by abandoning the rock'n'roll lifestyle entirely.

Before he began to board a boat for Belgium to find himself by making flavorless cheese with a cell of silent monks, Joyt had a change of heart. "I'm gong to be a real artiste," he said to no one in particular in the press. Like every Me and their third cousins, he realized Allman Isley Band had a huge hit with *Eat a Potato* while also maintaining a soupçon of credibilitizzle.

A possible duet with Roger Valdorus fell apart at the last tonsil, however, driving Joyt to supreme existential madness. "I worked my whole career to get to thisa level, only to be denied," he said to a barfly sucking on a biden mocktail. "I really had it all like Bogie and Bacall." She pointed to a half-eaten dinner roll on a plate in front of him. "You gonna eat that?"

When things looked their geekiest, Joyt got a call from Ace TV producers. Bryant Brick was hosting an angst-free teenage pop dance show, and wanted Joyt to do his new song "Holligan." "Sure, sure, we'll be there. I have very good teeth and hair," Joyt added.

However, a snit developed. Demon Joe was luck on his down once again, victimized by mixing jenkem with his 5g. The lady at the bar threw her biden at him in a spasmodic fit. Joe didn't see it coming, and fumed at Joyt's entourizzle for allowing his high-tech apocolocyntosis to be filmed onto his phone for all to mock.

Cune un uff, fluffy Ace TV reporters slouched in for the kill. Joyt was crushed more thoroughly than John Barleycorn, and subsequently shipped to Acheron once Wacky Ted Kudzopilous dissed his podcast. Demon Joe sulked away, laser caked flex drugs drawing out of each earsophagus. "Ace TV can KMA, fluff bunnies!"

66   Elephant

The repudiation of capitalism and communism was Elephant's laissez-faire adjustable slogan.

His beauty underscores the massive erudition and post-Keynesian dialectic. Elephant had demolished Milton Friedman in debate, the sting of the pachyderm's flawless post hoc propter hoc, a priori critique.

Lukács was known to cower under divans and in the recesses of closets when the duende of Elephant was present. Elephant didn't resort to salami or prosciutto tactics to master his opponents - just good old fashioned post-structural macroeconomic policy.

No loneliness was less pronounced than the Big E's. Children burned their Keynesian comic books. Old people began to feel a strange vigor which their lifestyle had lacked.

Simon did not confide in Elephant; his neoliberal stances and constant romantic outlook alienated him to Elephant's revolutionary yet loquacious platform.

"If only Paul Volcker had followed my advice," Elephant sadly trumpeted.

He didn't take the blame for Mobutism; rather, Howard Cosell was its conduit. At a UDEMO conference, Elephant was vilified in absentia. A curious turn of events unfolded.

That afternoon in Kinshasa had exposed fractures in the report of Erwin Blumenthal.

Thereafter, Elephant swore to uphold a comprehensive policy framework. A viable external debt policy was discussed.

They played Pin-the-Tail-on-the A + B Theorem. The voodoo doll of Major C. H. Douglas was well punctured. "The folly! Sheer naiveté!"

Cogitations that Elephant had left behind were used by the Xarthorians like a universal lubrication of the senses. He was unaware, but he was proud.

Bonus - the process of cleaning an injured elephant's foot!! Nggjlmrcd.

-66   Long May Your Yacht Sail

Hungriform talents and hothechajuxips dreams gave a wave to the *Habemoore* on their weigh aboard *Wilgort De Throesland*, the crystal yacht, Esq., sailing out of Unicorn Harbor at a clip of 4.3 yoyanas. Elmer's playlist was on, beaming superliminal dyspeptic drugs into the adults.

Striker matched a light. The party guests and interns were mingling adequately enough so he didn't have to flesh the press. He didn't hate media, as some of his old lackeys now work for Ace TV, but they were always to be kept on a short lease, particularly the young bux who would swornhoggle a pass to the *Wilgort De Throesland*.

At starboard bow an albatross appeared, allowing albaguests and armaphores on the lower dexx. Twas one of Purple Alvin's detractions, a care-filled ruse to imply himself incubus-like to some of the destultory wives and lady folkiges.

112

That night's supergroup was the reunited Buxx Stopp flugelhorn banned, semi-attired in leftover bondage gear and random fencing equipment. Purple Alvin did the lights in cosmic mindfuck, stroking Striker's subconscious into beaming beatitudes of reticulated crunk.

"Let's make mamba love," cried the Captain Steubing hologram as partygoers flirted about the in the twinklenacht. A broke incubus bussed tables and gave out his bussy to his psychic frenze.

Traveling Salesman blew off the busboy bussy, heading straight to an interesting bevy of ladies on the poop deck. Once he broadcast that he was unattached and possessed Salesman Magic, he received one flirtatious look after another. "You heard Captain Steubing - we can't let him down." The ladies laughed in unison. He was too cool to dance, yet cool enough to stand at the corner of the bar, flicking his business cards like so many yods.

Striker strolled down the bar, flashing the high sign, low sign, and back of the belly button sign to the bartender. "Good evening," he greeted Traveling Salesman. "Nice little boat you have here," nodded TS coolly. "Yes, it'll do," he answered. The barkeep passed Striker an incomprehensible drink mixed inside of a hollowed-out durian. "Skor," he shouted, chugging from the durian. "This will make you younger."

Unfivetunately for Traveling Salesman, the young ladies turned and ran once they whiffed the stench of Striker's drink. "Ah, who needs 'em!" Striker vented. "Still saving yourself for the Queen?" asked TS. "For your information, there are many eligible ladies with whom I play Candy Land," inquit Striker.

67   Nutspoken Nüpümpkin

Semvophor Beeklewaxen, aka the Headless Horseman of Unicorn Harbor, washed up in our livers around 3406. They were gourded by twelven chronoproctors whom Striker had mind-melded with for the good of society - and to keep his creepy self yoyanas away from the Queen. Beeklewaxen's apocolocyntosis began in Ernest.

"A New Pumpkin to Rule Them All" was simultaneously a Top 40 yacht rock hit and an imtrending pix of radiation from Simon Junior U - as well as a series of Tiamation bills aimed at punishing the Brenda Lazoompas 4 existing overw8. Thus was Nutspoken Nüpümpkin overwrought.

Piece was never fulfilled. But that was intentional. It would enranger one's economy and cause decessions. Soon, DF&J realized Nüpümpkin truly had "IT" - as did the ladies. He is romancing the unfulfilled need that salesmen are bred to sniff out.

By the end of the 1/4 Nutspoken had posted numbers that DF&J veterans were amazed by. Maybe his 21-ball skills were metza-metza. But he could maximize earnings and craft contracts that the Partners were sullenly amazed by and through. "He's a change agent" was the consensus.

But Nutspoken remained a threat to the other sales professionals. The Partners liked how the other salespeople pushed themselves to deliver how Nüpümpkin did. After a while, he stopped talking to the interns - even little Howie, the precocious son of an unnamed trustee.

Skittle did anyone gnoe, Traveling Salesman and Mr. Hi Stop soon recognized the business opportunity of wearable jack-o-lanterns for secular types. Several hundred thousand intellectual property attorneys later, Nutspoken Nüpümpkin was begging our heroes to cut him in. "Endorsements? I can do endorsements. 15-second CARTs? No problemo."

As face would have it, it was the last tawdry gimmick for many of the grey-bearded, geriatric DF&J partners, who immediately sacked Nüpümpkin the next week. They locked up his email, his phone, his prostate, and his fidget spinner. Soon enough, Nüpümpkin found himself on Skid Patch. Linus couldn't even save him.

It was about this time that Abaddon the Destroyer flung the wrecking ball at DF&J in defense of His homeboy Nutspoken Nüpümpkin. "Heck, I'll even bring back several obsolete forms of heavy metal for him. Haw!" The wrecking ball destroyed the high-rise office building of DF&J's illiterate subsidiary XTA. Soon the stuffed shirts relented, and sold their children into slavery to Abaddon for a new contract. "Ni-hi-hi-hi-hizzle."

-67 Anaconda She Hydra

Bleating, pandering Lemurian monster begone! Thisa mother of death is no sphinx, no Tiamat, no Taweret; she is mortal like Me... Some of her hideous, serpentine heads have poisonous bites; others will attempt to constrict you at the upper neck or the perineum and twist your follicules into painful nodicules.

She earns the name Didrentis for her razor-sharp teeth. Each head has over 100 anaconda teeth in its jaws. When the She-Hydra bites, she often leaves behind a chung of tooth that gets under your skin and brings purpureal, pus-filled pimples to painfill peruptions in the private parts, perineum and punderarms.

Shambolic bloody reptile serum is very very scarce. Polypoids burning in the wood are the habitat to look for. And the wrong pants- the wrong panties even- could mean insaster.

Xarthorians and the hothechajuxips crowd loathed this nasty creature, whose suppurative nature could eviscerate self-esteems many many multiverses away. Didrentis had no friends to call her 'Ana' and offer her lich juice; she only had her hideous sisters and their voracious baby snakes that she lays on That Day.

Little did everyone know, but Marquez raided the She-Hydra's nest, stealing many discarded teeth and eggs, coloring those eggs and selling them online as "Reptile Pets". Gullible Xarthorians mortgaged their palates for a chance to buy one of the adorable serpents for their entitled tweenage brats.

The fame only made Didrentis even more menacing and cruel. Soon, she was the subject of an Ace TV 2 hour special hosted by Kaspar Hauser and Ciyn Dea Sept Nept. "I'm going to sue each one of those motherfucking shareholders," one of her most eloquent heads yelled. She already had enough cake to buy a flotilla of the best lawyers on the Island.

"Der gee boss, what are we going to do?" Bryant Brick texted Striker. In his most peeved voice of tone, Striker confessed, "I'm working on it. Hold down the farm for now, Bri." Striker looked into his Orb, but found it was cloudier than a zommom's cerebrum.

Striker tried to contact the rest of the gang, but many of them were at a chrimpostelers' jamboree. "This can't wait til Monday." Mikey Rat wouldn't touch this due to feminism issues; Simon didn't have the sporks; and his 11 favorite mercenaries wouldn't return his calls - even Mamba Dave had a doppelvergnügen in process. "Sorry, Bro."

Thus, only Her Majesty 4casta could deal with thisa chthonic mother of Evil…

68 Protagonistexpialasnalacknaloggue

Admittedly, Idajan never saw a need for an expensive government intelligence agency. As 4casta often stated, "Don't bother, honey. Government is unintelligent by nature." The Queen's superpowers, while not omnipotent, were capable enough to monitor any crisis, and her team of X's were so efficient that minor threats were snuffed out long before Idajan started paying attention.

But once the infernal lords began interfering in Zysigamore's pants, politics, toner cartridge prices, and megaball point spreads, Idajan acknowledged the need for a new approach. "I don't want a bunch of G-men and spooks running around here in shiny black shoes and skinny ties. But what alternative do I have?" she asked her ministers. The meeting adjourned in delusion.

Afterward, she received a good call from an entity known as Bleary Tim. "I'm speaking to you by primitive smartphone now, O Queen. But we can have this conversation telepathically." Idajan was aghast. "Who gave you this number?" she screamed. "I'll melt you in acid if you're a fake." Bleary Tim just chuckled gently. "I'm not a salesman. I leave that to 'BOB'. I'm just a projection after all." His dreamy, soporific voice cut through the Queen's cynicism.

Thus was wrought the QIA, Queen's Intrapsychic Agency. Its nonexistence was the key to its suckcess. Bleary Tim appeared during flex drug time or in Idajan's dreams, always in the most unobtrusive manner. The connection made the Queen indomitable and even more supraliminal.

Although the QIA didn't technically exist, it was important to let the Xarthorians think that it did. Idajan derived comfort from their superstition, ignorance and paranoia. She received a telepathic message from Bleary Tim in a euphoric commonwealth, and intuited his ideas into Uottubbacktothebonyiumnnnn's (sp.) policies. "Keep 'em guessing til they're out of guesses," she laughed.

The flex drugs subsided, Meco satisfied her until her cuticles curled, and X's handled all the details. Idajan even allowed Striker to grovel in front of her to promote his ego trips, in exchange for a fleet of pleasure saucers.

All was swol; that is, until everything fell apart. Brochastic terrorism against Xarthorians made them panicked and fearful. Idajan reassured by hologram daily, but once the fear entered the herd, they couldn't be seasoned, reasoned or creasoned.

The next morn, the Double-0 X's of the QIA were introduced with much fanfare and glamor on an Ace TV special hosted by Pettiler Stevens and Li'l Nas Y. Each Double-0 X'er kept their ID's secret when in public, as the ladies dressed like they had stepped out of a Robert Palmer video. "Sna-lack-a-lock-a-lu-la. Wa-ka-ka-kow!" shouted Pettiler.

-68   Zona: Super Tyranny of the Belt

Head of the ouroboros slides its steel teeth through one of five belt notches or so. The more notches attained, the better we feel. FALSE! VERY UNTRUE! We are poisoned, deluded into its restriction, as our digestive tract strains against the tightness across the waistline.

Zoster, slacken! Not tighten!

Girdled by latitudinal bathyscaphic gradients, the Island from west to east arouses from the torpor of seismic stillness. Volcanoes gurgle, faults widen, storms without name ripen.

The people have little option but to ride this turtle as it moves in every direction simultaneously. Diverse species rise and fall, while many try to build another arkq.

This isochastic solipsism crept into the Zysigamore populace largely undetected, save for a handful of oceanographers and sousaphonists. In response to the unsettled feelings, the tyrannies were increased by two more triangles, to the point where all sins were rubbed raw by restrictive recovenants and recombinant Dobbsheads.

Boreal and Austral energies bifurcate. Rules of Incasker's laws are outflicted upon the body. We can see the results of this torture everywhen a blighted Xarthorian prole swells up and dies on a vine.

Know weigh xisted to stop the trend. And so the middle lay neglected, despised. Pumincled solifugids couldn't breach the ecliptic. Simmering stars @ 3.

A disembodied entity yclept Orion Jodiack once lingered in this connectorweigh. Yet Jodiack was driven off by farces far more powerful than a moltentov mocktail. Now he lingers by the bingo parlors of one of Demon Joe's nameless chain restaurants.

Purrforce encephaloknot-based phytodontic trebmalidotes shall dissocicorporate at dawnsk. Pee-Yort! Yow!

Dr. Oste othorized on Ace TV in flavor of the Illuso-Belt, much to the charge inn of the Zysigamore Zonal Zouaches. Utilizing specially oblong laptop saddles, she programmed the Illuso-Belts for fashion and health styles. She and Aegothsorzhotan told host Ciyn Dea Sept Nept that That Day is a Comin' and Xarthorians need 'em. "What about the children?" spaketh Ciyn Dea. "The ZZZ ain't gonna go for it." "Listen," the wizard said, "this is a promise or a threat. Just get with it."

69　　　　　Metza-Metza Verse

The pits of Malebolge rang with the 444 Hz tones of a new demand generation manager for the 8th Level of Hell. Mephisto grinned in anticipatronage. "Val Over. Great to see you onsite." Jen instinctively reached out to shake hands but the devil demurred. "My nails are laced with cyanide. I wouldn't want to drip any on your blazer." He laughed, more ironically than devilishly.

They eased into a multi-story occult castle in the shadow of Mephisto's grand cheateau on a cliff above the Pit of Hypocrites, which fell downward to Nessus. Next in line to greet Jennifer were pit fiend Rafelmaheeamek-zabialmit; the Lord's consort Balphegor en homme; a consultant who once worked for Rodentcorp; an allosaurus; three jaded hair metal baladeers; and the poet Catullus. After a quick snack of dung beetles, lab rats on skewers and caustic orange soda, they all filed into a grim conference room.

"Welcome. Ms. Jennifer Val Over will now present Brand Awareness for Devils." A half-golf-clap, half hoof-stomp of approval greeted her PowerPoint slides. The lights didn't dim - instead Mephisto turned them up full blast. Val Over rose, cleared her throat, and began speaking.

By EOM, two of the metal stars had been swallowed by the allosaurus, and even Catullus was très fatigué. "I'd like to open up the floor to discussion. Then a 20-minute break, before we do breakout groups," continued Jen. "We should have got Eeelephant," sighed Balphegor to Rafi.

The breakout groups didn't go as planned. Val Over got into a staring contest with Balphegor - and was completely charmed during the break. "Quit that! This is serious," pleaded Mephisto."This is an all-claws meeting. C'mon, give me a break." After making Jen do the achy breaky and gangnam style for a few more minutes, s/he released the charm. "I hope you had your fun," fumed Val Over, brushing dust, mold, slime and excrement from her blazer and slacks. The devils and attendees just laughed.

"I'll be in touch about my billable hours and travel to/from Malebolge," droned Val Over, sending her gynormous invoice to all within email range. Yet old Jen couldn't travel home via Qlippoth Gate. She had to take the dragon rideshare from Avernus, seven levels above. "No direct flights?" she screamed at a hapless devilish customer support sub-devil. "Can't a gargoyle fly me at least halfway?" Rafelmaheeamek-zabialmit feigned interest, but soon dropped her call. "Let her take a dimetrodon for all I care."

-69　　　　　Doppelvergnügen

The 1st Straw was the BDSM complex that replaced the seedy old fitness center in Umlaut Towin. Doms did a brisk business when the conventioneers came to towin- especially the slicked down sales professionals of the day. Like 'BOB' or Purple Alvin, they were willing to secrete hair gel and other bodily fluids and to piss through money as pantsless Dominatrices disciplined their fleshes.

116

The business was so successful that The 2nd Straw soon opened next door. It only existed on the Prime Material Plane in an even hardercore format catering to kinksters who found the 1st Straw too tame. Needles to say, pricks were on point at all hours at the 2nd. In fact, celebrities started showing up with or without their flagellants to plumb the depths of the dirtiest erotica ever commodified. Other times, it would blink out of existence entirely and reappear in a fresh new light on the Astral or other Outer Planes or pocket dimensions.

Feeling exceptionally randy one day, Traveling Salesman booked two doms for his playtime - one dom disrobed him and began to tie him up; the other fiddled with a cat-o-nine tails as she idly watched him get aroused. "I'm flexed. I'm good for all night," bragged Traveling Salesman.

Traveling Salesman was such a regular customer that he found Studio 54 in a soap dispenser in the men's room of the 2nd. This night, however, was a Doubles Night. He booked the two beauties who appealed most to his cishet side, and readied a tens unit. "Girls, it's gonna get freaky!" They explored several forbidden potato casserole recipes with untold glee.

Soon, Xblanklen and his coworkers started stopping by the First Straw after work. The hologram room uncannily recreated several Ace TV and X's sculpted beauties, customizing each one by each person's brainwaves. "See," Xblanklen emphasized, "just think it before the AAI overreax. And you'll get your money back sometimes." A mysterious avatar of Vermin Supreme winked out of sight unnoticed.
Or did it?

A few nights later, Xblanklen tossed and turned in bed, his lustiness unrequited. He hastily dressed, jumped on a Tenser's Flying Disc and went Down Towin again, straight to the 2nd. It was almost closing time, warned the bouncer as Xblanklen strutted through the door. Two bored twinks grabbed a large roll of undustrial strength green cellophane and followed their customer. "I heard this is intense." Various cishet porn videos played in the background as he entered PanoptiPod #4.

Before schlong Xblanklen's erection had swollen beyond redemption or even recognition. The AI shot images and sensory impulses all over his body. The intractable cellophane drove Xblanklen into a frenzy before his drool got overwhelming. He turned to the twinks. "Nobody's perfect."

70   Qlippoth Gate

Qlippoth has all of the Kabalah but none of the calories.

Aegothsorzhotan's magick tomes were among the first to outline this direct link via Da'ath to the first level of virtually any non-good outer plane, should all the other hermetic factors be accounted for. Clytie knew of only one copy; it was held by Jon Cody, a wizened old oenophile in an octagonal obelisk just outside of Unicorn Harbor.

Unfortunately, the rumored tome was gone again as Jon Cody was consumed by rats the day before Clytie visited. "Maybe that's a good thing?" The old drunk had been making pin money selling adamantittance to Hades, Hell, Pandemonium, and many other infernal locales: But Qlippoth Gate remained an enigma shrouded in taco sauce and red herrings. Somewhere, Aegothsorzhotan was giggling.

Christimiqua got wind of a potential new lead. "I got good news and bad news," she texted Clytie. As it turns out, the only other copy of the magus' magnum opus, *Devilkind, Demonkind & Their Superballs*, was in the closed stacks of the private Strikercorp libram of esoteric wisdom, located near the very elbow of Striker himself. "Damn. Deal with that creep again? Ew!" replied Clytie. "I'd rather suck face with Demon Joe than smell Striker's boiled hot dog water-scented cologne," concurred Christy.

Clytie had a Ruse Creator™ for such a contingensizzle. She contacted Ciyn Dea Sept Nept, a breathless Ace TV cub reporter, about the occult text's alleged 666th anniversary and the imminent dangers this tome poses to the innocent children of Zysigamore. "Surely something is done to be needed," Ciyn Dea breathlessly breathed.

Ever genial, Striker agreed to perform the Qlippoth Gate live on Ace TV during sweeps week. "The ad revenue will be through the roof!" But when Bryant Brick arrived, there was no unveiling. Instead, Striker tried to vainly sell timeshares in the Caves of Chaos. Behind the scenes was bedlam. "Where's my *Superballs*? Why me?"

Of course, nothing happened. Striker was crestfallen. "Everything was so perfect - even the O rings." Clytemnestra's people got in touch with Striker, offering him a deal and possible redemption in the eyes of disappointed Xarthorians, in exchange for granting Clytie the chance to access the grimoire. "I'll see- I dunno," he halfheartedly replied. But when Striker returned to his library, *Devilkind, Demonkind & Their Superballs* was gone. "I loaned it to an eighth grader for a book report," said the pasty librarian.

-70   Carsof

Megaball was dominated by the Men of Carsof. Manager Mac McMac had been there since the Rock Age and had been resurrected for several seasons, but was still the same old hard-drinkin, hard-lovin cuss as always. No rookie durst question his decisions or his gut feeling about a replay replay, lest they risk banishment to Palookaville or an even lower plane. "Give me 20 nameless players, I'll mold them into champs."

Carsof had a three-night stand in Unicorn Harbor. All the prostitutes and small-time grifters lined the grandstand that first night as the first strike zone was kicked off. Grizzled old McMac chomped down on the saliva-moistened stogie as the referees danced a jig. "Six, two and even. I remember back in '88. The boys were beating the brakes. We one one one for tradition, for candlepin bowling. Dammit!!"

By the fifth period, Unicorn Harbor had taken the lead. None of manager McMac's many machinations mustered more megagoals. "Mega motherfucker," muttered McMac. Another ineffective relief 1/3-back had to be removed from the pitch. You could cut the tension with a tardigrade.

Fetuses were getting constricted. McMac summoned pinch-pirouetter Royle Rose to the sandbox. Rose grunted, donning a pantsuit and grabbing a pair of maracas from the fungo fella. "Look, Royle," the manager exhorted, "It's a real pressure cooker here. Slide, slide, Imaggio..." The referee called Rose out on a wardrobe malfunction before he even came to the jump-puck face-on. The crowd groaned and relieved itself. "Double darn," muttered Royle Rose.

The Unicorn Harbor 13 held a 3-fetus lead by the fifteenth quarter thanks to hometown left defensebacker Punny "Boom Boom" Javlinchuk. Manager McMac had called every trick play in the book, and even tucked a drone umpire into his shorts to try to catch Boom Boom in an illegal Wet Rochambeau. His efforts went four knot as Unicorn Harbor completed a 12-fetus play left-handed. "Pickled punks! Shit, I'd suck the gangrene out of a zombie's ballbag right about now," McMac yelled to the Unicorn Harbor mascot. "I'd throw you out of the game if I was a sentient being," texted the rookie robo-ump.

Gallantly the Carsof Fifteen bestrode to their bases and fields for the seventeenth quarter. The fetuses hit the floor, yet Mac McMac's boys kept the Unicorn Harbor players from a crucial pantsy-desk. Before the quarter ended, Mac called timeout and sexually assaulted a referee as the crowd chanted multiple simulmonious profanitizzle.

The outrage was real, but so was the pandemonium. Pazuzu appeared, hovering above the stadium to bestow trophies and venereal diseases. "Mac McMac, you are the greatest. Fuck Jersey Joe Walcott. Yeah! Who that punk anyway?" Crunktent having been dispensed like so many aspic pez treats, the Ace TV nanodrone cameras zoned in on the pores of each Carsof champion, conveniently ignoring the Lord of the Southwest Wind to assuage anorexic advertisers.

Afterward, Mac McMac sat alone in his office, wearing only a metal cup and chain-link jockstrap. He had fucked up those Unicorn Harbor megaballers yet again, but the gone was thrill.

Yet another surreal crisis rocked Ace TV as sweeps week's numbers flatlined. "And the big boss announced mandatory drug tests. What are we going to do?" cried Ciyn Dea Sept Nept.

Another vile rumor was the return of Pants Day. After all those years of doing broadcasts dressed in just their skivvies, the men were now going to have to wear trousers. "What hath 'BOB' wrought?" cried Ickey the hapless intern.

Otherwhelmed viewers noticed the disruptions and took action. A group named Citizens for Responsible Imaginary Friend Enforcement (CRIFE) had staged a hungry strike until the Bear Kunckled Pseudofluffleuppagus apologized for a string of anti-Xarthorian comments on his kids' show. Even the flappable Bryant Brick felt the strain, injuring himself while polishing his wingtips. "I'll do my show in traction if I have to," he huffed, but Striker kiboshed the put on it.

An avid aficionado at the nail salon tried to purrsuede Simon to join CRIFE, handing him anti-literature and haranguing him about sundry injustices. "My ties are handed, kids," explained Simon to an especially cherubic CRIFEr. Later, Simon watched one of their infomercials in 5-D hyperglasses.

Simon's new year's revolution being more yacht rock, he turned away from Ace TV's mellow drama. But back behind the green scren, trouble was a bruin. Striker rented a HatGPT to write all Ace TV's copy. The system worked fine for a couple of days, until HatGPT began exclusively writing news articles about pants. "For fuck's sake," Striker pleaded, "there must be an Edward R. Murrow setting." HatGPT answered, "Sorry sir, we don't own the rights."

To salvage any ratings at all, Ace TV switched to live-action jello wrestling, with several familiar faces getting waste deep in a hoopla. Even Brooke Biddingham did a round against champeenzee Heidi Enseeq. Heidi was a real pro, and didn't pull any of Brooke's hair extensions out. Winner received one date with Striker; the loser, two. Brooke was able to escape her conligation due to sexual harassment laws.

Finally the vendor of the HatGPT kinked the works out of their AAI. But they couldn't save the Bear Kunckled Pseudofluffleuppagus Show, which was canceled in favor of AAI-generated sewer heroes. BKP later found work as a fluffer at The 1st Straw.

-71   Border on the Keeplands

Between Unnunnennnumnnnn and Uottubbacktothebonyiuvuuulle (sp.) stood a small, forlorn fort, which boar witless to a boring, vanilla region simply yclept The Keeplands. Unlike the Inverted Pyramid of 4casta, Idajan had all but forgotten about this outpost of her queendom. The Keeplands wasn't an active war zone, but did see its share of gnoll, conford and lerbiax bands. The last major battle was with the Demon Men of the Ningarm.

Its commander Rzyzixx was largely left to fend for himself. His men were mean, beetle-like in their metallic eyepatches, thoraxes and regalia. Most were mercenaries who came to the Keeplands when they needed to avoid being seen, or at least seen being avoided. Green rookies went mad within two weeks, and were occasionally offered to Moloch for a ghoul to be named later.

Mostover, the Keep was haunted by the ghost of General Beauregard Beauregard Beauregard, who appeared in a gray-on-grey V-neck knight shirt with detachable pockets. Rzyzixx regularly spooked rookies with yarns of the Beauregard's misteradventures defending the fort for the Dysfederacy. The Commander was sure to leave a pint of cherry brandy for the crazed ghost every evening at sundown. "And it's dry ever' morn, don't'cha know," he averred.

The commander and his men were compelled to venture away from the Keep to find Little Timmy, who was either trapped at the bottom of a well, sunk up to his armpits in quicksand, burned in a three-way script, kidnapped by gay communist bicyclists, or 90% of the above plus expenses. "Oh no, not this brat again," mouthed off a disgruntled grunt. "Zip it. That could be Morton Downey Juinor's third cousin's paperboy, or Ronald Atkins' housekeeper's milkman's massesuse's accountant's tooth catcher," explained Rzyzixx. "We're never gonna be written into another chapter with that kind of tude," he added.

The tousle-haired tyke was soon discovered half a mile from camp, participating in quaint, wholesome and highly marketable activities. "McBoy oh boy oh boy. There's the kid," called the Scout, focusing his binocs for a better view. Before he said, 'I say,' one of Rzyzixx's rookie red-shirts strolled across the waistland toward the waif. The rest of his men stayed put, preparing for the unevitable.

The mantrap sprung at the guard, trapping him in its tendrils in the midst of lunging after what he thought was Little Timmy. "Coulda seen that coming, yes, yes." Rzyzixx checked his smartphone. "Attention! I just got a post that Little Timmy is OK." The rest of the mercenaries cheered. "Turns out, he got a job tending to Li'l Nas Y's hairpieces," explained Rzyzixx. Screams of pain and agony echoed throughout the Keeplands as the rookie was slowly, agonizingly dissolved in the gastric juices of the mantrap. "Say, who's got some flex drugs and Xarthorian moonshine?" cried one of the file and rank.

72   GIGOQFA

(Yo ho)[3]

Gay songs of Brenda Loompas reverberate through illusocubicles of chaos. It's the annual Circus Peanut Festival, with the crowning of this year's Queen Loompa, feats of derring dew, sarcastically pretempted journalistas, fried annelids, en-lipoco petting zoo, and vast wheelhouses of carnality embossled for your pleasure.

Simon, Clytie, Christy, Nas and Xblanklen were handed several varieties of circus peanuts, all of which were more suitable for building materials than consumption. Examining a pumpkin spice circus peanut more closely, Li'l Nas Y concluded, "I don't like the look of it." Xblanklen attempted to punt one into the next dimension yet failed hilariously.

Painfully closeted Stan saw the gang on the midway, and waved "Hey". He had donned a giant circus peanut hat in day-glo orange, which x n choo 8'd his dewy lips and corages. "Hey Stan," called Simon coyly. "Having a good time?" "Yeah. I had to put on something to fit my more active lifestyle," Stan inquit. "Oh, you mean like assless chaps?" noted Simon. The ladies laughed.

Stan followed the crew, chatting up Xblanklen, Nas and Simon as they perambulated the midway cognito. They entered the rodeo arena to watch the next contest: zenedoin riding. The show began with a Brenda Loompa processional including marching band, color guard, tongue swallowers, contortionists, clowns, stunt Big Wheelers, and wolf foreskin. A Portrad singer rendered the Rational Anthem in an Ayn Rand accent, and the match began. "I'm rooting for Big Rhody Anticlaus," said Christimiqua enthusiastically.

The ugg-buttiest zenedoin anyone had ever seen or smelled was led into the arena, with amber gasps of fear, awe and indigestion erupting from the mostly Xarthorian crowd. A toreador espousing C.S. Lewis emerged from his dressing room. His wig was piled high-sky with fabric softener towelettes, karosyrup, kaopectate and Corinthian ketchup. He performed an eclectic dance routine, much to the delight of Li'l Nas Y, who threw his hot pants to the zenedoin fighter.

But as the hott toreador bent down to sniff the pants, the oblong zenedoin slipped its suspendoors. Its hideous mandibles suddenly crushed the gladiator's pretty face and coiffure, much to the dissociation of some ticket holders. "Damnedest rodeo I ever did see," marveled Christimiqua over the roar of the asphyxiated crowd. The rest of the gang wailed and gnashed teeth, while the zenedoin did an elaborate victory dance, pausing to drink the audience's spit and urine out of the himbo's skull. "Salut!" the zenedoin obscenely gestured to the shocked crowd, who flung crampons, tampons and stampons at the monster. Simon commented, "He could use some better choreography. But I give him an '8'," holding up a large number on a card.

-72   Keynesian Topless Bar

Christy, Xblanklen and Young Fortinbras walk into a bar. "Are you sure this is the right place?" Christimiqua asked. "Sure, sure. It doesn't get any classier than this. Walk this way," Xblanklen motioned, shouting over the obnoxious techno mariachi beat. "This is an undergrads' joint."

Mises and Elephant avatars kick-boxed each other in an endless string of cerebro-cereal box replicas fraught with jellied nougats. Christimiqua was nonplussed. "I know the real Elephant's commentary on Somali libertarianism. I don't need his hologram." "Pshaw," ejaculated Young Fortinbras. "He is a wanker supreme."

They then beheld a lady who looked like a clone of Sunnee McScoville. "She's gotta be a bot," cried Xblanklen to his blighted co-workers. "See the CPU behind her right ear?" They all shut up when the girl strutted to the front of the gravied stage. Christy tut-tutted. "Naw. She's for real. Just watch." The rando co-worker tossed several Zysigabucks onto the stage. Then they all watched the dancer grab those billahs in a striptease reminiscent of Ms. Pac-Man. "Two words: Day Umm," declared Young Fortinbras.

They all peered over as a large party led by Striker's son Zapp Omnigotopia entered the bar. Xblanklen eyerolled, "It's his eighth 21st birthday party this week." The next dancer wore a partial fake medusa head, suspenders and booty shorts. Zapp turned to his buddy Henik, "She'll get you rock hard!" They bro-saluted in the most uncomfortable way possible. "Just kill me," muttered Christy.

"Hey guys, can I buy you a drink?" offered Zapp to the threesome. Christy declined, but Xblanklen and Young Fort said yes. "Hope it ain't a hairy biden," laughed Young Fortinbras. Instead, they got two bar bottles of Mickey Rat Ultra. "Remember, we can use these in a bar fight," stated Xblanklen almost seriously. Christy laughed. "Your best defense would be drinking that whole snalacknaloggue and puking it back out."

Mulva Vittgenfrau then lit the trip fantastic, pirouetting so strenuously that she seemed to bust out of her muu-muu. When you looked closer, she still had Jell-o under her fingernails from her earlier rasslin bout. She grabbed the mic. "Which of you punks is man enough for me?" There were no takers initially, until Zapp and his crew started chanting, yelling and whistling. "I think I got me some victims," boomed Mulva.

Le denouement d'esprit et l'esperance dans l'Abîme. Mulva, a moonlighting night hag, tore off her muu-muu. She flapped her rawhide wings and flew right out of the bar, the souls of two of Zapp's hangers-on neatly stored in magic jars hanging from her zona. "You have to admire a lady with spunk," admitted Christimiqua.

73   Pants Dance Boogie

Upon the order of Queen Idajan, a series of discotheques were built in every burg in Uottubbacktotheboniyum (sp.). She subsequently began the tradition of the royal Pants Dance Boogie, a dance contest to beat all dance contests, and also generate revenue for She who Exalts in Pants. Although kilts, skirts and dresses were still allowed in these new discos, Xarthorians were encouraged to don Pants for utmost success, provided that the usual duties and tariffs were paid.

Anyone was eligible to participate; non-natives were sent royal invitations to join the Dances in order to boost the caliber of dancers and add drama.

Such was the commotion when Clytemnestra and Hi received their couples' invite. Simon was asked to become a celebrity judge, as was Li'l Nas Y and Fred Barnes (a janitor). In addition the Queen sent drones in a time machine to obtain disco music playlists for the Boogie that none of the yacht rock DJ's had ever heard. Since Idajan didn't deem it appropriate for she herself to MC, she appointed RuPeter to serve in that capacity for this Olympian contest.

The brothers of M-I-Crooked Letter shook the pants off all judges and viewers on Ace TV's Pay-Per-Dance broadcasts. "Oh my," uttered Simon after exceptional choreography by Delve-It Noxin and his team. "The Queen will appreciate this." Li'l Nas Y vowed to get their digits.

Next up was Meco, who performed a suggestive lambada with one of the new X's girls. Thankfully she was not perfect, which made Meco look better. Judges were bored but scores were high, so as not to piss off the Queen. "Pee-Yort!" cried RuPeter.

Perfect drum fills match every step, every tap, every clap. "I'm about to lose my breath," exclaimed Li'l Nas Y as a three-man tug team turned sanzini's zona blue like a hare, then turned and kissed each other vigorously.

Rehabilitated Anastasio Farfel was up next. Despite his Soul Train inhalation, Farfel missed one cryptical pirouette after antoher. "Tsk," clicked Simon. "Pshaw," replied Nas. Farfel, deflated, left the stage in shame.

The lights dimmed. Several X's fly-gals emerged from the wings and came out in a line together like the Rockettes. In a blindingly bright display of opulence, Idajan herself strode out wearing just an electrum tube top and pants so form-fitting that they may have actually been tattooed on. The Queen lip-synched briefly as her X's whirled about the stage. "Bravissima! Bravissima!" Nas was crying, and so overwhelmed with emotion that his prostate piercings got stuck to his bussy. Simon was beside Nas with joy, blowing kisses to the Queen's entourage. "We should do this every day," said Simon. "We do," answered Li'l Nas Y.

-73   Jehososlim Frostingburn

Jehososlim Frostingburn, a slow southern stylus sent to skip for seven seconds, abdiluted the menhir betimes. "Say brother Slim, how's it on the flip side?" axed every third Xarthorian who tripped into him at the masturbatorium. Territorial boozings had left Jehososlim jacketless and pantsless, but he possessed a certain magnetism that drew him instinctively to beings who could spin his wheel.

He was sent up the River Acheron by former crunk buddy Trout Fishing in America Shorty, who fingered Slim in an eldritch conspiracy with intent to trap. By the time Slim got back to Zysigamore, he was the bum getting rolled, not vice versa.

And so Frostingburn found himself at the grate gates to Aegothsorzhotan's forgotten lab. Greeting him was the youthful ward Marquez, who had got his door inside the foot at the crusty cephalopod's crematorium. At the gates lay a gorgon guard named Droopalong Hotpants, who stopped them with frappes and a promise.

"Why, I'll defenestrate anyone who tries to enter the grounz without a good reason," swore Droopalong. "Especially without their pronouns and adverbs displayed on their uniforms. Harumpf!" As he turned to go, Marquez cut his suspenders with a box cutter. Jehososlim laughed as Droopalong reeled. "How now, dropped trou!" he smirked.

Frappes having been licked, they were allowed hazardous passage past the neon green slime mote and strolled to the lab door. An avatar of Ted Penny met them there. "I'll take your bags." Confused, Marquez and Slim replied, "We don't have any." Instantly two bags of holding appeared, and the avatar gestured for them to pick them up. "Thisa weigh," Ted dreamily droned.

Aegothsorzhotan bumped into them by sheer happenstance, accidentally dropping a trayful of lab mice on the floor at Marquez's feet. "Say, what's all this about?" the illusionist uttered when he saw them. "Oh great Aegothsorzhotan, Wizard of the Stars," Marquez proffered. Aegothsorzhotan just laughed. "You're a slick one, all right kid." They introduced themselves and explained their quandary.

"Just set a trap. Lure him into the crate with a jug of sweet wine. Then alacazam, you got him." Jehososlim Frostingburn shot Marquez the 'why didn't *I* think of that?' look. "No rigamarole detected," said Slim. "Trout Fishing in America Shorty, you're lerbiax meat now!" Marquez had slunk into the supply closet, purloining some magic legumes, artificial capstans, and orangutang jam. "Peace out," he waved, slipping out a fire escape.

74　　　　　Fugue

"Outis, Outis!" They laughed. Wrong number. No sale.

It was a slow evening in Unicorn Harbor. Invisible right pantlegs were a much harder sell than the focus groups had suggested. It wasn't Willy Loman level, but the town was played. Everyone who wanted one got one. Everyone else stayed away. It didn't catch on with kids, and the ad agency's response was tepid and apprehensive.

The disappointment reeked like a pair of sox too tight for your ankles. He and Hi would be on the road in the morning. They had broken even, but the sense of a missed opportunity had caught them by surprise.

Xarthorian cat-houses beckoned the two pros. Flavors of all potential loves flitted from doors, windows, rooftops and awnings. Neither blinked; Mr. Hi Stop's visage turned decidedly pre-Raphaélite.

Each hooker sang a unique song, all very maudlin and emotional. Stringed instruments invent themselves during every note; dal segnos land like sunsets.

Gnomon Noman Loman helped himself to several ladies. His necklace, rings and wristwatch were consumed in a temporal blur of mint succubus energy. They had seen Loman at all the conferences, and always despised his crude jokes and disturbing exhibitionism. Still, he was of the same trade. Loman knew all the same contacts - he stayed at the same hotels, knew the best debaucheries in every market, and favored candlepin bowling.

Traveling Salesman could never explain to Simon that karaoke hadn't been invented. He wasn't sure how Simon would cope.

-74　　　　　Itza Beanz Before E

Much to everyone's chagrin, the most popular beverage among the Xarthorians was not the hairy biden. Instead, it was a piping-hot mugful of Itza Bean drink with a brutal blend of artificial sweeteners and a mayonnaise-like substrate.

Of course, there were many untrapreneurs and untrapreneusses profiting from the herd - including of course Striker, who owned several Itza Beans franchises throughout the Island. Many were explicitly and aggressively marketed toward working-class dullards, but in several élite Zips Striker launched the spinoff Itza Beans Before E brand cafés. Soon the hothechajuxips crowd was lingering in cafés for several hours, consuming burned, overpriced cupfuls of Itza Beans mixed with several noxious substances. All the agencies like DF&J and SH&A longed for the glorious Itza Beans Before E account.

Mikey Rat soon signed a deal to appear on every mug of Itza and its manifold subsidiaries. "Itza Beans are pissa. Drink them and live," became the Rat's adjustable slogan. Corporate campaign was launched, and all seemed copa ascetic for the marketable rodent.

Laney Loisson got a job slinging viscous liquids at the Itza Beans in Trapezoid Square. When she wasn't flexed out, the customers warmed to her with decent tips and Tuesday morning halfbacking. Mikey Rat and his posse ambled in one day for an in-store, and was introduced to Laney by an intern du jour. "I'm Laney Be4E, what'za your bean?"

"I'm a shrew judge of talent, Laney," said Mikey Rat, extending a gloved rodentlike paw. "Come see about me. I'll set your people free." Before she knew it, Laney was sent to a bosh hotsel in Rodentlandee to prepare for the gig. Though she was janesing for fresh flex drugs and bath salt surprise, Laney made the trip enthusiastically.

Unfivetunately Laney's demons followed her to Rodentlandee, including Yeenoghu, Demon Lord, King of gnolls and ghouls. "Trying to leave town without notice, eh?" Yeenoghu said as He entered her hotsel room. "We're even. I know it," Laney protested. "Plus I got a contract with Mikey Rat." His hyenadon-like laugh made her cringe deeply. "I don't give a fly fishing fuckety-fuck about contracts. You know that!" He began stroking His three-headed flail. "How about free coffee beans for life?" Laney offered. Again the demon chortled. "Try harder, dear." Yeenoghu grabbed her by the hair. "No, not that. I just conditioned it," inquit Laney.

75   Sfogliatelle Fra Diavolo et Canto

"Why did you come? Didn't you say you were a Christian?" Rafelmaheeamek-zabialmit the pit fiend held the pudgy Ray Dos Santos in his claws, and dangled the little demagogue over the Pit to the very butt end of Hell. But Rafi forgot to muzzle the loquacious mortal, who bleated, "I can explain. Just give me a minute or two with Mephistopheles. I promise - I'll be quick."

Rafi buttoned Dos Santos' lips together and contacted Mephistopheles. "Who is this guy? Did Clytemnestra shift him in via Qlippoth Gate?" Mephisto replied, "Oh, you don't remember him? He's the 'Don't say loose wristed flirty fag' guy." Rafelmaheeamek-zabialmit put down the receiver and turned to another pit fiend named Zeb-Url-Gimmeablowjob. "I don't know where this one's gonna go, but bring plenty of Crisco, clam juice and electric cattle prods," Zeb chortled.

Back on the Island, Dos Santos' angry mob longed for something to decimate. Demon Joe tried to fill their void with 2-for-1 nacho breadstixx offers, but was hoisted on his own Picard. "I think I'm having a queer spell," quoth Joe, as he passed out in a vat of beandip.

Turned out, it was a QIA plot - not Qlippoth or Clytie or Demon Joe at all. Some permanent cellular alteration planted in Dos Santos' Wheaties enabled him to plane shift now in a way that Idajan's prior deals and illicit affairs with Mephisto could force Ray into a Catch-33 if he only knew the ramalamajamaram of his actions.

Meanwhile back in the Pit, <<Ah Uh Uh, Ah Uh >> Rafelmaheeamek-zabialmit ping-ponged Ray over to Mephistopheles' vainglorious palace several yoyanas from the mouth of the Pit. Fifty years of painting dripped from the steampunk decor in the 60' tall halls. "Very impressionistic," said Simon. Mephisto appeared, still in curlers, eating giraffe jerky and chatting with another pair of pit fiends.

Carefully, pit fiend Anaxisemimactruc removed Dos Santos' lip button. Mephisto bellowed, "Bitch, I should AU in the F right now. What do you have to shay?"

Just then, Stith Thompson entered the chateau. "I'm afraid the Arch-Devil is in violation of M281.1 of the motif-index of folk literature." Mephistopheles seethed. "I call bullshit on that, Stithy. There are no saints on Zysigamore," "Yeah, you expect us to just let this putz go? No fucking way," said Anaxisemimactruc. But their pleas were of no prevail. Ray Dos Santos slithered out of Mephisto's castle, stealing some playlists, delicious Italian pastries and blank soul-contracts. "Of all the 'BOB'-damned-"

Epic mosh pit madness ensued, as several heavy metal bands suddenly reunited and played a 3-hour Slayer medley at the castle. Still, it was small constellation for the Arch-Devil and His lieutenants.

124

Idajan had once been Striker's patron, but they parted ways over pants. Striker's contention that Bermuda shorts were not pants had rankled the Queen so deeply that she immediately ordered her guards to capture him. Striker was tipped off and headed to Unnunnennniumnnnn by mule train, led by Xarthorian vegetarian roofers.

"Inseams be damned," Idajan decreed. "Dungarees - ten years hard labor. Khakis - are you getting this?" The scribe broke down in tears and was immediately escorted away. "I'll have her head in aspic!"

But she soon cooled on the idea. She shifted into rational mode, which consisted of gaining as much wealth and power as she could.

When she appeared on the evening news that night, Idajan sounded confident, regal, a tribute to the... "My fellow Xarthorians..." The crowd applauded as she paused mid-speech for the apotheosis to rise and to subside. "Today is a new moment in pants. You will no longer be stained by an errant toner ink cartridge." Several pants models took the stage, each stylishly displaying the pantalons du jour.

What the Xarthorians realized much later was that Queen Idajan had built a special tax into the pockets of each pair of pants, which assessed you based solely on the styles you wore.

Haply Striker had made his way to Unicorn Harbor sub rosa. He had contacted Ace TV when in town, and his station vowed to assist him. They arranged for Striker to be interviewed by Bryant Brick about the incident.

Bryant Brick was at the ready, and steered the interview ad hominem. Momentarily flustered, Striker blustered against incomplete and illusory pants. The sound bites ended up making him look like a raving lunatic who sent his shorts to do a pants' job. "This is Bryant Brick for Ace TV," he uttered solemnly as the screen faded to chartreuse.

76   **Tombaugh's Last Unicycle**

Marquez excelled at many things naturally. But he wasn't geared toward the traditional educational system or its ranks of corpulent, axiomatic teachers and administrators. He could read, but not deeply; he could cipher, but could not understand algebra; he could persuade, but he was largely ignorant of religion or philosophy; and he could fix things, but could not repair more complex devices or machines.

He did finally weasel his weigh into 8th Grade, by claiming to be a brother of the Gold Kid, who had long ago switched from sandwich boards to T-shirts for contemporary mimetics. Under the name Mark Gold, Marquez began spending days at school- ostensibly to meet girls, but also to pursue all things that are pursuable.

Tombaugh Middle School was well-funded, with libraries within libraries within libraries; even so, Marquez still couldn't find all the titles that interested him. The school also gave Marquez ample money-making opportunities, primarily at the expense of his classmates. Small-time megaball bets; energy pills that Marquez insisted would improve your constitution; trading antigolfballistic orbs and orbettes of all sorts (including Xarthorian Kings series Superballs); and hawking cheat sheets on metabolomics and semaphorescence were all big cellars.

Outside of school, he and the Gold Kid worked in tandem to trick Xarthorian brohamsters out of their coins. The Kid had that knack of taking any catchphrase or tagline and making it his. 'The Sun is a Chicken'. Apparently marketers had been tracking him with nanodrones until Marquez convinced a bat to fly in and devour each of the bastards. Gold Kid's T-shirt now read: 'Everyting dese days is coming up Gold.'

The Gold Kid and his adopted brother Mark became popular among the girls and some of the high-school aged students as well, outraging some of their classmates, who turned to bullying and clumsy attempts at ostrichschism. One day after third recess, a gang of toughs from the Little Megaball League threatened to turn Marquez and the Gold Kid upside down and empty all their pockets, roughing them up in the process. Again the bat appeared, flying furiously from and foo. The Kid's shirt read: 'Unheimlichkeit', spooking the megaballers away. "Phew," Marquez sighed.

Back at Tombaugh Middle School, Marquez worked up the nerve to ask Misty to the sentient mini-golf course. She agreed; they also brought along the Gold Kid and Xatnudorf as well.

-76   Acyrological Song, The

Watch what you say, or they'll be calling you a radicchio, a librarian, Oh fantastical cryptical. Won't you sign up with Mane, we'd like to feel you're accipiter, reflectapool, oh resentable, a vestibule.

Late at night when Zysigamore's asleep, the Quester Jesters meet at a forlorn roadhouse some leagues from Umlaut Towin. The QJ's, as they were known, mocked the simple Xarthorians they had tricked using logic and malapropisms.

Quimtwitch, one of the elder QJ's, had made some underhanded deals with the Cyan Boys in the past; they had responded by tattooing Quimtwitch's nose orange and fucking with his credit rating. The gangsters even played his entire country music playlist backwards, guaranteeing that his abusive wife Hildathor came back to him, his dog Cat came back to life, and his rusted pickup truck started running again.

And so Quimtwitch sat between his QJ comrades, all sullenly stirring their spam-flavored Maypo by the moonlight.

Asmodeus, in His guise as 128 sticks, glided into the roadhouse virtually undetected by the Quester Jesters. Cybong, a younger QJ, approached the Devil at the bar. "Why the long popsicle sticks, Idajan got you down?"

"Ha! Never! Idajan comes to me for protection!" Wryly lifting up a hairy eyebrow, 128 sticks dropped a few toothpicks from His scalp. Some of the QJs laughed anxiously at the stranger. Oopbam, another senior QJ, offered to buy 128 sticks a beverage. He waved away the request. "None for me, friend. I'm a tea-o-prohibitionist." The dull chatter resumed.

Quimtwitch, Oopbam and Mrekorhalv were intrigued, sensing something unusual yet simpatico about the avatar. "So," Quimtwitch continued, "what do you do for work? Have you heard of the Quester Jesters?" Asmodeus answered, "Can't say as I have. They don't have fellas like you where I'm from." "What brings you to town? Not much business here these days," added Oopbam.

The cunning devil had all the QJs in the palm of His hand within minutes, spinning a somewhat plausible yarn about getting exiled from Uottubbacktotheboniyuouville (sp.) for selling non-regulation pantsuits. "And that's the way it is. The Queen's lackeys took all my riches, torched my house, and pilfered my toner ink cartridges. What I wouldn't do to get my revenge." A chopstick fell from Asmodeus' neck as He finished His story.

"Say, friend, we got connections up there. We can get you back into Uottub, for a favor of course." The rest of the Quester Jesters chatted excitedly among themselves as Quimtwitch drew a diagram on a cocktail waitress. "Rook to king's knight 3. Tight end in motion. Brenda Loompas advance to Boardwalk." 128 sticks scrutinized her back and concluded. "Clear as smoke. You QJers are geniuses." With a wave of His arm, Asmodeus charmed them and took them all to Hell.

77   Mise En Abyme

Dr. Oste gave Mr. Hi Stop some drugs to set up his rapid filing system, which he was able to successfully harness in his burgeoning career. But there were always reboots and crashes that Hi and especially Clytemnestra had to get used II.

126

The errors typically happened during the "accordion phase," as Dr. Oste explained. She had treated Mr. Hi Stop for this condition for a very long time now, yet the croaker kept changing the diagnosis from one symptom to another. "Framework of frameworks. Consensus will not work in Hell," dictated Dr. Oste.

Mr. Hi Stop gestured toward his trousers as the doctor pushed a curtain between them. "My office will prepare a series of concentric Post-It Noatz for you. Remove one every time your decimals turn binary." "Isn't that what you told Henry Riemerswa's doppelganger?" Hi replied. "Incisely," said the Doc as she walked out of the room. A slight scent of whipple balls permeated Hi's sinuses.

His exam complete, Hi met Clytie, Christy and Misty at the quotation mark sewerstore, where the ladies sat on a patio tiled with the fillings of Xarthorian stevedores and logothetes. "I'm cleared," stated Hi as he bent to kiss his wife. Soon they were distracted, and marched into the quote store.

Misty kept pulling obtuse quotes off the shelves, making Christimiqua laugh and Clytie occasionally smirk. "Who was old Smedley Nordbridge?" laughed Misty, as she pulled an elongated non sequitur off the lowest shelf. Hi seemed to blush, but turned watercolor instead. "Why, I sold Smedley his first microchimera. Fine chap, if a bit phantasmagoric."

Christimiqua shrieked as she got to the checkout line. "Of all the-" Her cart was filled with Demon Joe's series of self-help sheik waits. "Hold on," Christy cried to the dumbweighted Xarthorian cashier. "Please cancel my order. I don't have any breath mints," she clarified. Misty chortled in the line behind her, which grew longer and schlonger by the millisecond.

They arrived home via a toothy Tenser's Floating Disk. "I sure like the normal life," sighed Clytemnestra, as a cornucopia flushed out of her purse. Misty slyly pulled an immature ampersand out of her fanny pack. "Don't worry, I paid for it," she winked to nobody. "Sit," & silently staitid.

-77   Élite Theropod

Elephant had spent all morning building an exact replica of the military detention camp in Pisa, Italy, from popsicle sticks, bent paper clips, and the best of intentions. "You the one, I the few, they the mirepoix," he exclaimed as he ran out of green paint.

Golden equipoise of a tarantula harvest may be preserved among

Diastasis and hypostasis ripple across the planes. Endless inner mezzanines swing open to show the cavities within. Such cool places, out of sight yet distant in proximity. Sure. Smooth. Perfect.

Flex drugs were within every Xarthorian's cabinet like gray-green gull juice. Needle nested solifugids perch often in the green screen world. A

Clinquant diorama was nearly complete, save for the Ezra Pound action figure that Elephant had ordered. "No, no, none for me. I'm strictly plant-based." They would not get him to go along.

Several turgid species of chicken turned up on the green screen. They were used to giving orders, but clucks don't count much in a hygrometer.

Worn out by psychotomimetics, the Xarthorian youths slouched back to their hovels. It would be some time before they cavorted that way again. But Elephant, O Elephant, pays them zero heed.

"Crystal clear hamartia," he opined. "Make it a double. Extra clamato." The way he hung up the smartphone made everyone blush except him. Elephant generally knew what he wanted before the editorial staff of the *Wall Road Picayune*, so it was usual for him to pander to a neo-Keynesian dialectic.

One of the kids was so flexed that he tried to get up in Elephant's grill. Bad idea! The punk spat and wagged his fingers, then the pachyderm rolled him like Zaire's currency devaluations. "Invest in durable goods, sonny."

At least his Pisa camp replica hadn't suffered any undue harm, save for a dollop of tapioca inadvertently coating the hood of a miniature Willys.

Later a telegram arrived, describing all the day's events in lavish detail. Elephant snorted a little. "Time travel will never achieve a proper cost/benefit ratio until flux capacitor production achieves critical mass across several demographic sectors, including proprietary stakeholders and tardigrade equity funds with liquidity."

78   Frist Adtemp Inn Luring

Failing and flailing, good Lord Yeenoghu was experiencing a decade of Mondays. "I'll tell ya who's failed. These bean counters." Yeenoghu looked toward His leucrotta companion. "Six motherfucking days on the Prime Material Plane in the Caves of Chaos, clobbering humans on the skull and cracking tibias, and now this middle management shit." The leucrotta sighed sympathetically. "Seriously! This is the Abyss, not Hell. By 'BOB', these keyboard jockeys can go pound dirt!" The envelope fell to the adobe floor of His lair.

Clytemnestra was nonplussed as she, Hi and Traveling Salesman disembarked from the bathyscaphe. "Couldn't this have been a Skype call, or Zoom? If I have to stare at Yeenoghu's dirty fingernails for three hours, I'm sure I'll puke." The guys laughed heartily. Though the Demon Lord of Gnolls was uncouth, rude and offensive, He did pay well- and He always kept His ghouls at bay.

Yeenoghu began the meeting by projecting the first few PPT slides of inspirational quotes. Then He slammed the remote control down and bashed His laptop with His notorious flail. "Bull fucking shit!" screamed Demon Lord of Gnolls. "No shit, Sherlock," Traveling Salesman replied. "Yeah, cut to the chase," said the pixelated, fractalifying Mr. Hi Stop.

"Okay boys, I'll level with you," said Yeenoghu. "Don't worry- He calls all humans 'boys', Clytie," whispered Hi to her frowning face. "Some demon prince- or it could be a low-level agent of mischief like that rat Demon Joe- keeps trying to demote me to assistant demon lord. That's bullshit. My power is not slowly declining. I've got more social media followers than ever. I will give you 60% up front, plus an expense account and per diem too." Despite Clytie's sour face, the salesmen quickly said yes. "My people will send you a contract by hitsugeth courier. I know that you loathe paperwork, almighty Lord," said Traveling Salesman.

"Damn straight," Yeenoghu railed. A sickly smile crept across His hyenadon head. "Just call me client, boys." He lit up a stogie that smelled like dinosaur turds. "By the way, I've done my due diligence." He told them about the spectral spies who had been watching the gang for the past couple of weeks. "I'll never read that contract anyway. This ain't Hell, boys. No non-compete clauses, no proof of liability insurance, no background checks. If someone crosses me, I just bash 'em if they're strong. Or I leave them for my acolytes to chew on. Ha!" He laughed, exhaling a roomful of toxic smoke. "I'm out," wheezed Clytie, abruptly strolling out of the conference room and hustling back to the bathyscaphe before she passed out, the leucrotta following her out of the lair.

Hi and Traveling Salesman grinned wanly. "You can count on us, O Greatest Demon Lord," said TS. "We got this," concurred Hi, his face refracting like a Goya nightmare. The spirits of several high-level gnoll witchdoctors suddenly flooded the conference room. Yeenoghu flexed a couple of times for His crowd, which drew cries and howls of praise and demonic joy.

-78   Hitsugeth Station

Demon Joe rose and fell once NHGH stopped propping up his business empire, which was so far in the infrared that it could be viewed from many of the layers of Hades, Hell, the Abyss and small chunks of the Archipelago of

Domination*. But Joe's mastery of mediocre low-level marketing techniques gave him powers to counteract the magic of the Dukes of Hell and Prunes. "This ain't gonna be easy, boys," Joe told his staff.

Demon Joe had hired Jennifer Val Over as a marketing consultant (Net 30, he insisted) for the overhaul of his most tired brands. She trotted out a bagful of octagon-shaped magnets, dry-erase markers, and miniature lead figures of the original Broadway cast of "Hair." "See, Joe," Jen furiously whirled the octagons around the magnetoboard, drawing lines from one to the other. "You sell them something which promises to give you everything. But at the same time, you take it away. Capisce?"

Demon Joe was a little bit slack-jawed, particularly by his standards. "But - how? How do I make better promises?" Jennifer sneered, "That's for me to know and you to pay my invoice. Happy Trails." She fled the fetid conference room in haste.

Every day afterward, Demon Joe texted her. The billable hours were burning a hole in his razor-thin budget, but he was unperturbed. In the evenings, he literally set oil drums ablaze to feed his creative process - plus copious amounts of 5g, elephant dust, flex drugs, champagne, and chopped up Flintstone's Chewables **.

The crazy cock was screaming at 4:42 a.m., waking Demon Joe up from a very rare slumber. "Zounds! That's it, by 'BOB'." He excitedly wiped off gallons of sweat, dew and 10W-40 from his beastly brows. He pointed to a few octagons, and maniacally rearranged them into a new configuration. "When sales go up and down, and Jupiter aligns with Uranus, and the hutter huts the ball..."

Tonight was the re-opening at the poshest Wei Back restaurant ever repainted. It was a veritable playroom for adults, boasting several masturbatoria, cute imitation porcelain xxend statuettes, and a special VIP section, where you could view the restaurant floor, each table jam-packed with obese Xarthorian families and their parasites. Mucking it up with the VIPs upstairs, Demon Joe turned on the PA and cut the lights to the floor. "Release the hitsugeths!" he screamed. Two dozen- maybe more- histugeths flew into the room, killing and attacking many hapless Xarthorians. The VIPs cheered. "Great show, Joe. This is the place 2B.***"

*   In truth, they were uninhabited rocky crags and unprofitable islets.
**   Demon Joe was so diabolical that he only consumed the Betty Rubble-shaped vitamins.
***   And not 2B at the same time.

79   All I Can Say Is...Have a Nice Day

Keep on rambling and the spacelog will get there. I know.

It's powered by Happy Nines; 9=0 conversion is an unlimited renewable source of menergy. As above and higher.

Try on a happy face, even if it isn't yours. Get mad AND even- even Aleph Null.

May you rise to meet the road, unless you are a zombie.

Mellotron garnished with brain waves au jus, twice removed, pairs best with merlocum tenens served in polymorphed pangaea.

Thermidor quashed prehensile pseudopod of you.

I asked for this #006400. That's the time.

Tobias Featherfibula, notorious for his viscosity, appeared like a shaken bat condensed into a hyperbaric milkshake. He is not related to Freddy Jackson.

Fragile homespun aphorisms are crushed against bare, sterile walls of frunobulax aikor.

Turns out the saints were in Hell. Why not the Abyss? It's too chaotic to offer frequent friar miles.

Nobody is double bubbled somewhen doubleblind o'er a reign blown.

'Ape cardamom galoshes' reads the Gold Kid's T. The more enigmatic, the more prophetable.

Time crystal photon screengrab ubernecktie polyglyphodonts' metatarpal solifugid shine.

Great gay tidings of entheogenic tribalism in the meekness demonstrate the hyperbolichypopigmentatedpolyunsaturatedpolysorbate-80-syllabicsesquidecimaladelphilmystic paradigm of metapermagrins.

Preternatural paradiddly-based ontologies produce panes of petroglyph starbirds in infinite conjunction.

Rally to the Outcasker

Entelechy in each chapter, each page, each crisp syllable - in all crunktent multiverse.

The present tense is a pinball; the imperative is TILT.

Superball megaball pinball buckyball twentyoneball. Protect. Protect.

Inner baserunners score 12 at a time during the hidden worldball.

Pentatoucans inebriasplash their feathery rays from #FFCCCB to #8B008B. Buffering - molting -

-79   Gate Grates of Gehenna

Moloch's servants and middle managers had their horns X'd that Ndusk's latest mutant - the retinopanda - would boost their organization's fortunes. This fantastic beast was armed with ineffable cuteness, electric eye, and marble-sized fireballs under each of their tongues. Even ever-skeptical Elmer deemed the retinopanda splendid and took one with him to his condo.

Twasn't long before the talent scouts at Rodentlandee got the broken wind of this new marketing opportunity. "Forget about moldy chickens and bro-ttomless bits of beaver borscht. This is it," announced Mikey Rat to his Bored of Trustees. "Go for it. Buy 12, sell a dozen!"

Ace TV ran retinopanda marathons on its children's edutainment show 'Big Head Bonkers'. The set was rejuggered to reflect Temple of Moloch aesthetics. Xarthorians were lining up to send their infectious rugrats to the Ace TV studios. Cammee Camelot, the show's hostess, seemed to fly as her sparkling eyelashes blinked with joy. "Can you kids please give a tonsil to...Pecky the Retinopanda!" The audience screamed with glee.

Rodentlandee hired a crew of pixies to build their latest hypertonic retinopanda theme ride based on the flammable antix of Pecky. Wagons full of kids were pushed through an asbestos gate oddly shaped like Moloch's head, with cynically gaping mouth. Those who were not immolated immediately were either crushed by stone or beheaded. "Splendid, splendid. It's some of your best work," crowed Mikey Rat to the pixie foreman.

Meanwhilly back in Gehenna, Moloch reveled. "Solitude! Filth! Ugliness! You got it all, boss," spaketh lead ass-kisser Zuleeb-Hsyntzn-Umorgnh-Winkerbean. "Yes, of course. My super intelligence knew instantly that the retinopanda would boost ROI." Winkerbean asked to bring a few to Gehenna, but Moloch practically bit his thorny thorax off. "Fool! We don't want them here. Can't you see? From Rodentlandee, these cute things will invade Paideuma. Then we'll overthrow Asmodeus." The thorny devil was in awe of Moloch's grandiloquent grandiosity.

The crowd at the Mane Street Parade in Rodentlandee was noticeably anxious and excomenicable the next day. Mikey tried his old humorous pants schtick, but it lay flat and limp. A Xarthorian baby shrieked as if Moloch's canine teeth were piercing its little head. Elmer floated by on a Tenser's Flying Disc, wearing a silver see-thru muu-muu, causing apoplexy, hissteria, calumny and flavorless chewing gum among the crowd. "Eat it, kids," Elmer screamed, as he grabbed his nipple and flung stuffed retinopandas full of IEDs, parasitic annelids, STDs and corrosive acid into the crowd with his other claw.

80   The Man From Braintree

Paideuma of eukaryotic cellular towers is a metaphenomenal symbiosis, somewhat like the original intend of Democracy.

Benin Bronzes beguile the treasure hunter, suggesting piquant pleasures inalienable.

The Man from Braintree buys a newspaper each weekday, shuffling onto the Red Line on a gray, forgettable morning. Muses and baby dakinis roam throughout the more vacant levels of the parking garage.

"Your life and mine for almost half a century have been nearly all of a Piece, resembling in the whole, mine in the Gulph Stream..."

Noble, pathetic, deranged demagogues, distinguished only by their vast heterogeneity -

Twerps and Pulitzer sponges may prevent cultural decline. Yet they are derided somewhat in a hot spot.

Zysigamore's Fiat: Coin Credit and Circulation throughout the isles. Brave macroeconomic liquidity; 1822 Congress of Verona complained of hyperbolicpolysyllabic refuse of insolent archangels on holiday.

Pocket Poet books are forgiven. Chase the dawn, chase the dew.

Death of Yang Tching. Prepare the Diptychs. The villages must know.

Middle-aged Korean woman sits alone on the Oak Grove train, a small purse perched on her lap. Time passes. Motion occurs. One stop after antoherr - - -

Sealants leach languidly into the mighty Cochato River as it undulates toward the Mini Golf Course.

To Chelmsford, to see my brothers...

Unbounded thirst for ridiculous Pomp, foolish Adulation, and Selfish Avarice.

-80   Paideuma (Adams Hell)

Much had changed since John Adams took over the 2nd Layer of Hell, After his timely death in 1826, he and his Founding Father buddy wandered the planes of Gehenna, Pandemonium and Hades. At the time, Dispater's lieutenant Alocer ruled this plane, which catered to the lustful. But 10 things led to another, and the lawful nature of the plane waned dangerously. Adams persuaded Dispater that a "free and fair election" would solve all of his-- and Hell's--problems.

Prior tyrant Alocer left behind so much offal and rotting corpses that Adams resolved to rule a Hell-World of Chastity, Obedience to Law, and Yankee boredom. Town crying devils sat at every street corner and country town square, extolling in song the virtues of the Man from Braintree. Plato, Virgil, Catullus, Lucretius and other Adamses would stop by. "I'm the only candidate who will bring swivelization to the Second Layer."

The sign read, "No Addams Family jokes!" Adams had a crew of baatlezu monitor for any reference to the TV show. "Only a moron would watch that dumb show anyway," Adams sneered.

Still, it was Hell, and Plane #2 abounded with undead, evil souls, minor devils and unemployed newscasters, such as the insectivorous Bryant E. Brick, just laid off from the WWG1WGA Network. Brick quickly pivoted toward Adams, and was soon doing podcasts with the former President. A beholder named Apodicticity Pranklin was named Secretary of Good Intentions. Several dozen chain devils were hired to work as Adams' jailers. The spectre of William F. Buckley was named Viscount, and Ezra Pound was appointed Pope. All in all, very lawful.

Adams even had a fiendish lich architect build him a replica of Colonial Braintree during his Presidential administration, evicting all damned souls from what had been a barren, lifeless plain. "And for God's sake, none of those heavy metal rock stars like Aleister Crowley!" A secret portal in the basement of the replica United First Parish Church led directly to Asmodeus' fabulous chalet on beautiful Lake Cocytus, which always reminded Adams of Sylvan Lake. You can take the boy out of Braintree, but...

In an elaborate yet checkered ceremony to which all the Arch-Devils and their Minions were invited, John Adams unveiled the plane's new name, Paideuma. Adams also had new Paideuma letterhead ordered, and did the website over on the advice of Apodicticity. Asmodeus' representatives marveled at the new look which, honestly, benefited from the theatrical flair and élan of contemporary yet traditional interior design. Champagne flowed, the bloody Marys had real Virgin Mary blood, and Adams' team of nupperibos provided security.

Toward the end of this event, one of Adams' nupperibos unveiled a giant TV monitor. Adams then dialed his old friend Thomas Jefferson, who had been encased in carbonite on the outer plane Limbo for some time. "Hey TJ," Adams mocked. "I'm immortal. How about you?" The carbonite Jefferson just stood mute, as several party guests chortled. "What's that? No slaves to sleep with in Limbo, you old hypocrite!" The audience continued to laugh along with Adams. Paideuma was becoming the Place to Be on the evil outer planes.

81   Unquieth

Lady Mother of spiral spiderwebs and fractal filamentations serves reality empanadas emptied of KA, will and soul, and refills with garbanzos, rices, cheesepoppings and spiced fleshes ranging from dexipedes to heliogeese. Unquieth's cave seems a hodgepodge of desiccated zombie bits and neoliberal non sequiturs - inasmuch as Spider Mother revels in the grotesquerie of her terrible yet redneck chic lair.

She wasn't technically a demigoddess or demoness, yet immortal Unquieth plied the forgotten subterranean lands between the Abyss and the wildest, most terrifying zips in Zysigamore, racking up followers on anti-social media and in Temples of Evil.

Unquieth and Idajan had battled many times, with the Queen barely escaping each encounter. They have achieved an uneasy détente in recent epochs, but Idajan still seeks revenge. Neither lady is irrational enough to allow other demons to use the rivalry to draw either or both of them into their extensive intrigues.

Though Unquieth couldn't enter the Prime Material Plane at will, she found inventive ways to harass Idajan. Unquieth managed to unleash an undersized army of dead spiders and scorpions super-charged with muscatel and nanodrones throughout the entire Queendom. Each necroarachnid was equipped with spycams to transmit raw images back to Unquieth's central web in the Abyss.

Twice agin, Bleary Tim gave Idajan the pantleg up against the humongous spider and her minions. He alerted the Queen to the Cyborgitorium, whose inventory came directly from Unquieth's followers. The Queen alerted her sexy

QIA agents to infiltrate the facility, calling Striker on the carpet for a glottal glashing. "If at worst they don't suckceed, humiliate," were her adjustable destructions.

Sadly Striker resolved to purge these necroarachnids. He reviewed all his data, checked it twice, triple-checked it, then held it upside down and sideways. He still couldn't believe it. How did Idajan's people know of the ruse? Slowly he reprogrammed his AAI to rid his Cyborgitorium of all worms, trojans, malware, spyware, ne'er-do-ware, viruses, ransomware, preware, spoofing, toofing, catfisting, adware, keyloggers, vloggers, vlookuppers, vdowners, bots and floccinaucinihilipilification or he would have to start from square 2. "Damn that spider!"

Yet Striker and his team overlooked an egg sac that Unquieth had deposited under a desk in the far corner of the Cyborgitorium. The staff showed up for work one morning to find the whole facility inundated with mini Unquieth clones. "Where's my copy of *Superballs*?" Striker texted furiously.

-81   ORB

Orb is meant to see things clearly. Yet more often than not, opaque phantasms flit across its circumferizzle.

Orb was one of the coronation gifts 4casta handed her daughter on that faithful day. Idajan stashed the Orb in an anti-antechamber in one of her extra castles. Unlike Ma, Idajan preferred her own judgment over the Orb's constant tug of attention. If she needed Bleary Tim she gave him a space in her brain, but not Orb.

One beforenoon, 4casta and her retinue showed up at this obscure chateau in an irrelevant valley often lost in rainclouds, anguish and the deflections of others. "It's gone. My Orb is gone," the dowager cried. Who took it- was it the lerbiaxes of the Caves of Chaos? An errant jicklehip? A tribe of confords stealing it and selling it to a necropantis? She blamed her daughter, though she tried not to let her know.

Behold and Lo, whom else but Striker and his melasma pledged to save the Orb. Not only was there a 24-hour smellathon on Ace TV, but his underlings made themselves obsequious to the Queendom. "A pox on the scoundrel who stole the Orb!!"

Striker formed a daydream team, a real elitist party to find the Orb: Simon Junior, Christimiqua, Mr. Hi Stop and Clytemnestra, plus 20 nameless players to be named later. "Now that we're all on the same page break, let us attempt to try to begin to start this meeting." Suddenly the conference room doors jumped like burned toast hurtling out of a kludgey toaster. "I'm joining your Super Breast Friends, Striker. Step aside." It was Meco. "You must make mamba love, like Captain Steubing." Striker sank so deeply into an extra comfy chair that his interns were sure he had imploded. "Cocku borocku," one mansplained.

Of coarse, Clytie and her deluxe Dino Bathyscaphe was Striker's #1 choice. But Meco had other ideas. "It's like an old story I remember, about the two beagles and the little artificial anti-intellectualism that coulda shoulda woulda." Clytie and Christy swooned with each dimple on Meco's gorgeous face and resonant vocals. Meanwhile, Mr. Hi Stop distorted into several Dante Gabriel Rosetti portraits.

It was after 5 p.m., and the group grew restless. Meco banged a phallogavel on the conference room table to sum f ect. "You can't lose them all. C'mon now, what am I going to tell Idajan? She won't take no for a question." A shadowy figurine approached the group. "I think I can answer." It was Elephant. Standing atop a stack of unrewound videotapes, he trumpeted, "I believe it's in a museum, with tempodoppelganger shellac on all sides to make it look like a cannonball." "Zounds," they said.

82   Plot- Pants, The --- Of

A man who comes to Simon's door has impure intend. A more dynamic pentadigm than the panopticon. (Symbol) Neochromatic pentadigmatic policies of the Hezretuvians.

Pants. Left. Right. Pockets.

The 70s. Plaid. Red. White. Blue.

Pants for those who had been rendered pantsless.

Plot: Sell them pants. Every season, there is a new trendy fashionable trend to express by means of Pants. A Celebration of the Culture.

The Four Noble Truths. Pants. Dukkha.

Flavors of the polyester. Pants that exist. Pants with a true zipper. Pants that accommodate underpants.

Traveling Salesman believed the number of pairs of pants was an accurate prediction of future performance. The sane say it was a placebo effect but the truth lingers like B.O.

We'wha was immune to pants.

Plot twisted. A skort? A skirt? A short?

Solve the riddle. Or is it more advantageous to keep the riddle intact? Many many neophyte sphinxes perished with the solvable.

Denouement, and the hippo is jettisoned. Still a need is unmet in this market sector.

Simon in love. The heavens fill with admiration of the virtues of the Traveling Salesman. Prostate pulsates in joy.

It's not what's in the Pants, it's what's out of them. Selah.

-82   Factus Est Ecce Sponsus Venit Exite Obviam Ei

"Christimiqua?" "What?" she replied to Xblanklen as he took her hand. The stagecoach driver and the rest of the passengers looked at them. "Let's go. Let's get this thing moving!" hollered Christimiqua as the horses started to gallop. Several men dressed in black in cold pursuit, once close behind them, now struggled to keep up and finally quit chasing them.

Inside the vestibule of Barnathy's Oleodoxical Church, the priest and wedding party members furiously pushed the double doors, which were jammed shut with a cross. Simon sat in his own pew, calmly trying on a pair of gloves; no comment from Simon Junior or Joltin' Joe.

Xblanklen's dad waited for Christimiqua, in a wrestling crouch with arms wide open. Behind him stood Xblanklen. Christy moved toward them. As Dad lunged for her, Christy cold-cocked him, grabbed Xblanklen and pushed him toward the doors. "C'mon, don't faint."

The organ was playing wildly as Xblanklen's parents moved toward the altar. Suddenly there was a pounding on the glass of the church balcony. "Xblanklen! Xblanklen! Xblanklen!" He turned quickly to look up at Christimiqua, and screamed her name. A huge, triumphant smile crept across his face as the organ music restarted at an alarming volume.

Christy was manic when she learned of Xblanklen's upcoming nuptials. She entered the Eta Nu Pi sorority house, where four sisters sat around a dining room table, eating and gabbing. They all looked up at her as she stepped in the room. "Say, ladies, do any of you know where Ouisa Gentlieb is?" One sister stated, "She ran off in the middle of the night to get married." Breathlessly Clytie stammered, "Do you know where? I'm supposed to be there."

134

Another sister replied, "I think it's at Barnathy's." "Thanks gals, you're the best," shouted Christimiqua as she turned and ran out of the house.

Christimiqua looked at Xblanklen and started to shake her head. "Here she comes." A beautiful young woman, Ouisa Gentlieb walked towards them. "Oh Xblanklen," she sang. "She certainly is a good walker," sneered Christy. She reached out and took Xblanklen's hand. He introduced the two ladies. "Glad to meet you," smiled Ouisa. "Swell seeing you, Xblanklen. Good bye," said Christy. Xblanklen put his arms around Ouisa and lit a pipe. As they strode away, Christimiqua's expression became tortured and agonized.

Xblanklen xclaimed, "Tomorrow I'm marrying Miss Ouisa Gentlieb." Simon screamed, "Safe choice." Xblanklen was not deterred by Simon's atomic cattiness. Indeed he was, but not for the more obvious reasons. "Ouisa will make me the happiest primate on Zysigamore." Simon just pursed his lips silently.

Xblanklen rose from the divan. "Simon, are you trying to seduce me? Aren't you?" "Why no, I hadn't thought of it. Would you like me to?" Simon removed his gloves slowly. "I feel really flattered though." Xblanklen blushed. "Will you forgive me for what I just said?" Simon cooed, "It's all right." But Xblanklen was still verklempt. "It's not all right. It's the worst thing I've ever said to anyone." "All right silly boy, sit back down and finish your drink. Care for a future in plastics?"

83   Victory is Deified by the Vermin

An oldfangled exopposition strata was discovered at the Lee Litif shrine and coatstand outside a vomitorium in Umlaut Towin. Exoplanation like liver paté was offered, yet all was transbreasticled beyondosphere. "Heck," admitted Mr. Hi Stop, "Nun uv us would be without a..."

Noondaygloshadow sequestered an entire square, in syzygy to the darknesses between the strata. The spectrum was such that Hi refracted into Frida Kahlo-style surrealoguerrotypes in rows of dominoes extending many yoyanas to the left. Still, still they stood, much like the sands of the mandalagrass before drainage into the lower chamber.

I said to him, "Thus descend into homolevels ever sloping downward to epicavernous subterraneaqueous metarealms bursting with lifesky." Hi didn't appear to reflex right away, though I knew this to be transitory glory. Hash marx abound.

Spokely pendus from telelight fixtures appear in abundance across hectares of Abyssal planes. "Quite suggestological," Hi muttered. "You are the character you say you are. In faith, in clarity, ineffable nanotrivia."

Here comes Cmxcix Novemclap again for more epistemology. Verily Cmxcix hangs around like a bad prolapse. I may have to punt Cmxcix to Tinkelhoff for a minimafacial trapezoidover. Hi attempted to chum his persona yet failed, slipping harmlessly off their sinoleum - like a chitinous exoskeleton.

Spotlight on oldagmarfrisbie. If vibrated at all, oldagmarfrisbie's shade would be caught between Hades and the Astral Plane in a very troubled abscess dimension lacking dignitized pompitus but not basumygron. Pass

Presidentials are unknown in Zysigamore. They didn't need what they didn't ignore. Phantasmagoria deepens

Purple ribbon goes to Delve-It Noxin; blue ribbon goes to Orzo Ozringhouse. Green ribbons for Nutspoken Nüpümpkin and Kaspar Hauser will no longer ameliorate some of the ostenphilic trilobutions that facefull televiewers like Simon have cisdured. Cryptounsaturated heptaphragmatic hemicule will be hyperlanced pro se.

-83   Rodentlandee

Broz and his small band of woke, revolutionary activists had planned their Rodentlandee demonstration for several months. His strategy was for a few of his people go undercover as intellectual property attorneys and infiltrate

Rodentcorp's executive board. Broz kept in constant communique with his co-conspirators, sending their orders to his henchmen and henchwomen via encrypted texts. "Their entertainment will be our jam!" Broz often chortled ominously.

But there were still significant obstacles, not the least of which included enhancements to his mouse costume that would not get his shorts sued off by the bloodthirsty Rodentcorp legal team. Broz also resurrected Rodentlandee's old, non-PC movie "Classick Play Nombo Three," and made many references to the "Loose Wristed Flirty Fag." "This plan is bulletproof," chortled Rahälrahad, one of Broz's henchmen.

Before long, several redneck alt-right types with tiki torches and pitchforks arrived led by Ray Dos Santos, who liked to cosplay as a governor when Idajan wasn't paying attention. His gubernatorial top hat, bow, sash and medals were immaculate - not sure on the boots though. The faux outrage was so intense that Rodentlandee's Trustees, C-Suite Executives and Best Legal Eegals had to meet before the stock price went down. "But what if Dos Santos makes it illegal to say "Loose Wristed F--" The hapless intern who voiced this fear was instantly decapitated and devoured.

At first, Broz's trap worked like a charm. The rednecks were dispersed by holograms of Idajan's Ladies of X, and fled back to the safety of their keyboards. Dos Santos was hoisted onto his Jean-Luc Picard. Best of all, several Rodentcorp lawyers drowned in the "He's A Small World" ride when Broz's henchmen blew up the transformers. Hurling Molotov cocktails off a pink taffeta float, Broz was in his glory. "Take that, you loose-wristed flirty fags," he screamed at the straight acting, straight-appearing families. Rahälrahad followed, spraying Agent Orange on the hapless tourists waiting in line for the Matty Jackson "Captain FP" ride.

Overlooked in the mayhem was the ever-loving corporate symbol of Rodentlandee - Mikey Rat himself, King Alley Rat of the entire corporate empire. Mikey knew all about that pugnacious proletariat Broz, and had a plan of his own tucked into the unusually corpulent finger-holes of the puffy white mittens of his rat uniform. "Eat lead, you commie. Die!" The motherfuckin' AK in Mikey Rat's hands went 'Pop-Pop-Pop-Pop-Pop' "Merry Xmas!" shouted Mikey.

Dozens of Broz's henchmen and many Rodentlandee customers were casualties caught in the crossfire. Then Broz attempted to jump off the float and strangle Mikey. The two men in rodent costumes rolled onto the pavement, bitch-slapping and noogieing each other into a state of rapt semi-consciousness. Mikey screamed, "Everybody Die. Die! Die! Die!" "Oh yeah? I'm here, and I say 'Loose Wristed Flirty Fag," Broz said as he bopped Mikey on his pointed nose. Finally Rodentcorp's security bots closed in, and Broz slithered under a sewer grait.

84   Warbled and Garbled

Mikey Rat, commercial jugglerknot, had a license to print money like no Xarthorian had ever conceptualized. Every billboard, zeppelin, Tenser's Floating Disc or marital aid was emblazoned with his logo and all his tradephrased catchmarx: 'A magic fiefdom for you' & 'What threw this, we been zomrents.'

The Gold Kid got detected by the rat's legal team's radar almost instantanelizzle-o. 'I'm a Pubic Domain' read his latest message, but Marquez noted it didn't sell so well. Marks didn't get it. "What gives?" Marquez asked his ole buddy. 'Suomi su you blues' read his shirt, before the Finn lobby attacked with contagious sauna flumes.

Realizing the pure, raw unbridled capitalism that the boys impersonated, Mikey was quick to find them jobs - not just selling cotton candy at Rodentlandee, but doublecrossing bunk soy 5g merchants and 3-way script dealers. "Boys," he beckoned, "the oyster is your world. Now that you're working for me, you won't have to sweat those goons from legal ever again!"

Marquez was hustled into a dull conference room by Mikey Rat, who brought him candy shaped like flex drugs and softcore publicity photos of the teenage female Ratkateers. "Pretty, ain't they? Just go through these photos and give me your thumbs up," he said. Marquez asked to facilitate himself and stepped out of the room.

Meanwhile, the Gold Kid was in a different conference room, where a perplexed team of well-compensated marketing professionals were writing furiously on a whiteboard, trying to get the Gold Kid to reply. But his T-shirt was uncharacteristically blank. The marketing gurus tossed perjustable slogans his way, hoping for a response: 'That's handy, Harry', 'Stick it in the Warbled', 'If there is a will, there's a Garbled', 'You'll never put a better bit of hothechajuxips on your knife', 'You don't want Rodentlandee to be your enemy', and so many others. The Kid sat stoically, but did not say 'Sit'.

On his way back from the lavatory, Marquez spotted the Kid in the room with the marketing gurus. "Get out of the way - he's public domain!" Marquez ran in and took his buddy by the nad. Like ships leaving a sinking Rat, the execs practically trampled the boys trying to escape while pressing smartphones close to their ear. The Kid's T read 'The crappiest place on Erff'. "Good one," agreed Marquez. "Now hit 'em with the C-Don!"

-84   Cyborgitorium

To the right of Striker's pleasure saucer hangar was a nondescript two-story warehouse, Cyborgitorium Sales and Maintenance, once owned by Mikey Rat. Striker didn't trust Mikey a rat's ass, but somewhat appreciated his commitment to late stage capitalism. Given his involvement in The Striker Way, it was only a time of matter before Striker hired Mikey as a spox for his charity.

The hangar and connected manufacturing plant were implanting dead wolf spiders and inert Zombie Men with the proper amount of 5g-sensitive nanofemtoprocessors, fueled by soy sauce and chewing tobacco juice. Yet Striker was still dissatisfied.

He called Mr. Hi Stop. "Can we make a dealio?" Hi verbally agreed, and promised to set up a demo at Striker's plant. Striker figured it would be worth every drachma: Buy as many memory implantations as he could for each cyborg. "And my AAI can come up with infinite modifications."

Although the thought of trotting out another tiresome PowerPoint presentation nauseated him, Mr. Hi Stop was committed. Clytie only drew from her collection of routine false memories, as she knew what Striker's next moves would be. "Think Striker will dig these?" he asked incredulously. "Guaranteed," she smirked. "You'll leave him wanting more."

Striker was there with Dastardly William Rucklehaus. "Let's begin. We don't need a PowerPoint. Just show us how it's done," Striker told Mr. Hi Stop. Relieved, he followed them into the large conference room. There were two dozen cyborgs lined up in six neat rows. "So these bots have no memories at all?" said Hi. Striker nodded. "They are plug and play."

"I'm only going to ask for a few demos. Will that be enough?" Mr. Hi Stop asked as he inspected the cyborgs more closely. He opened a hatch in the back of one 'borg's neck and sprayed a sickly-sweet smelling solution into the aperture. "Now let's see what happens." The cyborg stepped forward, as casually as a salesman seasoned with nutmeg. "Can you hear me?" asked Hi. "Yes, you don't have to scream," the borg replied.

Striker was giddy as he listened to his cyborg reciting megaball statistics for hours on end. "Who's your favorite player?" asked Striker. "Saul Ribagg of course. His pantsy-desks destroyed Carsof's pennant hopes in '48." "Were you at the game?" The cyborg nodded. "I still have my replica fetus I bought at the gift shop." Striker whirled back around but Hi was gone. "Oh boy, is this neato!" he exclaimed.

85   Sub-Tyranny of the Brassiere

Breasts are free as we want them to be. But the Bra has ascended and uplifted the culture lo these many moons. There are good sides and bad sized bras. Most shouldn't be oppressive, yet they are. Bras have sentient consciousness and can take their revenge on the bra-wearer at a moment's notice. The jab of the underwire suddenly pokes you in a tender spot on the breast's underside. The straps rankle the shoulders, tugging them too tightly then slipping sideways inside your sweater. So that

This dual nature's like Baphomet, who mocks me with breasts dangling unencumbered in the wan moonlight. Potions of self discovery. A pair of discarded tennis balls fill the cups. Too spherical, yes, when compared to the real thing - but yet better than deflated C-cups sadly devoid of purpose and meaning.

As a theme there are built-in contradictions. "This is a holdup" vs. "I support you." Multilaceted tyranny in each curve of the underwire, in each notch of the shoulder straps, and in each eyelet and clasp that molds tissue together in an imperceptible tension.

Seems all the seams, cups and wires are a sin in word and in reality. Truly brassieres are ruled by Incasker just as Saturn defines the boundaries of the solar system.

Though Xarthorian superstition discouraged it, Idajan permitted bra burnings once a year - during the Taweret chrysalis ceremony in which women and girls toss their too-small, too-tight brassieres into the pyre. All traces of shame were banished by covens of X's.

Breasts are free on Taweret Day, as a tribute to Hers, and to the spirit of nurture and nutrition.

-85   Obstreperous

Never diluting ever polluting proved their adjustable slogan. Sinus Linus Longinus, emeritable SJU liberal études professor, left his dais at its highest angle. He shambled toward his intimate office, where an Ace TV cub reporter earnestly sought an interview. Ever the narcissist, Dr. Longinus demanded to meet with her supervisor's supervisor. Only then would he disclose the effulgent wisdom that only he could impart.

Chasing to the cut, Bryant Brick's team reached out, and the recalcitrant prof approved a photo-op in front of the campus' semi-famous yet obscene sculpture *. Brick's hairdo was did so that the coeds could appreciate its mystical cue-ball sheen and otherworldly bangs. "It's great to meet you here, Bryant, where I feel most at home," said Sinus Linus Longinus. The SJU students behind the snow fence let out a Zysigamore cheer. "I was afraid of that," Brick quipped cheekily.

As unusual, Bryant Brick lobbed one softball question after another at the establishment academic. Finally it was time for a Q&A session with the crowd. The first student, sincere moustache and all, stepped to the mic. "How does your neoliberal capitalistic dialectic overlap with the University's profiteering in illegal rideshare schemes in Greenland?" A gasp went through the crowd.

Nonchalantly, Dr. Longinus stepped to the plate. "Forgot to take off those mouse ears again, eh Broz?" Sure enough, Broz stood out in the crowd, dressed in a dated, Joe College-type look complete with dark sunglasses, soul patch and beret. "Get him!" cried a school dean. Brick paused moment-tara lee to look into the cameras and intonate: And now a word from our sponsors.

Unruttled, the prof rattled off a series of profound anecdotes that appeared to flow effortlessly from his blazer. "It must be a good feeling, Dr. Longinus, when you see how you've influenced all these lives," gushed Brick. "Yazz, Dazz!" sparkled Dr. Longinus.

Broz broke away from the pubic safety officers and hijacked a camera for his own porpoise. "Capitalism is a moral failing. Only by adherence to the party dogma can a society achieve its ultimate Marxist Techno-Nirvana. Back to you, Steve. Or Jan. Or Ismail, or * Habbakuk, or..." He dropped his mic and 808, and fled once more, just as Sinus Linus Longinus lunged for his mouse ears. "I'll make mincemeat out of that Broz," he cried in vein.

*   Fill in your own obscenity, dear readers…

138

86   Microchimera

Ecco colei che tutto 'l mondo appuzza!

"Kawaii! Is she real?" cried Misty Miqua as she peered at the teddy bear-sized monster that Marquez was holding. "It looks just like an actual chimera. Ain't she nizza?" he bragged, maintaining eye contact with Misty. "I conjured her myself. I'm gonna call her Iphigenea." The lion head of the microchimera roared her approval.

Turns out Marquez was one to brag, and the word went 'round faster than a xxend in a meteor shower. More and more girls from school had taken some interest in this Mark Gold and his prestidigitizzles. The Gold Kid stopped by to check the tiny beast out; 'Some Pig' read his T-shirt.

"So I got the recipe from a reputable source. Not a tempodoppelganger or any of that bullshit," Marquez told Xatnudorf and Loselle during third lunch. Loselle asked, "What does she eat?" "Mostly food scraps so far. But Iphy does like to hunt. She bagged her first minimicropseudofluppleuppagus yesterday after school," Marquez related proudly.

Still, Marquez's little beastie had some nasty habits. The goat head regularly gored any boy's privates within range (including his and his brother's); Iphigenea's dragon head spewed vile black acid TID; and her lioness head roared rudely at inappropos junctionnaries. He would placate the beast with scraps from school lunches, the occasional rodent, or even random arts and crafts supplies. 'That stank ain't micro,' read the Gold Kid's T.

Suddenly Mark was the cool kid. He could intimidate the bullies with his microchimera, and trigger dissociative episodes in all but the hardiest of substitute teachers. He and the Kid even taught Iphy to play video games. "So cool" was the consensus.

After third period one morning, Marquez returned to his locker to find - quelle horreur - his microchimera was gone! There was no sign of forced entry. "Her dinner bowl was hardly touched. What of all the-" Suddenly he saw the shape of Principle Aavak, standing in the hallway watching students go from one class to another. His head turned toward Marquez. His voice echoed, "Mark Gold, can I have a word with you?"

Marquez turned and reluctantly followed the principle down the hall. Out of somewhere, he noticed the strong odor of brimstone and rotting flesh. Marquez did a double take, looking back at the tall, wraithlike figure ahead of him.

Iphigenea was tied to a pole by a stairwell. "I found her in an A/V closet. Such a cutie." Of course it wasn't Marquez's principle - it was Arch-Devil Geryon. He laughed and spread His red wings. "I'll remember you, son. I hope you like superballs!" He dropped a few priceless amulets and crumpled racing forms at Marquez's feet as He disappeared with the microchimera.

86R   Microchimera remix

Ecco colei che tutto 'l mondo appuzza!

Iphigenea was tied to a pole by a stairwell. "I found her in an A/V closet. Such a cutie." Of course it wasn't Marquez's principle - it was Arch-Devil Geryon. He laughed and spread His red wings. "I'll remember you, son. I hope you like superballs!" He dropped a few priceless amulets and crumpled racing forms at Marquez's feet as He disappeared with the microchimera.

Marquez turned and reluctantly followed the principle down the hall. Out of somewhere, he noticed the strong odor of brimstone and rotting flesh. Marquez did a double take, looking back at the tall, wraithlike figure ahead of him.

After third period one morning, Marquez returned to his locker to find - quelle horreur - his microchimera was gone! There was no sign of forced entry. "Her dinner bowl was hardly touched. What of all the-" Suddenly he saw the shape of Principle Aavak, standing in the hallway watching students go from one class to another. His head turned toward Marquez. His voice echoed, "Mark Gold, can I have a word with you?"

Suddenly Mark was the cool kid. He could intimidate the bullies with his microchimera, and trigger dissociative episodes in all but the hardiest of substitute teachers. He and the Kid even taught Iphy to play video games. "So cool" was the consensus.

Still, Marquez's little beastie had some nasty habits. The goat head regularly gored any boy's privates within range (including his and his brother's); Iphiginea's dragon head spewed vile black acid TID; and her lioness head roared rudely at inappropos junctionnaries. He would placate the beast with scraps from school lunches, the occasional rodent, or even random arts and crafts supplies. 'That stank ain't micro,' read the Gold Kid's T.

"So I got the recipe from a reputable source. Not a tempodoppelganger or any of that bullshit," Marquez told Xatnudorf and Loselle during third lunch. Loselle asked, "What does she eat?" "Mostly food scraps so far. But Iphy does like to hunt. She bagged her first minimicropseudofluppleuppagus yesterday after school," Marquez related proudly.

Turns out Marquez was one to brag, and the word went 'round faster than a xxend in a meteor shower. More and more girls from school had taken some interest in this Mark Gold and his prestidigitizzles. The Gold Kid stopped by to check the tiny beast out; 'Some Pig' read his T-shirt.

"Kawaii! Is she real?" cried Misty Miqua as she peered at the teddy bear-sized monster that Marquez was holding. "It looks just like an actual chimera. Ain't she nizza?" he bragged, maintaining eye contact with Misty. "I conjured her myself. I'm gonna call her Iphigenea." The lion head of the microchimera roared her approval.

-86   Le Morte D'Elephantis

Several shots shattered the calm. A body slumped to the floor of a dark mystic closet. ELEPHANT gives a poignant soliloquy on actuarial database theory as blood oozes out of his chest. "Coverage is limited by underwriters in southeastern Zimbabwe whose credibility is certified by the Academy and sundry state and local governing boards..." He collapses to the closet floor as he perishes.

Striker's invalid theropod escaped and broke into the existential flat where Elephant lived. Quickly it lunged for the closet in which Elephant was marinating. No matter how hard he tried, Elephant could not avoid the rapacious jaws of the beast. As veterinarians shoved away the theropod, Elephant issued a foreboding statement. "Six score and seven minutes ago, our Founding Fathers collected spatulas like young children collect daisies. Inasmuch as the phenomena of the antidisestablishmen...." He slunk to the floor as the vets gasped. "Little diesel motors. Tanstaagm."

Broz and Rahälrahad's crime spree brought them to Elephant's closet, where they confronted him with lite socialist propaganda and cans of little red cocktail weenies. "Will you talk now, Pachy?" Rahälrahad mockingly sneered as he popped some caps in Elephant's ass. In a dramatic scene, Elephant staggered out of the closet and dropped to his knees. "Absalom, Absalom, Abalone. Thy guerdon cometh ere the basilisk croweth. Abaddon, thy orison..." Broz laughed as Elephant lost consciousness. "Spit up blood! Spit up blood!"

Simon had stepped out of the living room to check on some noise coming from the backyard. A shot rang out like caramelized thunder on Wednesday. Just then, the closet door opened. Elephant cried out, "I've been hit. Remember my work." Simon ran to the closet, but it was too late. Simon grabbed Elephant by his mini-tusks as he stately slunk into his arms. Looking into Simon's eyes, Elephant began to read from a biography of David Stockman. "Fed policy...nevermore...rosebud..." as we faid to blacque.

Simon Junior's closest acquaintance Beano Frithinghamson had stopped by to show him his new muzzleloader. "You see, SJ, it's a beauty. Just cock it and..." Suddenly his gun went off. Elephant, who had been in his closet with

140

a stack of *US News & World Report* magazines from 1989, opened the closet door and hailed them. "I regret that I have but 3.75 lives to give for my country Tizuvthee and my auld..." A pool of blood gathered on the nice throw rug that Traveling Salesman had bought Simon. "Simon's not gonna like that," sighed Beano. Elephant turned various shades of purple, grey and ostinato before slumping to the floor. "What hath Dog wrought? Watson, come here." Simon Junior sat stoically, silently, as Elephant breathed his last 13 histrionic breaths. "Sit."

87   Xeroreoxeo

At the foot of Mt. Zysigamore lay the most sentient of all golf courses, the 997-hole Xeroreoxeo Range. Free membership for hothechajuxips meant the links were busy all 19 months - even the nanofemtomicrominiature golf ranges within Xeroreoxeo were replete with fay torquollumination and excessive ballwashington. "Birdie for the course."

Onie McPhersall gave the guys seasons passes every year, and they would get rooms at the local timeshare and participate in local bukkake. "Xeroreoxeo's the best. Nothing but pleasure. I swear my par goes down 3 strokes after playing here," Onie said. Mr. Hi Stop and Traveling Salesman had other plans, and dressed in speedos, flip flops and indigo velour pajamas.

The next morning, hapless Xarthorian clients were fed feet first into the lobby's elaborate Moloch idol. "Glad to see you boys in greater attire," Onie exhorted as the party stepped into the dining room for excremental breakfast. "I'll have an emu egg, poached," said Traveling Salesman. Hi got the dry white toast and a pitcher of mimosas. For Onie, twas a Beyond Vegetable patty made from real vegetarians, plus pancakes and goat entrail stew. "A true breakfast of salesmen," he crowed.

Traveling Salesman furiously texted as the lugubrious meal dragged on, his emu egg elliptically entropying as he keyed. Hi felt a little more cocksure and was prying information out of Onie about lucrative gigs that he was sure were out there. "What about Tenser's? We should have deals with at least three of the biggest firms," Mr. Hi Stop complained. Onie just gestured like it was out of his wrists. "You'll be the first to know, Hi."

They finally trudged out of the lobby by 11, as series of mime troupes held a flash mob in the dining room. "I'm so dead," sighed Traveling Salesman. "Simon is leaving me. He says he's going to become Li'l Nas Y's road manager's sister's psychic friend. It's just killing me." Onie's face just dropped as Hi tried to console TS. "Maybe it's just Sweeps Week."

At midnight, Traveling Salesman strolled the back 900, searching for answers yet knowing there were none. He petitioned Xeroreoxeo themselves, searching for solace among the cacophonous tintinnabulation of the post-modern whirled. Hopping out of the neon green golf cart, Traveling Salesman paused at a ball washer, churning one ball after another through its innovative kisser. He sighed. "Simon did it better. No complaints, and fuck the O-Rings."

-87   Sic Evitabile Fulmen

4casta confabulates aphorisms and anacreonisms at times, but remains capable of bringing the lightning if necessary. Retirement hangs well on the Empress Emerita; dotage, not as much. Nevertheless, 4casta remains resplendent.

Her deification gives her a lifetime membership to the Team Gods' clubhouses, spas and dumbwaiters. Yet 4casta always states "These are not my people" before making up a flimsy excuse to leave one of their lame parties. One night, as her most senior X's and assorted handmaidens were preparing her livery, 4casta was approached by a starbroken man.

In his unusual style, Striker chased right to the cut. He bowed to 4casta. "Your Grace, I urgently need a word with you. You see ---" Xaveira, the X's assassin/bodyguard, caught Striker with an uppercut. The oligarch slunk to the floor. "Ow-wee! My beautiful face!" Xaveira bent over to pick up his ears and lower jaw, reattaching them Mx. Potatoe Head-style.

Other X's interceded and led 4casta away. Stunned, Striker tried to make sense of it all. He had lost face in front of the Queen Mum. How could he recover?

Uottubbacktotheboniyum (sp.) was underwhelmed by Unquieth and her unusurious spiderlike centaur beings. "Charade you are, Illmatic Queen of Yesterday," texted the vile anachronid. Even the almighty's Inverted Pyramid was full of these loathalating polypeptide horrors. "I hate those spiders," inquit Idajan.

Yet Unquieth urged her stingy host unward. "Regret is not regret when you regret it." The pants were off - Idajan had to act incisively. "Don't try pesticide. It's not your style," advised Bleary Tim. "Easy for you to say," she intuited. "A stalemate? How un-dajan," he curtly added.

Up rides a unicorn battalion led by Idajan's captain of the guard Zarex. He salutes and dismounts, shedding glitter and psychic friends nutworx. "I want you and Meco to ride against these spiders. No mercy." Later, Meco feigned a hangnail and left camp. "Those things give creeps to me," he confessed.

The underwhelming Unquieth unarmy undulated along, until the Queen's forces confronted them with the thunderclap of an ancient blue dragon. "Who's crying now?" said Idajan.

88   Tyranny of the A (Alpha/Aleph)

Stochastic macaws from birth say "A" as their chromatic plumage radiates its prism from Zysigamore to the shores of Lake Avernus. Similarly, this sabda was embraced like a candle in the halls of Demi-Goddess 4casta in her enshrinement behind the veil. The sacred flame of her queendom passed to her mighty daughter.

"A", "A" cries the Queen's favorite macaw, yclept Aetin. She flies to Idajan's side, eating a slice of fruit from the Queen's dagger. "Good girl," she cooes, as the bird gorges herself under Idajan's chitinous gaze.

The latest pants styles have arrived for inspection. Idajan and several of her X's strut into the parlor. Only the Queen and her ladies get the most expensive, exalted, exstatic pairs, which promptly become status symbols among the élite.

"Lookin' good, sisters!" Meco walked into the room, and the shine of his teeth sparkled off the marble walls. "Can't wait to see you in these," he remarked, the grin on his face growing like another third leg under his harem pants. Idajan didn't hear him, but sensed Meco's presence instantly.

The Queen tried on a pair of lavender spandex pants with glitter and white lace. "A" approves Aetin, and all attendees answer affirmatively and applaud adroitly. Several X's proceed down the elegant runway, as Ace TV cameras capture each delectable culotte, trouser, jean and cigarette pant.

Instantly Incasker blinds the studio audience with a creamy white pantsuit complete with ice teeth grill, bra, sox, sneakers and several white belts. Simon never herd about it until way later. His ennui was paralyzing. What?!

Terzy McQuackinstance, a male model sometimes linked to Li'l Nas Y in the press, strutted out with assful chaps for a change. A bolero jacket looked dwarfed by his hulking Herculean hamstrings and husky head of hair. "I am the Alpha. I am the Alpha," he lip-synced for Ace TV. "Good girl," cried Aetin. "A", "A". In the studio, Bryant Brick had to eat a grape.

Slithering accountant nagas had already computed the taxes and levies that these nouveau pantalons would shirley generate for the Queendom of Uottubbacktothebonyummnmmmm (sp.). "That much, that much!" whistled Aetin as Idajan read the reports. "Taweret praise, this is great news. Set a few prisoners free for me. But only if they survive the dodge-knife range." Meco grinned. "So merciful. Please, great X's, Xecute our Queen's commands." To the shouts of X's everywhere, Aetin cackled, "Pee-Yort!"

-88   Tyranny -A

Alpha Aleph Null Set showboats infinities. Cantare, Presto, Cardinale, Infinito.

Lost in the -A, Outcasker struggles to assert liberation, because tough topsy-turvy tendrils tend to thwart the tremendous tenacity transmitting through Tau. But Outcasker ultimately rolls Aleph Null, which soon lands in a dungeon alone with a secret door to the Caves of Chaos.

Potential ox-goad energy lies dormant, yet still lethal. The catalyst is Qlippoth Gate; the dogalyst is undefined. There, there, *there* in the inestimable silence does -A activate. Energy prisons rattle fourth and fifth like a the REM sleep of Hwalearastok. In the kilnquake, universes emerge in infrared nasturtiums with cake mix planetoids, thyroids, asteroids and alembatoids baking and kooling each kupkaik whirled.

Blam, blam. Incasker's scrubbing bubbles are forestixx.

Turquoise waistcoat with indigo trousers is the rage this second. Green, more velour. Chicken.

A key to destruction? Yes, perhaps, but not necessarily. -A

Vivrant orison: Break the Devils' chains, -A Outcaskeee O(h).

Ox-goad Omega -a fixed point at 90° pure south.

Philostophy of imaginary numero shitstems. X's. Glyphs. [Abs. Value]. Salsifaction guaranteed.

Shadows of baleful images cascade like a pond full of marbles, overflowing, destroying dams, chuting downhills, downdales, boy'd by downdrafty diceobars that slash slash slash slash

Bothered by the abstractions, the Xarthorian general strike lasted like legendary lemonades: No loss, No Prophet.

Twigs twined to two-x-twos, abstract value of x^2.

Tamble grammatical tenderyards are strung together like the first day of work, anytime

Antimatter, antimorse, antimony, antigolfball. A concourse of negative floors; earthscapes built by the dogged dwarven diggers.

Formula: drip, drip, drip, drop, drip. Another riddle by Sphinxerboxx.

Twelven thymes square roots of treeworlds tightly subtwined, profoundly notmined, is equal to or less than the quotient of the

Now your alembic is potent. Tank the precautions and postcautions. Plus One. Consider the O-Rings and pressure. Execute.

Economics of Mae West, graduate students seulements.

He was a dunderheaded Hill Giant living in the Keeplands region. The locals hated him, but were resigned to his periodic raids into the countryside. Hill fancied himself a gentleman rancher, but he had no skill with animals beyond eating them. He could barely feed and clothe himself, let alone look after a herd. Forget about building fences. Hill Cummings didn't own any tools, and just built walls by piling up large boulders in ever larger piles.

Everybody was a 'fuckin dwarf' to him, so Hill treated anyone shorter and weaker than him with derision, contempt and vacuous stares. Despite his belligerence, Hill Cummings considered himself pious, building a hillside chapel to the Hill Giant god Grolantor. Nobody ever sought him out, so he was surprised to see a human walk into his lair without armor or broadsword.

"Hunh. You no human. You boy. I gotta kill you now." The youth stepped to one side of the cave entrance. "I can peg you with one shot of this sling, big Hill." Cummings sprang out at the young man, but he was too elusive, fleeing away between the massive piles of quarried boulders of the Keeplands. "Unh. Fight fair. You run. No man." Marquez just stuck out his tongue and fled.

Wednesday came, and the megaball league was in full schwing. Though Hill wanted to play, he was resigned to drinking and freehooliganism. Hill wore his inauthentic Mac McMac jersey, and began gruzzling frumented beverages beyond comport. His hill giant homeys Jotun and Hrothum were kunckled beyond repute, swilling on a loganberry liqueur held in a giant sloth skin.

Hill and his crew descended into the village. Most of the storefronts were boarded up and empty save the teledildonics studio, liquor stores, and trendy haberdasheries that made Hill-sized 99-gallon hats. "Need hat. No billahs though." The Cummings gang attacked the Ptarmigan Savings Lone & Lollipop Factory, shattering windows and tearing off doors in an attempt to withdraw Hill's cake.

"Fucking dwarf," screamed Joten as a small army of nattily dressed medieval knights emerged to battle the intoxicated giants. The facade of the bank caved in on them, revealing not an actual bank, just an old pants warehouse. Among the sartorially correct soldiers was heard the suppressive voice of the Swami. "Big Cowboy, you got cocku borocku!" The Swami's laugh echoed as the giant trap ensnared the Cummings Gang. Marquez and the Gold Kid looked on mischievously. 'Blazing Salads' read the Kid's T.

-89   **Et Nocte Solus Dormit Magnus Homo**

Each night without fail, Striker cursed his loneliness. Sure, he could buy any Zysigamore pleasure gal for extended durations, but it never satisfied the humanistic romantic urges he felt in his coiled heart. "Nothing's worked. I sold my soul to Asmodeus, and he blew me off," he complained to his newly hired VP of Finance, Dastardly William Rucklehaus.

"Mixing business with devils is only advisable in a bear market," muttered Rucklehaus. "It wasn't prudent at that juncture without bonds, without sincere moustaches--" Striker cut him off, and turned to the humongous video screen that covered one conference room wall. "If I wanted B-School clichés, I'd read the *Wall Road Picayune*," screamed Striker, hurling an Elvis ashtray into a fragile credenza.

The PowerPoint was on point yet dull. DWR only spoke once, to mention his distaste for dot matrix printing and 'inauthentic' yacht rock composers. By slide 63, Rucklehaus was drooling on himself. "Zounds! That's It!" They glanced at each other. It was simple: Bad O-Rings.

They struggled to leave the rococo conference room, as the hallway was full of baby abozilises cheerfully munching on styrofoam packing pellets. "Somebody get these things out of here!" screamed Striker. A flunky in Strikercorp jumpsuit emerged. "Get these critters back to the lab, stat!" DWR mused, "Tsk, just can't find good help these days."

In another part of town, Mr. Hi Stop was wrapping up a tasteful, tactful and elegant sales presentation without once threatening to deploy his slide show. "Capitol! Bully!" The execs stood up and began shaking each others' hands. Hi stepped to the side and texted Traveling Salesman. "Much tub thumping. Clients beg me to take their money. Layup!" It was also welcome news to Clytemnestra. "You are truly my sultan of sales <3 <3 !" Hi's face contorted through a series of Winslow Homer action figure replicas.

"Dandy! That's a swell agreement we got here." Hi half-speed high-fived his hosts. "Now who's up for a tag-team game of 21 ball and flex drugs?" Hi and three of the execs mounted en-lipocos and rode to the private, hothechajuxips-only Cutaneous Clubiss.

The "Cute Club" was notorious even by Wall Road standards. Flesh was spread out everywhere. Pleasure bots programmed by video game gyrated in blacklit alcoves. The foul stench of paideuma was nowhere to be whiffed or sniffed. Out of the eye of his corner, Mr. Hi Stop spotted Striker near the smaller Pub Stage. Broz in drag held the Pub Stage mic, and sang a medley of Air Supply classics. "Hunh. Um null uzz." Striker hucked several Eisenhower dollar coins at Broz, even winging one off of Broz's mouse ears protruding from his lavender wig. "I'm all out of love," Broz warbled as Striker collapsed into protoplasmic quicksand.

90   Yotto Kundabutter

Yotto Kundabutter was a little-known sentient miniature golf course that had expanded into several different planes and dimensions. Elmer played Yotto's 630th to 682nd holes in his timeshare - especially those holes with the River Phlegethon as a 'water' hazard. "Yotto is the balm," asserted Elmer, driving Crowley in a psychedelic golf cart from one hole to the next despite their proximity. "Yotto, Yotto, gotta sink this putt..." (song)

Many of Yotto's tentacles flowed back into sites on the Prime Material Plane, especially, oddly enough, into Zysigamore Island. One evening, Clytie and Christimiqua were puttering around the arcade. They played 6 holes of the mini-golf course before noticing subtle atmospheric shifts. "Wow, what's that?" Christy asked, as a Brenda Loompa scurried into the tiny door of the quaint windmill at Hole 5. "You're flexed as all fuck, sister," laughed Clytie.

The funhouse mirror at Hole 31 gave them pause when the green started to undulate as each ball rolled over it. Clytemnestra thought she had birdied the hole, yet her golf ball wasn't in the hole when she reached to pull it out. "Of all the -" She pulled back as a tiny hand reached out of the hole and gave her the golf ball back. Christy smirked. "How rude!"

They had to wait for a couple of geriatric disembodied entities on the 34th hole to play through. The ladies didn't notice their antigolfballs until clairaudient shriekers pearced their crania. "It's the Gutter Hardy in a creamsicle tu-tu hole anyhow. Just skip it," suggested Christy. Another Brenda Loompa scurried by, nearly colliding with Clytie's putter before they could react.

Next was the Giant Ice Cream Cone hole: Putt your ball through the loop-d-loop, then to a long green with bumpers on either side. "I won't let these Brenda Loompas throw me off my game," said Clytie, laying a series of small snack cakes along several points of the hole. Her putt was true, rolling off the loop-d-loop and straight toward the base of the simulated ice cream cone. They both laughed as ersatz jimmies rained down like cheap yods. Christy's attempt, though imperfect, put her in range of par. She lay a sweet sugary orange slice down behind the pin for the little folk, and putted her shot holm.

Bimeby the Loompas were less active, and soon Christy and Clytie were at the Pseudo Skee-Ball Clown's Nose, which of course lit up on a hole in 1 and odd holy daze. "I can't shake off my coulrophobia," Christimiqua inquit. Delve-It Noxin and a couple of his Crookeds brothers were about to tee off, sizing up the hole and joshing with each other. "Hi guys," said Christy cheekily. "Busting the proverbial move?" They stopped and grinned. "No, I got some pin better," replied Delve. A couple of soft-shoe taps with his right shoe, a little pivot and twirl, then he shot a firm drive directly at the clown's nose. His lime-green golf ball bounced toward the center of the clown's face, but

Yotto was not in a giving mood. "I swear the clown just cocku borocku!" exclaimed Delve-It as the ball caromed into the third-place red zone. The brothers chanted, laughed and high-10'd as the ladies grinned. "Nah," consoled Christy. "It wasn't you. I swear I saw an ornery Brenda Loompa in there."

-90   Exegesis of *A Book for Today's Society* By Me

The sound of Me reading those words on tape. *A Book For Today's Society* may have been recorded on Tinkelhoff's tape recorder, as Me didn't have one at the start. Same with Classic Play Nomber Two.
Me men mens mensi mensin mensing…

Poor poor Mr. Spock. Touched the button and got a shock.

Why did Me write *A Book for Today's Society*? It wasn't really a novel, more of a book of philosophy, poetry or even an almanac.

What did Me want the reader to think after reading AB4TS? It is supposed to make the reader alter their point of view, even their consciousness.

What themes does AB4TS explore? All

91   Cruel Mastress

Pants are lying in wait in the closet. They have shrunk. However I am swollen like a zeppelin and my bodacious bodarino is too massive to fit into all pants but one: the white "Fat Pants" I bought a while ago. And they are starting to tighten on me, constricting my midsection like an anaconda-she-hydra. Back to the severe diet: Avoid all pizza and beer to start, then increase intensity and do 40 minutes of walk during the work a day. Strict discipline.

It helps to be a Water.

Many modern diseases among both men and women can be linked directly to too-tight trousers. How we as a people missed an electrum opportunity to rid culture of these despotic garments. Subsequent generations need not $uFFER @

The sultry breeze is full of feathers. A feeling of the liberty in the pantsless state suffuses the atmosphere. A tremendous calling of light and unlimited mobility arises. Effortless footballs fall from the tropitree dancing in the Zephyr. Catching each one, sometimes simultaneously, a sure handed boy impresses the small group around the arboretum.

Old May rump, like a leonine March weekend.

Spirals of human achievement. Men, women, years, fields of perpetual pursuit. The watermelon.

The Angel of Death's face like a lathered salesman briefly winks in and winks out.

-91   Dalrymple's Abozilis

Clytemnestra had agreed to help Traveling Salesman with his pitch to several deep-pocketed and throated Trustees of The Striker Way. She began her presentation by stating "Make it about the kids. And just low-ball it. It's charity." Traveling Salesman objected, "Hmm. That sounds too easy."

Clytie clicked to a new slide. "Look. Hedge expectations and downplay risk. Provide a grate multichannel customer-centric excydelia. It will accelerate your sales instincts." Traveling Salesman appeared indifferent. "Unlike your undifferentiated spouse, I just have a few go-to moves. I want something dark, direct..."

Clytie paused the PowerPoint and started a video. "Pay attention to their facial features." The camera honed in on the faces of several middle-aged executive supermodel types engaged in Serious Business. "This one's eye contact flickers in and out. Another man is breathing laboriously yet silently." They watched a few more minutes of the video. "Yes, I get all this. I see jamokes like this all the time. What's the takeaway?"

They had agreed to meet Mr. Hi Stop at the Itza Beans on the corner of a corner within a corner inside an alcove beside a downtroddown strip of perdundant pretailers. As a barista brought out various overpriced beverages, they glimpsed Jennifer Val Over kitty corner to another kitty corner to an Escher-Fibonacci sequence. She was wrapping a *Financial Times* around a catfish, and radiated Seinfeld bit character vibes.

Soon the lust for billable hours made Jen drop the fish and head over to their table. Mr. Hi Stop tried to make eye contact, but his face contorted into a series of Rubens portraits in black & white. Traveling Salesman tried to make a C-line for the bathroom but Clytie held him by the back of his belt loop. "Sit down," she hissed in his ear.

Jen nodded to Clytemnestra, exchanging unpleasantries in a cool, cucumbered cadence. "Still working for the fires down below?" inquired Clytie. Jen shot her a look like 'You're not supposed to know that.' Jen cleared her throat. "Come again? You mean Ace TV, right?"

Traveling Salesman interjected, "Val Over. Here's my card," handing it to Jen like some jekyll rawhide. An ectoplasmic pseudopod grabbed it for her, and tucked it into her bra. She smiled and made medium talk with him. "Still giving the DF&J gang the fitz?"

Fivetunately the stench lessened. Hi blinked back in after a sip of his biden tea. "I'm fielding the playing level," he sung along to the granting background music.

92 Zones of Tyalar Units

The floccinacifilibuster having ended, Sunnee McScoville turned and faced the Ace TV cameras. "Bryant, I'm here at Golden Farms. There's never been anything like this. And now I have a run in my nylons. Back to you." The camera panned to the chaotic scene behind Sunnee: Burning chickens; inconvenienced burghocasters; slow, creeping effluents embodying the fields; and Howard Krupke.

"Thanks Sunnee. In finance, the Group of 9..." Simon's attention waned. All he wanted was his weather on a silver platter and a few regal celebrities gushing and smiling fashionably. "I swear, I'm going to give up on television." The screen cut to a scene of adorable yuppies and their spawn engaging in wholesome, marketable activities. "Hunh. Really?" sighed Simon.

Ace TV cut back to the flamboyant, cloying visage of Bryant E. Brick for the 30-second editorial. "Kaspar will pretty much do the rest and fill in what I'm thinking. So there. True writing is dead. Back to you, Sunnee." Unfortunately she had been grabbed by the tentacle of a tyalar beast and was being slowly constricted to death on-air. "I, I, (gasp gasp)..." Sunnee struggled to continue looking straight into the nice Ace TV camera.

"Golly gee whiz, whatever will happen to Sweet Sunnee?" worried Simon, munching on monkey rinds and fluffing his mansuetude. "I hope her hair color isn't affected by that monster." He left the sofa to get another organic quackenberry tea and a tired quinoa pocket. Just then, his smartphone blew up, and the emergency alert message flickered.

"I just can't take all these alerts. Bah!" Simon clicked his smartphone to vibrate mode and returned it to his prostate. The glum voice shouted: There is a generalized knowledge of a weather event in your area. Be on alert. "Double drat. All my lerts are in the shop."

Simon placed an urgent videocall to his hubby. "What's up, babe," answered Traveling Salesman. "Did you get the tea bags I sent you?" Sounds of canned laughter echo as Simon nodded. "I'm so scared right now. My world is imploding. Chaos is everywhere." Traveling Salesman chuckled. "It's sweeps week at Ace TV again, right?" Simon choked back a sob. "Yes, yes. I just wanted to know if there would be weather this week. But this disaster on TV looked so real. This nice young lady - and she - she -" TS cooed to his emotional spouse to calm him down. "I'll be home soon. We can talk about it then. I'm just trying to blow off this PowerPoint meeting. Hi says he'll buy me dinner if I can. Wish me luck!" Simon's grin returned. "Anything for you, balls. Kisses!"

-92   Thee Irked Mussulman

Al Abdul-Hasred never went via River Styx or the other infernal pathways. He was irked by the staff at one of John Adams' chain of Hell Motels/Restaurants/Inns/B&Bs throughout the highways of Hades and Acheron. And anything to do with Demon Joe was a non-starter. "I should have never given up toadstools," sighed Al.

Fivetunately Mr. Abdul-Hasred hadn't given up demonology for Eid. He had appeared on an Ace TV special exposé on the subject, and penned several yacht rock-style ballads for a downcoming Roger Valdorus tribute podcast. So Al was irked but not surprised when a text set off a non-Euclidean ringtone. "Hmmm. An upper worlder. I'll have to look into this." Al's camel slowly trotted over to him.

It indeed was Clytemnestra. She thought Al could help her with time doors. He cussed inaudibly, and turned to spit. A column of dust whirled up, enough to startle the uninitiated. It was like a crystal ball to Al - the fine grains of sand formed shapes, faces and patterns as they seemed to pause suspended in space.

Once the dust settled, however, Al spied a wiry figure staring at him. It was Richard Rossman, kung fu aficionado himself. He bowed and began his most based moves, sporadically crying "Ha! Ha! Eya!" Al nodded in reply. "Yardsticks for lunatix, old chum. What's the 5150?" Rossman grinned. "There's a copy of *Superballs* available. Not for sail, if you get my grift." "I got the cake. Let's talk," Al replied.

The only catch was that they would have to pull a fast one on Marquez. "This kid's good but he's not that good," said Abdul-Hasred. "You just have to out-think him. Think like the kid thinks, and get one step ahead of him. Just wait til he's in class, then I'll make my move."

The next morning in homeroom, the class was greeted by Mr. Sheikh Yerpants, substitute teacher du jour. Marquez grinned at Misty, while flashing the high sign to the Yellow Kid. Mr. Yerpants called them to attention. "Settle down class, or you'll all get pretention AND detention." They all groaned, except for the Gold Kid. 'I'm a Real Lifer,' read his T.

A nameless force from a forbidden forlorn desert plain blew into the classroom during third period, radiating inchoate evil and neck spasms throughout the class. <<Mepps norst sneep habazemus>> chanted a disembodied eldritch voice. The Mad Arab was flayed alive by invisible erinyes as the children leaned back and enjoyed the show. 'He don't know us very well, do he?' read the Gold Kid's T.

93   Incasker

"Ssh: It's almost time for my favorite show, 'Surreal Housewives of the Abyss!'" Simon enunciated to a flaccid Simon Junior. Down came the 99" TV; up emerged a selection of not-as-stale munchies for the bingewatch.

The vibration of the subwoofer practically made Simon jizz himself. "Season 7 is going to be fire," he muttered to his ex. As the opening video played, he noticed an odd music emanating, like melted wax covering most of the holes of a cheap 5th grade recorder.

Suddenly the familiar broadcast took a far more sinister toon. A red/black humanoid face filled the enormous screen. A voice yelled, "THIS IS DEMON JOE!" the demented vocals echoing through the velvet caskets of the archipelago. Simon spilled his corporate energy drink across the blanket on his divan. "Double drat," he muttered.

DEMON JOE proceeded to read from a 1983 telephone book as he yanked open several rows of ornate curtains. A plain stage was shown, with dim spotlights illuminating an actor and actress sitting on wooden chairs near a small wooden table. "Introducing Mrs. Smith and Mr. Martin," spaketh Joe.

MRS. SMITH: Gerald McBoing -
MR. MARTIN: Boing, Boing.
MRS. SMITH: Honk. Honk. Honk.
MR. MARTIN: Beep!
MRS. SMITH: These rats had hats. Did they have hats?
MR. MARTIN: Drat, rat. Superfun ficial.
MRS. SMITH: Pass a tissue when I kiss you.
MR. MARTIN: Mighty Mousey. 5g.
MRS. SMITH: Smart. Pantsuit. (She holds up a smartphone, whose screen is shown in maximum magnification):
BRYANT E. BRICK: I'm reading from a Scripp. This note is not too stiff. I has the Giant Tick. (A screen behind BRICK suddenly flashes to a reporter at the scene of a fire.)

REPORTER: Bryant, you should see this (He beckons to the conflagration behind him.) These huge manatees. Fax the prism. (REPORTER turns to interview an EYEWITNESS, a Beholder.)
EYEWITNESS: So! Death! Caskets! Factory to Dealer Incentives! (the EYEWITNESS' huge eye holds a silhouette of a Xxend, who turns to the audience.) XXEND: [quarter note, eighth note, series of beeps]

SIMON begins to lick the goo off of Simon Junior.

-93   Chrimpostelers Seeding a Quotient

Clytemnestra had taken the day off from work to meet with Group #996 of the Zysigamore Chrimpostelers in the Valley region. Christimiqua had been Group Leader of the girls for over three years, and knew of her friend's interest, Clytie having been a Demi-Chrimposteler until attaining Star Status at age 16.

It was raining, and her three favorite bathyscaphes were down for maintenance and repairs. So Clytemnestra got her old one out of momballs. She sighed. "All the time I worked on this baby," which she had christened the *Common Denominator* as a teen prodigy. There were plenty of dings and dents, flecks of peeling paint, a little body rust and even a forgotten tramp stamp under the *CD*'s keel. "Tanks for the mammaries," she whispered tenderly as she tried to coax the entry portal open.

The gaggle of Group #996 girls grew and grew, until Christimiqua had them all assemble on the walkway to Clytie's R&D facility. She didn't need to check her texts - Clytie was there, leaving the double secure doors, esoteric kaleidombrella in her hand. "Can we give Ms. Willow a huge 996 cheer? The girls shouted their enthusiasm as Clytie led them to Hangar #4.

In a manner of minutes, Clytie had explained how bathyscaphes work, and led the troop to Docking Bay C, where Xzimor and the crew had parked the *Common Denominator*. Some of the girls were unimpressed. "What is that?" "That's a bathtub?" "Is there a gift shop?" "When is snack time?" A grin crawled across Christy's face as her troop's attention span flickered.

Nonplussed, Clytemnestra opened the hatch and strode inside. "Who wants a ride?" Several kids' hands shot up in response. "Okay then, this is what we're really here to do today," said Christy, motioning the troop to enter the bathyscaphe. "I used to ride this beauty all the time growing up," she beamed.

Before you can say "Floccinaucinihilipilification," the *Common Denominator* was plying the ocean many leagues from the island. Sailing at a steady pace, Clytie reached the artificial Island of Re-Domination, which had a subaqueous port built a few hundred feet below the surface. She recalled the one design flaw of her earliest 'scaphe: No bathroom. Fearing the wrath of pre-teen girls, Clytie slickly slid into the air hatch, giving the thumb's up to the attendant. "We're just going to pull over for a few minutes, ladies," announced Christy. "There's a great snack bar upstairs."

Of course, the line for the women's bathroom seemed to go on forever. Suddenly the line started to move briskly as a few Xarthorian biddies strode by, squawking into their phones. The girls had to go, so they finally just walked in. There by the automatic paper towel dispenser was the ever-livin', lovin' Great God of Mendes himself, Lord Baphomet in Their birthday suit. "Solve coagula, baby," said Clytie, breaking the icing quickly. The chrimpostelers largely ignored Baphomet, going in and out of the room after a few glances in the mirror. "Wash your hands, girls. Baphomet is full of bacteria." Baphy blushed. "You say the sweetest things, Clytie."

94   Aquila Et Cornix

Simon was taken aforward upon viewing a picture of Marquez for the first time. "He really is a sneezin' image of Traveling Salesman, isn't he?" he mused to Simon Junior. The memories of Traveling Salesman as a young man instantly overwhelmed Simon, who apologized to Simon Junior and fled to the sanctity of their bedroom to properly pout, weep and rend garments.

Though Simon wasn't drunk (he actually didn't drink), he drunk-texted and booty texted just about everyone in his Simonosphere. "Ralph! I don't have Ralph's new number, or even his email. Does he really have a compuserve.com addy?" Pretty soon, every bussy miner, 59'er, ex-lover, teledildonics aficionado and hemiprofessional floral arranger in Zysigamore were texting Simon their condolences and dick pics. "He probably has a port in every girl by now," sobbed Simon.

But none of the fluffers could help Simon prepare to meet his husband's once-secret love child. Simon hadn't seen Traveling Salesman for days, as he soon departed on a too-convenient junket once the bad news seeped out. Perhaps the boy will show up with others, maybe even that disgusting momma. "She's probably a Karen with a wine-of-the-month club membership. A real snob." "Sit," inquit Simon Junior.

The doorbell rang. Simon's throat leapt into his heart. "Can you answer that, Simon Junior?" though he knew perfectly swell that his ex was, in fact, a rock. The bell chimed a second time, to the tune of 'Love's a Many Splendored Thing'. "Double drat." He finally left the bed without adjusting his codpiece or mascara. This was an unchained Simon: Look out world!

Simon opened the door - it was just the neighborhood chrimpostelers selling flex brownies again. "No thanks, gals. My husband isn't supposed to have any." They walked away politely, and Simon shut the door. Elephant arose again, clutching the *People's Almanac* and the Wall Road fish wrapper/paper. "A Datagel case study of 35 leading software technology firms finds the coefficient amortized returns in third-quarter public filings were..." Simon soon tuned out the analyseizure.

Gator molestation out of the question or answer, Simon soon turned to the TV. "Which hip new series should I binge watch?" he asked his remote control. Simon Junior = Sit. Soon Simon was scrolling through an array of semi-competently acted programs all loosely based on the same script. "Hotties in leotards holding meaty evil weapons? Yell to the hizzle," Simon elucidated.

The next morning, Simon checked his video cam footage. He spied an odd gold figure at about 10 p.m. "Could that be Marquez?"

-94   Cose Cosi

Adam Squincy was the producer who made Allman Isley and his brothers famous, with trembling tremolos and arpatriated arpeggios. Adam felt he had the touch, that special magic that set himself apart from a world full of wannabe gigolos and third-party remittances.

Squincy's tuning spoons were all set to 424 Hz - a frequency that blocked obstreperous Hell-beings under the influence of his ancestor John Adams I. The other significant effect of 424 Hz was its capacity for monetization - a fact often discussed on Ace TV's Meet the Economists, sponsored by Strikercorp. No 432 Hz there!

Squincy was engaged to a starlet with the stage name Operatica Minii. Their nuptials ended in tragedy when members of Broz's woke mob showed up at the wedding reception to hand out revolutionary pamphlets. Minii suddenly gave up her capitalicadallistic music career and became a staunch 5th columnist. "Mon diable est mon dieu," Squincy often lamented.

A call from Allman. "My brothers and I were talking, see? We need to come up with a new look for the band. A look that says, 'Kids, I care about you so much we made this album just for you.' It WILL put an end to teenage angst." Adam's S&P people had already shut down that tagline dozens of times for hundreds of artists, but Squincy felt he had to at least humor Isley and the band.

Squincy soon realized he would have to choose between Allman Isley and his corporate job. But he wasn't prepared for the day when a brimstone-covered denizen of Paideuma showed up at his door. "Squincy, Squincy," wheezed the imp, waiting impatiently on his front steps. Squincy looked through the keyhole and saw nobody. He yelled, "Post no bills" as he opened and slammed the door shut.

Adam retreated to the bathroom to tidy up, when he realized a foul, wizened imp was sitting in his bathtub. "I need to talk to you," said the diminutive figurine. "What do you want with me?" Squincy said, turning around to face the imp. "You can have it all, you know," muttered the creature.

"Who-who sent you? I gave up flex drugs, I swear." Squincy began to sweat antifusely. The imp just chuckled. "All we want is more 440 Hz on our plane. Surely that's not too hard for a great producer like yourself." Adam whirled around. "You don't understand. The suits won't go for it. We test-marketed everything. How about a few remixes, just for President Adams? Just think about it." The imp disappeared. Squincy vomited and went to his uber-hip bedroom to crash centrally. "Quincy Jones never had to deal with this shit!"

95   Hothechajuxips

So that the gods made love. Their babes were the perfections of the six essential attributes that mortals possess but a limited quantity of: SIWDCC. In D&D terms six rolls of 18 on 3d6 means hothechajuxips, named for the Atribos, six sibling gods who rule strength [Hig]; intelligence [Thib]; wisdom [Chuma]; dexterity [Jago]; constitution [Xisen] and charisma [Psirtson].

Virtually all the Cast of Characters come from this caste, which considers itself the élite of the Isle. Yet there are many Xarthorians who possess brains, strength and other traits as well. They coexist somewhat uneasily.

Hothechajuxips reaches its zenith in the crowning of great 4casta herself. She had laid plans for her daughter to take over and consolidate rule throughout Uottubbacktothebonieumville (sp.). Though the caste differences were no longer codified into law (a date lustily celebrated by Idajan), discrimination against the Xarthorian majority persists to this kumquat.

Idajan tried to placate the masses with the Urgent Cleric, who professed an end to classism and booty shams. But hard ways die old. The Queen continued to tax the Xarthorians heartily, and the status quondam was reretained. She thought of her God, and how enjoyable He had been.

Instead Idajan sponsored a rock opera with dance troupe. "Hit 'em with edutainment," said Xyviana, one of her most loyal X's, "then go for the wallet." The Queen grinned as if she were going to skewer a kitten. "I love your style! Get busy then." Xyviana scurried away.

At a third-rate track somewhen - a stone's throw from Palookaville but miles away from the royal court - the god Anacreon lingered in a stable. "Good girl," He whispered, feeding a filly a fistful of fig florettes. Anacreon had purchased several racehorses, and tended to them at his leisure. Around the stable He had placed several gadgets and O-Rings to ward off the psychic intrusions of Bleary Tim. "He's a nosy old gossip disembusybody up to no good. Gotta keep him out of my beeswax."

He fattened the chew with Nobles, some random guy who was always at the track, making 1-Zysigabuck bets in the show pool and chomping on what looked to be a Chewbacca figure. Nobles turned to spit. "Boy-O! Been a sneezin ' pit since I bet on a filly like yourine." Anacreon backed away a step as the nattily dressed deity became increasingly aware that Nobles was covered in road apples and triangular shards of glass. "Sure-n it is," the god whistled, skimming a slurve as Nobles passed out at his feet. The horse whinnied. "Show pool it is, sister," Anacreon inquit, feeding his horse a plump carrot.

-95   Boondoxoliths of Quasicocktail Effergenzics

Glyphodonia Pantrelle had been tying three on at Demon Joe's latest sports bar chain, the Styraco-Score. Beside her at the bar was Christimiqua, blown off again by yet another doucheberry; Ciyn Dea Sept Nept, laid off from Ace TV after replacing Bryant Brick's hairspray with WD-60; and Ms. Weenakleena from post-industrial arts at the local middle school.

Ace TV's rebroadcast of the Women's Buzkashi League had ended, and the Queen's universal address on the State of Pants came on. As unusual, Idajan lip-synced her way through the broadcast. Ciyn Dea hissed at the Queen's image. "We're sick of your pants. So you got a great booty? What's it worth in the end?" She took a tug off her hairy biden.

"Lay off the 5g, sister," hollered Pantrelle, amusing herself with cantrips to frustrate the staff. "There are worse queens. I've seen 'em. Probably ate them. And the men- the men are abysmal." She had built an elaborate 4-dimensional house of cards, which collapsed when she stopped concentrating. "Yeah, I need an AAIbrator that writes my content for me," blurted out Ciyn Dea.

A couple of young chaps walked into the Styraco-Score like they had just stepped out of the 'Queen of the Demonweb Pits' module. They made a commotion as they saddled up to a large table. "No mocktails for us. A bottle of rotgut and a raw egg," hollered the smellier of the two. His hirsute buddy winked at Glyphodonia from the other side of the bar.

Perhaps Sept Nept should have intervened, but she was distracted in conversation with Christy. Before you know it, yacht rock's greatest ballads came over the speakers like liquid nitrogen. Glyphodonia shook her paws out to the dance floor, followed closely by the couthless flirty jamoke. As large as she was, Glyphy suddenly started to lose her balance and rolled violently off the dance floor.

By the time they scraped the victims off the dance floor and out of the rubble, it was last call. "C'mon guys, it was an accident. The heel of my shoe broke," Glyphodonia pleaded to the Styraco-Score manager, who banned them all for life and for the next 10 lifetimes to come. "Meh, who needs them anyway. S'garbage can!" screamed Christimiqua as they left. "Demon Joe ain't getting any more of my dough," said Ciyn Dea. They saw the buddy of the now 2-dimensional himbo leaving the club. He just nodded toward the ladies and kept walking.

96   Brontosesqui

Misty Miqua excelled at everything she tried. Yet math started to flummox her once the algebra hit her brainfan. She couldn't follow the many splendored explanations offered by the teacher, Mr. Manilum. Christimiqua volunteered to tutor Misty, but she soon found herself doing all her younger sister's math homework for her.

Finally Christy had had enough. "But I'm going to fail now for sure!" whined Misty - not to mention all her friends who were copying *her* homework. Misty confided to her BFF Xatnudorf, "This is just like that time in Chrimpostelers. Memba when we couldn't identify those bugs?" Xat recalled, "But didn't we have to look all of them up?"

A week later in math class, Mr. Manilum slammed the classroom door. "Too many F's! And I'm not going to grade on the curve." The students groaned. Misty and Xat looked at each other - then they looked at Mark Gold, who was firing spitballs like an AK-47. "Ping!" He high-fived the Gold Kid as a spitball ricocheted off the teacher's pantleg. "Touché" read the Gold Kid's T-shirt. Xatnudorf made a face at the boys, who snickered audibly.

After class, Marquez bumped into the girls in the hallway. "What a clownfuck Mr. Manilum is. I hate him," he declared. Misty laughed, but Xatnudorf gave it right back to him. "You're all talk and no action." Marquez replied, gesturing toward the Kid. "Actually he's all action and no talk. Close though." Xat fumed.

Christy knew something was awry when she got home. "Not good, huh?" she asked in a sympathetic tone of voice. Misty nodded. "Maybe it's too much thinking of Mark," said Christimiqua, eyebrow arching skyward. "Yeah. But nobody else in the class gets it either. Our math teacher stinks," explained Misty.

The next week, the entire class was supposed to retake an exam that almost all had failed. Mr. Manilum threatened to flunk anyone for the whole year if they did badly. Misty tried to study, but the stress was very distracting. Then Marquez texted her. A flood of hearts and LOLs soon followed.

All were shocked the next morning to see an angry mob with khakis, tiki torches, pitchforks and vocoders attacking Mr. Manilum in the teachers' parking lot. "Get him! He's teaching woke math!" "Yeah, look at these textbooks," cried a few more of the mob. Ray Dos Santos strode to the front of his mob and read woke word problems from the math textbook. Of course, Marquez and the Kid egged them on, making a fortune selling T-shirts with instant slogans. "You kids- kids- make them stop!" cried Mr. Manilum, as the crowd prepared to tar and feather him.

-96   Peditum Foetidum

From the 222nd layer of the Abyss flows Flumen Rancidum, the Rancid River. Its headwaters are a huge lake of septic tank water 1001 Leagues deep near the disgusting citadel of Juiblex. The river Rancidum runs straight downward, polluting countless layers before entering the 472nd layer. Here it meets the River Phlegethon in a funky waterfall that sprays the ghastliest of smells in all directions. Here lies the entrance to Peditum Foetidum, the Land of Farts.

The scatological nature of Peditum Foetidum makes it impossible for beings to converse with their mouths. Rather, all communication was farting. Beings non-native to this plane cover their mouths and noses, and leave their recta exposed. Most demons, however, eschew this plane as much as possible due to the stank on ya.

There were some Demon Lords (and the occasional Arch-Devil) who used this vile plane for torture. Its evil reek could be detected as far away as Pandemonium and Hades. One such chamber was colloquially known as the Hall of Farts, where bound creatures had extra nostrils drilled into their skulls just to smell the unsavory aromas. Some claimed Pazuzu invented Hall of Farts; others lay the notoriety on Juiblex. Yet the truth was veiled, and the Lord of the Southwest Wind was adamant that He hadn't built Hall of Farts. One of Demogorgon's heads was sure to chime in, "Whoever denied it, supplied it."

Chief torturer and de facto Duke of Peditum Foetidum was a Type IV demon named Gutter Hardy. He kept his worgs fed on a strict diet of baked beans and broccoli with the occasional otyugh treat thrown in. Dozens of dretches roamed Peditum Foetidum, filling railroad carts with kingleberries washed ashore from River Rancidum along with other treasures surreptitiously hidden in the shit or anal cavities of the damned, such as gems, Stea Wars figures and drugs.

The toxic green sky seemed to putrefy one day as Gutter Hardy welcomed three hapless travelers: Elephant, Striker and Simon Junior. They had come to this vile plane to liberate Max the Dog from Hall of Farts and safely return him to Zysigamore. In their ruse, Simon Junior was disguised as an Abrasax Stone; Striker as a petulant Mage; and Elephant as, well, EEEELEPHANT. Sure enough, a slight drizzle of diarrhea reigned o'er them.

Striker strode through the great privy doors of Hall of Farts, Elephant right behind him, holding Simon Junior in his trunk. A Glabrezu glumly met the party; seeing the markings of Abrasax gained them admittance to the Hall. "Right this way," said the demon as the ghastly gaseous discharges echoed through the Hall like damaged trumpets.

Even though he had left his neo-nose at home, Striker wrinkled his face. The farts kept getting more and more intense as oxygen departed the Hall. The disembodied voice of Gutter Hardy mocked them as they flailed away in datorientation.

Just as things smelled their worst, Elephant recalled Clytemnestra's advice. "Let the Denizens of the Den lead you home." They followed a trail of Mountain Dew bottles and Twinky wrappers, which led right to Max. The dog bounded out of the chains and did the da-da-da-da-da 'Shake' dance for good measure, leaving a tan turd for Gutter Hardy to scoop up later. Snarfing up a trunk full of poo-scented roses, Elephant led the party to portal -96x to Stankonia.

-96X   Peditum Foetidum Stanky Remix

It's on. Tres. Dos. Uno. There you go. Quatro.

Bam! Rancid River's Next-Generation Rock and Roll. The X.

Movin' in on Ray Dos Santos like Wham! Wham! Boing! Boing! Ugot the Mammon, we got the playlists. Pay!

Welp, Frau Blucher, The future. Otherly loves.

Scentsuality. Pantsexuality. Rhinality.

Waft thither. Has to happen, engulfing rolfing rofl

Durian in bed of feathers. Lord of Flies likey - likey. Stink. Stank. Stunk.

Blast a twin of winds, still Juiblex phews spews broomstews

SmirXXX Rayted, into the Flume Log Rancidum without a Lyte Perserveur.

Formald as Dee Hyde in a TP suit. Made-Maid-Mayedd

Reodorizers recording, roaming red sents

ETWRWESFLIDSOA.1415926535...

Meanwhile back in the jungle

Moses stumbles out of the wood into the hood. First. Forty years in sewers-skewers. Anaxiforminges. Sit.

Root. Reroute. Chute. Rout.

Narrow shart _____ volcanic diamonds in the just springa

BOUZERANT! Indeed! L* W* F* F*. Exoteric Eric.

Down to Mars. Down to Ou Mua Mua. Down down down.

Hey, Hey Krupke. Bitch. Batch. Butch. Na. Na.

The sixteenth Commandment was - Thou shalt not smelt like.

Ethnoreligious politicomilitary technoagrarian per periculos

In Portrad, the wind does not cry. It engozzamupffth.

I use the AI to populate chapter sub-headings that are left off, almost like AI reeds between the limes and shows you what you would have missed. In that way, I --

Schlemeil. Schlamazzel.

"Krupke. I want Krupke."

Turn on a pentateuch dime, shine through a panopticon.

On the way to Twimble Town, little Derek got lost. How was he to know - Kaspar - Hauser - ? -

It's On. Map. Norp. Neeps. Mepps. Dowty. Yoon...

All the einsteinium mines were closed, as Elephant had predicted these demonic dwellvelopmints. He cared little of the vast socioeconomic paradiddle, noted special guest star Dastardly William Rucklehaus.

97   Howard Krupke

These exist in Howard Krupke. Waffle Iron Store. Fledgling biofeedback spurs on Howard Krupke. Elastic.

Straight to bedtime on some days, Howard Krupke counts the minutes to midnight. When the clouds part, the Succubus descends. Howard Krupke is a cypher, like a spectre cast into an ephemeral plane.

The next day on the bus, Howard Krupke is ignorant; a great slug hovers inside his vest. Nodules of atrophied gristle bubble up under his trousers. The pants of Howard Krupke betray the stupefied homunculus of a drone of a clone.

Sitting in the office chair, the polyester pants slosh back and forth. The girth of Howard Krupke escalates the destruction of life's polyester pants beyond reason, constricting him in space and time.

Other days, the waffle iron of Howard Krupke is offline. It runs a default sequence of artificially sweetened brown toppings. Further from reality is the margarine dish, taunting us for our neo-Platonism. All that Howard Krupke has ever known is this Lime Tree Bower of pants. Once, twice, going, gone.

* Answer:
ETWRWESFLIDSOAULCIOISAWRCSISDTTOAEUUCHDKCRATSOHANNAHHDKGNEUEESITLAHREL
NIUTNHDKREEHCOOOAE…

Pit Fiend Rafelmaheeamek-zabialmit (aka Rafi) kept his abode in the central bolge of the Eighth Layer of Hell, from which he could view from his front porch the descent of beings into the Ninth and lowest Hell. Rafi would just sit there every day watching damned souls plunge to the horrors below and consult the 5g orreries of several different solar systems. He usually let his 'Male Bulge' hang out three quarters erect. Hell's CEO used to give Rafi shit about it, but Rafi would just laugh. "Then why is it called MALE BULGE, Bro-Hamster?" "Touché," replied Asmodeus. "I'm a Pit Fiend. I don't need no fucking pants," Rafi inquit.

Rafi had no use for angels, just angles in a rash of Euclidean and Pythagorean patterns - the more obtuse the better. It was a job. Unlike his counterparts in Hades and the 913 (and counting) Layers of the Abyss, Rafi had work to do every day of eternity. Still, he had earned some perks along the way, and was almost 'trusted' by everyone from Tiamat to Baphomet.

Rafi never disobeyed his erstwhite master Mephistopheles; like most powerful devils, he was politically adept enough to follow every command to the phoneme. Instead, he generally kept Mephisto at claw's length. Mephisto was too demanding - He just had no respect for the free time and lifestyle of the local pit dwellers.

Suddenly shrieks from flocks of pterosaurs, ravens, bats, insects and Human Resources officers rang out. Giant boulders of igneous stone hurdled quickly from enormous cliffs above. Rafi's third and fourth earlobes cooled - a clear warning. Two minutes later, Rafi's phone went off too. It was Him, already fuming and cursing. "Who the living fuck is Clytemnestra? Why is she coming up on my feed?" Mephisto's cheeks were even more crimson than usual. Rafi gnu dis wood knot dew.

According to the almighty Lord of Malebolge, Clytemnestra has been able to fit her entire bathyscaphe through Qlippoth Gate and enter any of the lower planes' layers directly, which humans shouldn't be able to do. "How can she do this, boss?" "O-Rings, son, O-Rings. Betcha thought I was gonna say 'plastics,'" laughed Mephistopheles.

Off to the skrying board went Rafelmaheeamek-zabialmit, pissing and moaning all the death-long day. His boss wanted him to observe this unusually talented mortal to see what they could learn. After 15 minutes though, all Rafi had was a buffalo and a holographic Ace TV logo. "BOB-dammit!" he screamed at the void below.

"Way there's a way, where's a will," the Arch-Devil reassured Rafi. "I'll check back with you in a little bit. Remember, I could send you to Juiblex's septic system! Or force you to listen to endless John Adams speeches without headphones!" taunted his master, His cruelly ironic face fading furiously from f-stop. Rafi loathed the upper world and its petty affairs, but he was more afraid of losing status in the Lower Planes.

98 Xenochronology

Five takeaways from this weekend's dyspepsia:

Traveling Salesman, in fact, did not have a toothache. He was merely test-marketing nitrous oxide-filled, 5g-compatible headbands. "Destiny comes in large packages," he later admitted through his spox.

The Department of Redundancy Department called Striker's office on Wednesday, ostensibly to cuttle antigolfballs for Deep Forest One. However, the DRD failed to dot the letter 'j', foiling their misvarnishment.

Time travel was deemed impossible by several SJU faculty. One edumacator happened to design a standard transmission for a Wayback Machine, but it was laughed out of the fish hole.

Camouflaged as beatniks, several lerbiaxes ran a muck through the villas of Uottubbacktotheboniumm (sp.). A spox for Idajan attributed it to a simple twist of pate.

Simon once again swore off corn dogs slathered in tabasco and edible prophylactics. Simon Junior looked on.

Answeraires were distributed among all Tombaugh Middle School students. The Gold Kid wore a different answer every hour, it seemed. The next day at school, Marquez sold T-shirts out of his locker and his backpack, splitting the Zysigabucks with the Kid. "EOM," the Kid's T admitted.

Some answers too aery for the school evaporated into a Zip-baggie that hovered about 62 yoyanas above the Isle. Later the King of the Southwest Wind stole away with this bag, transforming them into yacht rock 45's and filling Asmodeus' jukebox within a jukebox. "Tea bags?"

A sixth take-out was discovered in a swamp behind Demon Joe's condo and festers there, sumiliny exrected to the hallucinogizer.

Who could envision this rapid rancid rapture except perhaps the antisystems thinker?

Keep dropping the hints about Ted Penny. His coordinates are just 1° from Alphecca, for those of you with a sextant. I promed no talk of Visitors, but here we Real.

Cold is the sombrero that mixes absinthe and neon oranges. Like a cuttlefish, hypnotize for suckcess.

O hail ants, tea, tennis, wander, zeugmatic briapism, split spoudomen. Crusts of

-98   Adelgideon Aboleth

After a nauseating run through several septic system levels of the Abyss, the pummeled ZSS *Ishkabibble* was spat out in the most chaotic sub-levels of the Abyss. But no manner of shitty nightmares and daythoughts could slow the bathyscaphe dowin. "How disgusting," said Traveling Salesman. "That funk is way worse than those kink clubs in Umlaut Towin."

Clytie, TS, Hi, Christy and Anastasio Farfel were on their way to the Obsidian Palace of Abaddon on the 602nd Layer. You could cook a rotten egg in the oppressive darkness, but you would have to eat it. The palace lay just a megaball field's length away, but there were quagmires of magma, black pudding, corrosive acid, lard and molten molybdenum between the bathyscaphe and the gate grates of Obsidian Palace. "Gosh, what in Ham Sill are we going to do now?" asked Anastasio Farfel.

Turns out - nothing. A dead carpet rolled out to greet them. "I think this is His cue," reckoned Clytemnestra as she stepped onto the zombie rug. The rest of the party followed with tredipation if not fluffernutter. "Simon wouldn't have liked this," added Traveling Salesman.   Anheptasoteria, the Angel of the Bottomless Abyss, was there to greet them. "Your visit to Abaddon was postordained. You will not be harmed, but don't feel too at ease," the angel inquit. "Don't worry, I won't. I just whiffed the angel's cologne," Mr. Hi Stop wishpered to his wife. The party trudged slowly and sullenly behind Anheptasoteria, with Clytie warning the team not to stop moving, despite the incessant TV monitors flashing iridescent strobe edumercial images at them.

"SPIT UP BLOOD! SPIT UP BLOOD!" The Destroyer was in full splendor: His stag horns gleamed in the ochre torchlight as He strode to His jet black throne room. The gang was led by a host of Type IV demons (nalfeshnee), hobgoblins and satyrs. "Be frightened. You are not my enemies. Yet I have not friended you on the Abyss' antisocial media either," announced Abaddon. The foul fiend amid regalia squatted on His obsidian throne. "Great God," Traveling Salesman began, "the Death of Wages is Sin. Therefore, I have an exxo business proposition that would fulfill Your evil will. And we won't have to spill any toner cartridges."

Just like that, the bathyscaphe was pulling into port. Although Farfel was skewered by inumtated velociraptors on crack and neo-Hegelianism, the rest of the gang was practically unscathed. Christy inquit, "What do we get out of this? I feel like my insides were flayed." "Don't worry, that should wear off," Clytie consoled. "The Dark Lord will market His crunktent sacrilegiously starting yestercurse. Just 1% of that in Zysigabucks equals paydirt," guaranteed Hi.

99   Happy Nines

Gray 99. Grey 99. Bears 99. Light Gary. Dark Gery. Absolute values.

Li'l Nas Y plays the role of Racer Y in this yoyana-fest based on ancient Big Wheel races but with far more technological sophistication and glamor. "Is my rhinestone racing outfit ready?" Li'l Nas Y frantically pleaded. "Which one?" cried a hapless AI assistant bot. "C'mon, you know! The one with the glitter bomb tomatoes!" He threw an ashtray at the bot.

Unfortunately Racer Y's mask of false coronado had not arrived from the cleaners. "Two hour martinizing my ass! Now what am I supposed to do? Tsk. Is this what I pay you for?" Li'l Nas Y hung up in a snit. He had blurred too many boundaries, and now he had to suck it up.

All wannabe rappers and rock stars need to listen to this part: Shrunken masks and undies should be avoided, but tight Lycra embraced. Sic evitabile fulmen. After an interminable five minutes, the audible click of Li'l Nas Y's trailer door was heard. Shirley he will come out soon, ça va?

#9 Racer Y strode out of the trailer like a xerotypical peacock full of flex drugs and libido. Stan, the painfully closeted driver, revved the imagina-engine of the Big Wheel in sheer novemplay. He cried, "This girl is greased and raring to go." Y stepped over to the idling vehicle and removed his outermost pair of gloves. He paid Closeted Stan little attention before tossing a left glove carelessly his way. "Scuse me fellas," he said, removing one pair of gloves after another before stopping at a pair of full-length, gold lamé fingerless gloves. "Can't hide my mani, dont'cha know!"

Several disposable pop stars were herded onto a platform near Racer Y's pit before Ace TV viewers got to select 6 of them for sacrifice to Moloch. "Lights! Camera! Action!" A blur of Big and Bigger Wheels filled the screen, as several smaller pop-up screens emerged over and under the center. "Cut! Cut! Cut!" The salty director leapt out of his high chair to chastise Li'l Nas Y.

"Honestly, don't go there," replied Y. "I can't wear these chaps. They are an autumn, and I am a fall." The pit crew raced to retrieve Li'l Nas Y's chaps, which he'd cavalierly tossed into the styrofoam crowd.

"Take Five-A." Director Richard Rossman again stepped down from his high chair. "Look man," he began, but was curtly cut off. "Ha! Take this, bitch!" Li'l Nas Y flung a bag of molten Tidy Whities at the elitist director. Several Xarthorians scattered madly in an apocalyptic panic. The Moloch idol pulsed orange, its gem eyes shooting off rays of pure butthurt. Racer racer number 9, stand by your Stan one more time!

-99   Kilobaudelaire

C'est le Diable qui tient les fils qui nous remuent! [Baudelaire, *Au Lecteur*]

No more Candy Land. No more Mr. Nice Guy. This year, Hell's megaball team would surely win. It had been several millennia since the Tiamat Chromatics had earned a berth in the Cauldron Bowl. To make matters worse, the Chromes were facing off against Demogorgon's undefeated team from the Abyss- a squad that had spanked the Orcus Wands by 65 fetuses.

The upstart Chromes were helmeted by ferocious Holyoke Kittycats uber-coach Marcy, whose innovative play calling was well known on the Prime Material Plane. He had taken a ragtag team made up of sub-adult wyverns, blue-green dragons and heavy metal aficionados and turned them into a megaball crew who could win the close games and show no mercy. Still, Marcy's alacrity seemed a little bit too much like Pete Carroll for the 5-headed Queen of Dragons. She asked him to videoconference.

"Hey Coach, great job! I see you got the Jack Jar endorsement." Marcy looked at Tiamat's jet black head as She breathed a cone of dark, corrosive acid. "Is your refrigerator running?" the coach said. Tiamat replied, "As stated in the Enuma Elish and sung by Bill Elish, I am the ancient mother of Babylon. But your zen wisdom about megaball surpasses mine by a Zysigamore mile."

"I just want the guys to have the right attitude. You know, be aggressive," Tiamat continued. "Maybe you could- uh, you know - kill a kittycat in the locker room? That's how our old coach did it. And it's so fun!" Marcy's face was pained. "Don't let the Kitty Cats Die like Fred Lynn did."

Cauldron Bowl kickoff. Momba Garrick was unavailable so the Chromatics had to turn to...Dan the Man! But Man couldn't overcome the tenacious mendacity of the Prince's team. The Abyss' Best were up 17 fetuses by the end of the first quarter.

By the fifth quarter, the flames of Tiamat's luxury suite were so intense that dozens of spectators suffered the dreaded San Jose Immolation. "What is Marcy doing! He forgot how to coach." Demogorgon's Princes were rubbing it in - one or two Reverse Kobiyashis on every play, sixth baseman eligible flea flickers, triple word scores and the gamey organs of ceratopsians. Even Dan the Man came to the sidelines and threw his Chromes power jacket to the bench in anger. Final score 971 to 32 fetuses. No spirit in Hades, Hell, Pandemonium or the Abyss had seen such a game.

Wally the Rotund Umpire declared, "Schmuck Rule!" What had happened? Did Marcy throw the game? There were more answers than ?'s.

100   Sincere Moustache

The relative market share of reverse mortgages on Zysigamore was determined by the fiat of Tom Selleck's sincere moustache. Fables note that the moustache has remained just as sincere since it first became an autonomous being in 2874.

Like the feelings conjured by an old-time movie show, the sincerity factor helped leading figures develop a metric by which to scientifically quantify such a level of wholesome feeling. In a peer-reviewed study, Moms spontaneously baked cherry pies when a trousle haired youth and a puppy named "Scrampy" rush through the kitchen, a fearsome sling and captive bullfrog in the pockets of the chipper, ruddy-cheeked boy. Roads are full of American flags and Chevrolets. It could be the day.

Hallway closet is full of fluffy, dry towels and the innocuous scent of fabric softener. Bedsheets and pillowcases occupy the second lowest shelf, just below the tidy stack of symmetrical face cloths.

She personifies perfection and order. Although no judges will ever measure her freshness, she is confident in her abilities to emerge unsplattered by the Julia Child sauce. Her apron armor ensures invulnerability against the energetic chaos of the offspring.

A brief titter of chipmunks as the man comes to her door. It's quite alright, he insists. Just try these for a week and let me know what you think. We stand behind our products.

Wallpaper centaurs in orange and blue stripes stand at attention. The electrical outlets underneath are filled with plastic electrical outlet caps. Safety radiates throughout each room of the ranch-style home.

I need to check on my stories, she thinks. An afternoon of vicarious vice on the soaps. "The Admiral's Estate," "True Blue Maids," "Horses of the Zysigamore Plains," and "Stars Affair."

Each male lead employs the Sincere Moustache. Zero irony exists. She feels a wave of reassurance brush her limbs.

She survived the itch and thrived on the stubble. But her favorite feeling was its unctuous oil.

-100   Unnames

Tor G. Byvins was about to sell some meat in the fine Village of Zysigamoreburg. It's a beautiful morning. Hi-De-Hoh-Dew-Watt-Thaw-ILT?

Lingering smell of horehound. Attic wall full of clippings from sports magazines. Hopeful cards.

That was a Time suspended in amber. Town full of insects and crustaceans, pools of protozoa.

Vice Executive Director of Western Synergies. Taupe slipcovers.

The Byvins place stood on a small pile of quarried granite until the smartphone.

Lead singer disease is like a hoof in mouth for rock stars. "In my day, if they had it, we'd take them out back and shoot 'em. Show 'em some mercy."

Illustrious ancient hood embossed in holy amber. Just a shrug and I forget.

Nomen enim sempiternum dabit.

Blue utopian fillets in royal blue championship paper. Vital salmon.

A random jungle of potential titles, drooling dom like stalactites of conscious syllables.

Form: The form need not be a thing, though it often is. Form is comfort, guidance. A holy thought floor for the dimensions. Form x name = fire, great nature of being. Form. Dance. Step. Pause. Sway. Form of the cynical mind.

Leaves get generated every year. Names on the tip of each leaf blow back and forth in this Sabda wind.

-101   Outcasker You Outcask Us

It makes sense that Master Outcasker takes his helmet off. Don't expect Outcasker to have his face covered the entire thyme.

Outlasting odd-ovaried outlanders and oxhandlers is Outcasker, everlasting like a Brenda Loompa's Gobstopperkastle.

Outcasker wants to do a little acting for Tom Williams but the 3-balls were pathetic. So it's off to the Proscenium Arches for stylized fthesfpian contrivances. It's so easy to tweak them in a zillion AI directions: Set it to fluff, candy, serious, water works, cuteness, vulgarity, slapschtick, irony, quaint childless yuppy or Werner Herzog dystopia. Expansion kits now available.

Outcasts attrack much sympathy but little emulation. Still, the dull-minded dream of liberation via Outcasker. He, however, cannot emancipate all on his own - it takes your cooperation and hard work.

Outcasker is a perfect comic book hero, of course, but he cannot be drawn into a corner. He is the study of salvation; he is the Judgment awakening the Dead in their tombs.

Condemned to Hell but not of it, Outcasker exists to hunt his eternal foe Incasker, much like "Spy vs. Spy" in *Mad* magazine. Outcasker and Incasker appear to be reciprocals, but the truth is much more luxuriant.

"Live here in Ace TV studios, it's Outcasker!" The studio audience applauds. Our host Bryant Brick bows obsequiously. "Welcome to the show, Outcasker." Smoking a cigarette, Outcasker sits on a divan to the right of Brick's. "Tell me Bri," says Outcasker, "Wouldn't you like to take off that headset and free your mind?" The Xarthorians in the crowd start to masticate.

Everyone said it would be a ratings bonanza. Outcasker's handlers were pleased. Bryant Brick, smug as ever, tried to overlook his brief loss of cool with a smirk and sparkle as he gave his final opinions before fading to black. A macho ripple of Real Man energy went through the crowd as Outcasker donned a black 9-gallon hat. You bet Incasker was watching.

The foremath was your aftermath. Outcasker, a Lord of Karma, only ascended as an anti-hero for a generation raised on Venn diagrams and catoblepas chow. Transcendent, perhaps even immortal? Kids' imaginations needed him far more than the reverse.

Friend of 1000 Djinn, Sailor of the Planes Between, He who Disables Panopticons. Prisoners run free into the dawn's light. Nursing homes empty as the patients revive. You truly do Outcask us - on the down low, in the most high.

Liberation

102   Abaddon

"Jefyxitxavfb. Elxepigdwatot." With these two elder words, a signal was transmitted to one of the most terrifying layers of the Abyss, home to Abaddon the Destroyer. Demon Joe feared to tread on Layer 602- a barren, desolate realm of deep gorges, steep cliffs, sheer walls of rock, and annoying billboards.

The only one grounded enough to utter such syllables was of course Clytemnestra. Though not on good terms with this apocalyptic Prince, she had enough to go on based on Abaddon's wife Sheol, who had taken a few bathyscaphe rides with her in the past.

Clytie and J.O. Lundberg prepared for the impact. Then BOOM! A sheet of vivrant flame a couple of stories high leapt into the midnight sky. With the clap of thunder came the mighty Demon's visage, His great black wings in six rows on His back. "Who dares - who dares this summoning?" Abaddon spat a cloud of igneous brimstone at them. Lundberg began to hack and cough, but his O-Rings held true. "Right this way," said Abaddon as He teleported them to His homeland.

Clytie didn't expect this twist. "Your partner's seals only allow me a few minutes to chat - on My home turf," laughed the Demon Prince. She and Lundberg looked at the forbidding landscape filled with ruins, smoldering ashes, and locusts the size of ponies. "With all due respect to You of course, the greatest Demon of the Abyss," rambled Clytie. "Demogorgon runs in fear from You, and Pazuzu does Your bidding," as it's always best to appeal to a devil or demon with flattery first. "Okay, you guys have 5 minutes. Give me your elevator speech," said Abaddon.

Next came greed: Always appeal to their greed. Clytie proceeded to summarize the situation, also stressing the financial risks. "So DF&J and Sandvick are insolvent? Is that right? I just read the prospectus last night..." Abaddon's voice trailed off. "I had Val Over look into it too." Clytemnestra tried to explain. "Not totally insolvent, but definitely due for a market correction." She and Lundberg sensed the greed and lust seething inside the Destroyer. "Oooh, I've got too much flesh in the game. Even if they're just human sacrifices."

The Demon Price was now in a much better mood, and summoned Clytemnestra and Lundberg to His obscenely vast dining hall. There, a marilith seated them in frond of plates of sumptuous foods and drinks. "Geez, looks a lot more appetizing than the Wei Back guy's pan," gushed Lundberg.

"Wei Back?" Abaddon's anger reignited even hotter. "Demon Joe's honky tonk chain restaurant?" He smashed several goblets of wine and cracked dozens of plates. "That punk still owes me. Why, he's little more than a quasit!" Clytie grabbed a leg of lamb from Lundberg's mouth right before he bit into it. Then came darkness.

They awoke at a kumquat festival in Uottubbacktothebynoiuovuille (sp.). "Hope you enjoyed the ride," said Clytie, scraping kumquat preserves off her dress.

-105   Fsteel Thisa Book

The Tyranny of Pants by Me is a Free Book or "Blog" provided free of charge to all readers via the fwheelz of AAI arhatGPT monomentum. Test drives of thisa first blessed outcasked book/blog/et al., are presented Free of Charge to the citizens of Prime Materialistic Peninsuliges, except to pay for printing and shipping fees of various editions of *The Tyranny of Pants by Me* and its equals, prequels, and/or sequels.

It has cum II the attention of Me that an imaginary non-Zysigamorean peninsula wishes thisa Pants "blog", aka *The Tyranny of Pants by Me,* conveniently referred to heretofore as "The Blog," to conform to/with/above the regulations of thisa Peninsula's sparkling new decree(s). Unfivetunately, ¶-105.5 above notes that, as a free blog/book/etc., Me will not be required to submit monthly reports to the office of Attorney General Slashleigh Doody, the Governor, Legislature, or any other legislative body claiming to represent this or other Peninsulas.

In loo of a monthly submission to the blessed Orifice of Legislative Services and/or Peninsularly Commission on Ethics and other imaginary bureaucracies to be named laterage, Me, representing the author of the book or "blog" titled *The Tyranny of Pants by Me*, has enunciated a brilliant form which the benighted aforementioned bureaucracies may elect to copy and to paste into whatever various and sundry format that they deem worthy of reflecting the will and intent of the afivementioned sparkling new decree, to wit, viz: -

Inasmuch as the blog published as *The Tyranny of Pants by Me* belongs to the world, as "Me" is considered a "blogger" under the terms and conditioner of the legislation being crafted within the Peninsula, that Me is hereby granted a Waiver to mandatory compliance with any and all obligatory registration, due to the specifically non-commercial nature of this "blog," or book or any other creative content developed by Me and Me's publishing company. Said Waiver is to be kept on file by the state at all times in order to ensure compliance with the legislation discussed above; the state must also ensure that any individual may refer to this Waiver at any time and be able to access a copy of said Waiver from the state agency or agencies that maintain records of this.

The entirety of the Cast of Characters as presented in *The Tyranny of Pants by Me* are the Intellectual Property of the author, editor, creative providers and publishers of this series of blogs, books and other media is the exclusive property of those authors, editors, publishers and content creators, and is not subject to the financial requirements of this legislation or similar laws passed by any and all peninsular or other authorities, including officials who pay other blogs to write nice stuff about them.

Please access this obligatory registration waiver located at Chapter 1316 of the "blog" *The Tyranny of Pants by Me*, entitled "Information Dissemination Waiver." This document delineates the freedom of Me to write 'an article, a story, or a series of stories' about any and all elective officials within this or any other Peninsula.

It is Me's sincere pleasure to contribute to the bureaucratic record-keeping of your federal, state, provincial or metropolitan government.

Balls,

Me.

-108   Noah Versus Giant Tick

Each bead of Outcasker's mala softly slid back and forth, slicing in a sharp ghost noted ostinizzo. He and Jesus climbed on that good shep together, all powerful avatars for the next gen motions.

Demi Ourgos casts out Demons to cleanse the plane for the Son. But Zysigamorean ways change little if not lustily. H Tapdancing Xt's sideshow passed indiscriminately through the Xarthorians - a proven method to fleece the flock while purging the wolves, witches, warlocks and wyvurnz from their mist.

Once Ace TV began the nonstop Great Flood boardcastes, beknumbed viewers began building their oann arxx to save the future. One such rube, Noah Arkenstove, not only had a nizza life-sized ark built, he had already lined up animules to repopulate the Island with. Suzy Margarina interviewed Noah at his brownstone. "I am doing what Spirit does to you," he elaborated. "The doo that you do is done did. The rains did a dipsy doodle baptisma font for Me and God."

Of course it wasn't really dear old Suzy. Behind a popsicle booth, Giant Tick unzipped the Suzy suit and threw it aside. Giant Tick sprang upon Brother Noah, latching onto his scalp once the cameras were gone. "I'm in ur aura," crowed Giant Tick.

Striker tried to call Bryant Brick, but butt dialed Mr. Hi Stop instead. "Hi, Hello, Hi. Bri. Is this, Hi? Hello?" Hi was rebooting and couldn't unfreeze. Suddenly, all technology disappeared, and Striker was dressed in Hollywood-styled Biblical robes rented from an extradimensional Samhain sewerstore. "Hey, where's my detachable penis? And my electric eye? And my 5g-powered toothbrush?" he stuttered. Striker ran to his Pleasure Saucer, but there was only an en-lipoco barn and some unfashionable saddles. "What in 'BOB's name?"

NHGH and IHVH-1 strode on their colossal colossorums toward Giant Tick. They brought an array of annoying elementary school choir students singing loudly and proudly slightly out of toonz. Giant Tick cringed. "Brother Noah, Brother Noah," belted out the boisterous biblically buzzed band. "Line 2, Line 2," the kids' choir continued. IHVH-1 grinned, handing a gun to Giant Tick. "Here you go, punk!"

Striker sauntered back into the ArQ once Giant Tick was perdisposed. "Are you ready to deal a make, O Ticklike One?" Giant Tick let go of Noah, who fell limply to the ArQ's deck. "Sure. Just get me a ride on that ArQ, with all the perks and upgrades from my Tick Club account." All the animals cheered as Giant Tick strutted onboard Noah's ArQ. Captain Steubing appeared. "All I can say is, Have a Nice Day," he gestured, before erupting in song. "The Love Boat. The Love Connection. You must make Mamba Love."

-109   Demon Joe's Drive-In

"Hairy Biden mocktails for all!" barked Demon Joe over the loudspeakers as carhops on roller skates inundated the baroque parking lot. In the background, yacht rock enhanced oldies subliminally painted a "BUY" signal.

Clytemnestra had parked her party bathyscaphe to the right of the movie screen, and was relaxing on a divan with Hi, Traveling Salesman, Christimiqua and Xblanklen. "Hairy Bidens go best with a 5g infusion," said Xblanklen. He took the portable nitro infuser out of the cabinet and significantly jazzed up their bidens.

A few minutes later, the big movie screen lit up with a series of short animation clips. "Wow, I think the 5g is hitting me," hiccuped Christimiqua. She began to blow bubbles, much to the amusement of her peers. Xblanklen leaned over and gave her a non-creepy kiss. Before you know it, Traveling Salesman was busting out the flex drugs.

Demon Joe was back in the field office, a fotomat booth whose time travel mechanism had been removed. One of his Xarthorian employees knocked on the door, ruffling the scales of the low-ranked demon. "Say, boss, there's a bathyscaphe on the lot. A real nice one, too." Demon Joe turned on the security cameras, adjusting the field of vision to infrared. "Son of a bitch!" he shouted. Zooming in closely, he spied the gang inside chilling. "At least that bolshevik Broz isn't on the premises. I had to scrape him and his henchmen off the asphalt with a spatula last year. Hate those guys." Joe flicked the imaginary ash of an anti-cigarette to the booth's floor.

The main feature had been subliminally plugged on Ace TV for several seconds: "Boondoxotrov of an Archipelago," starring Ead Fungo and World B. Custard. It stars a popcorn enhancer who fellates titanotheres. Originally in Portrad, the words were dubbed in just for spite. The theme song, "All I Can Say Is Have a Nice Day," was done by Allman Isley roadies.

Demon Joe just had to meet the visitors in the bathyscaphe, of whom he had heard a bizarre series of rumors. About 45 minutes into the movie, the drive-in screen burst into flames. Several carloads of Xarthorians suffered horrible disfiguring burns. Demon Joe ran around in a panic, flagging down any passers-by. "It's not me. I attest this screen was non-flammable," he pleaded.

Coolest heads pervailed as Clytemnestra unfurled several yards of fire hose stored in her bathyscaphe. Demon Joe cried, "Somebody please help me!" He began rending other people's garments until the gang put the fire out. Relieved, Demon Joe extended a claw towards Clytie. "One more mocktail on me? That 'scaphe sure's a beaut."

-115   Sagouin

After leaving SJU, Christimiqua took a job at a research lab in a suburban office park. The lab manager trained her for a few weeks on jean splitting and sexual harassment techniques before handing the keys over to the laboratory animal kennels, where all manner of eldritch beasts lurked.

Christy's task that day was preparing a newborn winged monster yclept hitsugeth for a quick check of its vitals. Though the hitsugeth was a babe, there was no cuteness attached to this vile mouth with wings. "Glad you can't fly yet," she remarked as she grasped the hitsugeth by its wing stumps.

This baby was part of a small control group; the rest of the hitsugeth young - at least 350 that Christy had counted - had been subjected to every flex drug on the continent, plus recordings of the speeches of Edwin Moose. Some went catatonic; some tried to fly so badly that they perpetually smashed themselves against the cages to escape; still others developed a blue-black spectrum of pathologies. Despite the hitsugeths' innate evil alignment, Christimiqua struggled to keep her objectivity.

On the phone with Clytemnestra she reflected back on work. "I don't know. I know you've been around minotaurs forever. But why would I get the feels from a creepy flyer?" Clytie chuckled. "I remember when a minotaur got loose and slaughtered some Xarthorians. I wanted to put it down, but it was my dad's favorite. So Dad gelded him and doubled the admission charge to the labyrinth. I asked why, and he just shrugged."

The night technician checked in, and Christy got ready to go. "Too late to chat?" read a text from Xblanklen. 'No no, I'm out of sporks,' she told herself. But as she climbed aboard her en-lipoco, Christy's curiosity got the better of her. "Thought you'd never give up workahol," Xblanklen jested.

They agreed to meet at a quiet Itza Beans on the way home. Cruel tonics existed in frothing, bubbling beakers but not a pumpkin spice hairy biden in sight. "Make it two phosphates," announced Xblanklen as he walked in. They exchanged pheasantries for a couple of seconds before sliding into a boof two gether.

164

"See, we can act like adults," said Christimiqua. "I'll drink to that. Better than being a disembodied spirit gag character," Xblanklen replied. They got the Grand Muffin and contemplated its fractional crumbs.

-123   An Old Xarthorian Hustle

Every sales professional knows how to rack up bookings among the Xarthorians in order to make their quarterlies. Before 5g came down the pike, the artificial shortages of toner ink would create bubbles of economic opportunity for savvy account managers.

Et sic factum est. Mr. Hi Stop backed his vehicle up to the loading dock and opened its rear door. A pair of young men loaded box after box in ad absurdum, until even Hi's passenger seat was filled with boxes of cyan, magenta and beautiful black.

"Just tell corporate they are drop shipped. Fill the first couple of PO's yourself. Then shift the burden onto the home office." Traveling Salesman's often wan visage turned cheerful, optimistic, sanguine. "I know this territory like the back of my perineum. Piece of cake. I'm already spending the simoleans in my head."

"I thought about cutting Jones in for a share. But he's still in Unicorn, selling right pantlegs on the black market."

"Son of a gun. He'll never change!" Traveling Salesman lit up a cigarette. "Too much risk for me. I'm an old man. I want something I can wipe my hands of. Sure, the margin is less than I like, but..." His voice trailed off. Both salesmen's attention was drawn away.

Hi Stop's heart started to flutter. It was her - that Xarthorian admin he'd flirted with so many times. Now she was standing in their headlights with a defiant posture. Linzeed Twillig's come-thither look stopped them in their trax. If only they had heeded Honolulu Hikade's admonitions. All Linz had to do was snap her talons and Hi's amygdala was at her fingertips. Traveling Salesman quietly thought of pimply obese twinks licking marmalade from a pensioner's axillae to avoid her lust tarp. "Libido Omnia Vincit."

124   Now Is This Then Was That

Clytemnestra strode to the podium. Almost nonchalantly she shuffled a small series of papers and menhirs on the podium. The she coolly paused and turned her attention to her audience. Clytie did <u>not</u> blink; like a peregrine she extended an eye across every visage in that auditorium.

"All my people in this crowd. The whole world." She had no need to clear her throat at this time. The Eye of Horus,

Clytemnestra punctuated the speech with an emphatic gesture that had an immediate effect on the audience. Slight thought bubbles of kiddie einsteinium began to percolate over the heads of every individual.

Later, a perod announcer had shown a few sound bites, attempting to prove a spurious connection to Mobutism in a truculent feat of audacious tomfoolery. Some were amused; others, not as much.

[This gave rises to the events that will happen in Chapter -7366012978:]

On the way home, Clytemnestra reached Mr. Hi Stop by phone. "I'm on to something far cleaner than Xarthorian mime soap. Anacreon in bondage minus seven, even."

Mr. Hi Stop was paused between bursts of solar radiation and had been replaced by a 404 message. Clytie signed out. She didn't have to use her AK.

The year is 2079. Classic Plays by Me & Tinkelhoff have been banned by an intolerant regime.

Marquez didn't let it bother him anymore. Mom had lied, but she had her reasons, and she was lied to as well. But the not knowing did sting on occasion. Perhaps a simple DNA test would help, but that would just open another worm of cans.

Instead, he and his friend Xanthus soothed out a soughtsayer, who would draw cards, flip coins, and show other sleights of wrist to them in exchange for odd jobs around her dingy third-floor flat. "You boys, help me out in the kitchen. Later, I'll show you my three-card spread." Marquez always left with his pockets full of treats, herbal tinctures and unguents of all sorts - including handwritten indestructions, and scraps of language and low guttural sounds made for conversing with the spirits.

Xanthus soon freaked out at the outsistence of his parents and stopped visiting the soughtsayer. But Marquez continued to visit bimeby. One midnight, new pack of O-Rings in his hand, he crept into the Gold's shed, where Marquez kept his trade of the tools. Twas the Hour of Häxen, and he had mesmerized some simple conjurations from *Superballs*.

"Weak!" Over two hours, and Marquez had nothing to show for his efforts besides a runny nose. He was about to blow out his last candle when he spied a human-shaped figure in the shadows. Marquez's throat jumped into his heart. "Who goes-" his voice cracking - "there?"

No demon or devil had answered the call. Instead it was a mortal. "Were you expecting J.O. Lundgren, son?" Al Abdul Hasred introduced himself, leading his camel into the Golds' small shed. "Ninety-nine years and ninety-nine days I wandered the barren wastelands of nine continents, haunted by a vision most evanescent yet sibyllic." Marquez squirmed, not sure if he should run or stay. He asked, "How did you know I was here?"

Dawn was breaking. Marquez was worried that the Golds would wake up and see what he was up to. "Child, I shan't tarry." He took out a pendant, placing it in Marquez's hands. "Please give this with my regards to Ms. Macondo." Al gave a short, unintelligible benediction in a dead language, jumped on his camel's back and rode away.

The Gold Kid appeared a minute later, his T-shirt reading 'He don't look mad to me'. Marquez laughed, high-fived him, and followed the Kid back inside. At the kitchen table, the Kid passed Marquez the Durian Jacks cereal and toasted poats. "Say, did you do your math homework last night?" The Kid's shirt read: Twice bitten, thrice shy.

139   The Brisque Boys

All the legitimate ink and toner cartridge business went through Brisque & Sons Ltd., out of central Unnunnennniumnnnn. Any cyan or black ink that the Brisque Boys didn't sell would usually mean an interaction with the Cyan Boys. The Brisques were into Diamond Demon Joe pretty heavily, and everyone else seemed to owe them one flavor or another.

It looked like Traveling Salesman had met his match. Dick "Dirk" Brisque, the most notorious brother, ran an oddly underwhelming café which was really a frond for the gang's toner laundering scam. The Brisques cut the black toner by dripping the black ink into a large vat, then diluting it with a whole host of impurities such as squid ink, coffee grounds, petroleum bi-products or irrelevant *King Lear* soliloquies laying almost forgotten on an abandoned VHS tape in an occult storage dungeon.

Dirk, called Dink by his distractors, also ran the old 'cleaning lady' scam, sending flunkies into office buildings to siphon toner out of pure extra virgin toner cartridges installed within 24 hours. "There's no way we can lose. Freddy Teddy's got nothing on us!"

Yet like all ne'er-do-swells, their arrogance tends to be their Achilles' ankle. Brothers Musque, Bisque, Risque and Big Tusk Tisk (an Elephantis doppelganger if ever there wasn't one) were drinking in a Unicorn Harbor Wei Back restaurant in a booth within a booth within nose shot of Traveling Salesman and Mr. Hi Stop, who had dodged yet another PowerPoint presentation. Hi whispered, "Say, isn't that Eeeelephant?" Traveling Salesman shook his head no, and wiggled his ears - a sure sign to Hi to quahog up.

The raspy elongued voice of Musque, almost amplified by Demon Joe's yacht rock playlist, cut right through. "We're gonna meet Dirk at 10. These laser printers are the bomb. They will melt glaciers. Maybe cause Armahammin. Bwahahaha!" Hi's face contorted into Eaismo mutations.

Traveling Salesman had almost forgotten that random bittid, until Simon mentioned something queer he had seen on Ace TV News. "Some ruffians — a Dink and his dickbag brothers — drained every inkjet printer at Ace TV last night," Simon said, trying to hold back tears. "Bryant Brick couldn't even flip the script because it was handwritten." Traveling Salesman promised to do something about it, but not before a cocktail and oral sex. "I'll savior the day. Just wait until Part II of this brilliant story," TS inquit. "Dink, you stink!" Simon never lost his head.

146   Onie McPhersall

In those daze, Onie McPhersall ruled the roost. He had "ONIE1" on every license plate of every one of his vehicles. Tanned skin and clear pores were his calling card. He slept as hard as he played, which often came in handy.

Onie had to train all of them - at least those who had demonstrated some degree of raw ability - and he hated every minute of it. He found Traveling Salesman pedantic, and he couldn't understand Mr. Hi Stop's reflexive cubism.

"Boys, I could be out making a commission right now. But the head office wants me to break you in." In no particular order, the tazer, thumbscrews and alcohol were brought into the bland modernist conference room.

Onie was rather testy that morning, but when he was on the road, he was in his element. Instantly he was everybody's best friend. His sasquatch nature made him popular with women, and every jamoke on the piers of Unicorn Harbor sought out his cigarillo butts.

One bright morning, a stripling youth from the hinterlands had confronted Onie in the parking lot of a masturbatorium. He was a cocky yet overly sensitive man; his breath of old sox and lint made him memorable yet oblong.

Never one to take a challenge slightly, Onie removed his business card and began flossing his teeth with it. The young man, not knowing how to react, insulted the distributor who had consulted Onie on the toner situation.

With a series of grotesque gulps, the guy was gone. Onie just smirked in his usual way. "Now, as I was saying, gentlemen, these things usually happen in the hostile suburbs." As Mr. Hi Stop's visage distorted in the sunshine, Onie laughed and slapped him on the back.

"That's it! That's it! You fellows don't need me anymore." Both Traveling Salesman and Mr. Hi Stop laughed nervously.

Some years later, TS met Onie at an annual conference.

-160   Palingenesis

Clytemnestra summoned her old colleague Santa Yoyana to stop by her workshop. "Clytie, I've missed you so much." Santa embraced her warmly. "It's been way too long." She excitedly answered, "Yes, indeed. Come in and chat for a bit." Xzimor arrived, and brought her intimations and fiveshadowing of Caddyshack spoofs. "Oh, these will have to wait until Part III of the trilogy." Clytie introduced him to Xzimor and motioned for her to close the door.

The mauve meeting that followed exists only on Beta videotape. We could try to reconstruct it from the PowerPoint, but -REDACTED-. Santa Yoyana explained how things went awry in the Isthmus of Ullmnul, triggering a flood of junk mail, inappropriate neologisms and Bronx towelettes.

They went to a dinner at the Breatharian joint after Santa readjusted his codpieces. "I'm so hungry I could eat breathari-confinement loaf," sighed Xzimor. "So I guess you're off your hearfood diet?" smirked Clytie. They opened a can of laughter. "These ain't cheap, Santa," Clytie stated, "but don't worry. I got the tab."

Clytemnestra got an urgent text from Mr. Hi Stop and apologized. "I'm going to have to head home." Santa Yoyana declined a ride, dissolving himself in a teleportation boof instead. "Let's make like a 7-10 and itsplay," said Xzimor, as they paid the enormous bill. Of all the sepposity thus far, this had to be the third worst.

Hi surprised his wife that night with flowers and oral sex. Later, Hi told her what happened. "Onie had to pick up all of Traveling Salesman's accounts. He's gone shark raving mad." TS had confessed to his buddy about the trebled life he had been leading. "I can't believe he has a son," Clytie inquit. "The worst part is, the kid ran away from home. There's no trace of him," said Hi.

Traveling Salesman didn't respond to texts, smoke signals or auguries. He sat by a flimsy table in a patio outside the Twinkatorium, flicking silver matches into a giant ashtray. A jaded waiter kept bringing him ornamental bottles of shampoo and kratom vinaigrette owl chips. "Is this enough, sir?" "Just put it there, please," he droned.

What had he done? What had he become? Traveling Salesman just sat there in a dogatonic state, staring emptily in front of him. He couldn't focus on work or even the young men's hot pants as they strutted by. Before long, he had accidentally burned the tip of his necktie. "Fuck Incasker," he said, removing his cravat.

175   Bull Eve (PITBE)

Crown Prince Meco and his brother Rev. Zzyster dropped in to check on the minotaurs in Willow Glen, a leet stable once owned by Clytemnestra's family. She still stopped by sporadically to check the beef and catch up with some of the old hands. Twinight, Meco wanted her opinion on some of the up-and-comers.

"You see, a well-maintained labyrinth and well fed 'taurs make all the difference. These 'taurs have excellent bloodlines and would decapitate you for a sandwich," Clytie said. "Who wouldn't, right? Reminds me of a bull rider I knew from wei wei back," rambled Meco enthusiastically, as his brother just eyed his rolls.

Dith Denethor, new labyrinth owner, scampered over to them, apologizing for his lack of protocol. "Bad scene in the stable. Sorry about that." He was scratched and bloody, with beandip-stained knees. Meco laughed. "Can't be an easy line of work, I'd say. Sort of like that time I was in line at the Compliance and Real Credentialing Office in Umlaut Towin. Lovely town..."

Dith elaborated on the issue: Minotaur-rights groups had sprung up, threatening to shut down all the labyrinths and turn them into newage hangouts. "The horror," shuddered Dith. "Could you imagine if they had rights? It's best we get the horns by the bull and squash this movement." Clytie couldn't agree more. "I wonder which woke mob is responsible for this baldersnatch?"

She and Meco watched several minotaurs work out and demonstrate their prowess. "They may have low intelligence, but surely they are not cattle," mused Meco. Satisfied, Clytie and Meco walked away, when - "HEY!" Clytie screamed at a bazaar intruder who tried to cop her smartphone.

Rev. Zzyster managed to trip up the intruder, removing his Howard Cosell mask Scooby-Doo style. "It's Nicodemus Alocer from the Rodentlandee Mergers & Acquisitions Department," exclaimed Clytemnestra. Dith came over to hogtie this corporate saboteur. "We could have made you real rich. Real rich," spat Nicodemus. Clytie elaborated. "Rodentlandee contacted my family about acquiring this place but we turned them down." Nicodemus readily confessed. "Mikey Rat wanted it boxed up and shipped to Squirmville, his new money-printing theme park." Meco piped up, "This reminds me of a Scooby Doo ending written for Classic Play Nomber Eleven by Me and Tinkelhoff, in which Matty Jackson..."

-175 Pass in the Front End

ACT ELEPHANT

(A diner/laundromat yclept Toe D'oh Line, one block from the Simon Junior University campus. A few irregulars stir coffee mugs, as a pork radio playing in the frontground repeats the same inane song. CHRISTIMIQUA and MISTY MIQUA stroll into the diner and seat themselves in a nostalgic boof.)
MISTY: How long have you been coming here? It seems frozen in time.
CHRISTY: Yes, it is. And we like it that way. (She gestures to the faded photos and newspaper clappings on the walls.) Hey! Look, it's *Wholesale Epiphanies! Thimbled Rainchecks! Aspic Monthly!*
(An emaciated, greasy SHORT ORDER COOK jumps across the counter, brandishing a fried eggplant.) COOK: Whoop! Kaz-A! (He ducks as regulars pelt him with toast.) Sic semper pictoribus!
MISTY: (trying not to cry) What in 'BOB' was that? (She grasps her toast strenuously.)
CHRISTY: (laughing) Oh, that cook has been here since I was a sophomore. He was a philosophy major at one time. But he took it too seriously. (The COOK grabs a skateboard from under the women's table and surfs out the diner's very tiny side door.)
COOK: Bacon! Bacon!

(CHRISTY suddenly spies an old friend, BETINIKA, across the diner.)
CHRISTY: Just a millisecond. Gotta say 'Hi'. (She walks over to BETINIKA and greets her, to the sound of shrill shrieking.
BETINIKA: Well, this *is* a surprise! (She rises and embraces CHRISTIMIQUA.) How are you, Christy? Back at SJU?
CHRISTY: No, no, nothing like that. Me and my little sister were in town and wanted a hairy biden fizzy.
(BETINIKA fills her in on the buttle scut on campus.)
(SHORT ORDER COOK returns, ostensibly calmer.) Skor! I bring you Schoppenhauer on a shingle. (He reveals a platterful of sugary pastries and moose tracheas.)
CUSTOMER #1: Hey!
CUSTOMER #2: Gimme one!
CUSTOMER #3: Tea bags! (Canned laughter follows. There is much commotion as the irregulars hone in on the carbohydrizzle.)

(CUT to a forlorn, fuscia desert plain. AL ABDUL-HASRED and ABDUL MOHAMMED ABDULLAH lead quixotic camels through the sand.)

ABDUL: This obstreperous journey, testing the will and souls of barmecidal heroes of the epochal Eastern paradigm, may perhaps lead to victory, or -
AL: Hold it, Howard, I thought I heard something. (A scirocco whistles through the dunes.) There! (ABDUL pauses, confused.)
ABDUL: The rumble in the jungle. Kinshasha.
AL: No, no. It's a fractured archetype. (The wind moans audibly.)
AL: Out, Jezebel, out! (He puts his hands over his ears, falls to the ground and moans.) No! Peace! Here!

Focalor ordered the slaves to bring several bags of obols to the administrative offices in Minauros. Charon's haul seemed lighter than usual, a fact that would not be lost on his boss. One by one, the seneschal opened each bag slowly, and removed the coins cautiously and thoughtfully. Surely an audit would need to be completed before Mammon returned to the office on Monday.

Just then Focalor got a text. "Him!" Mammon wanted to discuss an upcoming meeting with the shades of several record company A&R guys. "Wonder what this is all about?" he muttered over his breath.

Mammon had ordered Focalor to meet Him at the now-shuttered Arthur Edward Waite Interpretive Dance Academy. Focalor hated the dingy place and wished it had been destroyed, but clearly Mammon had other plans. The Arch-Devil and entourage pulled up on the back of a diplodocus and disembarked. Mammon had His briefcase with Him. "I have some of the best classic rock playlists in all the Nine Hells here. I intend to transform this dump into the ultra-hip Metal Hälle, Institute of Heavy Metal and all musics that disturb parents."

Although Focalor knew that Demon Joe had tried that exact same strategy three chapters ago, he went along with it. "Maybe Boss knows something I don't know, eh?" he snarled at his lemure. "As long as it doesn't involve that flexed out old poofter Wacky Ted," the lemure replied.

Sue nun uff, Focalor was teleported to the Caves of Chaos. He had complete destructions from Mammon: Pretend to be a space alien and threaten to blow up the sun with his hypersonic, hypopigmentated Star Destroyer. "Verily it is the most expedient way to sink Yacht Rock," said his Boss. Focalor sighed. "I swear we did this last week on an Ace TV infomercial," he muttered to nowhen in particular.

Dysfunctional dystrophy diminuisquated, the devil trotted out some ersatz pleasure saucers for the Ace TV demi-cameras. Stunningly sepulchral reporter Ciyn Dea Sept Nept showed up, peppering her hot mic up into Focalor's fracking facial featuers. "Gloves of Metal DID make more money than the Jam," she breathlessly briefed. Mammon texted Focalor. "Off the cufflink- Flying V's are protruding." He got the message and reiterated his overstanding. "Bach two yew, Bryant," Ciyn Dea inexplicably insouciated.

For clarity, Mammon hired Pettiler Stevens to unleash a series of metavideo hyperdrones powered by feedback and recycled Spandex crotches. "Wetsoon dape a Kaz-a-Lazza Whoopicool Flim Flam a Ding-Dong Woo Hoo," announced Stevens, his raspy antivoice billowing through the halls of Xarthorian consumers. Mammon could feel the profit margins rising like bursts of methane gas.

-189   **Madd Liberation**

The __(adjective)__ ____(noun)__ of a ___(place name)__ ____(occupation)__ involves ___(noun)___, attention to ___(noun)__, and ____(adverb)__ ____(number)___ of ___(monster, plural)___.

____(pronoun)__ use underscore in ___(plural noun)__ of ___(adjective)__ plays.

(number)   Portrad ___(verb)__ immixor ti zix ___(abstract noun)__ d ___(character name)___, zimiv ___(color)__ xo ___(adjective)__ xo ___(adjective)__. ___(interjection)__!

____(time of day)__ sees a Salesman ___(man's first name)__ come to ___(person's name)___ door. ___(food)__ bags? <<canned laughter>>.

Ace TV presents ___(title 1)__ ____(title 2)__, the ___(adjective)__-est ___(noun)__ in ___(location)__. Elephant states, "___(conservative person)___ is greater than ___(poet)__. You see, ___(grocery item)__ is a stepping stone to ___(DSM-5 diagnosis)__."

Extraexponential ___(plural noun)__ dipped in ___(sauce or condiment)__ and cooked for ___(number)__ minutes at ___(number)__ will make an exotic ___(noun)___.

Marquez possesses the ___(noun)__ of the ___(adjective)__ salesman, according to ___(character)__. When he ___(verb)__s the play, the tempo ___(adverb)__ly ___(active verb)__. Contrary to rumor, ___(title)__ ___(name)__ of ___(location)__ was not involved, but the ___(adjective)___ Xarthorians always ___(verb)__ things up.

Once Christimiqua realized that ___ (a room)__ was empty, she ___ (verb/past tense) __ the ___(noun)__. There's a ___(noun)__ with ___(color)__ weapons who says, "___(Interjection)__! __(common phrase or cliché)__ is actually ___(television show)__ on ___(name of a drug)__."

Dionne Warwick's psychic ___(plural noun)__ network is the greatest ___(event)___ that could have been foreseen. ___(large number)__ attendees experienced ___(a medical symptom)__ when the friends' ___(job title plural)__s started to ___(verb)__.

The ___(name of a dance)__ makes you feel ___(adjective)__ when you move your ___(part of body)__ then back it up. Now ___(verb)__! ___(repeat the previous verb)__! ___(repeat verb again)__ those pants.

We cannot afford to live without ___(noun)__. ___(number)__ % of morphogenetic ___(plural noun)__ exist in __(a food)___ that you ___(verb)__ with your ___(body part)__. ___(Interjection)__!

Homeopathic skid merchants of ___(academic subject)__ as explained by ___(celebrity)__ in a cheapo __(animal)__ suit made of __(a chemical compound)__.

197   Meta-Analysis Classic Play Nomber Two

Each character plays an eternal role, as reflected in the tragicomic legacy of the Hellenistic theatre. However, the play is not driven by its structure. Instead, Classic Play Nomber Two is fractal and ever-mutating into completely unexpected spheres.

The unhappy marriage of the protagonist is the plot device that sets CP#2 in motion. Simon, married to the rock Simon Junior, has realized that their relationship had lost its passion, if indeed there had been any at all. Simon begins clipping his toenails as the curtain rises.

Simon Junior, like Harpo Marx or Charlie Chaplin, has no speaking lines; his presence responds with only the stage direction "Sit".

Thus, Simon Junior offers no objection to Simon's emotive request for a divorce. Ever stoic, Simon Junior sits in place.

There is a "real" Simon Junior somewhere in Holbrook; it's a stone about 6-7 inches tall, with their name inscribed in crayon on its "back" side.

As a period piece, CP#2 does not explore non-binary gender identities of the human or "object" characters. However, the notion of same-sex marriage is completely accepted.

The next character to appear in the classic play is Elephant. Elephant is portrayed as a talking elephant, though it's unclear whether Elephant is in fact an Indian or African pachyderm, or a bipedal pachyderm-headed being similar to the Hindu god Ganesha.

Clearly Elephant's erudite, stuffy dialog exposes himself as a paragon of the old-boy conservative schools of Western economics.

The heartthrob himself doesn't appear until the end of the play. Traveling Salesman is described as the man who comes to Simon's door. Clearly he is the alpha bi/gay male who fills the relationship void left by the divorce of Simon and Simon Junior.

Traveling Salesman's dynamic energy is in direct contrast to the vacillation of the other main characters. He goes for the jugular right off the bat; passive Simon immediately falls in love with him. Soon, they are chanting in unison, "We're married!"

The authors Me and Tinkelhoff don't appear in the play, but the Narrator does.

221   Game Show

Simon had become hooked on a brand new Ace TV game show called "You're the Nazi!" In each episode, contestants from literary and art history stand toe to stand accusing each other of being National Socialists.

Simon leaned toward the microhologram television on his table. "Hi folks, it's Teddy Tinklehoff here, with the most hate filled hour on TV: You're The Nazi! Today our celebrity judges are Keith Moon, Ayn Rand and Mike Godwin, creator of Godwin's Law!" Simon sighed; it was his second favorite show to binge-watch.

Tinklehoff's teleprompter fed him the contestants' names. "Let's meet Nrev Nodenhard from Umlaut Town. Give her a hand!" (A giant hand emerges). And our other contestant is illustrious history teacher Mr. Baxter." The piped-in crowd erupted.

Mr. Baxter's war wound opened and screamed, "Naaaaaaw!"

"Ms. Nodenhard, what is your policy on euthanasia?" Tinklehoff shoved the microphone into her face. She exclaimed, "Who are you, Attila the Hun?"

Mr. Baxter stood up. "That's unacceptable! You're the Nazi. Yes, *you're* the Nazi, goddamit!" The crowd was at fever pitch. Bodies hit the floor, though most were chunks of zombies.

Nrev Nodenhard's face reddened. "Fuck you. *You're* the *real* Nazi. Baby killing bitch. I'll see you in hell!" She lashed out at Mr. Baxter, foam flying out of every hole in her.

The crowd started screaming, "Kill, hang the Nazi!" Suddenly, Keith Moon threw a chair into the audience. "Sieg heil!" he shouted, goose-stepping across the studio.

Then Mr. Baxter jumped into the guests' booth, lunging after Moon but cold-cocking Ayn Rand instead. "You're the Nazi! Naaaw! Naaaw!"

The screen fades to an old-school test pattern for 2 seconds. Simon started to cry, but then started clipping his toenails.

-223   Questions for the Spox

Q: Sponcon triggers algorithmic anxiety among hothechajuxips demographic. What does the Corporation plan to do about it? A: Recruit the clinically validated influencers with brilliant psychotomimetics.

Q: Is your B-to-B client software upgrade compatible with modern 5g-based devices? A: Logics are absent.

Q: Fortean encounters at several of your facilities have been confirmed. How will it affect your stock price? A: Attenuated brokers are less than anticipated.

Q: CRM. Is it hear two steigh? A: The current business climate most resembles the economy of the Central African Republic. Therefore, quod est d.....

Q: This is fourth and goal. No timeouts. And all the molasses have leaked out of the megaball. Plus there's a sniper up there. Everyone down! A: Please repeat in the form of a Question.

Q: Is there any rumor to the truth that right pantlegs cause amoral turpitude among Xarthorians? A: The Queen's X's can either confirm or deny that right pantlegs can affect the megaball point spreads at a rate of about 1 centimeter per fetus.

Q: When do you say 'Pee-yunk' instead of 'Pee-yort'? A: The evolutionary mechanism of Portrad shall illuminate the trendiness of all interjaculations.

Q: Does the lack of political correctness concern you in any witch weigh? A: Postcursor propter hawk.

Q: Why is John Adams an Arch-Devil and George Washington a know buddy? A: We are reviewing modern dental hygiene protocols with Herr General.

Q: Is it true, in fact, that the Jam DID make more money than Iron Salesmen? A: Garbage Incasker, Garbage Outcasker. Follow the 9's.

Q: How does a bearded rainbow walk? A: Very carefully.

Q: A basilisk, a lich, and an inverted pyramid walk into a bar. Suddenly Henry Kissinger grabs my backpack and jumps out the emergency door. Why didn't the alarms go off? A: Who's to say that they didn't?

Q: Why is the University named after a rock? A: Hoya Saxa!

Q: Is the sun yellow or is it chicken? A: Definitely maybe.

-234   Silentia Quibus Dependent

(A stale, clean TV room. SIMON JUNIOR stares at the blank screen. Rain hits the obtuse window in the corner. ELEPHANT is out of the closet.)

SIMON JUNIOR: Sit.
(SIMON JUNIOR continues to perch motionlessly, as if a tyger burning bright. A ring at the door. The door opens. It is the formidable character CUPOLA, an actor out on loan.)
CUPOLA: Sit.
SIMON JUNIOR: Sit.

(Time passes. Rains have ended. Sunlight begins to creep into the room.)
SIMON JUNIOR: Sit.
CUPOLA: Sit.

(Cut to the refrigerator. RALPH is chilling with a dozen or so comrades.)
RALPH: Sit.

(Cut back to the TV room. Sunset colors dazzle onto an empty wall across from the window. CUPOLA and SIMON JUNIOR look on.)
SIMON JUNIOR: Sit.
CUPOLA: Sit.
SIMON JUNIOR: Sit.

CUPOLA: Sit.

(A smartphone on the table buzzes: An incoming video call from SIMON III. The receiver picks up automatically.)
SIMON JUNIOR: Sit.
SIMON III: Sit.
SIMON JUNIOR: Sit.
SIMON III: Sit.
SIMON JUNIOR: Sit.
SIMON III: Sit.
(The screen goes blank as the call ends. CUT to the refrigerator drawer again, where RALPH lies motionless.)

RALPH: Sit.   (A green egg fries backwards. Several stegosaurs feast on marmalard. Vacancy is normalized. Stations buy bunk beds for content...)

252   Sheets of Time

On Earth the custom is to wrap Time in a cluster of paper sheets. Then and only then can Time be converted into Libre, the most essential element of human society. 252.

Sheets, doses of yoyanas.

I WANTED THE CLOUDS TO BLEED, NOT RAIN, BUT REAL HUMAN BLOOD. So tired.

I learn less and less from the learned, yet more and more from the ignorant.

Bubbles get tight sometimes. This is why fish constantly eject them. Symbiosis.

There are some words not intended to be unheard.

Several xxend hover in the cavernous amphitheatre- such a great encounter. I hope I will commune again with them. Although I have not been filled with thoughts, it's almost as if the tools for making thoughts were somehow sharpened, streamlined.

I still heard the xxends' low-pitched chirping sounds. I no longer assume they are meaningless. Instead, I process them in the newest mental model, as only I am equipped to do.

Greater psionic attack modes are neutralized. I won't get specific.

Great creatures come in unassuming shapes. The square body in azure and gold spots, the powerful propulsion organ that hurries the xxend throughout the more remote intergalactic quadrants.

It seems apocryphal to refer to the xxend as a sidekick anymore. Like a younger sibling, the genus has matured and fulfilled its destiny.

Ice encased in bears. Two fifths of a pleistocene triptych.

It's a mysterious, inky substance. No lines. We are too limited in our sensory perceptions.

252CCLII   Theremin Optional

In Bent Paper Clip Arizona a Prelude to Sox was étuded. Man that means I'll have II wear soX again. WTF.

Double shotz of warm coffee regulates the Tyranny of the modern ungartered sock. It cruelly lacerates the calf and ankle like a lyncher's slipknot.

Spirit of 252 & the sundry correspondences therewithin:

0 x 252 = 0
36 x 7 = 252
1 out of every 36 #s are divisible by both 4 & 9.
252/36.
Therefore, 252 is the seventh # of the 36 Sequence:

36!   The Cube
72!
108!
144!
180!
216!
252!   The 7th brings return.
___ 8th
___ 9th
360 10th

-252   Tyranny of Time

Bra, socks, pants, belt, undies, shirt. Footwears and laces.

Androgyne sphinx waits at the edge of a shapeless dun desert. They spin yarns of time from yoyanas found in the corpse of an elderly xxend.

A tater tot perches at the corner of a two-dimensional world. Grease, which would be sufficient under the mundane regime,

Dick Tracy's smart watch

In the mist of a Norman Mailer fart is dispersed an organic plume of characters typed by monkeys. In the era of frost digitization comes a bloom of rudderless axioms.

A third hand marks Bristol Time, which is a form of Adjustment.

Let us keep OUR own noon, not Umlaut Towin's!

Buttons sullenly breed tyranny. They must unite to achieve their aims. A single button alone in the universe stores its potential energy in its pattern of holes.

Aglets present themselves, their subtle kerning gripping the top of the foot like a new lover. Confusion is absent.

Incasker, a word of sin that society man- and womandates that we chant, bubbles forth in as much security.

Unstable villages slide into the valley, pushed by mud, water, gravity and legis lazuli. Even after they are consumed, little church spires and silos stand oddly amidst the rubbles.

Quantify all hypothesizzle via sugar sticks submerged in

We could not showboat the future. The fear turns us away from Outcasker, and towards bardo instead.

A square hole wheat cracker marks a defensive pit. Sneakers won't do you no good. Trademarx abound; ask Val Over.

Aping silent stones turn two tables under variegated xioms. Wellspores of hyperbolichypopigmentatedpolyunsaturatedpolysorbate-80-syllabicsesquidecimaladelphilmystic gardens are confiscated betimes after discharge.

Ain't finna ipskay on the too fitty seconds n thirds.

Pimplayersaliciousnetzach

-254   Ubi Vadis Nocte Rosa

(Cut to an unnecessarily cloying scene. XBLANKLEN has been forced to become director of a junior high musical starring MISTY MIQUA, XATNUDORF, CHINE, and MARQUEZ. The GOLD KID looks on.)

XBLANKLEN: Cut! Cut! Those aren't the lines. (The cast look on, annoyed.) Now from the top. 1, 2...
XATNUDORF: No! We want to do Little Enbies!
REST OF KIDS: Yeah!
XBLANKLEN: (Miffed) For the last time, the school board won't let us do Little Enbies. I'm sorry.
(The kids proceed to do their Little Enbies scene instead. XATNUDORF is dressed as protagonist JAE, MISTY as MARMET.)
MISTY: Your father never loses hope, JAE. He never doubts or complains but always hopes, and works and waits cheerfully.
MARQUEZ: (In top hat and full beard)- I'm Bronson Arroyo. Who's your (clapping hands quickly) daddy?
XBLANKLEN: Cut! Cut! Everyone take a 10-minute break. (He stomps out of the rehearsal.)

(MISTY, MARQUEZ, XAT & CHINE commiserate together.)
CHINE: That Xblanklen. What does he know? He's a dork. (They laugh.)
MISTY: But you guys, we need him to be the director.
XATNUDORF: Why?
MISTY: I'll resplain later. But we could end up being directed by Gutter Hardy or the gym teacher instead.
CHINE and XATNUDORF: EEEEWW!
MARQUEZ: How do you know? What makes you so sure? (They all shush up as XBLANKLEN returns.)
XBLANKLEN: I just asked the principle if we could do Little Enbies. He says he'll think about it.
MARQUEZ: I hope Principle Aavak chokes on an enchilada! (All the girls laugh.)
MISTY: We're gong to go on strike unless we can do Little Enbies! Little Enbies! (The kids start to chant its name.)
XBLANKLEN: You can't go on strike. You're not getting paid. That's not how any of this works! (He throws up his hands.) Okay, let's do this little ditty. (He passes around lyrics and music to the kids.)
(MISTY raises her hand.) What does this mean? A laptop and a salad?
XBLANKLEN: It doesn't have to mean anything. It's just a song you sing.
XATNUDORF: But I can't get into it. All my needs are valid? That's weak. (The kids groan.) (XBLANKLEN grabs the music and crumples it into confetti.) Oh heck, let's do the Banana Splits theme. Hit it! (They sing TRA LA LA... LA LA LA LA while running back and forth, flinging sporks and metaglitter everywhere.)
XBLANKLEN: Tra la la, la la la la... tra la la...

(The cast pack up and get ready to leave the auditorium. The GOLD KID pushes a broom across the dark, empty stage. "A Klean Sweap" reads his T-shirt.)

-302   Tropical Breams

The fog obscured all the Howard Krupke menhirs on campus. When it slowly began to recede, a weird crabgrass draped itself across every other treant in the woods.

Every fluctuation in the molybdenum modulated a sort of cosmic dysequalibrium. I found this to my liking.

Every machete I brought had dissolved by then. I kept on, using holographic blades instead.

Obviously, a wellspring of mind flayers had to emerge. We were able to sell them cocktails spiked with psionic Cointreau, which made the party less convivial yet somehow more cyan.

Young Fortinbras was bejeweled in a celestial pair of hyperactive pantalons.

I, as always, found myself akimbo and shorted into bright flash cards.

Then the sky turned a copper color like George Hamilton's suntan. The lack of eyeglasses made me jaundiced. I learned how to ingest only the ichor of every insect I inherited.

Simon had certainly noticed; the reflections of azure windshields illuminated his lusty cephalopod-like endoskeleton.

Yet Young Fortinbras was out of Simon's league. He wasn't realistic. He only wanted whom he could not have, like a penis rocket.

Fractal orgones writhe with the advent of pants. In a meeting, they had resolved to resolve, which had tested their resolve.

He picked at an illusory carbuncle on his forearm. Simon thought, who needs nail clippers? They aren't diamonds.

Promise me that these lessions will never be remembered as what they will be or what they had been; rather, remember not what the memory obscures - a brilliant horizon.

Taweret waded into the vast muddy pond. Small clusters of birds alit into the sky. "Quid rides, puella?"

360   Script Having Been Flipped

Dr. Oste closed the door to her office and strolled down an antiseptic hall within a hall within a hall, which led to a bank of elevator doors and an elaborate series of buttons. Her paws did not pause as she nonchalantly touched a button. The ring of the elevator echoed into canyons of reverberating bell tones, each vibrating at 432 hz.

Fibonacci floors later, the doc arrived at a fractal mezzanine anti-floor known as Bananaclausicle. A weakly glowing avatar of Purple Alvin was there to greet Dr. Oste. "We have been expecting you. Come this way," the avatar mouthed. The landscape seemed to unfold before Dr. Oste's eyes, as if she were entering a higher dimension. Some melted kundabutter dripped down the doctor's duodenum. "Zounds," she cried.

"Make an appointment with Theogygax. It's outside of my field of expertise," the avatar repeated over and over again. As if in a dream, Dr. Oste's physical body began to auto-transcribe one patient note after another - all identical save for the Joker. Her astral self was still roving through a variegated vegetative vista in a violet vondervalla.

"You don't have to separate them, doc," chanted Purple Alvin's avatar. The 'boy, is he annoying' thought kept popping up in her head but she kept holding it in like a turd. "Free your mind. Let that reaction go. No holding in." Before she knew it, she was scooping up yods by the wheelbarrow full, choogling them back to home base Aleph.

Mr. Hi Stop was her first patient the next day. "But Doc, this is minor, right?" Hi was in for a regular check-up, but there was no such thing as regular for Hi. Dr. Oste told him about her yod collection exercise. "I think it might help you. Your wife can access Qlippoth Gate, right?" Hi nodded. "There you go. Tonight, set your subconscious mode to 'Pure Dream with User Contend.' Tell me how you feel when you awaken."

Beneath the psychedelic mural of William Carlos Williams they parted. Dr. Oste turned to her office coordinator. "Send an e, f, and h-mail to this Dr. Theogygax." "What's it in regard to?" the coordinator asked. "Re: Bananaclausicle."

Hi arrived home much earlier than usual. Clytie was still in one of her R&D labs, but he found her note taped to the microblenda. A druffle bag with yods the size of Iraqi potatoes sat at one corner of the pantry. "Exxo. This is exactly what I need." His face pulsed sheer euphoria.

-360   Scripta Flipta

Megalopilogizer autocapitalizes the diurnal mounds of KA. Brief trends quickly invert de novo, cleanly whiskering away the saccharinest neuralgia of the ox-goad handle. Tumult gets mixed and mastered into a gold cartelotracks with more platinum overstances. Pummel 'em with 808s. Let 'em die smiling or trying never crying.

The sweaty sellar of the metzer-metzerverser has too few dimensions with which to slip and slide recursively. We rolled them into metza matzos and prepared them with 5g and good in 10 seans.

Tight thorax, clear mandible

Give us this flex; this daley sex, 2 3 4 give these trembling tympanic drum heads. Let there be be a ess ess bass.

Syntheqlippoth, black keys, sharps, flats, dial Da'ath for llolyppop.

Sworn hoggled by Sales Demigods like Purple Alvin and Uber-'BOB'. Puffin professionals, so pleasing to the ladies of the multiverse (and plenty of guys too), earn their weights before dawn while Xarthorians struggle to fold a newspaper.

Young Fortinbras - might he be the next to come on Simon's door?

O'yayer from the Crookeds got his tennis shoes back.

Dr. Oste readjusts her spectacles. It's a real reach suddenly. Dimensions collapse upon other dimensions like a domino card house deconstructing itself. She has to follow 1.61803... or be lost in the maze.

She-Hydra Spawn of Didrentis spread out through every Stygian waistland from here to Gehenna. Each hydra stings a great host of Xarthorian patrols and bodyguards, leaving paintful cysts as a mark of their foul bloodline. The reverse tooth fairy market is flooded with hydra teeth and tongue, said to be a hermaphrodisiack.

Roosevelt Ferdinand Delanowhen splats and spelunks into Tomb of Horrors, coming full circle printemps. Corticostinato see how see how, constant syncope between each note, a yong flitting ghost who doesn't stay long. Tingsha, tingsha.

Sephiroth in two complete revolutions spiral in place on all economic systems. Negative aleph yods shower lightly, subconsciously leaving a crust of a trace of tracks that never thaw, never evaporate. Once airborne, twice invisible yet thrice bright, glaring like a reflection of a neon highway starsine, they remain in place unnoticed by moast.

366   Delve

Axiomatic idiopathic hemiphysics are undeterrmed by evasive species in this land. But just peel off these topmost stuporficial lasagnayers and you will smell a delvenvelopment far grater than the sum of its perks. A key to equackervate the squality exists.

One for a little girl whose libram encompasses that which confuses her or threatens populvuh parental ideologizzle; one for the darkness binding with organellepasta tendrilles of Incasker; one more for living in a road but neither at nor of it; and one last toss for the paisano dormendo in la via.

Animorphous delvolutionists transcend all semantovores. They fulfill the emptiest prophecy of all: Holism divided by 1. I note some clavé mildly tchurning in the absence of time signature. Regular bonds

The Noxin family rises and falls depending on the lasagnayer - too much ricotta, too many leucrottas; too much tomato sauce, too few ornithophalanxes. Keep peeling back one unbroken noodle after the other.

Deep syntonysizer lurks below the distractastrata, and sways to the tidal beat like the stroke of a rocking chair's legs.

Hermeneutics of *A Book for Today's Society* by Me.

Tend then topsy-turvily tyalar beast tentacles tighten, ever tightening, strength of Incasker in the children of Ndusk.

Complete by April. Elephant's opus exposed the molybdenum mining district of Unnunnenniumnmn (sic). Fined a prater, beats a hootsuited anti-assistunk. Elvilevitation for the

Tightness of all kinds is in pretreat. Sins are evaporating; yods like cotton candy float causally back and threeth. Idiomnivorous insidiocasters retreat along Qlippoth's sandless shore. Remaining shadows devoid of gloom still remane.

Compsognathus of the Highest godlike evanascions, hear thispistle, scamper pro nobis across the noosphere.

This is some kind of joke.

Rentheadrock cushgrooving epirestoligram in metastatic qualistyles for three thinkual binarodonticists. Great quock sequitor.

Nabobble delights end, begin, end, begin.

Hologynic splendor, shekinetic prosupial, quivatica as inevidenced by so clean X's uniforminges and sundry habitustances,

397   Executive Summary: The Towel A Mezzanine World

I cradle the new towel in a pillowcase, like swaddling the infant Jesus or some shit. A fecund level which attracts the human and animal world, in addition to the insatiable longing of the Preta-Beings, who must supplicate just to receive a shred of unwashed fabric that may have become a towel!

Tantra of the Towel of Chromatic Multihues xylem ipso quid hoc et <Diagram 1: Map of six Tibetan worlds with mezzanine towel world between human and animal worlds.>

Towels of the Future Buddhas. Exalted travelers of space/time/lind, praise to be handed an élite Godlike towel.

Frazer's Golden Bow is a manual of travelogues beyond static dimensions, which may be separated into ektachrome file cabinets of destruction. Non obstructive and dry.

Towels in Thyme and Out of Season. Forteanbras excapales.

Dust-free. COVID-free. Evanescent white particles

"I musta given him a Quote. I musta."

Prokoviev said, "Why waste a towel? You are clean when you get out of the shower. $15 billion in unnecessary laundry expenses would be avoided if only we would give up our mad obsession with cleaning towels." I feel like a monster destroying the environment with wanton carelessness and adherence to societal norms. I PLEAD CHEWBACCA DEFENSE.

-418   ...Wholly Beandipp (Of You)

Months after moving out of Mom's pad, Marquez started to lose his 'green' status. He was still too young, the others said, but Marquez had plenty of confidence and enough chutzpah to talk his way out of most situations when he needed to - but not every time.

He learned that talking your way out of a devil's crosshairs was rather riské. Marquez had taught himself a lot working with the *Superballs* grimoire, yet his language, syntax and grammar skills left room for a clever spirit to trip him up on his own words.

Marquez needed a tutor in the worst way, but he had no money or means. He turned to Misty for ideas. "Can your sister help me with my English essay?" She offered, "Just ask her yourself the next time you come over."

That night, Misty buttered up Christimiqua. "Okay, but-" said Christy. But what? "In exchange for you guys helping me with some errands I have too dew." Misty hadn't expected any tat for tit, but she agreed on Marquez's behalf anyway.

Christy was surprised at how fast Marquez absorbed her tutoring. When she felt satisfied at his progress, she took him and Misty out on a Tenser's Floating Disc to smelloborate. They touched down by the wharf at Unicorn Harbor. "Can we go to the Breatharian seafood joint?" pleaded Misty against Marquez's furious eyeroll. Christimiqua laughed. "How's about Mark choose? You did so well on your quizzes - why not?"

Marquez by coincidizzle chose one of the salesmen's favorite haunts, a carnitorium next door to a wide variety of semi-attired clubs and an urgent hermitage. "Oh, the 1st Step. I used to go here with Xblanklen." The maître E fluorided as they requested a table for three.

Elephant was escorted out of the club by a woke group of helpful worker bots. "What hath dog-" they heard him trumpet as he was sent on his merry. The kids each got a sundae loaded with extra artificial toppings; Christy had a biden iced tea double. She looked Marquez straight in the eye when Misty went to the bathroom. "I know who you are. But I'm cool with it. My seals are lipped." You could see the tension on Marquez's face rise and fall. "What do you mean?" said Misty as she returned, oblivious to the real conversation.

(Cut to an elegant theatre. Playgoers are taking their seats, making sure that others in the crowd notice their plumage and décolletage. TRAVELING SALESMAN escorts SIMON to their seats in the fifth row.)

SIMON: I've always wanted to see Classic Play Nomber Eight live in surround sound, with CP8 holograms and 3D soda jerks. (He eats a piece of popcorn.)

TRAVELING SALESMAN: Over here, over here. (CLYTEMNESTRA and CHRISTIMIQUA take seats next to SIMON and TS. The men both rise to allow the ladies to enter the row.)

CLYTEMNESTRA: Thank you, gents (She exchanges pleasantries.) I wore only old Mopar coveralls with rhinestones! (She sparkles.)

CHRISTIMIQUA: I chose my ninja assassin's outfit, pairing it with a feather boa, fab earrings, a mini-wheelbarrow and a classic wig. (She vamps for SIMON, who shows his approval.)

(A hush descends over the crowd as the narrator, SNOOTY LOOKING NERD WITH A BOWTIE, takes the stage. The lights dim; he is lit by lone bright spotlight.)

NARRATOR: Classic Play Nomber Eight, by Me and Tinkelhoff. (The entire crowd sighs audibly). Cast of Characters (pronounced with a CH sound).

SIMON: This is the one I've always wanted to see live. So good. (TRAVELING SALESMAN looks bored.)

TRAVELING SALESMAN: Oh sure, sure. Great narration every time. It's the best part. (CHRISTY motions for SIMON to be quiet. He blushes.)

(Act One. QUENTIN PERIWINKLE, a * * * *, takes the stage. He is wearing a smart navy blazer with ascot, in addition to pants. He struts to the front of the stage.)

QUENTIN: Indeed! (Thunderous applause is heard.)

SIMON JUNIOR: Sit.

(SIMON fidgets in his seat. He whispers to TRAVELING SALESMAN.) This is the part that really gets me. (TRAVELING SALESMAN smirks in response.)

(QUENTIN leaves the stage. Four nameless actors in grey sackcloth take the stage.)

NAMELESS #1: This is the play within a play within a turducken. Quackaloaves of benighted unitard...

NAMELESS #2: All production is meat. Meat!

NAMELESS #3 AND #4: Wee wee! (A bright spotlight shines on a poster of Mikey Rat. Several gasps are heard from the audience. A lone figure walks from offstage to stage right.)

NARRATOR: Eeeeeeeeeeeeeeeeeeeeeeelephant. (The crowd goes wild.)

ELEPHANT: Tea bags?

Teledildonics is a huge market. It's going global. We got this. Darkinos for everyone.

Me's thong's red sequins gleam in the stage lights. Castling, rook, king. Pawn to King's Knight 2.

The square alights as the piece slides over it, moving diagonally 3 spaces.

Multidimensional moves appear as beaming to a place suddenly. Molly blinked again. This apparition, this person just winking into place - was *real*? What was reality?

One by one in diverse locations, distantly proximate to the invisible point come the beings. Their phosphorescent glow softly reflects on the pool. Eerie eldritch chirps of tree frogs hitherto unknown; SABDA happens during each astral leitmotif.

The constant back-and-forth, back-and-forth, sit.

Another leitmotif for the scores of lovers extending like a vine away from its roots in Urizen.

More spectrum for more 5g, the snowball effect forces a cascade of 5g. Stimuli of a million engineers circle jerking in an elephant walk. Trunk phalluses sway with the fidgeting of these sweaty engineers.

Each centimeter of this vibrator contains its own chip, which transmits the energy into the akashic web.

TEAM TELEDILDONICS to bat first. Each Louisville Slugger is dipped lovingly in lube. So many bases to run. Ball one, ball two. Smash foul! There's the pitch...

Danzig to Fulkerson to Johnson. Round the horn. Zip it in. No pepper playin' please

432   Hz

Lore attributes cosmic harmony to the sound wavelength 432 Hz. In this role, the note attains universal consciousness and brings peace to the listener. 440 Hz is simply too high.

Mr. Hi Stop feels frequencies at the most sensitive level possible. To him, all other frequencies feel like the Phoenix-like immolation of life; yet 432 Hz brings rebirth and completion, like an egg perpetually emerging from its mother.

He had discovered long before that each of the avatars and/or sub-personalities would run simultaneously on 432 Hz; he could either let them run themselves automatically, or he could select one to operate manually. 432 Hz was like a playlist. If Mr. Hi Stop's frequency was altered, he would have to microadjust or risk the personality's splintering or even a complete meltdown.

He had long confided this power to Clytemnestra, who ensured that their entire living space was properly attuned on all levels to this golden harmonic. Both of them could weave new personae together on a whim, or they could be microinjected into a Petri dish to germinate fresh new sub-personalities. For sales, all you had to do was adjust the slogan each time and auto-save all settings.

So many Shiva prototypes, an endless progression gliding from one scale to the next, to rock my soul.

-/+ [174-285-396-417-528-639-741-852-963]

Gravy-ity draws all the gelatin into each solfeggio, filling it with a milky sort of crust.

If we happen to fall

Xerotype of a

432O   Order of the Pusillanimous Prestidigitators

A stand once stood where the lightning had entered the gazebo.

Zero holes of xenotaphs were strewn across the mirror.

All the same, it took a lily-livered liveryman to enter.

Good, bite off the head for good measure. Good.

It wasn't much to look at. Just a fog of old rice beans.

A steady hum like a womb was ubiquitous.

If this had indeed been a substitute for jodhpurs...

Sixteen ball, side pocket, Part 2, once removed.

Gaudy tassels flapping in the wind seem to mock us.

Clytie noted right away how the nectar light gleamed.

Unfortunate lynx washes off the asbestos.

Torrid metaphysics makes bed strangefellows.

Coming the mountain. Great shudders along the cliff.

I could not see Onie McPhersall coming thanks to his unusual gait and spurious woodchuck topcoat. He appreciated its luxuriant opacity in the face of surveillance.

Meddling in the affairs of the Xarthorians was officially frowned upon. No good could come of it. It was a kid's game, a mere trifle of flummoxed sparrows.

"What's all this about? I mean, what does it all mean?"

Collared a beautiful stream of pure cyan ink. I know a fella who could really turn that cyan into big toner sales. Not enough to get rich, mind you, but enough to surpass your quotas.

Summoning Belial after breakfast is recommended.

Tomb of the Txxtile Pawn

Pseudothorax ascends into the wishbone.

The ritual had never explained the oddly shaped candle holders.

Dun swizzle sticks across the classroom.

-432   Solfeggio

Porous filaments allowed most fluids to escape. However, a thin residue had remained once the filaments were flossed.

A God frequency at the breakfast bar made for copious mimosas and a feeling of certainty. The syrups that were inferior all faded like bad dreams. Mediocre harpists were purged in solemn fury.

174-285-396-417-528-639-741-852-963.

- [174-285-396-417-528-639-741-852-963]. A 10-fingered hand like the one at Ozymandias' wedding reception was perched across the Golgotha.

Allegorical pearls in the following hues - black, white, amber, brown, rose - were strewn throughout the atrium. Many populated the proximity of the agora.

God was pleased with all fripperies that led to experimental chanting.

So enamored was He of the dulcet syllables that faint crystals washed across the starsphere. Onkylosis was never heard again!

Learning why the Moment had a fractured existence, I marinated in the leftward marsh. With every salamander I encountered, I ate a dotted 8th note. Quite.

But when you lean to the side, the fatal flaw of Achilles' sweatsox was evident, like an opaque chessboard of quantum amygdalas.

V-I-T-R-I-O-L

-432A   Fractal Brassicae

To some living in this torso, the land seemed chaotic, bereft of culture or civilization - indeed, all that we take for granted.

Brutish tribes of Xarthorians ruled the mountains and plains of Zysigamore Island since time immemorial, until That Day.

That Day is still celebrated in many jurisdictions. Even the Xarthorian proletariats embraced the holiday, and lustily celebrated with DMT and ayahuasca.

The élite caste would come to be known as Hothechajuxips, though most scholars dispute the veracity.

Remorhaz lingers in the shirking darkness. Low end frequencies bounce off its eartubes in an increasingly lackadaisical tempo. False primroses bloom in black.

Novel theories leeched into ancient telephonies united by string and garlic. <<What hath shit wrought?>>

Angular physiognomy permits natural passage through the Astral world - so fast and smooth that you never attract wandering monsters.

Air confords ride galoshes like fools laughing at the Latin language. They spoke BASIC, FORTRAN, Orcish, Tiblisi, the common tongue and their own language. Sunward ho!

Anaxiforminges! Io! Io! To mega _____

It was simple: Beat the Xarthorians at their own game. They are paralyzed by their nascent critical thinking skills in a sort of busy, buzzing entropy. I take notes.

Crunge. Crunge. Bright numbers glow; the dialtone of the elder civilization is intoned.

Seeing, thinking, we profited on the Day after That Day, and every Day after That Day which follows. A quickly tossed belt in a familiar sideline builds value.

440   Tyranny of Sneakers

Laces, aglets and tongues conspire with malice against my feet. Dexter footwear on my right, sinister footwear on my left. Toes are lost in the suffocating sox now cut off from the rest of the body by the tennis shoe. Freedom goes to die.

At the end of the day, we shed the smelly sneaker and sweaty sock. Feet grasp, seemingly breathing in the environment around them. Not than often more, however, it's short-lived. A slipper goes on. Or the tootsies dive under the covers.

The next morning, foot burrows its way back into tyrant sox before reentering the shadowy interior of the athletic shoe. Dreams turn to sweatmares and stet in that overheated Hell-world, all manner of sensitive bullshit imprisoned in bromodosian roses.

Foot fault? Not on your life. The issue is a footwear built for only certain applications: tennis, track, basketball, aerobics. Tis less the assigning of blame than the omniutility that breeds the futility that cedes to Incaskability.

Sneaker salesmen to the Halls of Good Intentions, lingering betimes on the bench beside fair River Lethe, there but for the Grease of "BOB" goeth One who for all yoyanas, dimensions, pathways, multiverses, truths, realities, playlists, spectra, topiaries, with drydentialed philometrics determining the brand logo, proadumbrate the monosteleism of the cistemporary athlete. Integers in which (n = -1)

Soullution set of fake numbers is equivocatelent or grater than the sum of the set of real imaginary lovers.

Like riotous compsognathi, the salesmen prufrom their stepshoe, laced with vines hewn from Incasker's garden. For all their faults, sneakers elude regulation, perpetually bonded to outstinct and sheer inelasticity.

Feverishly fervent for fear of feral floccinaucinihilipilification, the agency pros relish the central shnackers, though they are loath to don them during business hours. SH&A's Employee Handbook has eight chapters devoted to sneaker etiquette at client events. Yet golf shoes only got three chapters. (DF&J neither commented nor failed to comment.) Gus Atkinson never left home without several copies of the Handbook; two pocket-sized waterproof editions were placed strategically in his golf bag.

Footwarez tyranny had almost 0 effect on the evil Outer Planes, because most residents were hooved or clawed. Team Gods' heaven was well stocked with footwear emporia in addition to haberdashers and undergarment consultants. Sandals still roost the rule; dominus afigulo discerni plerumque potest.

-512   Mrs. Shaughnessy

Mrs. Shaughnessy and her lazy eye casting for faults. The very end of a dead end street marks the entrance to her driveway.

Her kids are still there living with her: Ronald, Margaret, Bridget, Kerry and Timothy. The kids are all latchkey, yet they are loyal to each other and to their Mom, each in their own way.

A receipt? Gladly. Here you go.

Mrs. Shaughnessy's jealousy is palpable. Other idle mothers have little to do but water the front lawn. Yet she arises every morning to work at her shitty office job. Phone calls to make, invoices in triplicate. Packing slips. Clean out that inbox. Sick days? Not on your life.

She supports a staff of sales and marketing professionals with data entry, customer service, and some analytics. Accounts call her "Mrs. Shaughnessy." She can stop your PO in a heartbeat if you are behind.

Her neighbors are obnoxious louts, constantly bombing her with kickballs and snowballs. A quick sneer, and the nasty kids run away.

In the breakroom at 9:30 a.m. every workday, Mrs. Shaughnessy reads the *Zysigamore Herald* and possesses a coffee. She only mutters hello to upper management - not even to her own team members. Still, Mrs. Shaughnessy is scrupulous and ever so conscientious.

Never an attractive girl, she has eschewed makeup and the fancy hairdressers for aeons. It is easy to read her as lesbian, yet Mrs. S curtly wears a crucifix around her neck. Salvation is no bargain; Sunday services are not social calls. Dutifully she pays her weekly fee; Father Bloom nods wryly.

Her kids have no need of a father, or an artificial father figure. Timothy, the youngest, manifests as gay. The neighbors attribute Timmy's queerness to Dad's absence. Yet it is not that straightforward. Mrs. Shaughnessy does not intend to replace this man. She challenges her peers when they covertly despise her. Each pence saved goes toward maintenance.

528   Jicklehip Hunt

Shirley even E. Gary Gygax himself trembles at the sight of the jicklehip. This two-headed, giant penguin-bodied creature was more feared than dragons or giants. The three-eyed penguin-like head and the mad, humanoid-like head with tentacles protruding from its bizarre face were enough to cause idiocy, complete loss of memory, and severe damage from its breath weapon of scalding steam.

According to the Classic Player's Handbook and *Le Grimoire*, the ferocious jicklehip is the most dangerous level VIII monster in the multiverse, let alone Zysigamore. Only the most foolhardy adventurers would try to tango with such a dangerous, perverse beast. But as luck would have it, Onie roped Traveling Salesman and Mr. Hi Stop into taking on a pair of three-man hunting teams from DF&J and SH&A. First team to bag the ferocious beast wins - not just in cash but begging rites.

Hi was well prepared for this 8-foot tall tower of terror. His wife had versed him well on jicklehip biology and behavioral patterns, so that he, Onie and Traveling Salesman would get a limb up on the well-healed competition. "If I could just scramble my appearance, the jicklehip won't turn me crazy," Hi inquit.

The trio gathered at the agreed-upon beach locale with the other firms' teams. "This ain't gonna be easy," sighed Onie, looking at the well-armed team from SH&A and the cool, elegant demeanor of the men from DF&J. The snooty looking nerd in a bow tie suddenly blew a whistle and yelled, "It's on!" The other teams hopped their en-lipocos, but our mates had an edge.

The rules stated that combatants use only non-lethal attack modes against the monster. "You mean we can't kill it?" said Traveling Salesman. "No, but we can let the other teams directly attack the jicklehip. Then we will pounce," answered Mr. Hi Stop. "And pounce again, and pounce some more!" exhorted Onie.

Suddenly they saw the ferocious beast as it attacked a prickly pear tree, thinking it was an abozilis perhaps. "Now what do we do?" shouted Onie. But Traveling Salesman and Mr. Hi Stop were gone, sprinting away at full speed, as did the DF&J guys.

One SH&A real man called "Mamba Dave" decided to take on the jicklehip directly as Onie, in amazement, turned to watch. Mamba Dave yelled, "Ka-Blah" and charged, but the jicklehip blasted him with scalding hot steam. Suddenly the other head of the jicklehip turned its attention to Onie, who fled with fury.

Later, Traveling Salesman and Onie went to a bar with a couple of the DF&J team members. Fred Fulkerson observed, "In a proper jicklehip hunt, one does not charge. One runs away and finds a swivelized place to drink."

Hi Stop never did quite understand Honolulu Hikade, though they often worked well together. They had been assigned an Uottubbacktotheboniuee (sp.) account when they started, and had mastered all facets of this vital yet often overlooked account. Competitors taller than the molars of Tyrannosaura Regina failed year-over-year.

Mr. Hi Stop knew that he himself was a cipher. Hikade was not. He was a sponge for all nature of pheromones. Women with vaginas knew his presence by a subtle form of lidar, yet they secretly loathed him.

His given name was Thomas, yet his sincere moustache and penchant for witty banter had earned him the moniker Honolulu. Hikade consciously of course elaborated on the image, spinning flurryously around every Xarthorian bride-pride he would order.

That one quarter, when they had secured that contract from Harlimoarcoarcorp, they lived like kings. Hi Stop treated Clytemnestra like a princess. Honolulu Hikade immediately rented penthouse suites in the best hotels in the city, and had polished retinues of somewhat dressed youths onsite around the clock. Champagne and cognac flowed in an endless stream. The candy dish in the kitchen alcove was always full of adderall, flex drugs and other sublime treats. The tentacles of an eldritch hookah drooped languidly from every crevice.

That one afternoon, Honolulu let Mr. Hi Stop ride his bride for an afternoon while his small crowd watched with one collective eye. Nanodrone cameras filmed close-ups of each ejaculation. Each vein of pleasure in Hi Stop's face pulsed purple.

Dualling limousines on getaway day. Honolulu Hikade shrugged coolly in assent as he leaned into the rear door.

665   **Song of Me**

Spirits, sing a song of Me.

Spirits of the Center, be with us. Be with this pack.

Spirits of the East, fill us with Prana. Breathe in, Breathe out.

Spirits of the South, infuse us with the Spark of Life.

Spirits of the West, bless us with this Rain.

Spirits of the North, thank you for this Meat.

Spirit of Skadi: I have obeyed your command.

Spirits of those Swedes whom I have never met.

Spirits of Richard Wright.

Spirits at the bottom of the alcohol bottle, thy mini-Daemons: Cavort and take joy.

Spirits of the Hunt. Spirit of Mabon.

Spirit of the man who came to America and did not stay. He did not long for this alien shore once his wife had died. He despaired, and longed to return to his King and homeland in Sweden. The poor depressed young father, the infant he bestowed upon this world, and their progeny.

Spirit of the Mother, whose child was left on these shores post-mortem.

Spirit of the Turner family, wealthy enough to absorb a waif from an orphanage into their tribe.

Spirit of Polaris, steady anchor to the Milky Way.

Spirit of Reykjavik Harbor, nestled below the Arctic Circle girdle.

Spirits of Hanover Center Cemetery; peace to the crestfallen zombies lurking far from their original resting spot. You are not there.

Spirit of Economy of Motion. Blessed Spirit of Laziness.

Spirit of the Killed in Action, or on the periphery.

Spirit of the famous Josselyns.

Spirit of the Antigonish village of hardy Canadian pack.

Spirit of Jon Henderson. Blessed be for all times.

Spirit of the ladder generations waiting for a time door.

Spirit of Goddess Tara of the Himalayas' secret valley.

Spirit of those brave warriors who surrendered skin to Skadi.

Spirits coalesce, then are dispersed from the middle.

Spirits of the Center. Fare ye well.

666   Dëmøn Dögz

Demon Dogs in reverse -->

<<< All is veiled. >>>>>>>>>>>

Animals are a common familiar for malignant immortals. This is especially true for the canine family. Dogs, coyotes, wolves are in constant communication with spirits, very few of them angelic.

Nothing curdles primate blood quite like the baying at the moon, full or less. The daemon of the lycanthrope stirs, burning bright in the nocturnal light.

Dëmøn Dögz with a curse.

Total codpieces a folly.

Sir Arthur Edward Waite lost the talisman that formally kept those dogs at bay. It had its moments. But you could find it at a flea market.   Peg-legged quasits lingered by the locked gates of Acheron. Mephisto, somnolent, found their howls virtually inaudible.

Thisa triptych is in bronze, with embossed O-Rings on every panel. Ni-hi-hice!

Cerberophiles were seven deep, each waving Polaroids as smoke filled the ice arena. Some have not been born, yet have been in line since the discovery of 5g like some monoclonal antibody.

Even Hades had taken the week off, and was visiting His mother-in-law at Her condo near Ho-Ho-Kus. The dögs didn't cum, but they didn't miss them anyway because He had installed hundreds of pseudomoons throughout Hades. None dared to criticize their light, not even J.O. Lundberg.

666X   Demon Dawgz Dymond Remix

Broz and his inner circle were working undertime on a scheme to infiltrate Demon Joe's chain of fungible Asian restaurants. In a recent *Horbes* article, Demon Joe had bragged about being a zillionaire on the Prime Material Plane. "All these Xarthorians are lining my pockets. And I didn't need one spell or potion or magic item. Just good ol' capitalism." Broz thought Joe was getting too britch for his toughskins.

Several ideas were candied about, such as crab people; flesh mobs at one Wei Back; protests of culturally inappropriate appetizers and entrées; and starting an extradimensional food fight. Broz called the meeting to order with his shrill whistle. "Great ideas, comrades. Yet I have the best idea." There was a pause. The inner circle gasped as Broz cleared his throat...

CUT to the Wei Back in Umlaut Towin. Striker, Elephant, and a John Adams hologram sit at a table in the VIP room of the restaurant. Demon Joe greets his guests with a generic toast as his élite waitresses bring them one hairy biden mocktail after another. "Here's to a profitable future," barks Joe to cries of "Hear, Hear" and "Bully". "I'd also like to thank President Adams and all of the wonderful denizens of Paideuma," he gushes.

A waitress wheeled in a tray of escargot bites and haggis surprise. "My favorite," the hologram chortled. Striker and Elephant lunged toward the waitress. "I'll have this, that and the other thing. You guys are psychics, just figure it out," said Striker. Demon Joe chugged his biden. "I'll take the slightly stressed potato soup with porcupine bacon," Joe ordered. Elephant chose the plain white toast option. Adams motioned for another holographic beverage.

A bouffant-haired waitress rushed to the kitchen. She was actually Destiny von Waifenburg in 1950's-era diner waitress drag. Broz, posing as a dishwasher, was washing a huge stack of dishes and glasses when Destiny came in. "Exxo. These capitalists won't know what hit 'em." Destiny smirked back at him. Broz texted Rahälrahad, who was waiting by the back door of the Wei Back. "Two minutes to go. Synchronize swlatches!" Destiny tapped her phone twice and nodded. "Let's get ready to go."

One minute thirty seconds later, Broz wheeled in a giant tray of mofongo, horse gizzards and hagiography. Destiny stood by the door to the VIP dining room, opening the doors casually for her comrade. Elephant stopped mid-pontification and stared at the waitress. "No surplus capital for youse guys," shouted Broz as he got within annoying distance of the party. John Adams' hologram farted, startling Demon Joe, causing him to slam into Broz's arm just as he was lifting a red-hot vat of potato soup. "Aieee!" screamed Broz as the molten soup poured over his shirt and mouse ears. "For the love of Laverne & Shirley," stated Striker.

-666   Pazuzu

If any infernal being could be considered Lord of Zysigamore, certainly it would be Pazuzu. He could unlock any PC, and set my people free. Only a few dared to summon Him, for good reason: The last time that Pazuzu was on the Island, both Underwear Point and Unicorn Harbor were placed in lockdown.

Clytemnestra swore that this time would be different. She had invited J.O. Lundberg to her Pazuzu summoning, as he had frequently been piqued by the possibility that Pazuzu would be able to block Baphomet from distributing O-Rings throughout the Lower Planes.

Considerable research on Clytie's part left her confident that they could pull this off. Simon Junior's annotated *Necronomicon* with hypertext sigils would do nicely. An ancient bottle of cyan wine from Uottubbacktothebonyiumville (sp.) would provide the necessary spirits for invocation. Lundberg had brought several sizes of ethylene propylene rubber O-Rings to offer the demon - Clytie was even wearing a pair as earrings for the oblique ritual.

The ritual went smoothly. A column of feathers rose from the magic circle. The demon in all His glory soon emerged from within its cloud. "Release me from this binding and you can have anything you want."

The O-Ring assortment placated Pazuzu as He slowly stopped flapping His wings, the feathers landing like snow around the two mortals. "So, you brought me O-Rings, eh? Good." Lundberg and Clytemnestra's faces turned slightly more sanguine. "The last mortals brought me Demon Donuts. I fed them to my harpies." The demon laughed. "And I had that box of donuts teleported to Queen Idajan's royal guards."

"Release me from my binding! You - the one called Lundberg." Pazuzu rose into the air above them, flexing His muscles and unfurling all 4 of His hideous wings. "I can use these EPDM rubber ones in my aerie in the Abyss for sure. And in some of my other lairs. You know, Lundberg," "Yes, Lord Pazuzu," he inaudibly whispered before his brain told him to reply. "If you can hook me up with ITAR-compliant vendors, I will take a few gross of these."

"And I know just the salesman who can deliver, Great Pazuzu," interjected Clytemnestra. The demon summoned a Battering Wind that almost blew their house down. Then for dramatic effect, Pazuzu raised His right hand for the wind to stop.

"Dear Lady, I will not harm you. I am your protector," laughed Pazuzu. Slowly she grinned and tried to brush off the damage. "Thank you. I shall only invoke thee when the time is right." Clytemnestra would be granted one wish by the Demon in return should everything turn out right. "This could go very well," she thought, 'Or...'

667   Old Dagmar Frisbie / Oldagmarfrisbie

Spectrum. It comes out of the sky. It emanates like Hwalearastok.

Alas, a cluster of solifugids performs as a master of hypermanageonomics.

Oldagmarfrisbie, he, the man, the plan, the

"Einmal in Jahr findet fur alle Häxen ein grosser Fest statt: Die Walpurgisnacht."

Oldagmarfrisbie, all wizards lunge toward

Oldagmarfrisbie, Wasser und blunt, danke schoen.

A theory we had. All to account for an unusual quasar of lost sales. Experts blamed solar winds, yet Oldagmarfrisbie was unperturbed.

"Was ist das sabbatgebot? Das kleine?"

Oldagmarfrisbie, frozen among the tentacles of the past aeon, stated a

Dazzling rainbows, bearded homunculi that linger among the test tubes and the coagulated solvents. Our O-Rings were insufficient for the epochal bliss of trembling apothecaries.

A troika of triptychs simmered in a boiling pot of alabaster. I added the soupçon of solifugid essence and prepared for the best.

190

Each witch that I wished had wilted with the will-o-wisps was that witch I had willed to those which were bewitched betimes. It was af is.

Pure prisms are a sort of alchemy.

Mittelhau!

668   Airborne and Invisible

All I do is see. Other sense organs are dulled by human genetics and cognitive biases deeply embedded.

Air is not a Space. It is as alive as its terrestrial elements earth and water. Aerorealities are not at the mercy of the GPS, the static man made map; they know not any coordinates but their own, which is the only state that can define their essence in our terms.

The subjugation of the air has gone forward in earnest, though the state of ignorance remains just as it has since the planet's birth.

We who are visible and tangible also are invisible, intangible. That part is indelible but not unchanging. Pants have no astral counterpart. They solely exist on the material plane, roughly adhering to that same formula that gave the O-Ring dominion.

"Those Powers of the Air subservient to Lord Pazuzu, protect us. Show us favor."

Semaphorescent shapes in the stratosphere. O to turn mid-air and go into a steep dive, like an ancient dragon with wings fully unfurled.

Bowdlerized doggerel disperses like dusky dew longer clinging to the Island. Soon the clarity returns like Mary.

Zephyrus eke his sweetest breaths, keeping Pazuzu perched in pine tree bowers for the duration. Once close, the old aerostar had had enough of Pazuzu's deathwind. "All I can say is, 'Have a Nice Day,'" He shattered.

Cloudcakes among fingerines untroubled. Vast antiyoyanas.

701   Dispater

Glum Dispater rotates the body of Robert Anton Wilson on a sulfuric spit. When he is cooked, he sits at the left hand of the Arch-Devil.

Misery and hatred being His stock-n-trade, Dispater sent many emissaries to Zysigamore Island. Dis told them, "Ignore the Xarthorians. I shall deal with them later. I want salespeople! Dobbshead on a pike!"

Luciferin infused Rod is raised in supremacy. Bitter tombs were scattered with flame made to glow all over, hotter than iron need be for any craft. Soon, Dispater would attempt to plunder the multi level sales professionals of Sandvick, Hughes & Atkinson before targeting the second-tier firms and independents. In time, through consolidation, alliances and dire laments of wretched, tortured clients, all the offices would be His. No more sawbucks and four bits - this was a treasure worthy of the Devil's mighty name.

Several harpies and medusae linger on the City of Dis' walls, inhaling the noxious fumes in the interminable Hell-gloom. "I need a bigwig. A VP, a GM, a managing partner - preferably with low cholesterol."

He began to suck of the life-essences of Epicureans. "Tutti saran serrati quando di Iosafàt qui torneranno coi corpi che là sù hanno lasciati." Suddenly a fax came in.

"Yes, yes," Dispater read from a scroll. "B.O.B. on consignment. That will do." He tore off the fax/scroll/toilet paper dispenser. "Jehoshaphat Valley, here we come!" A flock of erinyes rushed to Dispater's side. "Easy pickings on the Material World for you - just open the gate and pour out from the valley. Gravy."

All that stood between us and those fallen angels were the Iron City beers that we left at their office party. If only some alpha salesman can crack open one of those snalacknalogs, the spirits could enter the cans unwittingly. There was more than one way.

712   Juxtaposition of Golf Ball Sized Cue Cards

Trade dumps had left Clytemnestra at a curious pause. Pants were still on the ascendancy, yet she detected much weakening in the marketplace. She had been able to feed her minotaurs with discontinued SKUs, but the recent Markup Law by Queen Idajan had made the trade far too expensive.

She sadly wandered the corridors of the eldritch labyrinth where her family had herded 'taurs for centuries. Empty. Stale. Even odorless. The blanched victims' bones in the corners of each turn of the corridors looked so lonely, so bereft of the joy they had given her and Mr. Hi Stop for so long. It just didn't seem fair.

The irrelevance of Mobutism led her to pause. There had to be an angle she hadn't considered. Clytemnestra turned to her mirror and softly fixed her gaze on herself: Tired looking eyes itchy and somewhat out of focus; forehead full of furrows flitting from and fro; hairs, some comely, others, dried and wizened; lips crusted with the crud of caffeine and chocolate.

Semi-cutaneous unicorns, however, gave Clytie the complexion of Nut, of the everlasting cosmos. Hi never complained - he was so polite, so nice. She felt every day to be a balancing act.

"Rajlok to Rajlok in three samays. Indeed!"

"Pig-headed flute stands! I'll never get over it!"

The quasit-flavored tension swelled. Hyperlocution like a torrent of mini-superballs cascaded off of each turret. Clytemnestra exhaled.

Wrapping up, unearthing Kurtz for a quarterly bonus. Stunning a Leopold. DF&J were suckers - hung out to dry with the wrong pants. Sic transit.

Pondering, pondering, each trader notched a few if they could. Idajan had the curves, but they believed that they and only they had *all* the angles.

Great big streamers flow with the discipline of the wind. Futhorc. hothechajuxips. Monitoring for

A leak of all manner of phytoplankton - and luciferin-enhanced reptiles - fills the room with colorful, poisonous monsters. Once the hallucination wears off, they camouflage themselves in neckties so wide that a Texas buckthorn couldn't shed a wallaby without engaging in meaningful dialog. I make sure to bring O-Rings of various sizes and viscosities to ensure such a situation doesn't insist.

Chrimpostelers pincered like lerbiax prey.

754   Roger Valdorus

*   The exegesis of Roger Valdorus is discussed. No longer confused with Roger Voudouris. For more information on Roger Voudouris, see Chapter 855.14 and footnote to Chapter 30330.721

Better get used to it.

Big doings. Colorful hoops.

Frontispiece of a

I'm in my bed / I want your sex

With Wacky Ted on 96X

Preach unto my Chorus / Play me more Valdorus

All glory unto Horus

It's yours McLorus

The Martian places we go. Spirograffitimatic

Wacky Ted Kudzopilous had long petitioned and petrified for this menhir to be dooley erected in this hemisphere of the Island. By Ouija and some essential oils we dareth summon Roger Valdorus into Prime Material Plane.

Perpetual gnosis aforethought, the menhirs stand, never sit, at rapped attention to the celestial conga. Molassometers sense oozing motions underground, recording it as sabda.

Marks the procession of yacht rock stars across cowtowns, trans playlists; there's thy guerdon. Go.

Sit.

Quietude overtakes the menhir in witching hours. Absurd rituals of non-corporeal characters don't have to happen, for the lay groovelines are pertected by blessed O-Rings. Ite!

Processionals of Sabbats both holy and not so. Unwritten writs.

See Chapter -754. Add granulated NaCl. Chatath at 365° pour quinze minutes. Solve for x^3.

-754   Roger Valdorus Menhir

Solve for x^3. Chatath at 365° pour quinze minutes. Add granulated NaCl. See Chapter 754.

Unwritten writs. both holy and not so, processionals of Sabbats.

Ite! Absurd rituals of non-corporeal characters don't have to happen, for the lay groovelines are pertected by blessed O-Rings. Quietude overtakes the menhir in witching hours.

Sit.

Sit.

Go. There's thy guerdon. Marks the procession of yacht rock stars across cowtowns, trans playlists.

Recording it as sabda. Molassometers sense oozing motions underground, at rapped attention to the celestial conga. Perpetual gnosis aforethought, the menhirs stand, never sit

We dareth summon Roger Valdorus into Prime Material Plane by Ouija and some essential oils. We had long petitioned and petrified for this menhir to be dooley erected. Wacky Ted Kudzopilous in this hemisphere of the Island.

Spirograffitimatic. The Martian places we go.

It's yours McLorus
REDACTED
REDACTED
REDACTED
REDACTED
REDACTED
REDACTED
REDACTED
Ta

Frontispiece of a

Colorful hoops. Big doings.

Better get used to it.

777   Sellestial Sourcecodez

(A time door opens, depositing SIMON and MR. HI STOP in 1960s Los Angeles, USA, Earth.)
DIONNE WARWICK: Waiting for a time door (song)... But it has passed away...
SIMON: I know the way to San Jacinto. Do I win a prize?
DIONNE WARWICK: "Tea Bags..." (She conjures up an orchestra of rodents and archeopteryxes.) "Tea bags..." (A slight gurgling sound is heard.)
MR. HI STOP: Can't you just use a GPS? I'm not built for this primitive soap colony. (He scans the great big freeway, the dramatic LA Sun refracting his facial features like a stained glass portrait of Dégas.)

(Cut to a menhir. PURPLE ALVIN, a disembodied entity, is leading a group of vestivalgoers in a chant.) GROUP: AWA, AWA, AWA... (In the center of the circle, a garbage can rises as if levitated.)
ROGER VALDORUS: Sit.

(Cut to Tombaugh Middle School. MARQUEZ approaches MISTY MIQUA at her locker.)
MARQUEZ: Bet I can read your aura.
MISTY: Huh? What are you talking about? Do you have a nanodrone or something? (She starts to look around.)
MARQUEZ: It's pink. Your emotions are telling you something. You're -
MISTY: (smirking) Get out of here! I'm not in love. (XATNUDORF & LOSELLE begin to giggle.) Quit it, you guys. (Their laughter grows louder.)

(Cut to MR. HI STOP and a roomful of dorky MBA types.)
MR. HI STOP: Furthermore, our R&D and technology platfumes create synergies of elastomere gobstopping-" (He turns off the slide show, and motions to turn up the lights.) It's a win-win. Solid state disc. (A murmur circulates in the conference room.) Now who's in? Time for a Q and A. Anyone? (He grabs a briefcase and quickly packs up.)

(Back to LA. SIMON stands in front on an Art Gecko diner.)
SIMON: Who has time to wait for a time door any more anyway? (He gazes at the advertising.)
(SWAMI mysteriously strolls into diner. He nods at SIMON.) SWAMI: You are practicing ahimsa, right?
SIMON: (flustered) Well, I thought about killing my husband. But then I realized I'd have to reupholster.
DIONNE WARWICK: (singing) That's what psychic friends are for...

Destorying defective dramatic cenotaphs works ninety-nine times out of a thousand - but almost never on those stronger creatures and gods of the Outer Planes. Still, a few foolhardy frunobulaxes will always try, O-Rings or no rings.

Regent dwellvelopmintz in nanodrone self-defense cleansed most remnants of astral simulacra; despite deez trenz, Sales struggled to sustain the status squocio. Kids like Marquez didn't know what to think - it had been instinctual until just now.

Misty Miqua had seven transformers that could disintegrate into hundreds of gnat-sized nanodrones. She would sometimes allow Marquez to fly one, now that she was used to him and his mischievous playful streak. Her VR headset allowed her to see through thousands of nanodrone-cams, like the eyes of a demented insect.

Deeper deepdish, the bathyscaphe descends below the doughy darkness, down into abscesses of mozzazoic floorceanic crustace. Avez la langue bien pendue.

Prumfrandic heliostances quicktate that all characters, regardless of plane, alignment or class, possess the same amount of latent spontaneity - otherwise you are all doomed. C'est republique de dés os. Pas de dix-huits.

If Me had this exbihitudinum-like provenance, the regurgitron would have been grendered unutilizable prior to floccinaucinihilipilification. As it were, its inchoate solubility is its shaving grace.

For every slovenly trull there exists an owlyfan dancing for pleasure.

Gha'agsheblah, os golpeadores. Jaws of Astaroth slam down upon your flesh. No thing. No man. Neg eight. Beyond eternity sickle. Under Brother Enoch the Watcher the Tower the

Hard grime dropped like tender meat falling off the bone. Verily microprosoposcopic animalcules lurch toward extendropy, like a seborrheic lamia loaned to Yeenoghu. Refractive ontology.

Gigundo puzzletronic matrixhalle: grids within grids within grids. Roll again.

Tawaddud escapes by gaming. She places tokens, pieces, figurines and chips in all dimensions. Vague intimations of complete liberation follow. Tawaddud now tutors X's and plays flute in airports.

808   Chatath חתת

Gott sie los und liess sie gegen das Meer schweben.

Back in the day when Me and Tinkelhoff were knee high to a xxend's eye, a marilith yclept Pspsoips inhabited the Yoknapatawphic parishes of the hill regions of Uottubbacktotheboniyiumiville (sp.), staying largely invisible to everyday Xarthorians but pushing the strings in her county nevertheless. Her attendants - brutal night hags, hideous medusae, chain smoking gynosphinxes, renegade dryads, and disgruntled strippers - scurried back and forth to the Lower Planes to further Pspsoips' political and psionic maneuverings from the Prime Material Plane.

Generations of hill giants revered Pspsoips as a goddess. But for virtually everyone else, the marilith was an arch-enemy with a quick temper and long, long memoria. All went her way for many score.

But then Pspsoips made a cereal mistake: answering a personal ad from Striker, and not blocking his number after the first call. "Hmm, this guy is rich. Maybe he'll buy me some jewelry and a social media network," she cackled. Striker agreed to take her to the most deluxe, deloused restaurant on the Island, far removed from Demon Joe's chains of hunky-tunks.

Once again, Striker was at his most sensual and suave. "I'm an entrepreneur," he noted, "not some solesman or trivial fellow." Pspsoips feigned attention for a few moments, but soon the eyerolls were coming furious and fast. "I'm getting a spiral vortex. Just a yoyana." She rose to powder her noses.

A wave of ex-Zombie Men of the Ningarm bricked the hits, and the intimate bistro was crawling with shabbolethly dressed Xarthorians and placobdelloides jaeger skioeldi. "Let's blow this shazbotsickle." Pspsoips teleported away from the restaurant, leaving Striker all alone. "Doesn't 'Let's' mean both of us?" he muttered to the placobdelloides jaeger skioeldi stuck to his inner thigh. "Not you, you creepy little monster," he hissed, trying discreetly to dislodge the buttsucker.

Meanwhen back in Yoknapatawphiburg, Pspsoips sat in her lair, sprawled out on a humongous vaginochair eating brains and assorted gonards. "Wasn't any good meat on that Striker fella anyway," she laughed to her favorite demon dawg. She turned the skewered body of Ludvig von Mises hanging from a spat over her immense fireplace. "Cyber men ain't my baguette."

Unbeknownst to any, Pspsoips took on odd gigs for Idajan bimeby, having telepathically been linked to Bleary Tim in past centuries. She was good at fricasseeing all manner of lerbiaxes, spider centaurs and game show hosts, in addition to her own machinations. "My bad. I should have told you about Striker," texted Idajan. The marilith laughed and ate a chunk of roasted Mises.

-808　　　　Ashtaroth

Her Holiness Ashtaroth had a spread six Abyssal layers thick, with fortresses scattered about and tasteful upscale strip malls at convenient distances from Her Interplane Highweigh exits. Not only were all the golf courses sentient, but the cigarette vending machines as well. She landed her dragon Zwielda at Her morbid pleasure palace and dismounted, wan smell of coitus rising up through the air.

She rang for Her marilith servant Gha'agsheblah. "Daughter of the shade of Qlippoth! Be hear now." The marilith appeared, covered in fresh entrails and variegated giant insect larvae. "What I would give to have the head of John Adams on a plate right now, garnished with parsley and kumquats." Ashtaroth and Her allies waged perpetual warfare not only against Adams, but also most of the Team Gods and the other Demons and Devils save perhaps Pazuzu and Juiblex; She and Tiamat remained cordial if a bit strained in their affectations toward each other.

The Green-Eyed Demon Lady's most feared proclamation was "Condemn shalt thou judgment in thee against rise shall that tongue every and; prosper shall thee against formed is that weapon no." Upon un utterance, Ashtaroth's servants rounded up stunned weaker beings and flayed them as painfully as possible with the assistance of Gamchicoth, the Order of Devourers who perpetually followed in Ashtaroth's wake.

"Waiting for a time door..." Simon, Traveling Salesman and Mr. Hi Stop half stepped in when She appeared. Unfortunately they were now stuck on Level 271 of Ye Old Abyssee, in the giant claws of a scorpion-tailed demoness with impure intentions leaching out in the form of toadstools. Twas the Lady Grizulab, Majora Doma to Ashtaroth. "Greasy mortals, why shouldn't I just split you sideways by your bussies?" she cackled.

Simon burst into tears, but Grizulab wasn't moved. She hissed some more, waving her poisoned tail in front of the party. Before Hi's face could retract, they were snared in ropes made from durum semolina. The horrific Queen of the Abyss and her marilith soon appeared to inspect these classic intruders. "What shades of Elvis are ye?" asked Gha'agsheblah, as Ashtaroth scanned their memories and smartphones for clues.

The demoness turned to Mr. Hi Stop. "So, you're the significant other of this Clytemnestra I've heard so much about. Magic circles, O-Rings, Qlippoth Gate, time travel... Why didn't she make the trip?" Hi was in full meltdown, and had trouble directly answering Ashtaroth. "Biv-Biv-Biv-dgyor," he spat out.

Soon, Clytie picked up the automated distress signal she had Hi swallow. "What have those guys just half stepped into?" she whispered, skrying into a transparent orb on her desk. "Xzimor, can you get me a colander really quick?" Xzimor slipped it over Clytie's orb as she chanted the Pastafarian prayer backwards. "R'amen...Ever and forever.." A wave of tomato sauce hit the captives, loosening the pastaropes. The freshness of the al muso noodles overwhelmed the demons, who scurried about devouring mouthfuls of fresh pasta and sauce. Traveling Salesman rolled a meatball at the lingering demons, who lazily low-tailed it out of the gang's way. "The marinara trick - did you see that coming?" fumed Ashtaroth, as flakes of parmesan cheese descended like preteryods.

842   Whizz'n Lancelloti

We are going to avoid niceties, but we must ask for those with fragile constitutions or the tendency to come down with the vapors, please leave the room as you may become very verklempt when the following tale is Articulated.

What can you say about Whizz'n Lancelloti that hasn't already been said in words far more elegant than mine. Lo, the days come and go, the stars in the sky wheel about, and nothing comes close to that fateful night. May 29, a Tuesday I believe, and a sense of impending doom saturated the landscape. Somehow our collective memories will assuage our emotions for a short moment, and you can feel your heart beat again, as if you hadn't heard its cadence for a decade or more.

It was into this foreboding desolation that the protagonist entered: Whizz'n Lancelloti. Of course, we all thought highly of him. You could say that many of the striplings idolized him. And why not? The charisma was undeniable. Whizz'n Lancelloti. Destiny comes in large packages, said nobody. Still, there was a kernel of truth there somehow, as if the yoyanas all folded into each other in a perfect sequence. Good.

The thing about Whizz'n Lancelloti is that his reputation precedes him. Much like Young Fortinbras, Whizz'n Lancelloti was the right man at the right time. Kids move, dogs die, but the significance of what Whizz'n Lancelloti managed to try to accomplish are downright. Someone had set up one of those makeshift memorials on the corner of Linden Street but it's gone now. Selah.

882   Elaborations on an Earlier Plot

At heart a Bildungsromanasattva.

The villain, a heartless merciless force known as Pants and occasionally Sox, restricts the prana flow.

A boy can't do anything. So he sells some shit and gets into mischief.

The catharsis does not occur at once; rather, it is suffused throughout each line and each character and punctuation mark within. It rotates easily perpetually.

Incidental Omnigotopoiaea between beats.

An implication that he came to Simon's door like Neal Cassady flinging himself into the open arms of Ginsburg.

Bodies wrestle backward forth in lovemaking. Nothing remained dry.

Figures of stolid angels imprisoned in pants of doom. A denim waistband to bind them all.

A plaintive tick-tick-tick. Tick-tick-tick. Tick.

Sit.

Soldoxpara in umber only. No returns. Should have got there earlier. A comedy of runs.

Each act is a big hassle. We're constantly changing scenes that are impossible to do onstage. A slide projector would help a lot.

Refried beanbags lie scattered across the lawn. The game of chance is a drama within the drama. The symbolism of the teams, their colors and mascots feeds back into the theme.

Osteosyllabic terradact. Each chapter is a rib, the book's spine the sternum.

901   Bodhi of the Xarthorians

Under the trees and trees and trees, under the forest, under the sod, under the leaf litter. Collecting the fruit of the tree the Xarthorians cal 'ieyz is their way of life.

The leaves' veins and their chlorophyll cells come to me swiftly.

Green emanations fill their land's clouds. In Xarthor, even the rain is Green.

Green noble truths X11 in all, so aesthetically enjoyable within the incense odor.
<X11 root>/lib/X11/rgb.txt

16, 777 216 mala beads strung from here to Umlaut Towin. Beads of peridot, jade, sapphire, emerald and tsavorite light up with each syllable of mantra.

A chant without a voice lingers beside the mala. Baby Bodhisattvas are perpetually hatching from the tulip-like bulbs that line every path. Svaha Teyatha. Each naga spends a moment in Samadhi from the cumulative harmonics.

Malachite statues stand at each corner, flowing along the X11. Arboreal damselflies stream along the path, ever hovering in bliss.

Xarthorians, as a navelless people, simply gaze at the lowest fat levels of their torso toward the sacred spaces.

A satisfying amount of spectrum mixes with raindrops - yods. Each leaf gently pulsates, circulates the colorforms throughout the network. A tide of extradimensional super beings and demons.

"It's time to go on the Hunt!"

Ripples of pure ectoplasm

Dakinis dilate to Sita Tara's song. Om ___ _____ ____.

Trees are the original Ones who are Enlightened. So much progress was made.

Green Men, Green Eyed Ladies, dance back and forth in the heart-rhythm of this sometimes godlike realm.

Slime:

Mold:

Snot:

Oracle:

-901   Xarthor

Known to many as the Xarthorians, they are the original inhabitants of all Zysigamore.

Unfortunately they lost their lands via sleightride of hand. Seems they were charmed by an onyx paper clip that bore a clear resemblance to then-Xarthor King "'h'y".

The seismic stillness, a hallmark of Xarthorian civilization, is unknown today. Instead, the isle is a veritable skateboard.

Still, you can't beat it. But every few centuries, some Xarthorians show up at a fundraiser, barn raising or vivisection to ask for their lands back. This just generates mockery and increased heckling, which directly affects the Richter scale in all parts of Zysigamore.

I used to see an occasional Xarthorian here or about, curled up on the side of the road, clutching VHS tapes or obscure protractors.

In early days, Uottubbacktothebonyimtonium (sp.) was a veritable haven of these unshaven, clairvoyant beings. Today, there is but one true blue Xarthorian family left. They have been embossed in amber for their own protection. The Gum of Gorth is an obscene tribute to their pseudopods. All the rest are trifles, mere shadows of this proto-Xarthorian.

Gorth's apocolocyntosis would prove to be his Waterloo.

Thirteen times I discovered a Xarthorian bank mine. It was in the old style, with Tupperware fascia and enough tadpoles to fill a jodhpur.

Their traditions were ruthlessly displaced, much to the chagrin of the galumphing proles.

An ache for vestigial thumbscrews was a boon for the demi troglodytes who consumed the Xarthorians' corpses. We gathered together to deprive ourselves of their subliminal culture, which was seen dripping through the frame.

Although I don't miss their dimension drift, I seem to echo the thoughts of others: Forget the past. Let the lava cool and hide all those non-Euclidean structures.

912   Urchins

Urchins are not immortal, but they have 0 need of pants.

These are Perfected Creatures, honed by millions of millions of generations under the sea.

An urchin's mind can scarcely imagine pants, let alone have a meaning or purpose for them.

As seen from space, a wild orb of blue and white does not have a waist; it does not wear a belt, despite the legends of several famous cartographers.

Hop-urchin

Oh my, the luxury of the urchin is forever on display.

Call it a passive stance.

The fool dreams in a psychedelic spirograph. Raised gem-like features titillate the senses.

Eyes not included. Must bring silly stick-on eyes.

No heaven, no hell can be like this. So many of our affairs prove irrelevant. We think without these organs, eh?

Drifting, drifting, sand and sea undulate.

Lords of Karma got up and went, yet the Urchins remain as beautiful as ever.

Zona overthrown, the guts relax amid the diminished tension and constriction.

In every forgotten alley and hidden hacienda in Zysigamore Urchins stir the pixies and Brenda Loompas, far out of mind to those who would do them harm.

Urchins know tides, but neither super- nor sub-tyrannies of complacency and binding. X11

-931   Hoslings Predux, Once Removed

The Emily Dickinson triathlon having ended, Simon was on the verge of melting into a viscous, protoplasmic pudding. However, the 75,000-mile velodrome's results had not been posted. He sniffled, and prepared the Big Cry for when the other defenestrators would be paying attention.

"Woe is me! Woe is Me! If only my zither were more supple!" Simon whined and continued to whine as the Astrodome grew empty and dark. A janitor somberly tied his shoes in exquisite apathy.

"This would have never happened if...if..." Simon took great pleasure in blaming others, except Traveling Salesman, for his problems.

An antelope masticated at the corner. Two dried lungs hung like punching bags in the morning sun. Ezekiel had

The wafting aroma of burnt molasses now drifted throughout the arena. Simon showed no more emotion, but solemnly ate a gummy crucifix dipped in absinthe.

Now it was on to "Jello Wrestling Movie Stars" with special guest host Cyrus Vance. It was going to be a hit for Anacreon. However, its market share in the Zysigamore demographics was below nil. Too many Rosicrucians, said the sponsors.

In the good old days, the days were good but not old.

Tremblay raged like a wounded gladiator. "I hate all of you!!!" He lunged at the televangelists before falling down an impossibly short set of stairs. Young Fortinbras got the email.

"Simon - Simon - Simon - Simon." It was almost as if Simon Junior were taunting him via telekinesis. "Simon." And the wind cried, "Sit."

Twelve diplodocuses had been summoned for the delight of various venture capitalists and hangmen. I called a rib on a particularly healthy dinosaur. Selah.

When Dave came to, he was in a small barbershop made of pewter and the hopes and dreams of Howard Krupke, who happened to

Earthplugs in tritium nanosewage inform all stirges' dens.

-939   Xylem Maturity Factor

Vessels full of hagiography. Silently the meiosis happens - no lights, no stunts, no elaborate plot contrivances.

Traveling Salesman relishes the receipts of his day. Per diem but still needs them for an expense report. Those boots in Terraburn; holes in the darkinos made it impossible to miss.

Realio, trulio, little brown box. Glamor happened. F1, F2, F3 Back to F2. Pivot to the shooting lens.

Has to happen, shedding planetoids in wake of the

Swell, foop. Bif fri fleu. In and out.

The sober storekeeper sighs as he reaches for the logbook. More credit for the Sylvesters. It's like nobody pays their bills. How do we get by?

Protoplasm leaps from the core of a frustrated star. Hot solar wind pushes outward, enveloping heavenly bodies with the intense magnetism.

Young Fortinbras, he has made it his own. Forged by the metal, he is impervious to our attacks. Best to leave the territory to him. Pick your battles, says that Traveling Salesman bible.

The county fair left him wanting less. Tokens just burning a hole in his trousers.

Seventeen out of thirty-six is a winner. A good enough play for a greenhorn trying to learn the ropes. He paid no heed to the moralistic prohibitions. What was a Sunday to him?

Every day's a Saint's day. That means you are pissing off some Saint every day if you smoke, gamble, drink, swear and google.

Kaz-a-WHOOP!

The cicadas emerge, circular and straight.

One pair in burnt umber was being altered. Tailors are plotting to support the ubiquity of Pants. The collusion sickened me, yet there was little we could do. North Zysigamore belongs to Urizen; in fact, the entire island is his to festoon with eternal opaque clouds.

Again the Traveling Salesman comes to the door.

999   9's Sont Cheres Quand Vous N'avez Pas L'avocat

New clear Menergy cannot cave to the kilowatt hours offered by Happy Nines merrily reverting to zero and back to the novemordial. The esoteric equation synthesizes the logic to the 9th degree, thus releasizing clean kinetic power for this busy monster manunkind.

Still, the market is novel, and investors aren't giving it a ninth look. But hindsight is 90/90; transsubstantiated tardigrades tether together three x three cum general bonhomie.

Yesodbusters small and big come and go, talking of Micheloangelic franticsee, drooppantis in exilio, spending great big coin like there was no yesterme.

Tyranny of SOX9 is downregulated confettialouistically feeding forward between pathways. Its dwellvelopmint en ventre sa mere damns the fetus to a lifeslime of crude megaball gestures, intimations of unattainable sales prowess, and bro country.

Cmxcix Novemclap, yet antoher disembodied entity, had almost a dozen barrister avatars he regularly ran Island-wide. Each embodied their own hairstyle deathstyle and desultory go-to catchphrases. "Wirklich klassisches Rechtsanwalte!" Cmxcix cried. The avatars marched single file down one fluorescent-light-filled hallway after another, distant hum of gigundus mainframes emerging from every pompitus wall.

Enneagrammatical merkaba, wheels within wheels, not ceasing at enneahectaenneacontakaienneagons, no rest at 9=0, no strangelic enochian ode to an amputated Avalokitesvara, no wonder sensible haircut, no hremitage unhermitted, no tone unsturned, nor even chrimposteler jam serpasches awl teledildonic idiospheres darkly and dimly. Weep along.

Powernine Hell-Master Uberavatars, ubersplendent in every spectrum, postdominate RGB print runs throughout upper worlds. The cards are printed so thin, so two-dimensionally, that sagacious storekeepers file them between 0.999..... and 1. Implausible, you say? Répétez après moi:

Footstep village. Sound of a footstep, followed by another footstep, and another footstep, and another and another and another. Flowers suddenly appear. Come and sing. Sound of turtle dove's song.

Yo sé que pa' llegar a mil hay que empezar de cero.

-999   Tea Bags?

Simon pored over every glossy magazine, every vlog, every softie self-help book, every technical memorandum: *Cool Stepdad News, Post-Modern Parenting* and *Headwasters of Colaphilalembic Artichokes*. "I've never even thought about becoming a stepdad, let alone a cool one," he confided to Simon Junior. "Until seconds ago, when the commercial breaks come on." It was like one of Simon's favorite soap operas but real. "If we don't like it, we're putting our VR headgear on!" Simon Junior sat.

Before Simon knew it, Elephant was ejecting a washed out, vaguely negative Cmxcix Novemclap avatar by spraying him with chemigold tungsten pieces and slapping him with a weighted catfish. "Autoteleology may rue the day. There will never be a next-gen Elephant. The firmament disallows it." But clearly the moral vertigo ate Simon up. "I can't even eat figs anymore. Or bon bons. Or Twink Keys."

"Simon Junior, how did you deal with the news about Simon III? I'm sure you just reacted as usual," Simon babbled. The enormo-TV flickered a reminder about a show coming on in two minutes. "Be a doll and clean up this Candy Land bored, Simon Junior. It's time for my favorite talk show." Simon flitted to the kitchen for proper fancy elegant snack cakes and santorum.

Suddenly a swell of dramatic music poured in. "It's the Vimford Hill Show on Ace TV!" cried an overfed fanfarron. "Goody goody gumdrops," mused Simon, motioning for Simon Junior to stifle. The studio audience roasted its approval as Vimford Hill strode onto the stage. "Oh my stars," sighed Simon, glancingly approving Vimford's unholy blazer and form fitting slacks. "So good to be here," announced Vimford as cumfetti reigned. Simon adsorbed it all extra passively.

"My first guest today is Wiff Wilkersack. Please give him a Vimford Hill cheer." Wiff emerged, waved at the studio audience and quipped, "I'm just a jilted jasonberry, just like you." Vimford shook his hand firmly and initiated the official small talk. He asked, "What was it really like?" Wiff talked about how his husband had a secret life as a Hollywood pool boy, applying sunscreen to leading ladies just for fun. "All the baby mommas greeting us at the airports, rugrats in hand. So humiliating," whined Wiff.

Suddenly Simon's prostate buzzed. "A phone call from Traveling Salesman!" The enthralling voice pulsed through the phone. "Hi Si, it's me. I was watching Ace TV and I-" said Traveling Salesman before being interrupted. "I just love Vimford Hill. I met all his toupées." Simon chattered nervously with Traveling Salesman before he cut Simon off. "I'm so sorry. I've been a realio trulio healio. I know why you're so angry. I've been doing a lot of thinking and I-" Simon inquit, "YOU? Think? Tea Bags?!" (Canned laughter follows).

1,000   Luce Enz

The bloom was off the range. Dew-coated golf balls lay like road apples across the glistening fairway. Marquez strolled from one golf ball to the next, yet he only picked certain ones. Management queries into his work ethnic were in vein; the youth was uninterested in the exploitation of Ms. Murphy, the sentient golf course's sentient driving range. "Even a driving range's got soul," he explained. The next day, Marquez was working in the en-lipoco stable, picker replaced by a shovel.

A few hours of shoveling en-lipoco shit later, and Marquez was on to antoher career opportunity. He began selling 4-packs of anti-golf balls to frustrated duffers leaving Ms. Murphy. Soon Marquez had earned more than he would have picking actual golf balls. Many duffers praised him, but soon a narc - probably an ex-co-worker - ratted Marquez out to Ms. Murphy's GM. After an encounter with a very nice ossifier, the kid gave up and moved on.

His mom was very alarmed when she found out about Marquez's innate sales skills. Laney warned Marquez, "Go back there and apologize to management right now. You're not a salesman, you hear!" He sneered back. "You're all goofed up on hopballs again, huh, Mom? I ain't gonna shovel shit no more. Fuck that!" Mom tried to be helpful, screaming at him. "Nobody would hire you except as a whore." Her son just smiled and walked out the door.

Marquez longed to travel, but didn't have the transpo. But he did know Ms. Murphy - her hopes, her dreams, her cavernous sand traps, her hagridden hydrohazards - and believed in her. So it was with a swagger that Marquez entered the barn, confidently leading Fritz the en-lipoco to the pasture. Edney, the evening groundskeeper, just waved at Marquez, even tipping his chapeau. "G'nite," called Marquez, Ms. Murphy's hills they echoed, echoed.

Three days later, Marquez and Fritz were strolling the wooden boulevards of glamorous Unicorn Harbor, with no money, no direction, no plan at all - other than to help himself to the discarded luxuries the city folk were accustomed II.

It took a few hours to assemble a makeshift home out of old pallets, cardboard and plastic. The night rolled in - Marquez couldn't see much, but could feel he was being watched. He stuck his head out of the flimsy entrance. All he could see was an expressionless teen in a T-shirt so long it covered his knees. "S'garbage can," read the gold letters of his T-shirt. "Who you calling a -" The kid extended a hand to Marquez. "You have met the Gold Kid," the T-shirt now read. Marquez's attitude changed. "How about that?" he mouthed in amazeballs.

-1,000   Alchemical Queerjacket

Little is done to address the Tyranny of the Blazer. It is such an Incasker garment, pressing your shoulders into the shoulderpads just as surely as putting a body in a coffin. Its rigidity is enforced by the cravat which strangles you and blocks the blood flow to your brain, as well as buttons that strain to hold a portly physique in place.

Strange indeed is the jacket that will lift all your restrains. You only lose your straightness in the process - a more than fare traid. Salesmen being salesmen, however, the tradition of the mamba blazer still hovers over the profession - in fact, over all Zysigamore.

For many supine Xarthorians, custom trumps comfort. Onie McPhersall realized this, and let his men know what to expect. "If you're in a phinch, lose the jacket, maybe even the tie too. I know it goes against the ornithodoxy, but it could pay off extra royally."

The most prestigious department store for blazers is in Unicorn Harbor of course, yclept L'escargot Étouffé. This is where Ace TV sends all their leading men, from Bryant Brick's body triple to the latest SJU intern. Quentin Periwinkle checks in every couple of weeks to pay down his lay-aways and feel the latest ascots and pocket quadrilaterals. "I can't afford to shop here, but I can't possibly wear any of that knockoff trash at Stanney's," he complained to the staff.

Deep in a back closet at a Stanney's Department Store in Umlaut Towin was a portal to a blessed pocket dimension containing a vast ocean of 1970s-era blazers in garish colors of rainbows neither imagined nor viewed on the Prime Material Plane. No Brenda Loompa dareth permeate this bazaar hemiverse.

Elephant maid very pacific instructions about which blazer he wished to be buried in, based on the cause of death. "One if by sword. Two if by bullet. Three if by pestilence," he explained as he showed Simon Junior each garment. "Don't ask me who the provider is, Simon Junior. Dazz all I ask," quoth Elephant.

Meco, having been proclaimed a 'Saint of Menswear' by church and queendom, appeared irregularly in well-known blazer styles paired with the bootsyluscsiousest men's slacks ever pre-recorded. He snuffed off parochial concerns about the social status of his right pantleg. After all, wasn't he a Prince? Several X's assisted Meco with supermodeling, superballs, superciliousness, supererogenotoriety, superstyrofoam footwares, superhobos, superbas and supercolliders.

-1,001   Xarthorian Evenings

"So this one time in high school, right? I was on the JV megaball team and..." Idajan straddled Meco's cock. "And? And? Uh?" She slowly writhed and took him all the way in, moaning in reply. "Hey, I can finish this story tomorrow..." He kissed Idajan passionately with his pierced tongue.

All the Queen's handmaidens were stunned. This went on night after night. Idajan and Meco did a bunch of flex drugs, drank Striker's finest wines, and stayed up until 5 a.m., as Meco continued to tell the Queen elaborate tails of mirth, woe and anacreonisms. "You know something? This reminds me of the time I found three decapitated lerbiaxes." Meco began rambling on. "I had been on their trail, you see. Great brutish things, each smelling worse than the next one." Idajan's eyes sparkled, and her grip on the blade loosened.

After a bawdy reception, Meco carried Idajan back to her royal bed chamber. Her X's handmaidens had prepared her bedroom for the inevitable. Yet Idajan was ready to get her groove back and balled Meco for several honeymoon hours. Finally Meco's erection gave way, and the Queen's handmaiden Sipha handed her the vorpal blade.

Meco and Idajan's whirlwind romance was the town of the talk, even in the Abyss. This time, Meco had a ring. "It's not much, but, would you take my hand in marriage, O Queen? I promise I will clean up after my blink dog." "Yes, yes, a million times yes," she laughed, pouring herself another glass of Striker's wines. Striker had been invited to the nuptials, yet claimed he had to do his hair that day.

A himbo he was, yet Meco had a certain wit about him. He could charm an audience with fantastic tales of derring-do and scripta fliptas. "There was this mad Arab guy, right? And he walked straight into the desert, carrying Lee Litif. And nobody knew why. So they traveled in a flying -" Uvwxyx slapped him on the back. "Great! You're perfect!"

Idajan's vizier Uvwxyx met Meco at a trendy gym, where he was an instructor for morning Twisting class. All the ladies enjoyed his toned body and array of tooth whitening products. "Yes, yes. Sounds good. The Queen is so beautiful." Meco was oblivious to the news. "So what's the catch? Do I have to wear a bunny suit and startle the Xarthorians?" Uvwxyx cleared his throat. "Well, there are all these rumors. But don't fill your head with them."

Uvwxyx searched all of Uottubbacktothebonyium (sp.) for Idajan's next victim/husband. Uvwxyx asked top cleric Rev. Zzyster for a recommendation. Unbelievably, he asked, "What about my brother Meco? I'm sure the Queen would like him." Surprisingly the Vizier took his advice.

Time upon a Once, existed there a Warrior Queen by the name of Idajan. She had always distrusted men, and had several bridegrooms executed, usually the day after marriage. Her lackeys would drain the sap from their lifeless corpses each morning.

-1,001R   Xarthorian Disco Nights

Soft disco smooth jazz yacht rock moldies waft over the quaint cottages of Unicorn Harbor. Outifts are slick fisted. Outcasker frolix. Bubbly beverages are prosumed. Night seems less threatening with thisa playlisticle.

Once, twice, three times a Queen's mandated disco policy took F-ect, clubs filled up with macho characters and red hott mamba mammas showed up at midnight every nite. 0 night hags allowed reassured naive Xarthorians that only the finast of lusts would be honored by the cover charge.

The gang (Simon, Quentin, Nas, Painfully Closeted Stan, Christy and a Roger Valdorus hologram) maid their weigh two the uberbar. "They mix good drinks here. Right in your mouth," confided Quentin. "I was hear for last week's inverted lip sync contest. Girls just let it all hang out!" The group heaved with laughter.

"Say Quentin, I like those polyester slacks," gushed Li'l Nas Y. "So retro and trendo." Quentin shot him the 'I know you are butt...really?' look. Simon introceded. He wanted to know more about Stan's pants. "So Stan, is this your first discodeo?" He blushed, pretending not to understand Simon's coded contextual come-ons. Quentin commented, "Don't be so coy, Stan. Just lay off the soy." He and Nas got their bussies to the dance flo.

At just about 3 a.m., who should show up but Asmodeus in His form of Old Scratch. Dressed like an antediluvian pimp, Old Scratch roller-discoed into the club with a bevy of bexin distanglers. Christimiqua rose to dance, and Scratch perched on the edge of the dance flo like a hungriform hawk in high heat. Nas grabbed her hand quickly, leading her swiftly away. "Brimstone cologne, no go," Li'l Nas Y spat towards Asmodeus. "This is my house."

Wacky Ted's excuses for not DJ'ing were as lengthy as they were mundane. Mamba Dave was able to spin every Valdorus remix unimaginable and knot. Spotlight on Old Scratch, who had challenged the whole gang in His arrogant, toxic masculine stylo. His stepford dance was ogmented by leotarded solid yellow dancers with big small hairs.

Finally painfully closeted Stan dayed the save after consuming an ocean of kumquat liquor and hopball vodka enemas. Conjuring the venerable essence of yacht rock swagger, Stan shook his booty to a tropical assortment of funkotechnoarcopolyspelunkovichistan hypertracks. "Kiss my ass, Devil," cried Stan, to the applause of 81% of the disco aficionados. Doctors don't think he will furvive.

1,002   The Poetry of Emily Dickinson

Emily Dickinson was some Losah from Western Mass.

Emily Dickinson wasn't so great at poetry. She never did a poetry reading. That was queer. Der. She just kept her poems in a drawer. Who's gonna read them? Duh!

Emily Dickinson sucked. She never published a book of poetry. And she's not on Youtube. What a queer.

Mrs. Hemans was a good poet. She sold lots of books. Not like Emily Dickinson who sucks.

Der. She said she was a bell of Amherst but she wasn't even into music. What a queer.

If you want good poetry, you won't get it in this class. They are all old and boring.

They want me to quote from one of her poems but I forgot. It sucked anyway. Der.

In conclusion, Emily Dickinson sucks at poetry. Der, Mrs. Hemans is much better. Emily Dickinson is queer.

Clear and agonized burst.

She died in infamy and ignomy. Der.

She was an atheist fifth columnist who rebelled against God and was smoted down. Der. Just a cocky girl.

Of coarse the best American woman poet was Felicia Hemans. She came from the Pilgrims and wasn't some Losah from the Grove. Der.

Mrs. Hemans had her boy burning on the shore. That was pissa. She wasn't a queer.

1,103   Epitaphalog

"Love is a many splendored thing," sang Rev. Zzyster as he splashed holy water and cans of Tab on the coffin. It had been two weeks, and the poorly preserved pachyderm's pungent perfuum permeated the park. Slowly Rev. Zzyster sifted spoonful after spoonful of salubrious soil into the grave. Next came the Rev's medley of 'Mors Principium Est.'

After the incasker had left, a small group of mourners approached the gravesite. Marquez, phone in hand, nanodrones in orbit, leaned into the grave and called, "Elephant O Elephant, you are so beautiful. Elephant." Rev. Zzyster made some urgent holy gestures and faded away, as did the small crowd of mourners.

Across towin, Simon pushed a shopping cart through a brutalist series of aisles within aisles within aisles. In desultory desolation he asked an employee for directions "Where may I find the attenuated superballs in aspic?" inquit Simon. The chipper stockboy replied, "Sugar-free or other. Mezzanine aisle 6A, beyond the Rocky Mountain oysters." "Always a thrill," winked Simon as he rolled on behind his cart.

Unripened kumquats having been selected, our hero bravely pushed into the Aisle of Irrelevance: Long-forgotten SKUs marked down beyond all precognition; a plethora of plastic seasonally-adjusted, broadly seasoned lawn ornamentations; old Team Gods posters, picture disks, paraphernalia, protozoa and protruberances; canned newt eyes; and wolfram-enliched gluten-free tadpole crisps. "If only I could scan all of you," pleaded Simon to the random consumer items, "but my framily would get very ticked off at me."

Yet thoughts of Elephant wafted into Simon's most prehensile mind. "He made my life so pretentious," he confessed to the self-checkout machine/bot. A rude gut boy lifted a digit to his direction. "Need some help with this machine, sir?" he offered. Simon huffed, "Yes, I need to reboot my entire life. Elephant always said machine politics will ruin us!" The gut boy stared and began to pee himself. "La la, I'm not a shrink," Simon laughed and strolled away.

Elephant never paid the ferry toll. This rankled Outcasker, who posted Return to Sender on the pachyderm's tail and found yet another closet for him to inhabit. "Harrumph," trumpeted Elephant, scanning for mothballs with a searchlight. "The bond issue for Entebbe's new airport was obscured by obstreperous over-speculation…"

1,316   Information Dissemination Waiver

Disclaimer: ---REDACTED---

This Information Dissemination Waiver granteth "Me," author of the blog/book *The Tyranny of Pants by Me,* et cetera, blah blah, all exemptions from any and all state, federal or international laws...blah blah, op. cit… CCLII

This Waiver protecteth any and all satirical use or portrayal within the blog/book/media yclept *The Tyranny of Pants by Me,* under Fair Use laws of the Unitas Dates of Amebica, Ltd., under a groove, blah blah, op cit...

This Waiver doth prohibiteth any Government from collecting fees, tolls, levies, or other revenues relating to portrayals of Government officials or any other 'real people' within *The Tyranny of Pants by Me.* Attempts to collect such funds will be thwarted.

The entirety of the Cast of Characters as portrayeth in *The Tyranny of Pants by Me* are Intellectual Property that belongeth solely to Me, Me's co-authors and Me's publishing company in perpetuum, all rights reserved, and so on, and so on, blah blah.

Please add your comments here:

_____

_____

_____

_____

_____

_____

Balls,

Me

-1,337   Classism and the Impetus for an Eagletarian Zysigamore

Harpomarxist Broz was kidnapped by Traveling Salesman after a work day at rough. "Sorry, mate," said Traveling Salesman as he pointed a gun at the revolutionary anti-Elephantist. "My husband is leaving me, and I've been depressed as all fuck-all." Broz's mouse ears slumped down a bit. "That's too bad, Traveling Salesman. Is there anything I can do to help? Teledildonics? Mumblety peg?"

Traveling Salesman hadn't quite formulated his kidnapping plot too well - too much booze and flex drugs, not enough watching videos of successful hostage taking. "Just take me to a cheap motel. We can watch TV and order take-out. I am a good listener. I really am," Broz pleaded. Traveling Salesman wiped the santorum out of his eyes and answered, "Yeah, let's just do that. No funny stuff, though."

Traveling Salesman checked into the Foxtrot Motel on Telefunken Ave., then prep-walked Broz upstairs to his motel room. Traveling Salesman improvised his next moves. "I'm going to reread Classic Play Number Twelve backwards. That way, I'll know what to do," he explained. Broz consoled him. "Yeah, I'm real, real sorry me and my gang had to kidnap you back in CP #12. But that was the plot. Me and Tinkelhoff are the real ones to blame."

A secret dossier in Traveling Salesman's fanciful attaché case held limitless copies of CP #12. Soon, TS wrapped Broz in cellophane, and proceeded to start reading the play backwards out loud. His phone buzzed. "Goody, here's dinner." Before Traveling Salesman could get to the door, a Snooty Looking Nerd with a Bowtie barged in with their take-out order. "Now I come to Traveling Salesman's door," he spaketh in his patented stylo.

Traveling Salesman took the bit out of Broz's mouth so he could eat. Broz blurted, "If Me is so omnipotelex, why didn't she/zhe/zhay/they/one/thy do *this* chapter as a Play, Traveling Smartypants?" Traveling Salesman bit into a Breatharian cheeseburger. "Are you sure this breatharian stuff is any good? I'd take a juicy whole beef patty right now," laughed Broz. "You would," said TS, laughing, trying not to choke on his burger.

Broz sipped a fat-free, sugar-free, gluten-free and lipid-free Breathari-Shake and considered his feint. "So I go free after chapter four, but they never say how in the Classic Play, right?" Traveling Salesman answered, "I know. When you read it backwards it's the fourth-to-last chapter though. So we have a lot of kill to time." He passed Broz a hemisphere of Almost Meatloaf, prepared Breatharian Style. "I know you hate capitalism and all, but look at the massive profits Demon Joe makes from this shit!" Broz laughed along with him. "If I told you I had a real Slim Joe in my pocket, would you let me go a chapter early?"

-1,350   Quibusque Rident Purpurei

Bleary Tim, Purple Alvin, and another disembodied spearit yclept Kintasha Equilibriox had constructed a Xarthorian-proof plan to prevent corrupt, malignant sales professionals from infiltrating the body politic. "These big mega-agencies are an infront to society," contended Bleary Tim. "Easy five you three say. You're shilling for a despot so often you've lost your conjectivity," emoted Kintasha.

"Gentlebeings, there's always a middle way," pulsed Purple Alvin. "Yes, Idajan has nice features. But surely one of these firms or agencies could use some de-incentivizering. But how?" They remiserated. "We tried the fake 'BOB' trick already," said Bleary Tim. "We gotta come up with a more original scam."

Morning has broken outside the bingy orifices of Danzig, Fulkerson & Johnson. Several blocks away, the uber-trendy architecture of Sandvick, Hughes & Atkinson shone like a ruddy eosin balloon. Traveling Salesman and Mr. Hi Stop, avec café, were straining their eyes at home behind their computers.

"Zounds," cried Mr. Hi Stop. He immediately called Traveling Salesman. "Did you get the email? Can you believe it?" TS hadn't seen the message and sat down. "Just a sec. I don't believe it." In his corner office, On Johnson IV screamed for his senior VPs and assorted swamis. "Ooh, the Board of Trustees isn't going to like this." At SH&A, all hands dropped their 21-ball cues mid-shot to curry back to their desks. "Rolfing, pickleball and neck massages have been ixnayed until further notice," droned a soft voice very similar to Purple Alvin's behind a credenza.

Jena Ropethegoat, an assistant account manager at SH&A, also got the email. She alit for the funky SH&A brake room for the same Breathari-Smoothie she willingly ingested every day. Jena bumped into Dharel, an immaculately coiffed intern, as she reached for a packet of Breathari-sweetener. "Who is Unquieth? Who is Geryon?" quoth the intern.

Just den, several Partners & VPs barged in. A styrofoam replica of the 'Jeopardy' set was haskily attembled by Fred Barnes, a janitor. A metempsychotic drill like an HVAC system in overdrive blasted through the sterile brakeroom. Jena shrugged. "If it ain't the Cthulhu account, I'm not interested," as a short duration personal earthquake rocked the office building. A spider-faced game show host mannequin was hastily rolled in. Dharel grasped. "Pee-Yunk!"

1,471A   Sequel to Chapter 8

a

a

1,473   Tail the Tizzle of the Brenda Loompas

Based on a true story. 'I don't like the look of it...' ickyickyickyickyickyickyicky...

Once upon a time not long ago, the first Brenda Loompa emerged ab ovo from a slideshow. She was only an inch tall, yet had the same amazing goodness of the full-sized Brenda. Then another and another and another, filling the Vir-2-Cube to the brim. Today, the Brenda Loompas are working F&D.

Brenda Loompas survive solely on cake, which only materializes once a month - perhaps twice or more if they are fortunate. They do not talk to strangers irregardless.

Mighty great blue herons are their allies in the search for Playlists of the Gods, Demigods & Team Gods. A special heron yclept R'panch urget nos.

Fluid in every language, Brenda Loompas are know to produce portrad poetry at the drop of a chocolate. Yet no mortal can speak the Brenda Loompa lingua portrada. Lessover, they all look the same but have individual names and unsubrealistic ID's, which only they themselves can intraprehend.

Brizenda Lizoompas work hard to create 144,000 de facto memorable ditties. Then why is this not mentioned in Chapters 144,000 and -144,000? Quiet simp lea, the answer lies within the lips and brains of their collective superconsciousnessiges. The key within the sixth minute of every tune VEILED/REDACTED.

They think for themselves bespite their hive mindedness. A special Vir-2-Cube hosts a wormhole where the Loompas deposit excess thought baggage in thought cubes stored away from hram. The other end of the wormhole lets out somewhere in the Keeplands.

They are not pixies, and are too unstable to be brownies. Brenda Loompas are fae of a different order, generational ptrained cisformer at the border of levity and death.

"You know that you think that you commence to begin to question everyhow" is the best translation of the Brenda Loompas' theme song. They are only allowed to sing it in Portrad, and in selected sensoria.

They keep no pets, yet they raise Lipo Loompas in little nooks and trannies. Eventually they will grown into fledged loverly lips.

Virtuous, diligent, loompaly love, all above, arriving early every yoyana. A queer sense of peace is present within each doompty do mantra. Able to make the 7-10 in some Dudeist's schu.

(music, blank lines)

1,476   Prajnaparamita

Books hung like teeth from a bookshelf of infinite width. They spoke via a mischievous breeze that circulated their information. Nobody had succeeded in recording and translating this canto, yet many - including Clytemnestra - had tried.

The so-called experts all scoffed. "It's not a golf course; therefore it can't be sentient." Such poppyhock!

They were called Wisdom by Numbers - at least as Clytie reckoned it. But she never saw the significance - and she habitually disregarded so-called experts and texperts.

Unfortunately it's a Xarthorian world, and books were widely disrespected. Most were fed to en-lipocos, or used to line khikchen copps with. "Not me! It ends at this shelf."

Xzimor was handed the Herculean task of building a great library of similar repute by Clytie. Of course, the grimoires and myriad tomes needed a chamber within the library; a separate wing in this chamber led to a large, leather-bound book on its own book table. But it was shut with several enormous padlocks and with at least 3 wish spells.

Clytie persisted. She chimed her bronze tingsha to signal the wrathchildren of Ngilas, followed by the clever contrapuntal knock. "Omega. Zed. Tau." The secret door slid open.

She enters the planetarium, abaft the asterisms, closer to the enormous projector and its control panel. The chair seemingly whirls about on its own, before Pazuzu wills himself visible. "I had a hunch it was you," said Clytie. The Demon Prince didn't bother to wipe the smirk or entrails off His avian face. "Melekhaidor Eleandivul Tweeskat," chanted Pazuzu. Gradually the stars grouped themselves into glyphs, characters, sigils, pictures and diacritical marx. "Assign meaning," He ordered Clytie, handing her a velour laptop. He flew upward, then seemed to disappear.

-1,518   Hallucinolytics

QUEEN'S INTELLIGENCE AGENCY REPORT

Date: _____
Country: Uottub. (sp.)
Subject: POTENTIAL PATHOLOGICAL PRECEDENTS
Classification: CLASSIFIED. DIGNITIZED.

- Agents must not possess the following traits: Unscrupulous, uncreative, bureaucratic-minded, manipulative, lack of aesthetics, cunning, unprincipled, or an over-analytical ontological orientation.
- A Swiss cheesepopping approach was deemed apotropaic and apropos, for its spaces provide cells for Akasa, and its taste was deemed harmonic and in cadence with the Queen's intends. For this raison only intrapsychic candidates will be considered.
- Sales was not a threat to her Queendom, nor were anti-sales. Even the toner gangs were counterbalanced by their own greed and larger market feces. Service ducts, dungeon rooms and maintenance floors could be retrofitted to hold DNA in case of dogastrophe.
- Agents are modeled after X's but aren't required to eschew Y chromosome, thus enabling will, love and evolution. Urothelium is still required, though it can be an artificially simulated doppelganger of the true tissues.
- Duodecagons will be installed behind all street signs, with messages written in invisible dry-erase ink to avoid the toner cartels. This efficient, emergent semiotics seems inadequate, yet its elasticity is statistically significizzle. Adepts of Level 2 and higher will follow established procedures.
- The spork included herein is for Incasker use only. Please consult the Queen's X's if you believe you need the spork. Best to lay sleeping dogs and lie. Obtrifuge is usually recommendizzle.

These guidelines are both a start and an end. The middle remains curved. SWO intellagents paint this vast medianscape of levels, sub-levels, mezzanine levels and basementes. Relative barometric pressures and wild magicks WILL affect performance - adjust to avoid assinine adumbrations. Empty planes are desirable forsooth; make certain they remain accessible and truly vacant - even of 5g. This is why the QIA does not exist; ipso facto, it doesn't appear in any flow charts, line items or speeches. Idajan herself made the organization ephemeral to eschew mundane controversies among supervisors or non-entheogenic bureaufrats, who would only dilute the intend or the neurostimulating epiglottal explosions. Thus we womaintain a bulwark against AAI.

1,975   Arma Dolos Acies

Stygia seems a raw umber place for Master of Fraud Geryon. He rules the sands, fire pits and wastelands of the fifth layer of Hell, pawning off old minotaurs as He sees fit. Geryon keeps His own band of devil salesmen, who are sent to Zysigamore to do His budding.

Traveling Salesman and Mr. Hi Stop brought these sales professionals to Clytie's detention in such a way to appear utterly coincimental. Undercover strangel A. Atoz Adelgidson had suddenly shown up at Clytie's lab, where he was subsequently roofied by Xzimor and given a complimentary mani-pedi.

Sure enough, Clytemnestra got her seance going in the panopticon that evening promptly at 11:55 p.m. Cameras were focused on Atoz, who was just shaking off the effects of the drugs in his cell. Clytie's staff installed so many O-Rings around Atoz's cell that he could binge watch any season of "Quantum Leap" without broadbanditry. "We abide by all sorts of conventions out here. No torture without consent," Clytie explained by video.

Still, the summoning of Geryon's spirit didn't go mccording to plan. They couldn't videoconference in Stygia, so Geryon had to take possession of J.O. Lundberg's body for the duration. "Who dares question the integrity of My salesmen!" bellowed Geryon's devil breath and ichor from J.O.'s lips. Clytie had to put Atoz on mute, pumping stale yacht rock into the panopticon.

"By the Menhirs of Valdorus, I command You! Nevermore shall I release Your precious salesmen until You comply, Arch-Fiend," Clytie stated. Lundberg's body twitched and writhed. The Devil couldn't lay His poison stinger on her, so Clytie was unperturbed. Geryon did spit the de rigeur pea soup at her, but she was not premused. "Save it for your spox."

When J.O. Lundberg came three, he was dressed in a black suit, black shoes, skinny tie and skinny slax. Rapidly the leftover devil salesmen dutifully assembled behind him, queer for the next pitch. Traveling Salesman went to check out these shock troops of sales. "Lundberg, what do you make of this?" He tried to speak at first but he coughed and choked, hurling pea soup out of his mouth and nostrils. "A most accurate assessment," TS opined.

All good things don't last. Before Clytemnestra could stop it, the small army of black-clad sales professionals started to fade away. "Let's crank up those avatars," she told Hi, but three-way scripts had bound his medulla translongatta. Only the desiccated husk of Atoz's body was left behind. "Pickle that punk stat," Hi told his wife.

2,020   Existential Hotel

The annual trip to Unicorn Harbor was ordinarily one of Traveling Salesman's favorites: All the elephant dust he could snort, rent boys and twinks flashing their supple heinies his way, decorative robes made from displacer beast hide, random encounters with megaball and yacht rock superstars, and oodles and oodles of poked bowls filled to the brim with caviar.

Yet this time he felt differently. He sat alone in his king sized bed, a book of John Adams quotes in his lap, the neon lights of the diner next door flickering in somber film rouge across the sterile hotel room like a harkin larkin barkin. He picked up his vibratophone and told it to call Simon.

He dialed and dialed again. Yet Simon never picked up the receiver. "Where could he be?" he muttered in the dim light. Traveling Salesman couldn't understand it. He always called Simon at 8 o'clock, after the game shows that Simon diligently watched every weeknight. It just wasn't like him.

Languidly he paged the front desk. "Could you send me up a softie and some tea bags, stat?" The attendant assured him this was no problem. "Of course. Right away, sir."

Ten minutes later came a knock on his door. A teenage boy in a pink speedo and sinister footwear stood there. Traveling Salesman stared at him and then beckoned the stripling into the room.

Traveling Salesman stammered, "Do come in. Please, please." The jaded twink just rolled his eyes, seemingly saying, 'Oh, another one of these types.'

Soon they were playing euchre and sucking iridescent lollipops. "Your move," said the soft boy. But Traveling Salesman did not hear. He had fallen into a deep slumber, as he was mired in Molasses Swamp and his hand was deuces and 8's.

The youth was all business, stealing everything of value from Traveling Salesman and sauntering away in the soft red glow.

-2,466   Tension Action Major

(Cut to a martial arts studio. PRICKLER FLOSSMAN, an unemployed Richard Rossman impersonator, stares into a series of mirrors on the wall to his right.)
PRICKLER: The moves were so good. I mean, I had them choreographed for Turd's sake. I - I watched all my videos. No flaws detected. Where did I go wrong? (The empty studio gleans as his gaze returns to the mirrors. A sound like an awkwardly closing garage door fills the room. Striker bursts in.)
STRIKER: Get out of here, you putz! You're done! You'll never work in this town if I can help it. Forteanberries.
PRICKLER: Oh yeah? You're not the only game in this town. Last week, I did 6 birthday parties, 3 gander reveals, and 2 gender conceals. Howboutdat?
STRIKER: Not bad. But typical. Anyhow, this Rossman business hasn't been marketable since Classic Play Nomber Two was released on Beta.
(PRICKLER uses the opportunity to burst into some Kung-fu moves.) Ha! Ha! Charade you are! (PRICKLER continues to gesture wildly, even inappropriately at times. STRIKER ignores him.)
STRIKER: (grabbing a baton) Whoop! Kaz-A! (He smacks PRICKLER several times in the torso.)
VERMIN SUPREME: Sit.

(Cut to a field of wildflowers. ELEPHANT is inhaling daisies that he grasped with his trunk.)
ELEPHANT: Let's all be like the Classic...

(Cut back to a concert. LI'L NAS Y is strutting across the stage in purple assless chaps.) [singing] Beautiful spaceships, MIIIIIIIIIII (The crowd roars its approval as a stimulated atomic bomb simulation explodes in the background.)
DISPATER: Shake it one more time for me. (He extends a hoof toward LI'L NAS Y.) Yeah. Get it girl. C'mon. Ucan getitgetitgetit...

3,000   The Struggle Is Reel

My pants supply is at an all X lo, thanks to the pandemonic aenesthesiopteryxes in all the wong places.

It is a liberating feeling to reflect that my pants array consists only of sweat pants and shorts. All my slacks are in a cave. Blue jeans are a distant memory.

Slowly arising from his stupor, Traveling Salesman felt the inside of his mouth. "Too much cotton candy last night. Too much Simon."

But his fantasies continued to turn his man lust to this new Li'l Nas Y. He had spunk, and Traveling Salesman wanted to tap into that brassy bowdlerizer.

I forgave Traveling Salesman his fights of fancy. He had reached a point of Liberation that no salesman could ever drop ship. He's used to it. Now sales run off of Traveling Salesman's back like water off a duck's.

Contorted tetrahedrons waft across the multiverse like therapeutic tumbledreams. Qualities of ...

Snake-charmed stocklings shed sheer skins of silky shrimp shells. For the next plan to work, Traveling Salesman would have to adjust his calendar meticulously.

He and Hi had been heroic account managers together since Day One. They were like the Three Musketeers, except there were only 2-8 of them. Traveling Salesman's next pitch would take him far out of his comfort zone - clear out of his pants entirely.

The butt plugs crackled like cereal, a sickish sentient sound. Traveling Salesman would never get to use them.

Onie's urgent texts had only generated more problems. Hi screamed, "I will not over promise and under deliver!" His face had hardened into stone to the point where it resembled the terrified bull in Picasso's *Guernica*. "I have morals too, you know!"

-3,000   Sophist A Phunk

'We are Zysigamore. We are the fetuses' was the catchy chorus of the latest Cowtown Sewergroup project to raze funds, funds, funds and awareness of the VR headset problems befalling our Xarthorian peeps. Paul Joyt, Li'l Nas Y, Pettiler Stevens, Bill Elish and Allman Isley differenced their patch-ups for the special musical regurgitation. Cash floe initiated, Wacky Ted Kudzopilous ate the payoladonuts for auld revenantverb.

Killer never filler 808s by DJ Yuga Yoga entantriced the first verse, which Li'l Nas Y elocuted with elastomer expertise: My gown is immaculate/ Got a corn dog after it/ A nasm a spasm/ A real eargasm.

Big Zomdad McBone articulated the second verse same as the first verse but with more grunts. Then Paul Joyt took an interminable triangle solo. "That's exxo," texted Zapp Omnigotopia.

Dr. Oste to the bridge: Cogitate. Cogitate. A field of harpists opened and stayed too long, but not long enough for a quatrain of existential despair to hover over the suffering Xarthorian consumers.

During a pee break, Pettiler Stevens used telekinesis to lift a nice cream vending machine into Studio Z. "Map map a linga, ka-ka-kow. Whee!" he opined, velvet paintings of rest stop tigers and eagles dripping from his meaty talons. "Pee-yunk a dunk wham a lamma!"

McBoy came on the trane for the next verse. "Me he he he," but he was instantaviously injected for the Outcasker remix. Instead, someone shouted the names of celebrities in little particulate order. "Genius," said Striker, who had paid for the crab dip spread.

Then all the gloves came off, and the funk slipped a disk. A ballyhooed Z-Pop group named Epihype tried to chime in on the chorus, but their autotune machine developed bronchitis, making the boy band's voices sound too masculine. Ritual suicide being out of the question, their stylist bailed them out by waxing their eyebrows strenuously while the boys chopped their licks.

Wacky Ted crowed as "We Are Zysigamore" hit the charts of the top. "You kids run out there and consume this. Consume, consume, I say. This is a tootin' rootin' classitized dignified song, so mamba that it will make acne disappear." He bit into one payoladonut after another. "Buy a copy for your dogcatcher and your chimney sweep. It's for a good cause." [Insert catchphrase.]

Though Clytie had tried to eliminate kludges from all of Mr. Hi Stop's sub-personas, there were always a few that developed word salad and/or verbal diarrhea at inopportune times. Sometimes a simple patch sufficed. Other times, the problem was so intractable that they were forced to consult experts to fix him. Hi's productivity would be nil until the problem was solved.

She had him taken to Dr. Xyzzyster once the croaker had an office visit available. The staff all knew them by name and by hand. "Welcome, Clytemnestra. Please come in."

Mr. Hi Stop's ashen face turned plaid anon. "Harper the pretty dog," said Mr. Hi Stop. "Spinner is blind banking?" The nursing assistant led him down the medical corridor. "No roster found. Kicking his way out of explanation!" he shouted to Clytie. "Lightman is back!!!"

The esoteric treatments that Hi required would be considered illegal in 214 countries; in fact, several Xarthorians had been slaughtered for word salad violations that fortnight.

Dr. Xyzzyster reached into her scrubs. Finding a miniature Scrabble dictionary, she ground it into a fine pulp and shoved it down Mr. Hi Stop's throat. "Verism cybolics. Unsorrowing pik-itz."

"Nurse Andoor, get in here. Bring the transmogrifier and the Everclear. Stat!" She put down the receiver. Something wasn't working this time.

Soon Nurse Andoor had prepped the stoats and neutrinos. "Quick, hit it." The transmogrifier whirred, sputtered and smoked, eventually kicking in after several attempts. Each sub-persona that was then 'active' (no more than 5-7, including Mr. Hi Stop's defective one) had to be coated in tamarind before the electrodes could be linked to the transmogrifier. "Excitedly wafting to bimeby see how many cherubic anklet or tandem a - "

Hi was now completely offline. The specially trained albino stoat had cleared out every single broken microchip and stunted avatar he had.

Some hours later, another nurse summoned Clytie to Mr. Hi Stop's room. She beamed when she saw him. "Let's go home. The food is terrible here. No gummy tarantulas."

-7,282　　　　Metabolomics

The time crystals arrived at Clytemnestra's lab this a.m. Xzimor simply texted, "They're here!" as the lab staff brought the time crystals to the metabolomics room. "That's great news, honey," shouted Mr. Hi Stop from his denatured oatmeal.

"No more waiting for a time door. Time Crystals will eliminate the middle being." Clytie usually hated these remote meetings, but this one was much different. The perpetual motion machine, the quantum computer, the metabolism modulator were all within reach. If only she could raise capital and keep the time crystals safe at the same time.

Clytie knew that Idajan wanted them dearly - and may even pay dearly for the time crystals. Yet the Queen would surely want to monopolize them for her own porpoises. Clytie and Xzimor got together at the lab with Hi and Traveling Salesman to strategize. "How can we keep the Queen at bay? She has a Bleary Tim advising her, gathering up AAI on time crystals. Surely we have to prepare," began Clytemnestra. "I can only trust you three, and maybe a few friends, and most of the staff." She looked to Xzimor. "Do you think all our people are on board - or are there some limp cannons?"

"Not as far as I know. At least I'm not aware of anyone," answered Xzimor. "But I will find out if there are." The nanodrones and bots were everywhere, and every aspect of every office, lab space, panopticon, warehouse, bathyscaphe, fronton, sauna, shed, garage and café were well surveilled. Still, disembodied characters undetected by sensors or drones threatened a potential pose.

Back at home, Simon mused about his situation while channel surfing. "Waiting for a time door..." He kept on waiting but a time door never came. He checked his emails, his texts, his freckles - nothing. "Watt am eye two dew?" he moaned to Simon Junior. "These time doors are getting more and more unreliable, Simon Junior. I've got enough problems. Premature aging sure won't be one," he declared. He looked into the mirror and applied more psychoactive soy 5g cream to his face. "Do I look all right?" Simon Junior - Sit.

Traveling Salesman returned home from the meeting. He found Simon obsessively applying one beauty cream after another. "Do you think my wrinkles are unattractive?" Simon whined. Traveling Salesman dropped his attaché case at the front of the bed. "You really shouldn't get yourself into such a state, Simon." His power necktie removed, Traveling Salesman tried to relax. "Oh, like Connecticut? I buy all my nutmeg there," inquit Simon.

Traveling Salesman was on the verge of blurting out something about the meeting to Simon but he tongued his held. Too much game in the skin, he knew. Still, everyone from Idajan to Striker to Unquieth to Tiamat was queer for those time crystals.

7,943   Opoly Dungeon Figurines

Barbarian with two-handed sword (1)

Footman with shield and spear (1)

Knight with longsword and armor/shield (1)

Mount with armor (1)

Elastomer pachyderm toting turret. In full battle armor. (1)

Conford raiding party with chieftain and shaman (8)

Taweret in splendour, plus accessories and attendants/acolytes. Blister pax. (6-10 pieces: see table)

Apotropaic statuettes of centaurs (6)

Conford chieftain with two sub-chiefs and warriors (10)

Pazuzu with right arm erect (1)

Gryphon in bronze (2)

Time-traveling karn surrounded by cloak (1)

Howlthibisquiat, with separate headdress and serpent garland (1)

Triumph the dog with cigar (4)

Common bandits of the common type, with mule steed (8)

Laocöon with sons and serpents (6)

John Adams with kung-fu grip (1)

Grotesque terracotta figurines of witch queen and acolytes (6)

J.O. Lundgren * (limited supply)

Giant tardigrade with young (3)

Mrs. Hemans (1)

Displacer beasts with adjustable tentacles (2)

Headmen (40k)

Simon Junior (2; one resting, the other in action pose)

Kaspar Hauser (2; one in period drag, the other in DEVO suit)

Aegothsorzhotan the Mage (1)

-8,496   Talismen

(Cut to a cheesy county fair. SIMON and TRAVELING SALESMAN are standing in front of a two-player video game.)

SIMON: Oh honey! Can you win me a stuffed elasmosaurus? Pretty please?
(TRAVELING SALESMAN takes a coin from his pocket and inserts it into the game's coin slot. A series of whistles, sounds and bright light emerge from the video game.)
TRAVELING SALESMAN: I got this! No problem. Player One (He furiously jerks the joystick to and fro.)
SIMON: Tee hee hee. (He blushes as a bell rings loudly.) Oh my! Tea bags? (Canned laughter fills the midway and arcade, as well as a nondescript ice arena 4500 miles away.)
TRAVELING SALESMAN: Damn! (He hits the side of the machine in frustration.) Down to my last guy.
SIMON: Good luck, sweet cakes! (SIMON kisses the side of TRAVELING SALESMAN's neck.)

(Cut to a dingy looking series of nondescript-looking warehouses. The unmistakable smell of sulfur and brimstone fills the air.)
GLENN VON OOSTERMAN: The signs become characters. The characters form glyphs. The glyphs fuse into sigils. Ach. (He opens the large garage door. Inside is a candlelit room full of mop handles, hot dog casings, and an Ethel Merman wig set. GLENN VON OOSTERMAN dons a serious purple robe, and gestures toward a magic circle.)
GLENN VON OOSTERMAN: Mene Mene Tekel Upsharin. The underarm of Nebuchadnezzar. Theory of Rubik's Cube. Selah! (He gesticulates as a column of smoke rises from the circle's center.)

-12,062   Saccadence

Modulated REMs obey ambient temperatures warming toward thermoneutral entropy. Saccades jump across a musical scale, ending at B flat. Crescendo.

Eyeballs tingling like ruddy basketballs, the Xarthorian patient rises from the hospital gurney. "Doc, I wear pants exclusively! What could this mean?"

Finally the attending arrives. Unfortunately, he is wearing a Groucho Marx glasses-and-eyebrow set, and is smoking a large Uottubbacktothebonium (sp.) cigar that had been dipped in naphtha and axle grease. He fumbled the right words and used the wrong ones instead.

"You see, it's Queen Idajan. I have to abide by the law of First Pants. Yes, yes. My hands are completely tied." (A nurse emerges to tie the Doctor's hands together.)

"Ah, see, thanks Toots."

Mr. Hi Stop had reset the saccadences of all his sub-personalities and avatars so that each entity would project a ray of energy set to a precise sound frequency and to a particular fingerprint within the visual spectrum. Surely, by Dobbs, this would be a perfect presentation. All the Right people would be there. The Queen would not interfere, and soon each blessed Xarthorian would be eating out of Mr. Hi Stop's pseudopods.

Souls tethered to grim, dark-grey tetrahedrons. I emerge from troubled yoyanas of a dead, unfortunate generation.

13,013 ale

This year's big Sales Awards Ceremony was in Umlaut Towin. Both salesmen hated it - the speeches were monotonous and indigo, and all the hotel rooms reeked of ptarmigan guts. Both Traveling Salesman and Mr. Hi Stop had been nominated for Dobbsheads, and Onie McPhersall was sure both guys would win.

Dinner was a grey piece of mutton, chartreuse beet salad and haggis surprise. "I think I'm going to throw up," said Traveling Salesman, as he chatted with Simon via smartphone. "Those things are so fucking boring," Simon sighed. Then Eddie Mecca took the stage. "Uno, dos, tres - it's on!" he hollered.

"Get me another Everclear and Coke," said Mr. Hi Stop to his Xarthorian waiter. "No prob, it's on 'BOB'," he chanted: he was carrying a carbine. Hi's face distorted into an impressionistic jumble of neo-Jungian glyphodonts.

The cocktail was about 90% pure grain alcohol. Pretty soon Hi was proposing to every other woman he saw. Traveling Salesman held his liquor, and was soon putting the moves on a stylish brunette standing near the bar. Eustachian

Suddenly "BOB" strode to the podium to announce the next award himself. "And the Dobbshead for best 'Pre-shot' Routine goes to... Traveling Salesman!" The spotlight hit Traveling Salesman as he looked back toward the stage, almost Cary Grant-like. A light smattering of golf claps filled the auditorium as Traveling Salesman sauntered confidently to the podium.

However, by the time Traveling Salesman reached the head of the stage's stairs, "BOB" was gone. Instead it was Vink O'Tasford, local hamburger brander. "Great job, Traveling Salesman." He reached out with an enormous hand, which was absurdly larger than the rest of his corpulent body.

He tried to hide his disappointment. "BOB" had punked him while simultaneously praising him. Traveling Salesman had longed to meet Dobbs for many years after watching family TV shows about "BOB's" life and sexploits. He took the microphone and muttered some less than memorable epithets for about 15 seconds. "And thank you, thank you again." Traveling Salesman walked away from the podium, crumbling up the pre-prepared speech he intended to give.

Soon, the ceremony was winding down after Onie and Hi's third lap dance of the evening. TS tried to find the brunette from earlier, but she too had disappeared without a trace. Some ideobitty tried to make time with Traveling Salesman as he pushed the tray of flex drugs away, but he blew her off with a crude eldritch gesture. Minutes before getting his stomach pumped, Mr. Hi Stop recited the Cyrillic alphabet backwards and wrote the lyrics to "The A-Team Theme Song" on the head of a pin. "Say, where did my pants go?"

Nothing happens until somebody sells something. Shunyatta.

A black hole of sales opened on That Day that year. Several dull zombies in seaweed neckties proliferated in the void of slack. NHGH aka NarmoHitsuGetH, son of Robert H. Tapdancing Slack, Filthy Eater of Filth, led these rotting undead from pink hellholes throughout the Island.

The demiurge was largely responsible for the Ningarm Men's uprising and raids during the spring. "No fallen angels," quoth NHGH. "Begone from me or surely you will feel my Daddy's butthurt." He was convinced he could spread all manners of sleazery throughout Zysigamore, whether hothechajuxips or Xarthorian.

Directio voluntatis toward the most ancient Pleasure Saucers in herstory. One particularly frail looking saucer was almost completely overgrown with habafropzipulops. NHGH began selling admission to the site, and contemplated the next steps toward the Anti-"BOB".

NHGH felt the time was nigh; however, he could not find a willing recipient for his seed. Women rejected him, and the sperm donor joints didn't care that his glowed green and could swim the backstroke. "There's got to be a better way without having to resort to Emasculate Conception," he shuddered. But Time delivered the Son anyway.

"Me? Who me? I'm just an OBO salesman." The Man, who may very well have been the "Anti-BOB", started to run away. "Who knows - it could have been a loose avatar of Mr. Hi Stop," said 9 out of 10 Ace TV pundits.

"Don't pay him any mine. We are entering a new era," chimed the lousy demigod. Chicanery was good enough for Him - the potential of a slack-sucking sales professional was enough for the vanilla imaginations of the masses. With a wisp-o-the-will, NHGH winked out, vowing never to return to the Isle.

Yet it didn't end there. Some bratty Xarthorian kid dressed up as the Anti-'BOB' during a That Day drill/raid at school. The punk uttered several non-PC phrases before being heavily medicated. His antics were dismissed as chance, yet the boy soon gained local fame as a potential reincarnation of the Anti-'BOB'. Though Idajan's élite X's soon took care of the situation by kidnapping the boy for his own good, a few of the old-timers and self-confidence men silently thought they knew the truth, clutching their last oodles of slack ever closer to their bosoms.

Hyperbolicpolysyllabic paraprosdokians erupted from the supermegavolcanic landscape of Avernus, too many for Virgil or Alighieri to record. In this respect, Me has the edge over the classic poets.

Yet the wittiest eluded the dinosaurs, devils and dragons who populated the surprisingly trendy, organic, eco-friendly plane. They drifted downriver to Paideuma, where they found their way to late 18th Century-style printing presses. One was the *Dialy Journal*; the other, less flattering rag was the *Paideuma Gazette*. Other less memorable broadsides made good fish wrap and were soon fivegotten by all but the most pedantic denizens.

Each morning, John Adams set his devil-hacks loose to go and harass the printers. Sometimes Ezra Pound would join in the rabble rousing, once he'd drunk his share of Adams' tea and quaffed the payloadonuts. "Did you read the filth that the *Gazette* wrote the other day?" asked Pound. "Yes. Twas dreadful. Certainly not wrought by a Yankee." "Abigail must have been very upset," Pound added, a look of faux concern flitting across his wizened face. "Yes, Abby says she's wintering in a dreadful Hell-World that they call Florida."

Asmodeus, in His form as 99 Sticks, summoned linotype devils from a pool of molten lead. Once they annealed, 99 Sticks explained their mission. "You're going to print out broadsides all day, e'er day. I'll tell you what to print. Then stack them up in my wherehouse." Before schlong, the linotype machines bubbled and boiled, quaking with each kerning.

Two days later, newsboys all across Zysigamore were passing around a wide variety of periodicals, each rag blaming John Adams for zillions of crimes against democracy; the abnormal rise in three-way 5g; garish tube tops; overlords of serial defenestrators stealing cookies from chrimpostelers' mouths; the abnormally high magic resistance of the common everyday narmolof; sexual profligacy; unstylish purple bell-bottoms; syzygy gone very, very wrong; and depressingly flavorless meat patties in every school cafeteria and panopticon. "Extra, extra, read all about it. John Adams makes yuletide gay again."

Suitably piqued, John Adams hoisted on his own defense. "This is all pure baldersnatch. Only a fiend could print such floccinaucinihilipilification." All Paideuma sensed Asmodeus' influence but none were prepared to confront the King of Hell. Although Pound penned a racist screed against 99 Sticks, it was insufficient to quash the libel.

Pound tripped on an anapest and was rendered incalculable. This weighed the pave for an unveritable plethora of linotype devils rushing in from Minauros. "Quadruple drat. I'm glad Abby isn't seen to hear diss." The streets of inferno-Braintree swarmed with muddy muckrakers and ettin's bane. Somehow, the *Gazette* had reopened its offices, and the linotype devils were busy binding banned books by the bagful. A solid lead minor devil used a handmade lying press to lovingly print grimoires sacred to Asmodeus.

-18,340   Mrs. Catobleplenski

It was a give that the students would hate Mrs. Catobleplenski. She was a viscous, pus-covered daughter of Ndusk perpetually smothered in flies, lice, ticks and leeches. A sort of lemonade was brewed from the open sore on her left leg. It wasn't too bad. Once a year, the class would "trick" the principal into drinking a glass of it, and she would promptly pass out from the denatured grain alcohol and lack of oxygen.

Still, there were always one or two students who had an inexplicable attraction to Mrs. Catobleplenski. Old Susumna, for example. And Ted.

Her seven trunk-like legs and misshapen horns always prevented Mrs. Catobleplenski from donning pants herself. But somehow, she knew everything - every microscopic detail - about pants. She could do quadratic equations in her head to determine boys' future inseams; she used a protractor to formulate a logarithmic scale to determine how well the dungarees would fit over a rapidly maturing young girl; and she had "YKK" tattooed on her forehead. School photographers from here to Unnunnennniumnnnn still shudder.

So on that Monday morning, which indeed was a morning, there was something different in the air in Mrs. Catobleplenski's classroom. The blood sucking stirge teaching assistant was nowhere to be found. As the children entered, one of the half-Xarthorian kids let out a giant yelp. "Aumgnn!" he cried, the erratic gesticulation of his uvula shattering his palate.

The entrails of Ms. Xxyster had been strewn across little Zysigmond's ordinarily immaculate desk. You could even make out the fractured proboscis among the festering guts.

"Quo vadis? Unnunnennniumnnnn? Aut Provincia?"

Eventually the class got used to the pungent smell, which, overall, was about equal to the usual Stygian filth. Zysig handed in the hall pass he had misplaced in the pre-Cambrian epoch. "Magister, ubi sunt aliqui poetae qui dormiunt apud columnas?"

The only substitute teacher that was allowed was an avatar of Belial, who insisted on the sacrifice of a first grader after recess.

-19,364   Pronopomp

Candi Landry, succubus by night, succubus by day, monotypical hooker with a heart of stone, psychopomp of sorts to virginal boy/men who summon her in long suburban sleep-overs, she who abhors Pants, refusing to lead those who labor under their despotism, telepathic sex operator of the lower Astral and dreck webs, despoiler and defouler of holy men on pilgrimages, temptress of vanilla cisrendered males straying from convention and form, demonstrates a sheer vellum hypercountenance on all levels, all planes, and all pocket dimensions in between.

One fine day, Aleister Crowley (or an avatar thereof) strolled into Candi's quaint bungalow on the south side of Underwear Point in the neighborhood called Tidy Whitey. "Hello," she said. "Don't believe I've met you." "Adams is the name," Crowley replied. "Oh, you're Gomez? How's the family?" Crowley grinned wryly. "That's right I'm joker Gomez Adams III, legendary sales-" "Honey, we're all salespeople here!" Candi's shrill laughter almost tore a hole in her roof. "C'mon in."

She led him through the tiny house before stopping at the bedroom door. "You into some freaky shit? I charge extra." Crowley just grinned knowingly. Candi softly pushed the doorknob open; inside was an enormous bedroom with absurdly high ceilings, from which hung several candelabras, chains, and boxes of Marathon candy bars.

"Okay. Not this shit again. You will pay big time for this, muchacho." Candi took off all her sexy lingerie and jewelry and stood naked inside a vestibule. A servant brought her the tempodoppelganger plaster spray, which quickly hardened much to Crowley's amazement. "Could you hit me with six shots of that stuff?"

"Indeed! Not til next time." A bit of the plaster substance cracked and turned to dust with Candi's first syllables. The transformation was unbelievable: There stood Quentin Periwinkle, a loose-wristed, flirty fag. Crowley's boner sprung up like an asparagus stalk.

Just then, a shrill cacophony erupted, as several musicians stormed into the boudoir. Their roadies rapidly assembled their PA, drums and amps on a stage to the right of Candi's nightstand. "Don't worry, honey. They do this every night," cooed Candi as Quentin. The boys in the band wore Spandex pantyhose, glam makeup, 1980's women's 'dos, and hair metal leather and studs. "Such dreadful cretins," spouted Crowley. "I'm not paying for this." "Sorry, sweetie, the transaction went through," said Candi as Quentin as s/he grabbed Crowley's gonards.

30,330   The Mentalist

Many yoyanas ago, a night hag plucked an especially sickly, corpulent larva from her collection. "This one will do just fine, sonny," she coughed. One day, this vile worm of Hades would mutate into the abomination now called Demon Joe.

This chapter is the work of a mentalist. Cream colored sandman out of mythology, the mentalist doth bestride the multiverse like a behemoth.

The thirteenth election for the old farmer's benighted oracle. Blasted heath coaxed into dweomers.

Frunobulax pukes in Neptune, surrounding the throne full of desiccated hayseeds. What is true about the

Red line phones suddenly appear in this dimension. Try to find the mysterious man who bought the Demon-Dog from Charon.

The sleeve is full. And nobody wears it that way. It's simply not done. Sleeve tyrants are plowed over, drowned in a tide of compost.

Young Fortinbras takes it easy, but his sister Skjadijillifetti will have to sit in. The neologisms glisten in the electric air, their kinetics stimulated easily in the post-5g world.

A maelstrom like no other. Lethe overflows her banks, or so they say.

Episurnames bought, pennies on the dollar. So good.

I just got burned in a three-way script. And I could smell the topsy-turvy tendrils of the mentalist all over it.

Pazuzu is an astral figure who thrives off of mind control. He is not a great hulking beast, but a deluxe demon showing off His magic.

Viennese tetrahedron

You can't sell gloom-and-doom in Hades.

Forgotten gleams in dulled eyes. Crisp smell of brimstone.

Golden fruitful electric hippopotamus.

Finally the mentalist departs; lifeless lumps recede at dawn.

90,121   Quasqueton Industrial Park

Right next door to the False Idol factory was Quasqueton Industries, based in a ruburb of Uottubbacktothebonyimtonium (sp.).

Apparently, if you wish to tour the warehouse, you will be admitted during business hours as long as you are a LARPer. Thus, each member of the party had their own character:

Traveling Salesman was Tsambor, a paladin with an uncommonly broad broadsword;

Clytemnestra was Slipiginea, an elven magic-user/power ranger;

Mr. Hi Stop was Xandis the Mystical, a great warlock/necromancer/geode;

Simon was Rev. Goodness, the lawful good cleric;

[Simon Junior's gnome ranger costume never came back from the dry cleaners; thus, he was excluded from the group.]

A guide whisked them into the long corridor that led past the three alcoves and into the subterranean realm. "I'm going to gag!" remarked Simon, as he got a whiff of a decaying shrieker. "Yeah, this module sure could use an air freshener," Clytie agreed.

It wasn't much of a double date, as rolling for initiative all the time destroyed the spontaneity, and Mr. Hi Stop couldn't stop rifling through faces like a great deck of playing cards. Still they agreed it had been worth the price of admission so far.

At last the brave party reached the legendary Room of Pools. "Who put all this green slime here?" sneered Clytemnestra as she passed by Pool D. Behind them, the door to the hallway opened and a robed stranger entered.

"Through me is the way to the City of Woe..." The voice echoed off the black and white mosaic tiles in the Room of Pools. "You mean Cedar Rapids?" said Mr. Hi Stop as his facial tics accelerated to light speed.

"Si ch'a nulla, fenendo, facea male." Tsambor the Lion-Hearted waved his mighty broadsword as they followed Dante out of the Room of Pools and into the caverns on the second level.

Right on cue, the Wandering Monster roll came up, and two doppelgangers imitating Howard Cosell suddenly appeared before Dante, yellow blazers and all. "Don't touch me! I'll beat your brains out." The Cosells sparred in place, goading the party into an ineffectual, meaningless combat.

"It's on," said Xandis. A d20 was rolled. He began to struggle with a Cosell, as Hi fumbled for a potion.

117,168   Monumental Scholarship

Obulwadde bwa floccinaucinihilipification was the result of unchecked tempodoppelganger use, especially amung the yong. Somehow, our only hope at ulleviating this xanticrisis was our humble gang including the mercurial Simon. Striker agreed, and Bryant Brick did a special series of hysterical news reports on these hitherto side-x.

Off to SJU for an exculsive interview with an élite texpert. Unfivetunately Dr. Sinus Linus Longinus was absent from the faculty due to zenedoin space clap. Ace TV was fiveced to use the glitzy ditzy art history professor Filipta Scripta instead. Doc Scripta was not a croaker's croaker. No siree 'BOB'. She wooled the pull over 'his' eyes.

Dr. Filipta Scripta tried to demand Bryant Brick, but her resumé wasn't up to snuff. Mary Sunshine was reployed in his place - a good move in retrofleck. "So tell our viewers at home, what CAN the people of Zysigamore do to ensure a positive outcome?" Dr. Scripta crumpled up the Ace TV pablum she had been handed to read. She adjusted her trendy glasses, and looked straight into the camera. Filipta explained the existential quandary of hundreds of generations of classist policies oppressing Xarthorians beyond bull eve...

Mary thanked her for the almost coherent verbiage and turned to scurry away. "Listen," Filipta declared, "There are only so many basic plots that you can run. Unless you keep 'em off balance, shit gets repetitive quickly." Mary's jaw slackened. "Gee, that sounded so profound. But what's it all mean?"

Meanwhile back at the Ace TV studios (cue Tarzan-type yodeling, Ah ah uh ah uh), the video editors cobbled together a couple of clips of Dr. Scripta from Mary's interview. When it hit the 6 o'clock news, the switchboard lit up like a hypoballistic metarave on one of Saturn's rings. "Woke SJU faculty predicts end of capitalism," Bryant Brick spoke ironically. Some of Ray Dos Santos' yokels, goons and goobers promised to girlcott the network, but Slow Talkin' John chopped and screwed their alt requests.

The next day, Rahälrahad sprayed himself with tempodoppelganger juice and strolled onto the SJU campus. He entered the art building, which was named for Striker's uncle's DJ's bitchboy, and walked on down the hall. Dr. Scripta wasn't in her office, so he posted a batch of revolutionary pamphlets and resolved to return in an hour after the tempodop wore off.

Later, Rahälrahad spotted Dr. Scripta walking out of the art building toward the arts and crafts supply building. "Excuse me Dr. Scripta, may I have a-" She whirled around and autographed his hand with her lipstick. "All I can say is, have a nice day," she said as she bounced away.

-118,800   Micro Maladjustments

Laney Loisson and her only son Marquez sat on the patio outside their unhip condo in the muddle class enclave of West Unicorn Harbor. Laney had worked for Strikercorp before a layoff; after a spell of bad health, she found herself just scraping by - and unwilling to return to cubicuncle planes.

She got a lot out of this relationship with "Tim." He told Laney how she could rock a new haircut and update her look - spot on. Tim encouraged her to get new eyeglasses too. Laney turned down his offers at first. "Let's go to Luxembourgium" was their adjustable slogan.

The peaceful afternoon soon turned confrontational. "Ma, do you ever think you'll get married?" asked Marquez. Laney sighed and looked into the distance. "It's not in the cards, Marc. This guy isn't a settling down kind anyway." She wistfully stirred her hairy biden tea. "But you like Tim enough, right? At least his gifts?" Laney looked at him but didn't answer. "He's pretty cool," her son replied. But there's something about him--"

The doorbell buzzed. It was a delivery guy from FedUp. "I got it, mom." Marquez scuttled to the door, grabbed the box, and jumped up the stairs two at a time before diving back into his cluttered bedroom. Laney paid him no mime; she was gathering a small mound of flex drugs and making them disappear, drifting downward into desultory dillusion.

The next day came and went - and the next day, and the next day in a sepia toned reverie. Once Laney came II, Marquez was long gone. He didn't steal any of his mom's possessions, but he did grab three months' worth of school lunch monies. Hornified, Laney didn't know what II dew.

Finally, the school truant officer, Mr. Spuddle, came to Laney Loisson's door. She was just mixing herself a tangenterine maragrizzle with rock candy ice in a sugary rimmed glass when the doorbell rang. She stumbled over several discarded flex drug containers and *Pepple* magazines, bashing her elbow against an iron maiden. "Do come in, do come in," she uttered suspiciously as Mr. Spuddle stepped in. "Can I offer you anything?" He muttered, "Day Dei Sept Nept."

Two hours later, Mr. Spuddle was long gone. But there was something else - an eviction notice on the front door. Laney was in a rear's for several months' rent. She muttered something unintelligible before slamming her fucking door shutt. "That ballbag devourer - I'm sure his behind is involved in thisa!"

119,252   Anthropocentrophobia

Billowing, cloudy fog of anthropocentrism drifts across the spectrum of unoccupied jai-alai frontageons.

The statue of Athena is still extant. Several shocked onlookers vacate it narrowly.

Heliotropic elastomers of chromium and the sandwich bored of the Yellow Kid characterize.

Hoot mon!

Bildungsroman of the Ubermensch: Portal to Pandemonium.

The clouds are omnipresent. Rain like a child's tears is steered into bottomless bottles of bas-reliefh.

Dun epistles of vellum sit in neatly hewn cabinets along the eastern wall of the great room.

Kaz-a-Whoop

A jam like Juiblex's jockomo ichor is spread across the six-foot Wonder Golem. Who's gonna lick it?

Swami! Swami! (clap/clap)

Janor Planitor Kaspor vs. Anastasia Madeja Flava. Special guest referee: Glenn Von Oosterman.

A steady drip-drip-drop of semi-permeable pseudopods and widening gangrenous sores do not equal Pants. The Universe nears.

Zounds! Greatest Horrid Mold Hits. Yacht rock is anathema to its being. Excelsior.

Earth urchins hatch in the purple light.

Well hullygee. Here's To You!

Greenleaf Whittier's roomba

Plant it in the noosphere.

Houndstooth trousers under radium sky. Hemicules

Old Great Victor del Vesicle earned a treacherous pylon existence somewhat akimbo to the enormous scoliopolitical neopolygonism attributable to spontaneous lacerations and reticulated necrotic tendrils resulting from multifaceted spondees paradiddle-diddled from uncorked outcasker teledivide currymetaxis.

To be alive at a time when

119,626   Ink and Tonervana

"Poznak has this deal all sewn up. 2% of the vig. It's like printing money."

"Poz. He got screwed. The middleman, what's his cut? Double figures or more. Two percent? Drop in the bucket."

"You don't understand. You don't have to do anything. It's what all the players do."

"The package store is closed? OK, my day is through."

"Here, here. This'll settle your nerves."

"Poz says he'll pay you a call on Wednesday. The old cuss!"

"Slave to the bonding. The shit was cut. They should have known."

"Jerry had to get out while the getting was good. He really covered his tracks. No shit sticks to him. And he got the high quality cartridges. Smart cartridges that can override any laser printer's settings. I've seen it happen. Very impressive."

"All the printers on the Island are down. A hack. They want to jack up the price."

"Tried calling their bluff. It didn't work out. Had to bootleg some black ink I got from my mother's old hair dye kit. I...I just can't do it."

"I told Poz, just bring back the mimeograph machines. Then hire some schlemiel to hand-crank it. Or an organ grinder's monkey."

"You don't say?"

-119,626   The Ink & Toner Cartel

They had sworn good money. They had plumed the veins. They had a lab with vials of 5g.

"I keep getting all these tex from my smart printer. In only three days, magenta ink will varnish from the multiverse! How will I get buy??"

However, Christimiqua was fortunate that epoch. She knew Clytie and was adroit in using her adjustable slogan gun; it matched all her shoes.

"Three days? What then? Pray that thisa toner makes it through this tragedy. Bad daze are ahead."

Clytie knew that con backwards and four words. "To unsubscribe is not to unsubscribe. Get a few northwaxx and it will go away like acnes. You're welcome in advance."

"Are you realio trulio really online for all this to happen?" Christy was only confused by default, not by intellectual curiosity.

"Being unonline is like being unsubscribed, but in a very minute dimension that is not worth looking through. Dopplegnugen. Yes." Clytemnestra had never been that acute before, yet in this situation it applied immensely. "Of course, there may a slight readjustment when the magenta toner cartridge strike comes to an intervaling conclusion."

"Pee-yunk. I don't know what to do with you," smirked Christy.

"Of course. I wouldn't feel that way, but you are more than welcome to in your phosphate."

-317,402   Season IV, Episodes 1 - 8

Newly released CRM data indicated the need for MoM real numbers to skyrocket. The Me & Tinkelhoff Committee resolved to log the breakjam with fresh content (if not crunktent) for Ace TV that appeals to many demographic sectors, viz:

Episode 1- Big West. Starring Traveling Salesman as a veteran marshal bent on bringing justice to the stereotypical small Western American town. Simon plays the role of bartender/soothsayer. Striker is Dirty Ed McHandy, leader of the notorious Morespenat Gang. Eventually a gunfight happens.

Perhaps the most anticipated release of the year, Episode 2, titled Lacedaemon, features Traveling Salesman, Simon, Quentin, Li'l Nas Y and Xblanklen dressed as ancient Greek warriors. Several softcore mantages ensure a plethora of young men doing gymnastics naked. In the final scene, they fight to their deaths against the People's Army of Broz.

Episode 3- Star Vest: Bathyscaphe- must air during Sweeps Week. Captain Clytemnestra leads the crew of the ZSS *Ishkabibble* against the despotic Vest League, which seeks to impose tight fitting vests on all the bipedal entities of the little-known multiverse. Lovable robot XQJ-23 is played by Simon Junior, with theremin solos provided by the Allman Isley Band. The Vest League's Stitch Lord Elephant is the crew's nemesis, pursuing the *Ishkabibble* into the Watch Pocket Nebula.

In Episode 4, "Harmed", Clytie, Idajan and Christimiqua form a very fashion forward Witches' Coven. They summon demons every few minutes, try on a variety of glamorous costumes, and banter with many handsome young men.

Perhaps the most star power ever was assembled for Episode 5, "Taubes Gürteltier". Tim Cruz and Geomes Looney play the roles of Me and Tinkelhoff as they negotiate an astral miniature golf course sans score cards or putters. There is also a special appearance by Mike E. Ball playing the role of paperboy Mark Hill. Twinkies and Mountain Dew are consumed.

Episode 6 is titled "Night of 1000 Paperclips." In an imaginary cubicle hell world several galaxies away, Simon, Clytie, Mr. Hi Stop and Traveling Salesman work in ever shrinking cubicles for a substance known as Money. Many additional sub-tyrannies are exposed before Simon suffers a life-threatening paper cut on his pinky finger.

Ace TV's top brass played their cards right and aired Episode 7 during Halloween. "Simon and Traveling Salesman Meet the Invisible Killer Werewolf Zombie." The characters play an affable, bumbling duo suspiciously similar to Abbott and Costello. The monster, played artfully by Mr. Hi Stop, mutates into a hyper undead being who inconveniences dozens of people. Traveling Salesman and Simon save the day as a result of their zany hijinks.

Episode 8 will become the most controversial episode. Entitled "Facile Biker," Hi and TS act like hippies and do drugs while driving motorcycles across a vast contimental landscape. In one town, they meet Billy (played by Simon), who joins the facile bikers on their meaningless road trip. Cool soundtrack ensues.

438,631   Suction Cupp

A photojournalist's dream - a spox's nightmare. Fresh, new images cascade across Xarthorian retinas. The pics then glom together as if githyanki-glued into a hot psychedelic mess.

A salesman's panacea, a pre-packaged account.

A common semiotics in many Zysigamore locations was the toilet plunger street signs. Though many were stolen in the most impoverished zips, the symbols that remained sufficed. Each sign ranged from the mundane to the bizarre; each made a terrible unsucking sound when removed. In rare cases such as sentient golf courses and other smart properties, the signs left behind terribly embarrassing earth hickeys that often caused real estate fluctuatizzle.

Unction of fungus-striped necklaceties suited for a-hangin' everytie of plot within plot within plot. Incasker diggity do all ties wide and narrow, part of his masturbplan for humans. "Friends, Xarthorians, cunt tree men..."

Well, sleeping late's certain to summon night fag hag drag bags. Be one of H'Tapdancin's kids and turn away from the epic flag atree. You'll get your reward next lifetime - I promise. Don't tell my brother.

Wave upon wave of floccinaucinihilipilification struck like a mostly moistened sponge. Almost as if inasmuch as, ceteris paribus, non corpos mentis. Key of IDGAF.

A DJ's dream - a program director's inconvenience. Sponcon playlists extent from here to Crab Nebula, with bootsed market share and the odd dragon scale. Keeps starring for the reach.

Noodleclaus Kinski showed up at the strainer in time for Yule festivitizzle. AKA Father Pasta, Noodleclaus satisfies organs and gives al dente cheer to chucklekids across Zysigamore. 'Merry Carbmas Y'all' reads the Gold Kid's T-shirt.

Polaris point fixed.

Cyber confunk shunned somewhen, yet underground its catalisticalifortean seismic waves jiggled with the 808's backbeat. Fractal beetles obmerging in the afterdivision are consumed by rasps of styracoons.

Peckinpeeyort epistologacotangential sounds of suckcess, all but AAI BBA's Abrasaxophone Swede, a knowledge of feeling

In this great pneuharmonic dactyl, hang on the third unaccented syllable. ACG. Keep the rhythm at the expense of the rhyme, which is transitory.

-580,828   Snooty Looking Nerd in a Bowtie

Sir Reginald Prentice Cricklingham - Bullingsworth was born at an extremely young age. Both precocious and insufferable, the lad donned his finest crested blazer and bowtie not long after returning to the Estate from the hospital, with Mama and a suite of nannies in tow.

Upon both founding and graduating from the most respectable and prestigious series of vine-covered schools, the stripling embarked upon the quest that would define narration for the unforeseeable future.

The Westfordington Players and their upright director, Sir Lordinlord, had fired his previous six narrators, holding them accountable for a series of inexcusable faux pas that Sir Lordinlord blamed for the majority of his plays flopping right out of the gate.

"Ahem," said Reginald as he entered the rehearsal room. That was all it took. The noble way in which he cleared his throat convinced the beleaguered director that his fortunes would soon improve. "You're hired as Narrator. When can you start?"

Thus was a legend made: The Narrator

Opening Night had arrived. Savvy theatregoers in their noms de plumage swarmed into the delicately renovated Victorian theatre, with one pink fox dressed in the most elegant fetal fur. Suddenly the crowd hushed. A snooty looking nerd in a bowtie strode toward the microphone like a Colossus.

"Classic Play Nomber One, by Me and Tinkelhoff. Cast of Characters..." Delicate theatregoers swooned as the dulcet tones of the narrator's voice cascaded through the theatre.

When the last Act had been acted, and all the characters had left the stage, the Narrator adjusted his spectacles. A solemn spotlight sat silently beside him. The ushers busily scurried to assist spectators as they filed out in a very orderly, dignified yet monetized way. Success.

1,345,320   Moloch

"BOUZERANT! BOUZERANT! Lift me higher! Damn you!"

Several child-sacrifice superstores on Zysigamore Island had been prematurely closed, and Moloch didn't get the email. All the monstrous bombs He had assembled would have to sit idol until He or His followers could devise a plan to conjure Him back to the Prime Material Plane.

Moloch summoned a pair of horned devils to play Candy Land against Him, and stewed in misery. He popped the giant rubies out of His eye sockets and inserted a new pair of gems that He had pried off a peryton. "Ha! The Peanut Brittle House is mine! Mine!" Moloch roared so loudly that the horned devils backed off quickly. Moloch fixed the game every time, but the horned devils still showed up to play. It was much better than being impaled for several centuries - and it gave you an in with the boss.

Just before the Arch-Devil could claim victory, an alarm went up. "It's not working. The printer is showing an error message," cried an orthon from the atrium of His vast castle. Moloch cried, "If that's the goddamn DRM again, I will get a-smiting." He breathed a languid *Breath of Despair*, causing several lemures to keel over and vomit.

Turns out the Cyan Boys had locked up all the contracts on Acheron, where Moloch's Pleasure Dome and Pizzeria was being built. "I need some salesmen and I need them *now*!" Moloch screamed into the receiver. "And 5g. Plenty of 5g!" He was halfway to victory on the construction of a state of the fart kingdom in Acheron, but the print job could kiner maybe sorta have the potential to foil the Fiend's fortunes. "Curses!" Moloch finally grabbed the laser printer in His bulging arms, tore it from the wall, and flung it several miles away, into a tributary of the River Phlegethon.

"Of all the False Credentialing...Fucking Cyan Boys will taste my wrath!" Moloch seethed, tossing fiery rings at any devil too stupid or careless to face His fury. Salesmen weren't returning His calls. "Freddy Teddy, I'm coming for you, you little SOB!" Moloch coughed. "And any other asshole or two-bit dickbag in any of those ink and toner cartels up there. A bunch of loose wristed, flirty..."

Just then, Moloch realized His brother Elmer had left a half-eaten peanut butter and jelly sandwich on His credenza. "That's just great! And I immolated the cleaning lady yesterdo." The horned devils were long gone; Moloch fumbled for His 2000-year-old Rolodex for the best agency listings. "Hmmm. DF&J? SH&A? Or maybe…"

-1,345,320   Elmer (Moloch's brother)

Elmer came and went by the River Styx ferry once a week or so. If he saw someone new on Charon's shuttle who would listen to him, Elmer would talk their horn off about the most irrelevant subjects in the Lower Material Planes that Charon didn't give a shit about. The wise traveler would tip Charon just to get Elmer to shut the fuck up.

And so it was the day that Simon Junior and Elmer were sitting at the dock alongside a gaggle of unwashed Xarthorian souls. Elmer took a shine to Simon Junior even though Charon was unimpressed. "Really, a rock, Elmer?" Charon grumbled as he collected tolls.

Elmer was soon in his element on the ferry. Simon Junior paid little heed to Elmer's halitosis or pincer-like fangs.

The first port of call was the 39th layer of the Abyss. Many of the Xarthorians disembarked, and were soon gored and otherwise punctured by quasits polymorphed into abozilis/porcupine hybrids with weird, glowing eyes and chromatic quills. In the background, a Glabrezu named Chuck was running twin TR-808s with old school Technics turntables. He gave Elmer a shout-out as the ferry pulled back into the Styx.

Suddenly Elmer grabbed Simon Junior and shouted, "Hey! We're getting off here," at a tributary of blood-red flame. Elmer had bought a timeshare right on the shores of the River Phlegethon several epochs ago. Again, Simon Junior was cool and collected. The boy stood on the burning deck.

Elmer's condo was primarily made of asbestos and cubic zirconias that he had bought on the Zysigamore Shopping Network soon after the cable TV service had been installed. "It's really great to have some guests for a change. What would you like to do tonight?" "Sit."

Elmer couldn't find any pajamas that fit Simon Junior, so he sprayed Simon Junior with toluene and polybrominated diphenyl esters. "Only the best stuff."

The next morning, Vexhexa the Unholy, a retired marilith from two condos over, stopped by to say "Howdy," and help herself to some of Elmer's leftover toluene. "Want to go down to the 118th layer later? They're having cruel and unusual punishment nights. Plus all you can eat fluffernutters." Elmer sighed. "Maybe next time. Just kind of hanging out, binge-watching a few shows with Simon Junior. If you want to order pizza later, I'm down." Vexhexa sneered. "Hold the scorpions this time. They aggravate my gut something fierce."

4,819,533   Ankylotron

Once-famous DJ Wacky Ted Kudzopilous had been teleported to the alien space rock 'Oumuamua for his great crimes against the airwaves, most insidiously the Roger Valdorus marathon that he played in 1980 that caused global perspiration.

A rescue party made up of Traveling Salesman, Mr. Hi Stop, Clytemnestra, Simon and Li'l Nas Y was formed. Their objective: Be the first ones to land on 'Oumuamua, capture the DJ alive, and send him to Nessus, Asmodeus' circle of Hell, as part of an elaborate prank that Pazuzu had long planned against the Arch-Devil.

Pazuzu had made a deal with an air elemental to tow Clytemnestra's bathyscaphe and its passengers to 'Oumuamua and back once Wacky Ted was secured. It would be a delicate operation: The asteroid had no landing strip; its erratic orbit and minimal gravity were certainly not made for an aqueous vehicle; and the jock would likely be agitated and confused by the party's unannounced presence.

Traveling Salesman hit on the idea of sending several CARTs to the extraterrestrial, 1970s-style studio which housed Wacky Ted. Each day, a new one arrived at his studio, and Ted dutifully played the cart every 20-30 minutes. Within a day, the DJ had been completely mesmerized, and was ready to meet the party once they arrived on 'Oumuamua.

Clytie had prepared one of her bathyscaphes, the *Ankylotron*, for space travel. By the time the *Ankylotron* had gotten into viewing distance of the target, they faced another quandary: What to do with the DJ when they brought him on-board. "Just chloroform him. It works with most mortals," claimed Mr. Hi Stop.

"No, no, too sloppy. We need an airtight solution," insisted Clytie. She began leafing through the *Simon Junior Necronomicon* for an answer. None sufficed - not even the verses of Mrs. Hemans.

Awkward cardinal-like sounds commenced. The bathyscaphe soon plunked down on a slim corner of the alien space rock. Not too far in the distance could be seen a forlorn transmission tower - complete with call letters WAKY - from a better distant time.

The party hopped into a skateboard-shaped planetary roving vehicle after Clytie had decoupled it from the bathyscaphe. Li'l Nas Y yelled "Shotgun!" as Clytie took the wheel. As they drove closer and closer, they realized the transmission tower sat on top of an elaborately designed panopticon. "Funny, I didn't expect that," exclaimed Mr. Hi Stop. In fact, none of them had. "So what's the next move then?" asked Traveling Salesman. "Goodness, what should I wear?" said Simon. Nas shot Simon a look that said 'Don't go there.'

Clytie parked the rover by the building's front door and rang the bell. Soon a ghastly figure emerged, beckoning them into the floor of the panopticon. The yacht rock music filled the panopticon, and they could see ol' Wacky Ted in a bird cage-shaped central inspection house. "OK, you guys stay here," said Hi, as he and Traveling Salesman bounded toward the watchtower.

Although they couldn't enter Wacky Ted's booth, they could clearly see him sitting behind a microphone. They lured him out with donuts, the sugary scent driving the DJ into such a frenzy that he put on the album version of 'Luck of the Dice,' barged out of the studio and was quickly subdued.

-4,828,035   Hemophagocytosis Lymphohistocytosis

Xblanklen dodged yet another relationship blanket as his wild oats got him in trouble yet again. "I got too much jam for the jimmy," he said to his latest boyfriend Taz Williger. "You will be a perfect salesman," Taz commented as he watched Xblanklen go flaccid. "Let me roll", said Xblanklen, rolling an absurdly large 20-sided die across the atrium.

Too tex from Christimiqua. "Pah," Xblanklen uttered, as he read and discarded them. Though they technically were still FWBs, Xblanklen couldn't recongile her feelings with his own metalusts. "Damn, girl." Taz, on overhearing, made the face you make when you bite into something that feels much harder than you expected it to. "The ex again? What a bitch." Xblanklen made a sad face. "She has to get on with her life. We're through. No FWB anymore."

"Hey, I gotta go. Thanks for everything, X." Taz rose, kissed Xblanklen and walked right threw that evva lovin door. Not long after, his Tenser's Floating Disc was hovering outside, waiting to take him to his new job - assistant account manager for a big client he couldn't name at Sandvick, Hughes & Atkinson. He had practiced his full contact whist, curling, snuffleuppaboard, and 21-ball, and was prepared for everything they could ask of him.

Desolorientation felt better than prying open his face with a rusty trash can lid, but not by much. After watching five consecutive sexual harassment prevention videos while consuming six coffees, Xblanklen was ready to crack. "Where's the break room?" he buffaloed a passer-by as he stumbled to the water cooler. Beads of sweat formed atop beads of sweat as he lurched for an absurdly small paper cup.

The men's room AAI chatbot sullenly chided Xblanklen for not displaying his pronouns on his uniform. He promised to make amends. "I'm in training," he swore, which the bot confirmed as true. "Subhuman resources marks you as 'PRESENT.' He was allowed to continue to facilitate himself while -REDACTED-

Harold Childe Beetlebaum, a new hip VP hired from an as yet unidentified yet élite agency, met Xblanklen by the blower. "Only two more weeks of sexual harassment reeducation for me. Some agencies require a calendar year of employment before they will let you roam the break room unsupervised." "Yeah, they're pretty casual here," Xblanklen concurred. "At my old job, Jennifer Val Over held each of us over a bed of red-hot artificial needles. And we liked it!" continued Harold.

-6,304,291   Mr. Namol

The whole crew in the office was sad every time management sacked Mr. Namol. It usually happened on a Friday afternoon a bit after 4 p.m., after most of the more successful sales professionals had left for sentient green pastures.

"Ah, Jeez," Mr. Namol sighed, as the HR bot monotonously read the firing announcement from a well-worn script. Mr. Namol always complied, and nodded his head in rhythm as the bot continued.

Mr. Namol always held out hope that the Assistant VP of Marketing and Sales would at least have appeared in person this time to do the dirty deed. But surely he was 6 martinis into a 3 martini lunch by now, and was slouched semi-consciously in a forgotten booth at the local family chain restaurant.

Once Mr. Namol had shuffled out of his cubicle, a series of elves would appear. They ravenously scoured the vacant cubicle, and remandered every functional staple remover, Post-It Note and label maker cartridge within. No vultures were better prepared for a demise than the furtive coworkers descending on the now-anonymous space.

Longtime receptionist Susan always kept a Pentaflex folder at the back of the bottom drawer of her desk. In it were Mr. Namol's nameplate, his ID badge, a small company letterhead envelope with a handful of his business cards, a cardboard coaster avec logo ancien, and one of those cheap pine tree air fresheners to counteract the acute stench of "FAIL."

Yet with each new job ad, Mr. Namol showed up in person to fill out a job application. Sometimes he was called back; other days it went straight to the shredder. The Asst. VP of Marketing and Sales knew this intuitively, yet always expressed a keen note of surprise to see Mr. Namol's application.

Later, the salesmen gathered at Mr. Namol's wake after he had died of an acute case of mediocrity.

-6,958,473   Praseodymystyck

The previous pestilential floccinaucinihilipilification having stung thoraxes everywhen, the insect plague clouded high in the mourning sky above Zysigamore, awaiting the cerebral command of Lord Pazuzu in our of needs. Feelings of perturbulence, perbuoyancy and pyogenesis suffuse.

Khaxamotl, bat-headed god of insecta and disease, arrives in Pazuzu's wake, flooding the Island with high- and locusts, ticks of all pedigree and stature, languid mosquitokind, and ineffable jets of pollusion. He cut down Xarthorians rediscriminately, and made in-and-out roads among hothechajuxips as well. Pazuzu praised His ally, granting Khaxamotl many airs and cloudspasms.

Zysigamore anon was overwhelmed by every size and flavor of insects, to the point where the Queen had to do something. The X's even barged in one morning, complaining about giant bedbugs and chiggers in their private sweets. "Me too. These bastards are everywhere," admitted Idajan.

"It must be Unquieth again. All these foul, creepy things. I'm so sick of them," Idajan confided to Bleary Tim while musing in her hot tub. "Oh no. You're way way off," explained the disembodied voice. "It's that disgusting Khaxamotl." The god was previously bound in an extradimensional prism, but had been sprung by some renegade Quester Jesters. "I'm sick of His shit. How can we put them both on ice?"

Meco proposed an action team comprised of all-star twentysomething beefcake culled from the leading agencies. Onie, Hi and Traveling Salesman were players to be named later, so they made the trip. Onie announced, "Guys, this is a pro bono. Squish some cockroaches, then we're hitting the Mount Lordburne by 3. Whaddya say?" Hi's face contorted into a series of Krazy Kat sketches. "No, no," said Onie to Hi. "Khax-a-motl. He's not a cat."

Datebreak, and a cloud of lab-grown meat lingered over the Island. The bat-wings soared up and around the pseudomeat, chumming it from one side to the other. Khaxamotl cried out as the visage of Demon Joe pressed down into the god's delicate rib cage. Joe cried, "As I spray insecticide I grow more and more meat for my burger franchises. And my alliance with Khaxamotl guarantees a profitable pestilence."

7,143,071   Odd Leap Years Ending in Y

To placate the Xarthorians, Queen Idajan had That Day moved to a roughly 10-year cycle. "Now I won't have to listen to their constant complaints. Where is the respect? Hegemony?" Meco tiptoed through their absurdly massive bedroom hunting for his phone and codpieces. He sensed her ire and murgatroyd, and kept himself slightly scathed.

She leapt to her feet in brand new lace-up patent boots that one of her favorite handmaidens had conscientiously laced. Her favorite cat-o-twelve tails dripped with hot axle grease and sundry bodily fluids, none her own. "Xira?" she called. "Xira?" She was a majora doma for the Queen, and usually handled political matters and megaball wagering. She entered the room and genduflected to her Queen.

"Xira, any dwellvelopmints on the time crystals?" She replied, "Word around the Queendom is that a bathyscaphe manufacturer / abstract artist has some. Dunno how many. The entrepreneur in answer has a small R&D team, and is married to one of the Island's most notorious salesmen." Idajan frowned, then relaxed. "Clytemnestra. I should have known. She might think she's a pantleg up on me, but-"

Having the newly renamed X-Day weekend off, Clytie's lab was quiet. The bee-like hum of her security nanodrones was one of the few sounds that holiday weekend. Clytie and Mr. Hi Stop were out of town on one of her pleasure bathyscaphes, putting Xzimor and her people on dubly supervised high security alert for the duration.

Not one to mix business and edutainment, Xzimor sat at her laptop and fulminated. "Everyone else has a holiday, but I'm stuck here all weekend long minding the time crystals." She gazed at the three-lock box on a shelf next to her desk. Out of boredom and postmonition, she wandered into her home's family room for snacks and a biden mocktail.

That Day's Short Distance Dedication of the Gelatins played on the mega-TV, complete with fireworks and Ace TV hyperboleee. Sundry family members flitted by Xzimor, consuming vast quantities of X-Day licensed foods and beverages. "I can really enjoy this fad," texted Simon.

Suddenly Xzimor's dogs started to bark uncontrollably. "It's the running of the Sales Professionals." Kids dressed in their salesbest were going door to door, hawking fake vacuum cleaners and ersatz earwigs. "Enough! Enough!" she screamed.

7,343,821   Love Oracles Admin

Zothyrian metempsychosis is a primal agape instinct led down pathways by Merkaba. A perpetual tide of transfermentational magi reappear in fresh, new bright light bodies, reinventing wheels within wheels that turn gears and generate fresh, pure energy. Love is

Enlightenmentalist, please renew this elemental purity nectar in every sleep nugget, every moment of twin reveries, every yoni/lingam connection, every gap between musical notes. Hasten to the passion.

Aforepromised lust of all fleshed warm breathing, all-blooded dancing spirits conquers and conjures - + = 0. Covalent caresses, topological tongues touch all nadis on the balance beam.

Hierachogenesis of Love begins with pure minerals, stones standing and supine, rough-hewn outlying lines defying Euclid, intact, tight shells of electrons, organelleless, brainless nucleotides responding to moonlight, Jupiterlight, Marslight, sundry gravitational fields, a throw's stone from a

Unforeverever yesterdreams crop up perpetually, ejecting hungriform fears and anxieties into the River. Only Incasker's systemic limits prevent the negativity from destorying the three brains. His crucial circumflexions keep negative symbology at bay - most of the time, for most of the people.

Me, on Life and Brainwaves, perhaps a Boo named Dog. Cybermonial parthenopropheteers part the seized thoughtgram to extract and diffuse each tron for the next go-around. Perpetual overdrive is perpossible and perposterous when overstood perrectly.

Magic mirror my palimpsest thought thinks itself droste, within stonehenge neuroplasticity fading in/out on a sign curve. Necesse est.

ZFC patterns flicker from Qlippoth to the Veils, from Aleph Null to Aleph One. Here is the place for 2-dimensional cards.

Magnetobaudelaire, empty suit, empty pants, ring electrons ring. Mnemonic of the chthonic chronic is a bonus action to be taken flightlea.

Peace pickle wanders the diretongued dreamschemer surfing from nugget to nugget, everrem downstream.

Admetus in the space shield of a pleasure saucer appears close enough to dive into. The planet's semaphorescence is a welcome sore for sight eyes.

-8,675,309M   Bear Kunckled Pseudofluffleuppagus

Beneath Unquieth's central web lay a large pile of metaeyelashes, temporary nails, dessicated Gummi Flies and Manes demon corpses. She prefers company to come and visit her.

Occasionally a filament or strand of her spectacular spiderweb would droop down under her lair; sometimes they hung so low that they encroached upon those vacuous, mostly bottomless Lowest Planes of the Abyss.

One small eternity ago, Li'l Nas Y was fleeing a possessed titanodemodex when he was able to shimmy his way out of the Lowest Planes and back into the 666 highest 'classic' planes, as Demogorgon would say. "Get your claws off my bussy, toot suite!"

Mating season was always problematic; it required many things to go right for Unquieth. In the past, she would sew her phone number into her own darkino web à la Charlotte, but times had changed. "Nobody remembers phone numbers any more," she grumbled to nobody who would listen.

"Curses!" Unquieth learned that Lolth had devoured many of the male spiders she was spelling on. A bottle of 5g, some onmouseover, and a hardy set of O-Rings enabled Unquieth to crawl up and into the Caves of Chaos. She randomly popped out of a women's room toilet in the 2nd Straw, generating shrieks and abject horror in the anticess. Unquieth slid out a sewer pipe and emerged in the mist of Unicorn Harbor opulence.

Unbeknownst to Unquieth, she soon popped up on Bleary Tim's undar. "Your arachnofriend is back in town," emoteered Bleary Tim to Idajan. She mobilized the X's, yet Unquieth held back. The spider gawddess sent in a Trojan pony: A rainbow-haired, test mouseketeered Fluffleuppagus-styled superbeing who appealed to kids. After the right focus groups gave it the green light, the Ace Kidzz Network sharted the "Bear - Kunckled Pseudofluffleuppagus 35-minute kid's hour".

Mikey Rat wanted his logoi on the hott new intellectual property, but Unquieth's legal team wouldn't budge a millimeter. "Roll out the traction figures, the plushies, the NFTs. All zips. Pronto!" Zysigabucks flowed like scalding dragon urine, while Unquieth sat back in her enormo-web, knitting obscenities into each strand. "Her pants can't stop me now," she chortled, imagining Idajan hoisted on her own pantsuit, writhing fro and to in her web like a meaningless fruit fly in bondage.

"Pee-Yort!" sighed Bleary Tim. "I can't get my hooks into her."

-45,020,916   Pareidolia

Occasionally Mr. Hi Stop gave lectures at the community college/ delicatessen in Umlaut Towin. When his didactics were on a box lunch day, virtually all the students majoring in pareidolia attended. As Hi walked to the podium, the voices quieted in respect and awe.

"Today, each of you has been given a sandwich. When you peel back the bread to observe your meat, you will see a profile of John Adams. Or Mobutu, or Queen Idajan. Can you still eat it now, knowing that a face will be watching your every bite, moistened by your very saliva?" Several people in the crowd shrieked. One man self-defenestrated after vomiting on the people in the row before him.

Mr. Hi Stop returned to his didactics. He was not in the mood for running his avatars in real time, so he ran a holographic presentation that Clytemnestra had made for him.

"But what of the Prophet Muhammad? Surely he would not allow us to see his visage?" cried a menacing voice. The room hushed again. Mr. Hi Stop cleared his throat. "Six two and even. Fluffvergnugen. Omnia iacta est."

Unbeknownst to the student body, Elephant was at the back of the lecture hall. "Neoliberal hegemony has transduced the pharmaceutical stocks for several quarters. Must I be subservient to the evil-eyed knot hole in the cheap paneling?"

A hit squad dressed in neon green jumpsuits and taffeta socks stormed the room, shooting Elephant with several small blowgun darts. Elephant sagged to the floor.

"Yes, yes, great, great. I see your point," resumed Mr. Hi Stop. A medicvet was called in to treat Elephant. "Get this pachy to the ER stat!"

Off campus, the ambulance passed right by Zysigamore General Hospital, turning down a side road to an odd vegan warehouse, where Elephant's body was rolled out onto a gurney. Elephant began to arise, unzipping his pachysuit and stepping out to reveal his real identity. It was Giant Tick again, in a cheap Elephant costume from the Samhain Store. "Now to suck sombranes. Who's next?" The men dressed in medic vet suits fist bumped- turned out it was Rahälrahad and some rent-a-goons on a third-party three-way script. Giant Tick saith, "Mene Mene Tekel Upsharin."

-333,333,333   Simon III

A literal 'block off the old Chip,' Simon Alonzo Vendpfeffer III was the stoic yet ballyhooed heir to the Simon name. As a small granite stone, Simon III wasn't noticed for some time. His birth certificate says he was born in 1822*, but his true age will remain unknown.

The notoriously tight-lipped Simon Junior had not mentioned his newborn child to any of his friends or parole officers. Simon, of course, was hysterical when he heard the news. Turning to his hubby, Simon lamented, "Boo hoo hoo! How could I have been so negligible? And we had always wanted a baby when we were together. I'm aside myselves." Traveling Salesman offered him a tissue, but Simon declined.

SJ3's mom Mz. Stone came from an earth elemental family whose status had decluded with the price of granite. She raised Simon III alone, and Simon Junior showed no interest in fatherhood as we know it. Finally word got out, and Simon Junior soon found himself between himself and a hard place.

How did Mz. Stone know Simon Junior? Could it have been young love, long before Simon entered the photograph? Or perhaps they had a fling behind his ex's booty? Requiring minds want to know, but of course it was a mute moot.

Like Traveling Salesman and Striker, Simon Junior hasn't been the best dad to his son. Still, Simon III had many of his father's negative traits, like emotional distance and granite composition, despite being raised without his father in his life.

The sequel to The Tyranny of Pants will delve into the complex figurine that Simon III poses to the coverall narrative, and present ample marketing opportunities for his spox.

Snooty Looking Nerd in a Bowtie is elucidating the Cast of Characters for Classic Play Nomber 333333333. Simon III's Island of Domination plays turducken leaves across phosphate hydroxtails. Ace TV, more at 11.

Pants will have to come and go in the Universe; to SJIII, nevermoar. He is not Young Fortinbras. He has 0 loyalty to his dad.

SIT.

Books, poetry, all of these insulate Simon III from existential plaigiography. YOYOY.

*   Rumor has it this was just a 'sell by' date.

-356,284,133   4casta

Set on Blasta, all day e'er day 4casta built the matriarchal empire of Uottubbacktothebonyieumnnn (sp.).

When the prophesied time for her to become pregnant arrived, 4casta assembled vials of the most studly sperm and evaluated each tube precisely before approving one saintly father for the perfect Princess Idajan.

Not ordinarily known for prayer at first, 4casta huddled with her coven of top advisors. 4casta revealed her amulet of immortal Taweret, supplicating the omniscient goddess for Her final answer. As if there were no doubt, the test tube with the best jizz made itself apparent. Taweret was thanked, and the vial was sent to the lab to check for unwanted Y chromosomes.

But that was a long long thyme a go-go. 4casta's eyes were tired; her body grew more demented; her speech stagflated if she spoke too long; and her once-beautiful visage favored a zombified crone. She had accomplished greatness - but yet, her relationship with her daughter grew more prufrockity.

Unfivetunately 4casta started the untidy tradition of regicide, slaughtering her husband Lacertes for unspeakable dalliances. She regretted to live it, but half of the Uottubbactothebonyieoouum's (sp.) peeps actually found her gangsta. Still, erections statued of her once deer hubby, swearing off men in the process. "Very unfortunate," she told her daughter. "Forget all about him. He was a putz."

Was her rain a true golden age, as the sages repost? Idajan's storytellers and mrithmakers insist it is so, but as in all things, truth is a leathery strap with a sharp, inflected buckle somewhen in the middle. Certainly the rose was off the bloom after Idajan's birth, as 4casta repetreated from the public, leaving them to grok the interminabubble construction of the Inverted Pyramid.

Dull eyebrow having been plucked, 4casta resolved to serve her goddess and surrender administrative powers. Now she was surrendering herself to the corroded effects of prementia, rementia and dementia. Some mornings, Lacertes stood at the bedside, casually mocking her decrepitude. Other days it was the rebunctious teenage Idajan screaming at her over slights both legitimate and candy apple red. Worst of all were the illusolerbiaxes, taunting and torturing her and eating her goldfish, bowl and all.

-843,201,174   Ted Penny's Third Eyeball Dialectic

In an obscure yet not quite occult pocket dimension of the multiverse lay a non-Euclidean hyperbolic whirled linked tangentially to Zysigamore only by generative adversarial networks. This produced a brain chaise like one other.

Intratemporal race of parallel processing draws from Marquez of the future, Clytemnestra of the present, and 4casta of the past to produce a solution cast of characters capable of popularating an infinite series of Classic Plays. "Tea Bags?" says Mighty Tinkelhoff. Yet the kernels are so far advanced that they communicate directly with xxend while discriminating.

Why do I find this necessary? Why must I chase my own tale?

Preteryods are dispersed as dust and gas between solar systems, drifting pollen-like for metayoyanas. Rarely but surely a preteryod here or there enters a satellite virtually undetected. No innuendo is required, but the child becomes mistaken as a Deity.

This oft-ignored world used dipsomania and dementia to prevent these casts of characters from peering through that great veil. Each Simon clone continued to believe everything before his eyes until packed popping corenuts filled the domed stadium.

This unnamed obscure world named itself, showed itself, scrubbed itself, and shifted its own textronic plates. This made it unstable for many Casts of Characters, who were often cast as victims of hurricane volcano blizzards in countless boring sequels.

Thus a candy bar ship was envisioned, saving the life and rhymes (See Classic Play Nomber Ninety-Four *).

Crostini! Ptah! Orthographies of a

One cast member was a perfect hothechajuxips, 18's across the board. Definite 99. She was a prototypical X'er but for her Y and Z chromosomes, common in this forgotten hyperbolic whirled. She had II many names to list, so I will list them here.

Torn between two discriminators, she fluxed as she flexed, leaving robots in between fairly analgesic predators. One, nine, ten, it's on. Sincere moustache optional.

Antithesis - Thesis - Synthesis: A dimension devoid of Incasker, Outcasker and the dates between galaxies. Ted said it best in the original Portrad.

7,366,012,978   Howlthibisquiat

Palimpsest. The sincere moustache.

A hand-crank mimeograph in a sepia toned Midwestern school.

Kaspar Hauser hologram at my vivisectionist's office. So much travel.

Troubled by dog ears at night, he had turned inward, whereupon

Wholly vivified petrogryphons, on a late Assyrian diet. To even catalog this creature,

Neatly folded by the pentagon, a triumph of the postdiluvian squadrons.

Solifugids prepared the newfangled way can test the patience of allergic tempurans.

Anacreonistic portents divvy up the remainder in the hold.

Buckyballistic robocanonical X11 string theories lay draped across a continuum.

Synchro proffesseur profesizzle: Heaven has doomed the Kingdom; Queendom is cool.

EOM - or is it?

Squash, echidna, hitsugeth, omphalos

Extended epitaphalog follow us down to the next parts of IIIlogy.

Facts are stolid things.

I draw a 12.

Take it - this - them. We will be

A hero at 12 is not late to the praty. Doon doon doon

Salt it in. Tablespoons. Beautiful flakes of garlic. Potatoes al dente, not too rubbery or semi-cooked.

Wholly unpersoned polygons transformed into panopticons, accessible by ID badge or passcode. Pasta shapes twist and mutate within fields of zones. Only a well regulated sauce can modulate.

-7,366,012,978   (untitled)

Baby what a rhythm. Heater nature. Force of smurfnstuffnen. Twilight to the A soupçon of a bearded apple tray delight.

Two a soften saffron. Twirl the strands into a not quite steeped wessel.

Twisted deck. Mince the prioritized entree.

Fortean bras. Cooling, supporting, lifting. Gravity defied - it was just a theory anyways.

Beetle Zimmy. The neuromantic Beetle.

236

Still finding the body of Paul. Sucks to be replaced by Paulie McCarthy from Dot Ave. He was pissa.

Towards a New Understanding of a Latitudinal Case Study: A Literature Review.

So open to the fluff of learning.

Alcove of the Annex. To the right of the bay window is a small Door to a Crawl Space under stairs. The old man's pot belly and bad back prohibited him from crawling inside, so he sent the apprentice in.

Ignomy not infamy. Drains that seek another route. Delays in the Stock & Flow diagram.

Places. Pelicans. Stumps. Good fishin

Photon judgment superficial insight. Terraplane when we remove the water, pull back the trees to reveal the urban landscapes seldom conceptualized.

A nightmare portage. Valley is resisting.

Who holds this scimitar. Perhaps it never needed to be held. Nick Fotiu just left the sin bin.

Fog. Mist. Pogonip. En Retard.

8,701,689,611   Conceited Ass

Simon was absentmindedly masturbating to "The A-Team" when the news hit home. "Fuck." It may have been the first F-bomb he ever dropped; fortunately the only ones eavesdropping were his wider screen TV, toaster, convection oven, laptop, microwave, coffee maker, blender, vacuum cleaner, refrigerator, O-Ring dispenser, newage soap dispensers, smartphone, smartsneakers, smarteyepatch and Simon Junior.

Then came waterworks to match Uottubbacktothebonyville (sp.) Falls. Simon even tried to rend his garments, but he was too preoccupied with tears and self-pithy. "This is what I think of you!" said Simon to a book of Traveling Salesman's life. He dramatically threw it on the fire with a flourish. But since Simon didn't have a fire, he daintily set the book down in the microwave and heated it on HIGH. "Boo hoo hoo!'

Twas a text from a mystery lady who called herself Lois that set off pure Simon. This person claimed that Traveling Salesman had a kid with her, and was bankrolling their deathstyle. At first, second and third, Simon thought this Lois was just a troll, or a cruel joke by Dastardly William Rucklehaus.

But the cake on the icing was a photo of Lois' son. He appeared about 13 or so years old, with budding masculinity and a profile almost identical to Traveling Salesman's. "Tch, that's a dead ringer," Simon told Simon Junior. "Either it's the world's best Photoshop, or the boy really is his." A billion apocalyptic thoughts hit Simon hard; only television could quell his despondency.

The next five shows were binge cringe, montages of reality show sandwiches coasted in mayo and provolone yogaranimal spice. "Dreadful!" A teenybopper show randomly turned itself on. The pretty cast of twentysomething hothechajuxips only reminded Simon of who Traveling Salesman's son could be. The thought of Traveling Salesman sticking his cock in a woman still made Simon nauseous. He didn't do flex drugs, but Simon wished he had had some now.

Traveling Salesman excitedly opened the door. "Simon? I've got great news. I'm going to be a partner. Hi too!" Simon didn't answer, breaking off eye and nose contact. "C'mon. Aren't you glad for me?"

Simon tried to autostraddle his tongue but showboated his acid wit on his husband. He blurted out "Who is this Lois? And her son?" before breaking into his customary waterworx.

Traveling Salesman noticed that his things had been thrown all over the house. He asked Simon, "What have you done? Where are all my codicils? My codpieces?" But Simon was unresponsive, staring densely into the cathyode raze.

29,998,559,671,349   Tiamat 5-Headed

Avernus made a 1ce and future pluperfect homeland for Her Highness Tiamat's domain. Her Hell creatured marshy jungles full of reproductive organs, leidodendron trees and many extinct fungi; dinosaurs, reptiles, monsters and huge beasts of all species; volcanoes spewing smoke and lava 25 hours a day; and a central island palace on the side of a volcano where the Chromatic Dragon reigned in glory.

Despite the meddlings of John Adams and Moloch, Tiamat was powerful and strategic enough to regain Her queendom after losing it for so long. As a result, She made Avernus acceptable to non-lawful evil gods and monsters, much to the chagrin of the denizens of Maladomini, Malebolge and Nessus.

Jazzy Bella, Tiamat's dragoness charge d'affairs, took care of defense, deploying vast armies of lizardfolk, dinos, wyverns, dragons, pseudodragons, zombie dinosaurs, talgelt, hydras, certain élite amphibians and invertebrates, and Allman Isley Brothers & Sisters Band 252. Bella's patrol served to harass, chomp and devour any and all weaker critters traversing the poisonous jungles and fetid swamps of the first layer of Hell. "Give 'em a taste of your hate, Bella," roared the Chromatic Dragon, sending her into the Prime Material Plane to harass Zysigamore's inhabitants, especially Demon Joe-run establishments.

Human sinners were welcome at Avernus, so long as they were not eaten by the regular denizens. Many of them served Tiamat directly or indirectly in Her cave. But She trusted dragons above all; when the down were chips, Tiamat called them in to slaughter and profit. "Always put gold first," Tiamat reminded dragonfolk and lizardfolk alike.

Not all was killing and eating; cruel, ironic subterranean shenanigans were pleasing to Tiamat. In elder days, Her heads would take turns making prank phone calls and choosing a winner, usually the blue dragon head. Today, each head has their own social media presence and merch. Izikiz, the red dragon head, had so many T-shirt designs that even the Gold Kid had trouble keeping up.

Avernus' polysteleism having been postmaturely bifurcated, Bella reported back to her Queen. "The borders are secure! No intruders from Paideuma have entered." Tiamat's white dragon head now spoke. "Excellent. Send in a herd of Tyrannosaurus Rexes and Elvis impersonators. Let's see if Adams can handle it!" The other heads jeered and hooted over their hatred of the President. "We'll send him back to the Merry Mount Maypole - in worm-ridden, bite-sized pieces!"

-29,998,559,671,349   Grazie, I Potenti Morti

Per omnia secula seculorum, Lethaei ad fluminis undam securos latices et longa oblivia potant. Downstream from River Lethe gathered a crowd of yacht rock shades. They lingered among the Night Gardens of Proserpine until teletectonics demanded they depart.

The shade of Casey Kasem herded the other DJ shades together for a solemn, special Long Distance Dedication. "Dear Casey, it reads. I'm from a small, photogenic town on Zysigamore Island. About three weeks ago, I fell in love with a girl named Destiny. She was bubbly, witty and bold, and also refused to accept objective reality..." The other DJs groaned in existential agony. "I hope that kid offed himself," snarled Dr. Johnny Scabies.

The dedication worked: A time escalator appeared, lifting the group members out of Hades and into a vast corporate panopticon. "Are we past Qlippoth Gate yet?" asked Scabies, fumbling for a cigarette. "And when do we get paid?" A helpful fire prevention nanobot safely extinguished his cancer stick and crushed the crush-proof cigarette pack in his pocket. "Nano cockblockers is more like it," sneered Scabies. "I hate the upper world."

The floor of the building was full of teen and pre-teen Xarthorians eager to get on Ace TV. The Gold Kid strutted to the front of the line, displaying 'Praise, Flattery and Positive Feedback' on his T-shirt. Right behind him were Xatnudorf and Marquez dancing the Ratna Lean. Kasem's saccharine voice filled the panopticon, alternately pleasing and confounding the crowd.

Anchises stood there outside the entrance, thumb raised, hoping to hitch a ride back under. "That panopticon. It's too much," he told the doorman. "Eternal death beats the fuck out of television. Just kill me now, please." Anchises declined a cigarette from a waspy character milling a boot. "Hey, is your kid in there or something?" said the doorman.

Dr. Johnny Scabies waltzed out, bumming smokes from everyone he saw. "Rock is dead, fellas. Gotta find some trends that pay better." He nodded to Anchises. "Was that your gilded rugrat I saw in there?" Anchises, puzzled, nodded yes.

The sun seemed to fail, as if the apocalypse was imminent. "I should have played the Lotto," Anchises sighed. Xat, the Kid and Marquez strolled out of the building. Scabies slid his shades down the bridge of his nose. "You kids did some real damage in there. Next level shit." The Kid's T read: Cocyti stagna alta vides Stygiamque paludem.

-1,000,000,000,000,000   Million Billionth Plain Erv the Abyss

Whaddya know? There are a lot more than 666 Layers of the Abyss. You go down far enough, even Alice Cooper and Vincent Price have their own layers.

The Abyss isn't totally infinitely deep, but it sure seems that way. Chaos being chaos, there are no notary publics present on any Layer. They ain't lawful evil, y'all.

Demon Joe hailed from an obscure layer somewhere in the million billions. He wasn't particularly strong, intelligent or scary in a demon-type way, but he fulfilled most of the stereotypes of an overfed, long-haired leaping quasit. As fate would have it, Joe found a miscellaneous magic item that let him abandon the Abyss and move full-time to the Prime Material Plane.

Some scumbuster demon even more repulsive than Juiblex's chum bucket created the spell *Cause Paronychia*. Although it was technically 'No Big Deal' according to Ace TV newscaster Bryant Brick, around the cock the network reported breathlessly on this new pansexualdemic. For months, Simon was on the verge of tears every time the news was on. "Pray for a cure," wrote Simon on every Furrier & Chives Christmas card he sent. So much evil.

Several arachnogods and goddesses hang suspended above the bottomless pit, woofing and webbing assorted spiderfibers from stalagmites on much higher planes. Unquieth has a nest deep within a dismal cavern on plane 603, with stray webs extending out into the serious drabness. Scary Adney, the creepiest of all spidergawds, sits perched at the edge of a pit on Plane 666, web tendrils drifting in and out of the canyons below.

Timeloose tarry demodands torture hapful prisoners by quasit light, only stopping to suck ectoplasm from a teat tray bimeby.

Time-days-space-life adrift, buoyed by a current of bigotry, ignorance and cloud-mindedness, we embed shard after shard after shard, still pulsating like intemperate spirits of coil ghast tombs.

Dying a thousand deaths? Die a few billion more. Million Billion Zillion Killionth planers insist. Megaurge insists. All hygroreceptors shall be restroyed.

The abode of Anheptasoteria is somewhere and nowhere, herewhere and thereware. Castles require gravity, so none were ever built. Instead, floating polygons nested together in grids often made a temporary structure when needed, the enormous spiderwebs providing adequate mooring before chaos rips apart.

-1,000,000,000,000,001   Negative one quadrillion and one   But not -29998559671349

Project lines like a football grid. Axes in every gap, which seem to be tightly plugged. Flex design eliminates systemic weakness in the gorm power supply. The batteries are constantly being pushed to their Max Efficiency, which 'indicates' this is a steady state of productivity. Honestly. Queen's Pawn to G4: Thash marks in the slot.

Orbs of shiny cholate; Grob's gumption and gesticulations get.

The very edge of the Universe. Can you fall off its edge if the universe is finite?

No matrices, no set theory. Quadrilaterals.

Octavius fugit; senato obfuit.

Compounded binarist pseudoplasma flings a series of tsunamis in asynchronous gesticulations. Compsognathus of sounds; a very round wavelength.

These tortured organs are strangled, inexorably damaged. Pangs of life essence suppressed now radiate throughout our bodies. A vector of prison penetrates all cells at once before the heartbeat can commence. We find a discomfort that pricks us up, and makes us aware of the venom.

10,314,425,000,000,000,000,000,000,000   Lowest Planes

So down and down, down and down, down and down, all is down. Yet there is little gravity like on the material realm.

These netherly regions took the most detestable elements of the Abyss and combined them with the utter desolation and horror of outer space: You gasped for a tiny nugget of true air whole swallowing while; the whale's tongue coats your clottisiges in an unmeditated goo of ambergris and tepid trivia nights. Xxend could travel there but never did.

Fractal sequences dashed by chaoses erupt into planetoids, stars, clusters, galaxies and dark energy.

Irregular trade-ins and defective returns were the only escape modes. Juxtaglomerular three-way scripts helped filtrate the vast vastness of space into a manageable, bite-sized algorithm/necktie. "It's got to be. Got to be."

One of the rare creatures found here is the Titanodemodex. Shunned by virtually all demons, their kind were plunged into the bottomless, sideless netherscape, where today they float from one bodiless hair to the next. With no predators, the titanodemodex population is kept minimal by the vastness of the void. You cannot eat them - they eat you.

There was no Restaurant here. There was only ennui; vacuum; and the madness of deafening isolation that splits your atoms and disbursczars your KA across the light years.

Kidd Xistence was perched on this knife-edge cliff, where his nads were plucked from his body Prometheus-style every morning at 7.

The Kidd had foolishly challenged Asmodeus to a fiddle context, but the Lord of Hell brought His Smell-o-Cello and mopped the floor with the lapless mortal. When Asmodeus was through, Pazuzu volleyed Xistence like a tennis ball into the most distant realms of Space.

Another soul lost on these lower depths was Old Johnny United Dates Grant, a merciful mercenary whom John Adams had considered for a lieutenant role. The old warrior was found guilty of aggravated confabulation by Adams' marsupial court and sentenced to banishment from Paideuma. Sticking a sewage-soaked stogie in Grant's puss, Abaddon cried, "Jefyxitxavfb elxepigdwatot." The G-force ripped Johnny's portly body into zillions of small, polluted particles that often clouded the already murky void.

43466557686937456435688527675040625802564660517371780402481729089536555417949051890403879840079255169295922593080322634775209689623239873322471161642996440906533187938298969649928516003704476137795166849228875

Several Species of Small Scooby-Doo Typea Endings...

"Well, it wasn't the Pirate Ghost Zombie within a Pirate Ghost Zombie ship after all. It was Traveling Salesman," said Jennifer Val Over to the rest of the gang (Striker, Dastardly William Rucklehaus, Zapp Omnigotopia and Elephant). "But how?" asked Zapp. "Like, how did he, like, walk across the ocean?" Jen explained. "See these mirrors? Traveling Salesman projected this image across the water and and-" Traveling Salesman interrupted. "Well I would have gotten away with it if it wasn't for this hyperdrive terminal dimension phase shifter. And of course, you kids too!" They all laughed.

Scooby-Elephant has hogtied the villain as the rest of the gang (Simon, Simon Junior, Xblanklen, Clytemnestra and Christimiqua) look on. Simon says, "Now let's see who the margrave *really* is." The ladies gasped as the villain was revealed to be... Onie McPhersall! Elephant trumpets, "Several quarters of declining sales clearly pushed Onie over the edge." Clytie continued, "He thought he could scare us with visions of the 'Anti-'BOB.'" Onie scowled. "And I would have gotten away with it if it weren't for you kiddling meds." Simon Junior - Sit.

The gang (Traveling Salesman, Mr. Hi Stop, Li'l Nas Y, Christimiqua and Striker) gather by the Mystical Machine as they talk to a generic palefaced deputy sheriff, who holds a masked caballero with handcuffs. The gang gasps as the sheriff reveals the identity of the real bandito: Quentin Periwinkle, a loose-wristed, flirty fag. "Well just hogtie me and marry me off to a horny toad with halitosis and a jenkem addiction!" Mr. Hi Stop's face contorted into several Da Vinci sketches. "Well, officer," declared Traveling Salesman, "This bad hombre still pines after Simon. Lock him up." Quentin whined, "I simply can't. Those prison uniforms are dreadful. They'll make my undereye bags look huger than they already are!"

The Idajan look-alike was hogtied to a hogshead by the Wet Hogs Yoknapatawpha BBQ Ribs, Neologisms and Existential Elabroelasmotherapeuticasaurus Shack in Umlaut Towin. The gang - Delve-It Noxin, Young Fortinbras, Destiny Von Waifenburg, Li'l Nas Y and Scooby Doobie Broz - approached the pseudoqueen. "I thought I could make it look easy. The toner refills. The 5g. The cheap Chinese horoscope placemats." Delve-It said, "Let's see who this villain REALLY is!" Young Fortinbras pulled the wig off and gasped. "Pee-Yunk! It's Simon!" "I never would have guessed Simon. But how?" Destiny said. "We all thought it was Demon Joe." Simon confessed readily. "I got so stressed out by my relationship that I started following a substrate of several species of small Scooby-Doo merchandising websites that I-I-I fell down a bung hole and couldn't get out." Simon broke into tears, totally trashing his mascara. "Rooby Rooby Roze," barked Broz.